PRAISE FOR
# *MASK OF SHADOWS*

"Get! Read! Now!"
—Tamora Pierce, #1 *New York Times* bestselling author

"An intriguing world and a fantastically compelling main character make for a can't-miss debut. Miller's *Mask of Shadows* will make you glad you're not an assassin—and even gladder Sal is."
—Kiersten White, *New York Times* bestselling author of *And I Darken* and *Now I Rise*

"Compelling and relatable characters, a fascinating world with dangerous magic, and a dash of political intrigue: *Mask of Shadows* completely delivered. Fantasy fans will love this book."
—Jodi Meadows, *New York Times* bestselling coauthor of *My Lady Jane*

"Uber bloody and action packed, *Mask of Shadows* is the book for anyone who loves a heavy dose of grit and gore with their fantasy."
—TeenVogue.com

"Miller's gritty, lightning-paced debut features a rough-and-tumble yet movingly vulnerable protagonist: Sal is uncompromising in their convictions and doesn't hesitate to kill when necessary but wishes to be more than just a weapon of vengeance. A complex but intriguing start to this planned duology."
—*Publishers Weekly*

"This is a memorable, sharply written character. While readers who identify on the GLBTQ spectrum may be easy fans as Miller handles Sal's identity with aplomb, that's certainly not the only point of note here; the impressive, intricate worldbuilding, tense action, and fierce competitors are equally strong."

—*The Bulletin of the Center for Children's Books*

"Gory, well plotted, suspenseful on every page, and poised for the sequel."

—*Kirkus Reviews*

"This fantasy's genderfluid protagonist, Sal Leon, makes Miller's book worth picking up for diversity's sake alone. Her treatment of the gender issue is most notable in that it isn't really an issue... Violent and action-packed, this offering by first-time novelist Miller will circulate."

—*School Library Connection*

"Teen genre fiction featuring a strong genderfluid main character."

—*School Library Journal*

"Miller's setting is vividly drawn...a solid addition for libraries hoping to expand the gender diversity of their shelves."

—*Booklist*

"It is fabulous. Go forth and read the Hunger Games–like craftiness and intensity, Kaz Brekker-ish determination and moral questionability, and utterly charming romance."

—*LGBTQ Reads*

# RUIN
## OF
## STARS

# RUIN OF

# STARS

## LINSEY MILLER

sourcebooks
fire

# ALSO BY LINSEY MILLER

*Mask of Shadows*

Copyright © 2018 by Linsey Miller
Cover and internal design © 2018 by Sourcebooks, Inc.
Cover design by Nicole Hower/Sourcebooks, Inc.
Cover art by Bose Collins
Cover image © yulkapopkova/Getty Images
Map art by Cat Scully

Sourcebooks and the colophon are registered trademarks of Sourcebooks, Inc.

Published by Sourcebooks Fire, an imprint of Sourcebooks, Inc.
P.O. Box 4410, Naperville, Illinois 60567-4410
(630) 961-3900
Fax: (630) 961-2168
sourcebooks.com

Library of Congress Cataloging-in-Publication Data

Names: Miller, Linsey, author.
Title: Ruin of stars / Linsey Miller.
Description: Naperville, Illinois : Sourcebooks Fire, [2018] | Series: Mask of shadows ; 2 | Summary: As Opal, Sal now has the power, prestige, and ability to exact revenge, but must first identify the murderers while ignoring the fact that Elise is a virtual prisoner and the queen may have ulterior motives.
Identifiers: LCCN 2017057879
Subjects: | CYAC: Assassins--Fiction. | Kings, queens, rulers, etc.--Fiction. | Revenge--Fiction. | Robbers and outlaws--Fiction. | Gender identity--Fiction. | Fantasy.
Classification: LCC PZ7.1.M582 Rui 2018 | DDC [Fic]--dc23 LC record available at https://lccn.loc.gov/2017057879.

Printed and bound in the United States of America.
MA 10 9 8 7 6 5 4 3 2 1

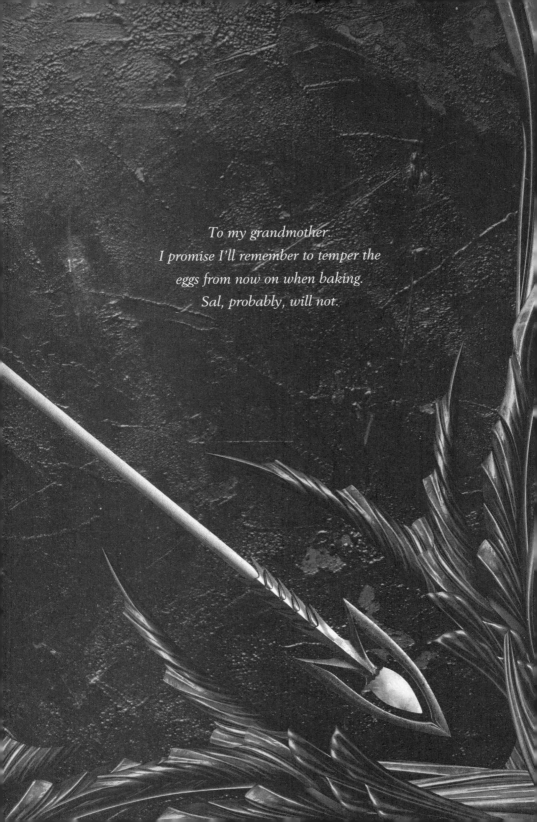

To my grandmother.
I promise I'll remember to temper the
eggs from now on when baking.
Sal, probably, will not.

The Blue
Silk Sea

Lynd •

Erlend

• High Water          Hinter •

Nacea                Bosque de Lex •        Aren •

• Field de Contes        • Willowknot

Tulen •

Igna

Poppy Green •

Port da Abreu
•

Verre
•        The Sun-Drenched Coast

Berengard

CHAPTER
ONE

A hand snuffed out the light. I leaned over the edge of
the greenhouse trellis, wooden beams creaking beneath
me. The guards, as they had done every night I'd been spying,
left soon as Lord del Aer tucked his daughter in, and they
followed him through the halls of his estate. His daughter's
room was left unguarded except for the ones patrolling the
grounds. He couldn't comprehend someone killing his child
to get at him.

I could.

I could because of him.

Lord Mattin del Aer was a good father and a terrible leader.

*North Star. Deadfall. Riparian. Caldera. Winter.*

The five secret names of the Erlend nobles who allowed
Nacea to be destroyed by shadows. I knew only North Star,
Caldera, and Winter by their real names—Gaspar del Weylin,
Mattin del Aer, and Nevierno del Farone. I heard his name in my
nightmares of the massacre he'd caused. I felt it on my skin every

time I wore my Opal mask. I tasted it every time I muttered the last words my targets would ever hear.

Caldera. Caldera. Caldera.

The fourth Erlend lord on my list to kill and only the second one to die.

I had carved their names into the inside of my mask. Our Queen had named me Opal, her assassin and protector, and given me leave to kill my list. I'd the whole of the Igna court to help me hunt them down.

And the hunt was on.

He was predictable as an Erlend. He rose at dawn, flipped through reports sent to him from the other traitor Erlend lords who'd seceded from Igna barely two months ago, woke his daughter for breakfast, and spent the day with a series of advisers, guards, and tutors, each more boring than the last. He did not hear his citizens' concerns or worries.

He didn't talk to them at all, just told them war was upon us and the time to take up arms and reclaim Erlend was now. Didn't even speak to them in person to draft them. The flyers went up overnight, and the rangers from North Star's stronghold up north went out hunting for dodgers the next day.

War. Again. Always. Never ending so long as North Star and his Erlend lords still clung to power and greed. There'd been no attacks yet. Only the dead, stripped of clothes and skin and life, strung up across the trees near the border.

We figured they were folks speaking out against the war. Wasn't much left of them to identify.

Wouldn't be much of Caldera left either after I was done with him.

Caldera's daughter snored. I slid a knife from its sheath, slipping the point beneath the glass pane of her window. She slept on, and I pushed the window up, the oil I'd squeezed into the tracks last night keeping it quiet. A paper shade or shutters would've been easier, but this worked just as well. They'd wonder how I entered with no shades cut or shutters broken. They'd think the killer a shadow.

I looked like one at least. The Left Hand of Our Queen— Emerald, Amethyst, Opal, and Ruby—were her royal assassins and named for the rings she wore. And I, the new Opal, had been gifted six masks. Three of bone white and three of pure midnight blue, the sort of purplish black that made you think of deep caves and missing stars. I'd carved my list into each one.

*North Star. Deadfall. Riparian. Caldera. Winter.*

The Erlend nobles who'd let the shadows tear my family to shreds, who'd ten years to atone for hundreds of thousands of deaths and done nothing, would know me as I knew them.

Bitterly. Painfully. A wound so raw it still ached in the night when the dark twisted like mage shadows. They'd made my whole world a nightmare.

And I would be theirs.

Caldera's daughter shifted, blankets tumbling to the floor, and I crawled into her room, knife slicing through the leftover smoke of her reading candle. The key to her father's study, one of only two, hung from the chain round her neck. I unhooked the chain from her head and took the key. I had to return it.

It would be better, Our Queen had said to me, one hand clutching my chin, if Caldera's fellows thought no doors or locks or guards could keep them safe.

"Let Erlend think we have made shadows anew and sent them after the nobles who betrayed us," she'd said. "After all, they made you the same way they made the shadows—through violence and fear."

I'd not given her an answer, didn't think she'd deserved one yet, not with so many deaths staining her soul, but she was right.

I was Our Queen's Honorable Opal, and I would kill Caldera as she saw fit.

If I did, she'd let me have the other lords on my list, and I wasn't passing that up.

*North Star. Winter.*

They would be mine and mine alone.

I tucked the blanket back around Caldera's daughter and left. I could comprehend killing his kid to get at him, but I wasn't him. Caldera's daughter was no more at fault for her father's deeds than Elise was for hers, and only Caldera was dying tonight.

The hallway outside her room was empty. I pressed my ear to the door of his study, the only room with a lock on the outside and inside. Nothing. Too thick for me to hear through and too thick for folks to hear Caldera scream. I unlocked it, muffling the click with my hand, and darted inside. The mechanisms reset behind me.

Caldera was talking to himself. He gestured to the windowless walls, hands flying through the air and back to me. A map twice as tall as me and even longer detailed the continent in deep forest greens, wheat yellow, and spring-water blue. The sliver of coastal land to the east of Erlend was labeled as Erlend too, but instead of rolling green hills, the cartographer had scratched it out in black and labeled it Fallow. Only the northernmost tip of

Nacea, the little snaggletooth of land embedded in North Star's mountain range home, was green. It was labeled as Erlend.

"Absurd!" Caldera flung the letter he'd been reading aside and ran his fingers through his long, light hair. "That woman is absurd."

I walked up behind him till I was close enough to taste the gold-cold scent of his gilded form and the lantern behind me cast three flickering shadows against the wall. He froze.

"Don't worry," I said. "You won't have to deal with her much longer."

He shrieked and tried run. I grabbed the back of his shirt and yanked him down, sending him flailing to the floor.

"No one can hear you, Caldera." No windows. No guards. No threat of being interrupted since the only two keys to the door were in this locked room. "No one is coming to help."

He crawled to his knees and pulled a chair between us. "How did you get—"

I pulled out his daughter's key.

"How well do you know your daughter?" I dropped it, let it clatter between us, and pulled out a second knife. "I watched the shadows you let loose in Nacea flay my family. I know every bloody part of them. Do you know what your daughter's bones look like?"

He whimpered and I lived, furious and alive, Sallot Leon, auditioner Twenty-Three, and Opal all crushed together by his hands. He didn't know fear like me. He didn't know anything.

"Please," he said. "Please, I don't know anything. Don't kill me."

I leapt over the chair and grabbed him, dragging him to the center of the floor. He was tall and broad, healthier and heavier than most folks I'd fought, and he ripped from my grasp once. I let him know freedom for a breath.

"Help!" He stumbled into the wall, knocking over a lamp and leaving the room at the mercy of one single candle. "Help me!" He pounded against the door.

I laughed, and it echoed between my mouth and mask. The sound died too quick to be natural.

"You're Caldera. Your old flame Lena told me. No one likes you." I leaned over him, and my two shadows flickering at my feet followed. "She only nodded when I said you'd been responsible for killing a whole country. Said it sounded like you. Was it you?"

Lena was one of the only Erlend nobles to stand with Igna and pledge her loyalty to Our Queen again, and she'd given me Caldera's name. He'd tried to marry her once, to get ownership of her land back when they'd both been Erlend and Erlend land could only be inherited by Erlend lords, and he'd told her his secrets to make her fall in love.

"It wasn't my idea." He choked on the words.

I stepped on his ankle. "But you agreed to it."

"I'm sorry." He flinched. "I'm sorry. I am. I have been since it happened, all those people. I didn't want to, but they made me."

"Who?" I asked, and when he shook his head, no names ready, I pulled out my knife. "Who went by the names Riparian and Deadfall?"

"I don't know." He raised his arms like a shield. "I don't know. Other than North Star, we never shared."

He took my silence for consideration. "I've regretted it since. What do you want? Whatever you want, it's yours."

"You've nothing I want." I took his tear-streaked face in my hands. "Apologies won't bring my family back. They won't clear the shadows from my mind. They won't change anything at all except the weight of your guilt."

I pulled him up.

"And it's not heavy enough for what you did."

I jammed my knife into his chest, watched his last breath leave his lips, and dropped him.

"If you were sorry," I said to his corpse, "you'd not be doing it again."

The gaping wound in my soul that never healed and ached with each breath only grew deeper at the sight of him. Each breath was cold and empty, a sharp pain between my heart and ribs. I was split—the Sallot Leon that could've been if Nacea stood whole, one that knew all of their nation's rituals and words, and the Sallot Leon that was, one that knew only the press of five names against their face and the fractured bones that came from offering mercy. I'd let Winter live at Elise's request, and he'd thrown me from a window. Folks devoted so deeply to themselves never changed.

They stole and stole and stole.

"Nothing can fix this." I rifled through his desk and shelves, turning over every scrap of paper for anything Our Queen would find useful. "Nothing can help me, but I can help the world."

Erlend had reduced us to nothing, to casualties in a ledger. They would do it again. I couldn't let that happen.

A fake wall shifted under my fingers. I pried the thin wood away from the bottom of his desk drawer and shoved my hand into the space. Papers crinkled. I grabbed them all.

Scraps and envelopes heavy with broken seals tumbled to the floor. I bent to pick them up.

Not seals. Not wax. An ear.

A tattered, runed human ear.

CHAPTER
# TWO

The ear didn't rot. I'd seen plenty of dead things and rot always won. During the civil war ten years ago, after the shadows had razed Nacea, Our Queen had banished magic from the land. Losing magic had destroyed the shadows, ripping apart the runes stitching their bodiless, mindless souls together, and every single rune within the borders of Erlend, Alona, and Nacea. Without magic, the flesh the shadows stole from the dead and tried to stitch into some broken memory of their faces rotted and stunk. I'd always been able to smell them coming before I saw them.

No one had been able to use magic since then.

It was why historians had named that date the first day of the Empty Age. Magic was gone. Shadows too.

But an ear that didn't rot meant Erlend had alchemists who could preserve body parts good as magic. What else did they have that we didn't?

"It's faded," I said to Emerald once I got back to the palace grounds two days later. The jagged edges were lined in ink, like someone had traced out where to cut before setting the knife to flesh. "It was darker when I found it. Now, it's more gray than black."

Nacea hadn't used runes, hadn't dared use the magic making up the Lady, and I'd no idea if these were proper runes. Sight of them set my teeth on edge.

"It's a child's right ear." Emerald turned it over, plated nails scraping across my palm. She'd met me in Willowknot, her cloth armor simpler than the exquisite dresses she used to wear, and when she turned away from me, she looked no different than the city guards she'd been talking to. "Did Lord del Aer do this?"

She wanted to ask if the person who'd cut off a kid's ear was dead. She loathed nothing as much as people who killed children.

"Don't know. It was in a secret drawer." I had to jog to keep pace with her long strides, and the guard she'd made walk on her right glanced over his shoulder each time she paused.

The guard stopped. A new set of footsteps neared. I turned, and Lord Nicolas del Contes, Our Queen's spymaster, stepped from the path to our left. He bowed.

Took all my effort not to bow back. I was Opal, not Sal, and bowed to no one but Our Queen unless I wanted to be polite.

And I didn't. Not with any of them. Not with the whole of her court ignoring Nacea's slaughter to make sure Erlend didn't resist being combined with Alona to form the new nation Igna under Our Queen.

"What did Lord del Aer say?" Nicolas's voice was low and rough. He'd grown ashen and more frantic since the night I'd been named Opal.

The night Elise's father had been revealed as Winter and restarted this whole damned war with Erlend. He and Five had killed Ruby, tried to kill Ruby's sister, Isidora dal Abreu, abducted Elise, and nearly killed me. The next night, every Erlend noble except three had seceded from the ten-year-old nation of Igna.

Before the war a decade ago, before Igna existed, there'd been three nations: Erlend to the north, with Nacea tucked into its southwestern side, and Alona to the south. After Erlend's atrocities in the war and their hand in making the shadows, Our Queen had tried to start over by combining what was left of Erlend and Alona into Igna, and only the northernmost tip of Erlend had held out. Lord Gaspar del Weylin, the king who'd bow to no woman title-thief, still ruled those mountain reaches. His constant attacks on Igna were why the Left Hand was even needed.

Course, I knew him as North Star, the one who'd come up with the plan to let Nacea get slaughtered in order to buy Erlend time to escape the shadows.

"Lord del Aer said nothing useful." I handed him the bag from my shoulder. "That's all his papers."

I'd recognized names and maps but nothing more.

Emerald glanced at me, the muscles of her neck tight with a scowl. "People will know what happened."

"No," I said. "Made it look like he'd burned them. Made him look scared."

"We'll see." Emerald handed Nicolas the ear. "Runes?"

"None I ever used." He held it up to the sun, shadows peppering his gaunt face. "You?"

She shook her head. "Ask Isidora when she's up to it."

"How is she?" I'd not seen Isidora since leaving the infirmary. "Physicians cleared her to leave?"

She'd taken up teaching me to read, laying out books on the unused bed next to me, and had been a good teacher when she wasn't crying. I'd have holed myself away if I'd lost my twin twice in one lifetime too. The silence Ruby had left behind was thick and cloying.

"She's mending." Nicolas tucked the ear into his chest pocket—odd man—and took the papers from my hands. The servant who usually accompanied him to carry around his notes wasn't here. "She's glad we have no time to audition a new Ruby."

She'd not gotten to burn her brother before, when he'd been Rodolfo da Abreu and the war criminal who'd killed the Erlend mages responsible for making the shadows. Least he got his funeral rites this time, even if only a select few knew we'd been saying farewell to Rodolfo and not just Ruby. Was it worse now with his pyre ash still clinging to our mourning clothes? Or did it feel more final?

"You're to meet with Our Queen after me," Nicolas said softly. "I'm sure Isidora would love to see you alive and well after that."

He bowed again and left. Emerald grabbed my arm, fingers tight but not painful.

"You're being rude." She pulled me away from the guard to her right and onto the shaded path to the inner workings of the palace.

"You didn't make me Opal because of my good manners."

Nicolas was all right, teaching me to fence and turning over all his Nacean goods to me, but he'd still been part of the Igna court that had let Winter and Caldera and Coachwhip—Horatio del Seve, the Erlend lord I'd killed during auditions—take no responsibility for their hand in Nacea's slaughter. I understood the decision.

Didn't like it.

Emerald leaned over me, her breath puffing out from beneath her mask. "You should be more polite to the people who thought you the best candidate for Opal. We're not too arrogant to refuse the opinions of confidants." She let me go. "Which was my main concern about you. Your personal vendettas cannot trump the well-being of Igna."

As of right now, the northern lands that had been Igna's only months ago were under Erlend rule yet again, but people remembered the strict rules of Erlend society and were fleeing south. I didn't blame them.

Most were like me—their very existence outside of Erlend's fragile standards threatened the old Erlend way of life. As if my existence was a threat because I didn't hold to Erlend's narrow definitions of man or woman.

And they always said "or."

Those folks fleeing had no place in North Star's fight.

"I won't put Igna in danger," I said. "No more than you."

Emerald clucked her tongue against her teeth. "Clean yourself up before you meet with Our Queen."

I hummed to keep from speaking and ducked into one of the squat corridors servants used to traverse the buildings. Maud had acquired clothes and soaps and a dozen other unnecessary things for me while I'd been laid up in the infirmary with one arm splinted and my chest bound in bandages. It had been overwhelming, the options she'd given me each morning, and she'd stopped asking. There were so many things happening it felt wrong to worry over whether I was wearing wool or cotton.

She'd be in my quarters now, not quite used to the new white collar of her uniform that marked her as my servant, with more questions than anything, and I couldn't handle it yet.

I washed my face in a basin set aside for servants to clean their hands and shook the dust from my tunic.

Wasn't trying to impress Our Queen these days anyway.

CHAPTER
THREE

Our Queen of the Eastern Spires and Lady of Lightning Marianna da Ignasi, draped in an olive-green dress and silver scale armor, was more tense than impressed with me.

"I told you to kill him." Her fingers, opal ring casting white across the floor, clacked against the armrest. "I did not tell you to start rumors about Nacea."

I pulled up from my bow. Her gaze still prickled on my skin even with my mask between us. "You didn't instruct me not to. They think they can get away with it again," I said, "because you never called them out for it."

She nodded. The runes lining her eye flickered in the light as though they still lived, and the jagged shadow of her armored silhouette shifted. "Did you harm anyone else?"

"No." I shuddered and met her gaze. "I knocked out two guards with a tree branch. They'll think it an accident of nature."

"Good." The interlocking scales of her armor were runed and sharp, saw-toothed where one might grab her in a fight, and the padded leather at her shoulders exaggerated her strength. She looked all-powerful. "Do you know the others on your list yet?"

*North Star. Deadfall. Riparian. Caldera. Winter.*

*Gaspar del Weylin. Deadfall. Riparian. Mattin del Aer. Nevierno del Farone.*

"No." Deadfall and Riparian were mysteries. "I'm working on it."

"Come. You will escort me to our court meeting." She rose, trembling, and reached out her hand. "Or shall I call Emerald?"

Emerald was terrifying and overprotective of Our Queen, and I'd no desire to die at her hands.

"Of course." I let her grasp my arm. "How would you like to walk?"

She was careful not to cut me with her armor. "Slowly."

Nicolas had explained why Our Queen toned down the effects of her illness. Erlend's fault, of course. He had turned to me while teaching me history and said, "What do you see when you look at me?"

"A hawk," I'd said. "Or a stork, depending on how you're standing."

Isidora had laughed from her seat across the table.

"Erlend sees weakness." He'd laughed too—and smiled. "Nothing matters to them so much as appearing what they think they are, fulfilling their image of power, and I do not anymore." He gestured to his missing arm. "Our Queen and I share very different yet similar liabilities in Erlend's eyes. She must appear as their definition of strength in order to make them wary. We like them wary."

Our Queen stopped me at the door to the courtroom and straightened her claw-tipped gauntlet. She'd not held me with that hand. "This is good."

"Of course, Our Queen." I bowed again—best I put on a show for the guards—and let her enter the room before me.

It was not a large room. Wasn't grand either. Three of the four walls were bare, and only one large map covered the other one. The low ceiling was lit by lanterns, and there were no handholds to boost you up to the two rafters. I'd tried it. They'd designed the room for safety.

I entered. Emerald saw me first, shaking her head at my dust-covered clothes. Nicolas was at the table already, and the seat next to him for Isidora was empty. I paced around to the far wall near the only other door, the one servants used, and waited. The door creaked open, Dimas's familiar face peeking through. The cosmetics beneath his eyes were smudged.

He'd been looking rough. Lady de Arian had taken a liking to him after her stay in one of the visitor houses, and now he was serving as her personal assistant. Maud was furious.

"And he got mad at me for being in it for the money." Maud appeared at my elbow, her nose crinkling as she scowled, and handed me a spotless coat. "At least dress like you care."

I shucked off my traveling coat and pulled on the new one. "You leaving me to work for Lady de Arian?"

"Don't have to." Maud grinned and tucked my dirty coat under her arm. "My family's from her holdings, and she's been helping me figure out where we used to live. And look!"

Maud spun, braid smacking my shoulder. A gold hair pin with small green gemstones spiraling out like flower petals held

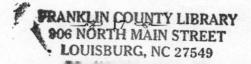

the strands of her hair too short for the braid. A hot, sticky weight filled my throat.

I'd offered Maud gifts, but she rarely accepted, citing propriety and privilege and how I was already paying her. I'd practically had to force her to let me help pay off her siblings' keeping costs and travel.

"You couldn't do opals?"

Her smile twisted. "My life isn't about you."

Lady de Arian entered and nodded to Maud, who bowed and grinned. I scowled.

"My guards took my pack to my room," I said quickly. "Can you take care of it?"

"Yes." Maud narrowed her eyes at me, nose crinkling, and sighed. "I'm glad you're back."

The rest of the servants filed out, Dimas pulling up the rear, and he glanced at Maud once, gaze skipping over me. She huffed.

"Thank you," I whispered as she followed them out.

"This will be quick," Our Queen said. Her voice carried across the room, and the members of the guard sat. The guards and Left Hand stayed standing. "Only one thing has changed since yesterday, and that is the number of living Erlend nobles."

Lady de Arian stiffened. "Mattin is dead, then?"

"Yes." Our Queen set her elbows on the table and her chin in her hands.

There were only three Erlend nobles left in Igna—Lord Nicolas del Contes, Lady Lena de Arian, and Honorable Lark del Erva. Each of them was vocal about their hate for Erlend's policies and history, but they still winced whenever we spoke of Erlend's fate and the fate of its nobles.

"Not to be crass," Honorable del Evra said, "but good. That man was a bloody battle in the making."

"True." Lady de Arian nodded, the tightly bound bun of blond hair atop her head wobbling.

She was older than Nicolas, maybe thirty-five or so, but they shared the same wrinkles at the corners of their eyes and deep worry line between their brows. Her hair hadn't started turning silvery white like his though.

"Nicolas will know more tonight, but we have groups moving into Mattin's lands now. Lord del Weylin will send soldiers, of course, but they will get there after ours, barring any complications."

Nicolas nodded. "Hinter is directly to the north, and Lord del Farone sent most of his west to the border. Only Mattin's troops are there now, and ours outnumber them."

"You'll be updated tonight once we have word of what's happened." Our Queen leaned back. "Other than that, I have no pressing matters that we have not already discussed."

I rocked from heel to toe, and a guard against the wall did the same. These meetings were always tedious.

Honorable Lark del Evra leaned forward. "What of the flayed corpses? The ones Gaspar del Weylin is using to claim we have shadows?"

"Isidora identified one by his teeth." Nicolas shook his head. "He'd had work done she recognized as by a local gnathic. He was a furrier traveling north for winter, and his flaying was done by hand."

I shuddered. Three's red, open eyes still peeked from the dark corners of my dreams.

"No way to track how it was done?" Lark asked.

"None." Nicolas shook his head. "It's almost certainly a scout or soldier given the type of blade, though Isidora isn't quite sure yet. She was going to wait to confirm it."

Our Queen winced. The guard pulled his sword from its sheath. I lunged, fear rising in me. Guards didn't draw swords in here.

Ever.

Amethyst and Emerald turned to me. The guard took advantage of their looks and darted forward. I sprinted to the table and leapt over it, sliding across the pages laid across it. Lady de Arian fell back and out of her chair. Our Queen turned. The guard raised his knife.

Amethyst got there first.

She disarmed him with a single hit, the sickening crack of his arm echoing through the room, and he crumpled. I slid to a stop next to her.

"Leave him." Our Queen stood with her back to the wall and Emerald between her and the would-be assassin. "We need him alive."

"Marc de Graff," Lady de Arian said quickly, white skin pale from shock. She grasped at the chain around her neck and spun the too-long key dangling from it. I'd never seen her nervous before. "He was one of Mattin's guards until four months ago."

Erlend had planted killers in our midst long ago, then.

"In that case," Amethyst said, pulling her arm back to strike, "we don't need him alive."

Lady de Arian grabbed Amethyst's arm. "We do. He has peers. Let them see what happens to traitors."

I looked down at him, the white expanse of my mask reflected in his green eyes, and his gaze slid to Lady de Arian and Amethyst. He opened his mouth.

"Knock him out," Lady de Arian said. "Arrest him. We need to find his friends."

I hadn't believed Lady de Arian when she'd told me she had been Elise's childhood mentor, but they shared the same measured shrewdness.

I slammed my heel into the assassin's temple and knocked him out. It was a dirty hit, maybe fatal, but the physicians could probably sort him out.

I was getting real tired of Erlend surprises.

We needed to find the other would-be assassins before they found us.

W hy bother with the Alonian-born ones?" I asked Emerald.
I'd learned patience during my fall. When Elise's
father, Winter, had tried to kill me by pushing me out of a
window, I'd not flailed about or reached out for the bare stone
walls and wooden windowsills flying by me. I'd waited for the
thorny rose trellises and thin wooden outcroppings. Emerald said
they'd slowed my fall enough to keep me from dying when I
finally hit the Caracol.

I shrugged when she looked at me. "It'll just make our search
longer." Course, I'd not had much patience to begin with.

"Because it sets a terrible precedent, breaks trust, and means
we're leaving half our suspects unchecked." She beckoned me
into a room with only the Left Hand, the remaining Erlend-born
nobles, and our assassin. "Igna is not a perfect nation. It is not
only Erlends who want Our Queen dead."

But only Erlends had ever sent assassins and started a war.

"Lena." Our Queen sat on the lone chair in the room and

yanked the gauntlet from her forearm. "How do you know the name of one of Mattin's old guards?"

Lady de Arian spread her hands out, palms up. "I know the name of every single one of my citizens working in Willowknot. I made it my business to know. It's why I was so surprised to find Dimas de Gaila and Maud de Pavo right under my nose. Start with my citizens. We will have all of their backgrounds on hand and it will be easier to rule them out quickly," she said, clipping each sound just so. "Should you interrogate Maud or should I?"

I scowled. "No one's touching Maud."

"Hush." Emerald's face turned to me, and I knew she was glaring by the tightness of her jaw. "The most likely candidates for grooming—who are they?"

Lady de Arian shook her head. "The best for making an assassin?"

"The easiest to train and mold to your will." Emerald gestured to me. "We recruit young adults. Who would Gaspar del Weylin have recruited?"

"Someone young. A boy, of course, as if Gaspar could conceive of a girl undertaking murder."

Honorable Lark del Evra and I laughed at the same time, and Lady de Arian ducked her head.

Lark, a stout noble with a penchant for bird-watching and from the lands east of Nicolas's, was practically Lady-sent and glorious. They were forty-two, married, and entirely done with Erlend's strict thoughts on gender. We were alike, not the same, but they were more than happy to spend all night talking to me about life when I asked.

I'd asked twice. They'd invited me to dinner and let me ask questions till I ran out.

"He would not even consider your possibilities." She laid a hand to her chest, fingers shaking.

Lark shrugged, pearl necklace clacking against their chest. "Yes, he hated me even before I rejected my original name and title. I was never enough for Erlend."

I'd heard the same from the folks up north and near the old border between Alona and Erlend. I was too emotional to be a man, too stoic to be a woman, as if my feelings determined either. Erlends and those who'd lived close enough to pick up their ways had been telling me for years I'd been doing "man" and "girl" wrong. Always *girl* too. Lark had said the same.

I'd been in too deep with my gang and its leader, Grell, to make friends as a kid, but now I could befriend who I wanted, and there were plenty of folks like me here, Lark included. It was just easier with them.

It was mostly Erlends, they'd said, who couldn't grasp people not binary like them. It was mostly Erlends, I'd agreed, who couldn't take my word for it when I explained I was fluid, that I wasn't both or neither. They existed in a world of pairs.

*Binary*, Lark called it. Said it had been the old word before Erlend had gotten tired of inclusion and burned the ancient libraries of Alona's ancestors.

"It would have been children. They always take young boys to be rangers." Lady de Arian glanced at me. I was short, sure, but still clearly young. "Children disenfranchised by Igna life ten years ago with ties to Erlend, ones he could make hate you enough to kill you. With less than a handful, he could keep it secret but make sure at least one or two had a chance of getting close to you."

Gaspar, the man responsible for pushing mages to create the shadows, doing what-have-you to kids to make sure they obeyed, churned my stomach.

Our Queen took a deep breath. "I had hoped that anyone Gaspar sent to kill or spy had been flushed out by now or won to our side."

"We'll change our standards." Emerald's voice, low and flat, wavered behind her mask. "The Left Hand was originally founded to proactively prevent the assassination of Our Queen when Gaspar del Weylin sent killers here ten years ago. They will not make it so close to Our Queen again."

Our Queen laid a hand on Lady de Arian's arm. "Lena, you will walk with Amethyst and Nicolas, and you will point out all the staff members from yours and Mattin's lands. We need to know if Weylin attempted to recruit them or anyone they know. You will harm none of them and threaten no one. Being born Erlend is not the problem; subscribing to Gaspar's ideas are a threat. We will not alienate our Erlend-born citizens. We are not better than Weylin if we repurpose his supremacy for our own nation."

A warm, prickling sweat dripped down the back of my neck. Our Queen would sooner die than that. Least some part of my hero was not a lie.

Sometimes, at night, when I'd nothing better to do than know this fact while my bones healed and the shadows crawled around my bed, it was hard to hate her. She wore power for others' sakes.

"Dimas and Maud, the servants from my lands, what will happen to them?" Lady de Arian raised her chin. Barely. A slight show of power.

Our Queen smiled. "They have been with us since they were children and have been exceptional staff. Unless they decide to kill me, no actions will be taken against them."

Lady de Arian's shoulders slumped as she breathed out, and her pale brows drew apart.

"Emerald, you'll stay with me." Our Queen rose and dismissed us. "Nicolas, make sure the servants and guards know not to talk as you go. I want no word of this to reach the ears of people who were outside of this room. Pull anyone who has heard out of rounds."

They all nodded.

I raised my hand. Our Queen caught my gaze, boring through the eye holes of my mask.

"The killers at the border, the ones flaying people alive." She held out her hand to me, and I crept closer, the shadows between us merging, growing. "They're yours. You will clear out the Erlend rangers and their captain, and you will flush out the killers from their hideouts. They are not only killing their victims; they're torturing them and the survivors still living in the memories of the shadows. If they cannot be arrested, they die. Understood?"

"Yes, Our Queen." I laid my hand on hers and shook as she shook, feeling the deep ache that murder left in her soul. "All of them?"

"At your discretion. If Isidora believes it is soldiers, I am inclined to trust her, and they cannot be allowed to carry on their torturous reign."

Our Queen felt it all as she'd felt the loss of magic, a hurt so deep I could see the way her orders ached in her bones and dragged her down. She knew she couldn't wear power without wearing death. She felt Nacea's loss in a way the Erlend nobles of my list never would.

"No one innocent or redeemable will be harmed." I bowed— nine out of ten on Ruby's scale if only I could keep my healing arm straight without trembling—and bared the back of my neck. I didn't love her anymore, but of all the monsters bearing down on us, I trusted her the most and would pick her every time. "Only the ones as soaked in blood as me."

Her hand stilled. "Good. Stay safe. Bring me any information you can glean from them."

She left me there, still bowing, and it was Lady de Arian who waited for me to rise.

"Did you find the others?" she asked. "Did Mattin del Aer tell you the true names of the others?"

She had not known either. Neither did Lark and Nicolas. No one did, it seemed.

"No." I took a deep breath, lungs full of the dust from carving a line through his name. "He didn't know who they were."

"I will be glad to be rid of those torturers lurking about the borders. They're entirely too arrogant and daring." She sighed, tension seeping from her jaw to her neck. "Was there word of Elise?"

"No," I said. "There was nothing from Hinter at all so far as I could see. I'm sorry, Lady de Arian."

Wasn't much. I could recognize *Hinter* written, but Caldera's handwriting had been jagged, too-straight nonsense to be letters.

"You should call me Lena. It will make our conversations

easier, Lady Opal, and I imagine we will have many of them in the future. Elise is fond of you. She is usually an excellent judge of character."

I winced, glad she couldn't see it. She was trying to be nice. And she knew Elise.

"Honorable," I said. We'd a title to keep our hold on male and female onlyness at bay, and it didn't take any extra effort to use.

"Apologies." She gestured to my tunic.

I shrugged. Ruby would have hated my rudeness. "It's not foolproof. I am as I am, and the clothing's a tool, not a cause."

Clothes had no gender, but people had a lot of thoughts about clothes, and I'd only been using those thoughts to my advantage.

Got tiring though, molding myself to make sure people weren't asses.

I'd asked Nanami Kita about it—wasn't the same but she'd changed her name to be easier on Igna ears—and she'd laughed.

It hadn't been a happy one.

Honorable Lark del Evra had laughed, too, when I'd told them about the exchange, but they knew what I'd been after.

Molding. Changing. Stuffing yourself into another person's ill-fitting idea of you so they didn't take offense. Got tiring not being able to just be.

It was nice having older folks somewhat like me to run to and ask questions, to get all the little worries out of my head. They'd lived their lives already. They'd answers to spare.

"I was the first person Elise told." Lena—it was only polite to think of her how she asked me to—began walking, waiting for me in the doorway. "She didn't know how to tell her father that she was courting another girl. I'm afraid I wasn't very helpful. Maud speaks highly of you as well. A pity I found her and Dimas only to lose Elise."

I ground my teeth together. "I'm glad Maud found someone from her area to talk to."

"I hope it helps," Lena said. "It will be nearly impossible to find all of the family items she pawned, but I'd like to help. And Dimas has some lovely stories about Erlend. I've enjoyed talking to him. It's unfortunate they don't get along better."

"Very."

She stared at me for a moment, blue eyes the same crackling pale of clear sea skies after a storm, and I cleared my throat.

"I am glad," I said softly, "that I have someone else to talk to about Elise, and I am sure Maud is happy to have someone around who knew her home."

Isidora had told me nearly all of her stories about Elise, and we'd talked our throats ragged. Elise had tried to raise chickens as a child, enchanted by the way they didn't move when she picked them up, and Lena had broken in with a tale about Elise attempting to sleep with them under her bed. Isidora hadn't known that one. I'd not known any of it.

I didn't know much about Elise at all, it seemed. Only that she was alive.

"Yes." Lena laughed. "She's been much more talkative than Dimas."

Like I cared about Dimas after the way he'd treated Maud.

Lena grasped my arm, grip loose and stance too wide for an attack. She didn't notice my flinch. "If you hear of her, if you hear of Elise, anything at all, please tell me. There may be word of Hinter or her father nearer to the border. I know you would cling to any news as I would. Please."

"If I hear anything, you will hear it." I pulled her hand from my arm and stepped away. She was too close. Too strange. She wasn't Maud, who'd earned my trust, or Rath, my childhood friend and thievery partner who'd stitched me up and stolen me breakfast more times than I could count. I didn't have to humor her. "I promise."

She would hear the news from Our Queen. From Nicolas. From whichever member of the high court blurted it out in a meeting first.

My news of Elise was mine—there was too little of it already—and I had shared too much with the world. The least it could leave me was grief.

# CHAPTER
# FIVE

O ur Queen's quarters were at the heart of the palace, and in the rooms around hers lived the Left Hand. I'd been given too many rooms to count, Maud to manage them and me, and a common room to share with Emerald, Amethyst, and whoever became Ruby next if Igna survived the war. My time in the infirmary had been eaten up by my days with Emerald and Amethyst, and the handful of meals we'd shared since had been strained. I was new and Ruby was dead. The Left Hand was three again.

I liked being Opal. I hated being Honorable Opal of Our Queen's Left Hand.

The huge rooms and their many corners, my new bed with enough space beneath for a person to crawl, and the constant need for new things—new clothes, new boots, new orders for Maud to follow. The emptiness closed in on me each time I stepped through my doors.

The only good part of the rooms was the lockbox at the

head of the bed I'd stuffed with Elise's notes from tutoring to keep the charcoal from rubbing away and vanishing completely.

Being Opal was more emptiness than fulfillment, more long stretches of empty time in empty rooms to think over all that you'd done. It wasn't a good job. It was a debt-laden weight on my soul I'd taken up willingly. It was a necessary job. It suited my revenge and me.

And I would continue to be Opal until the Erlend lords intent on murdering their way back into uneasy power were mine and Igna was safe. Elise, and the others like her once set to take over, would make sure the future Igna knew where it had come from. North Star had to die to make way for them.

"Shadows!" I flung open the door to my washroom—frivolous, useless space for the sake of space—and slammed it shut. "How do people pretend to be shadows?"

How could they bear it?

The wall rumbled, and the basin tumbled to the floor.

"More quietly than that, I imagine." Maud, impeccable and stoic with her white-collared coat buttoned up to her throat and the emerald pin from Lena still in her hair, stepped out of the closet in the corner. "I know you don't like anything in these rooms, but could you try not to destroy them every day?"

"Sorry," I muttered. "And I like some things in this room."

She pressed her lips into one thin, serious line and pulled a brush from the closet. "I hope you didn't imply I was a thing."

"I was talking about that big bathtub, but you're all right." I took the brush from her and swept up the shattered pieces of pottery, dumping the pieces into one of the buckets she'd set out to clean up another of my messes. "Sorry, really. I'm not used to having so much stuff to worry about."

Rath had been enough back in the day. Now I'd rooms and servants and jobs and Rath and Elise and Nacea all knotted into one taut tangle of feelings, the threads tightening with each bit of news from Erlend.

It made me itch, like every bit of me had fallen asleep and I only needed to move to wake myself up.

"A sentiment you've expressed time and time again." Maud sighed, nose crinkling. "Your rashness is not my favorite trait of yours."

Meant she'd a favorite at least. I wasn't good at this. The auditions were over and we both had what we wanted, more or less, and I'd nothing to fall back on.

"I don't know what I'm doing," I said. "Not really."

I wanted to move. Amethyst had me training every morning and Nicolas was teaching me to fence each evening. I was barely better at sword work, and he took every chance to remind me the Erlend lords would disembowel me without getting their sleeves dirty. We used real swords, and he never flinched when I nicked him. He never hit me though.

He'd perfect control, like a physician knowing how hard to push to set a bone instead of breaking it.

That skill escaped me. I was moving all the time but didn't feel it. My mind wandered. My hands trembled. Sometimes I felt like I was still falling and, on the worst days, like I was back in the woods but the shadows at my heels were real. Only when I'd a singular focus did the constant panic vanish.

*North Star. Deadfall. Riparian. Winter.*

I had to keep moving or else the nothing behind me, the yawning emptiness of Nacea and all my debts, all the lives I'd taken, would catch up to me.

"I'm all jittery." I glanced at Maud. "That make sense?"

She laughed. Loud.

"What?" I scowled, my face twisting against my mask. "Me being honest a laughing matter?"

"You having no idea what you're doing is not a revelation." She covered her mouth, braid swinging behind her in silent laughter, and stepped up to me. "I'm not laughing at you, really. I'm sorry. It's just—"

She paused. I nudged her knee.

"You're sad," said Maud. She moved as if to touch me and stopped. "You're sad, and you have no idea what to do about it. Or anything, but that's another issue."

Of all the folks who'd touched me today without asking, I'd have been all right with her.

"I'm Opal. I won. I got it better than most." I tilted my head toward her. "We're at war, Elise is in Hinter doing Lady knows what, and the borders are a bloody mess. Plenty of people have it worse than me. I'm not sad."

It was the only emotion I knew well as my own name. It had been with me the longest. But I'd nothing to be sad about now.

"Are you sure?" She laid her hands on my shoulders, squeezing gently, and knelt till we were eye to eye. "What did you used to do when you were sad? You could talk to Lady dal Abreu. She knows physicians who specialize in that sort of thing."

I wasn't asking Isidora, who'd lost her brother for a second time, what to do about me being sad.

I shook my head. "I just was sad. Wasn't much to it. Usually had a job lined up soon enough, anyway, to take my mind off it. Robbed anyone annoying. That was fun."

Maybe I needed to rob Winter.

Elise was too kind—she'd be at the front, making sure the people of Hinter, her people, weren't in danger. Not that she shouldn't have been, but it ate at me, wondering if today Nicolas's contacts would bring news of her death. Winter would never take the same risks she did.

Maybe I needed to rob him of more than his life.

"Fine." I groaned and patted Maud's arms. "I get it. I know what I need to do."

Caring for folks was nothing but fear, and I couldn't be afraid when I'd a knife in my hand and job underway. I had to keep going, keep hunting, and tear my way through Erlend until there was no one left to hide North Star, Winter, Riparian, and Deadfall. I'd nothing to fear.

I was Sal. I was Opal. I was death. I'd never needed anyone. Wanted, maybe, but everyone wanted something.

Maud clucked her tongue. "You sure you don't need to talk to someone?"

"I'm sure." I rolled my neck, the uncomfortable stretch of muscle under skin a welcome relief from sitting, and stood. "No more door slamming. Promise."

"Good because I usually snap a bunch of those pastry sticks with my teeth and eat them, but I don't think that would work for you. And I ate them all already."

I snorted. "I'd not even broken anything yet."

"Not you—Dimas." She groaned. "He told me I had no business being so close to Lady de Arian."

"You want me to kill him?"

She smacked my shoulder. "No. I feel bad about it. I'm certain she told him some less-than-pleasant things about his family—he's lost weight, his eyes are always bloodshot, and he's always asking her questions. I'm not thrilled with him taking it out on me, but I'm not letting you murder him."

I'd not asked Maud what Lena had told her about her family's fate, only let her share what she wanted, but I knew the family that had survived still had no interest in helping out her and her siblings.

"You say that like you could stop me," I said. "You're still throwing punches wrong."

"Who would I punch with you gone?" She shooed me into the parlor—we'd been the only people to sit in it so far since I had no friends left in Willowknot—and opened the cabinet she kept stocked with tea. "It doesn't matter. What I wanted to give you before you left again was this."

She set a topless box stuffed with finely scrawled papers in my lap. I knew the writing as well as I knew myself, so often had I traced the same words across my skin alone at night. Fingers shaking, I touched the first page and yanked my hand back. Elise's neat pen strokes shivered as the paper moved, and Maud laid a hand on my arm, patting my shoulder when I leaned into her. The curves of Elise's name twisted, black ink catching the light. The rest of the words were lost to me.

"What's it say?" I asked. "The title?"

What had she loved so much she signed her name to it?

"An Incomplete List of Borrowed Words and Their Histories in Alonian and Erlenian." Maud tilted the page back. "There's a subtitle about Eredan and Lona, but your lady is very wordy and I don't know all of the ones she used."

Eredan was the original home of Erlend's ancestors. They'd fled for some reason or another centuries ago along with hundreds of others from other lands. The Eredans had been welcomed into the nation of Aren, deemed the hospitality not enough, and taken over Aren in order to start over. And it had, over the years, become the land known as Erlend.

That had been my least shocking Erlend history lesson.

"She would write whole histories on only a handful of words." I laughed and choked. "I know I didn't send her there, but I've left her there. Every day I haven't gone after her, every day I've abandoned her."

Maud shook her head.

"I know." I sniffed. "She'd say that's nonsense."

"Actually, she does say it." Maud pulled a tattered piece of cloth from the side of the box. "Lady dal Abreu sent it to me. She said Lord del Contes is all right with you keeping it so long as you don't tell anyone else."

"What?" I held out my hand and didn't try to stop its shaking.

Maud cleared her throat and read, "I am safe. Weylin has drafted civilians and sent his rangers to recruit in every town. The worst of the lot have been sent to the border. People are missing. My father knows something, but I do not know what. The deaths and disappearances are being blamed on Igna. They say Our Queen has shadows, that Rodolfo didn't only kill Celso de Lex, but stole his work. There is talk of assassins living in Willowknot for years, waiting for word. Be wary. Do not send help. I will live. I'm sending Alonian-born citizens south. I don't know if they will make it past the rangers, but the only people missing have non-Erlend names. Help them. I'll find what I can and send word once I know more. Stay safe."

The note was small, and Elise's handwriting was scrunched together into thin, feathered lines where the ink had seeped through. She'd written it on a torn scrap of canvas.

"They don't want it known she's sending us news." Maud pressed the note into my hands. "Lord del Contes is hoping they'll tell her more if she seems fully in service to her father."

*I am safe.*

"Of course," I said, not really meaning to say it at all. Elise's words blurred. I squeezed my eyes shut.

*Do not send help.*

I took a deep breath. My chest ached. A great, crushing weight had grown within me since Winter had stolen her away. I'd dreamed of Elise drowning in snow, skin frosted till it cracked, and the drifts wept red. I dreamed of shadows creeping across the land like ants, wave after wave of nothing, and not stopping till their rotting attempts at bodies touched the sea. Erlend was an avalanche, and Winter had kicked off the first snow this time. He'd see us all, soldier and civilian, Igna and Erlend, bowing to Weylin or dead. A king of corpses but still a king.

Just like ten years ago.

"Can you draw me a bath?" I asked, hugging the box to my

chest and pressing my cheek to the edge of it. The dry burn of charcoal dust and old ink filled my nose. "I need to get ready to leave again."

"Of course." Maud brushed charcoal from her hands. "I'll lay out some supper and bedclothes. Don't worry about anything. I can deal with any mess once you're gone."

"Can you come back once I'm eating?" I shifted, trying to keep my blush at bay. "I want to know what's in these, but there's no way I'll be able to read them all."

"Of course." She smiled, wide and open. "I'll get some of those papers the archivists use too, to keep the older ones from smearing."

"Thank you."

Maud was the only person I'd entrusted with a key to my quarters—she was the most honest person I'd ever met. Not even Amethyst or Emerald could enter without my permission. Only Maud.

*Be wary.*

A lesson Elise and I had learned the same night. A lesson we were still paying for.

# CHAPTER
## SIX

M aud and I couldn't read all of Elise's notes. They were as flowery and fancy as her, the rhythm bouncy. I liked listening to Maud read them though, and I nodded off to a note about missing pages and inked-out words. The old Erlenian didn't make a lick of sense to either of us. Maud left and I slept. I didn't dream.

"What you know about rangers?" I said as I pulled on my pants and coat the next day. Hair slicked back and mask in place, I looked like Ruby sapped of red. Bone white.

Ash white.

I yanked it off.

"Very little," Maud muttered behind me, "and certainly less about killing them than you. If you would like me to help you plan a robbery, however, I will be of more help."

"How many robberies you planned?" I spun, scowling hard so she'd know it was fake, and waved my gloves under her nose. "Which one of us better at it?"

"Historically, me." She grinned. "I am the one who got you that nightshade extract."

I laughed.

It was nice. Sometimes, even when the world seemed all right, I didn't know if we'd all ever laugh again.

"You just wanted to watch me jump out a window." I tucked the gloves into my pocket, soft leather sliding from my hands like rain. They were poison proof and perfect, Emerald's gift to me the day I'd left the infirmary.

Course, she'd made them because I "didn't know poison from punch and was likely to die before midnight," but they were nice. And they were mine.

Leather work was time consuming, but she'd put that time in. Barely anyone ever did that for me.

"The others at breakfast yet?" I needed to ask Emerald about the rangers. She'd dealt with them before, and Amethyst would know how soldiers were trained.

Maud nodded. "Go eat. I'll take care of packing the basics, and we can deal with the other things after."

It was the simplest exchange we'd had in a while. Giving orders without sounding rude—Maud was always ready to say when I was—was harder than Nicolas's fencing lessons.

Least eating was easy. Our dining room was the only thing connecting each Left Hand member's rooms. Low, flat ceilings and brightly lit lanterns made everything feel safer. Even the table, carved with the true names of every member of the Left Hand, felt smooth and comforting under my hands. There weren't many names, but I loved them, memories of people I'd never meet. People who'd understand the bloodiest parts of me in some small way.

"I'd forgotten how long his signature was." Emerald sat across from me, mask gone and face crinkled in a grin.

Green was her favorite color, and she knew she looked good in it. I'd caught her crying once, after talking to Our Queen, and she'd spent the day prying up the metal covers of her nails so she could replace them with green ones. Made her feel more like herself, it had to. I'd drawn my own name and orange blossoms on my skin enough to stain it forever.

But it made me feel like me.

She reached out and touched the end of Ruby's name. "Such arrogance for someone so young. You're very similar."

Rodolfo da Abreu.

"Thank you." I spread too much butter and pepper jam over a potato cake and shrugged. "Your compliments mean the world to me."

She laughed.

Amethyst, next to me and dripping from her after-training bath, chuckled. "Very alike."

I'd have liked to know him longer.

"I'm sure." I stole back the honey from Emerald—she always used too much to be tasty—and stirred a spoonful into my tea. "I heard about Elise."

"Good," said Emerald, gaze stuck on the steam rising from her tea. "We should talk about the rangers and their propaganda. Elise's note provided context and certainty that she is, for now, safe."

*I am safe. Do not send help.*

Propaganda: Weylin's only constant export. Surely, if Winter had forced Elise to write the note, it would have been more kind,

RUIN OF STARS

but Elise was a star among fireflies. She was valuable, and Erlend liked value. So long as her value outweighed whatever trouble she gave Winter, she'd be safe.

"She'll be fine," I said. "She's clever."

"Exactly." Emerald peeled open an egg. "And if you don't do your job right, you'll put her and all of us in danger."

Lady save me.

"You could just tell me to get to work." I sipped my tea, staring at her over the rim and thinking of the way Elise had glared at me over the edge of her spectacles. "I was going to ask you about the rangers anyway."

"If he's still alive, there will be a group of eleven and a man named Caden de Bain." Emerald pulled the little slate we used for secret things into her lap and dipped her finger in the water pitcher. She drew as she spoke. "He's been fighting as long as I've been shooting, so imagine how good he is. You won't beat him in a fist fight. You won't beat him in a sword fight. You won't beat him at all if he sees you coming. I have a map for you to memorize, but don't expect exactness. It's as close as our scouts could get before returning."

She handed me the slate and tapped the dark, thick scar running across Caden de Bain's nose.

"All right." I wiped the slate clean. He'd three facial scars and a boxer's crooked jaw. "I'm not good with a bow, but I've fought plenty of people before—"

"No, you've fought untrained boxers and people with decade-old training they can't remember." Emerald set down her cup and fixed me with a spine-shuddering stare. "Erlend's rangers aren't soldiers. They're the men the Erlend army

—⁂ 43 ⁂—

thought too brutal for warfare, and this is the closest many of them have been to Igna in years. I fought in a war. I fought against the shadows. I served as Our Queen's Emerald." She leaned across the table, holding her spoon to me like a blade. "The fights I had with the rangers I killed were the messiest, hardest things I've ever done. You're the enemy, not a person, to them."

As if Erlend had ever seen Naceans as people.

"If you fail, if you are caught, they will use it as an excuse to march on Igna, to say, 'Here is what your enemy looks like; here is who they are.' If not you, they will find someone else, which is why you must kill them first." Amethyst drew a line through Ruby's name with her finger. "All the other Sals and Emeralds and Elises, the poor, the ill, those with an Alonian name or even only the looks of the Sun-Drenched Coast as Erlend sees it— how soon before Erlend declares them the enemy and only thing standing in the way of Erlend prosperity? Weylin's lands are floundering. He will not admit defeat. He will point at us and say we are the cause of their suffering."

"It's why Erlend destroyed all of Aren's and Lona's old texts," Emerald said. "It absolved them of their guilt and let them point at history and go, 'That's not what happened; this is what happened.' Aren's nobles took offense at Aren, Nacean, and Lonian society not subscribing to their ideas of personhood or inheritance or government, so they decided Eredan would be the only society. Our existence"—she gestured to herself and to me—"tempers Erlend greatness and prevents them from achieving their obvious destiny."

I curled my fingers tighter around my cup, skin burning.

Sometimes, when I was out with Rath and a bit of Erlenian caught my ears, I flinched before I even knew if they were talking to me. I was so used to their ideas about space and debt, who didn't want me around them, and who I owed answered about myself, my body was always in a low panic.

I whispered, "They'd kill all of us if it got them what they wanted."

Lady, they might kill us to prove they could.

"And we're here to prevent that with the least amount of deaths. We are killers to keep the worse killers at bay." Emerald sighed and closed her eyes, fingers still against the table. "Language and information are dangerous weapons, and Weylin controls both when dealing with his people. They know only what he wants them to know, and they know only the words he wants them to know. Erlend's old ideals, the Eredan traditions, are incompatible with many people's exis-tence. How do we end a system designed to kill us when we are also within it?"

"Don't give them questions no one can answer." Amethyst tossed a spoon at Emerald.

She knocked it away and lunged across the table, shoving everything between us out of the way. Her nose bumped mine. "Our entire world and the worlds of so many others rest on our duties as Our Queen's Left Hand. We cannot fail, or Weylin will see everyone like us, everyone like Our Queen and Nicolas and Elise, lessened and abused and killed to uplift unachievable ideals. Do you understand? This isn't only your revenge any-more. They will keep doing what they did to Nacea to every-one else if they get the chance. We wouldn't have survived the last decade without their resources and we thought they'd changed, but the leaders, the ones with a dependency on power, have not. We must succeed."

I nodded again.

"Good." She patted my cheek and sat back down. "Your list though, you'll get. They're bound to be on our list eventually whether we know it now or not."

Amethyst leaned over to me and said in my ear, "She does that to all of us new ones. Don't worry."

"I certainly did not say any of that to you." Emerald sucked her tongue against her front teeth, the little sound muffled by her tea. "I just told you to do your job because the ones of us Erlend hates shouldn't be the only ones doing all the work."

"I meant terrifying the new ones," Amethyst said with a laugh.

"I'm clearly not terrifying enough. All of you keep doing foolish things and dying on me when we are supposed to be the ones doing the killing," she muttered. "I'd never killed anyone before the war and had never entertained the idea until Weylin sent his killers after Marianna."

I swallowed and set my cup down, appetite fading. Marianna da Ignasi, Our Queen, was beloved by so many and once by me, but no one loved her more than Emerald.

I felt that sometimes. That deep *ache* of wanting to do right by someone so badly it hurt.

"There were four of us—all mages, all angry—and we decided that we were strong enough, that we loved Igna and all of its people enough, that the rest of the nation should not have to take on the darkest of jobs in order to live in peace, to do it this service. People shouldn't have to fight for the right to live.

People shouldn't feel bad if they can't fight. People should be people, and Weylin hates that Igna sees him as a person just like anyone else. We're killing a few killers to save many."

This was our debt, and I would honor it. I would bear it. There was hate in my reason, but she was right. I would not have gone after the Erlend nobles on my list so strongly if I had not loved everyone they'd killed and everyone they would kill. People deserved a chance to live, not because of who they were, but because they were.

"I get it." I nodded and traced Ruby's name again. He'd been prepared to die for sparing us the threat of shadows coming back. I had to prepare myself. "Can I ask you something?"

"Was the monologue I gave not enough?" Emerald glanced at Amethyst and grinned. "Young people are so demanding. In my day—"

"You walked up hills both ways through snow with no shoes and only one single wick to keep you warm all winter?" Amethyst asked.

I laughed.

"I grew up in the south." Emerald waved us off. "We had a single leaf among one thousand to use as a fan."

I groaned.

Amethyst laughed. "Roland here? Thought I heard him getting drinks earlier?"

"Last night." Emerald refilled her tea and glanced at me. "Roland is my friend and will join us for breakfast whenever he's done being lazy. He is familiar enough with the room, so don't worry about the blindfold."

Emerald hadn't bothered to explain the rules about guests to me other than all of them had to be blindfolded so they couldn't see us or the way to Our Queen's quarters.

"That's part of what I want to ask," I said and tugged the plate of fried, sausage-stuffed peppers to me. "You kept saying 'people like us.'"

Emerald had told me romance wasn't her style, and I'd had the little prickling in my soul that went off when I was talking to someone who got it.

"Let's wait for Roland." She twisted to the door to her quarters and waited. "He's a scout, and he's very good, but if you ever run into him, pretend you don't him. It's better that way."

Amethyst, stirring a bowl of porridge instead of eating it, cracked her neck.

"That man could sleep through anything," she whispered to me. "It's very impressive."

Emerald's door opened, and a guard from ages ago—one who'd led me to auditions and tripped me in the forest, one I'd been all set to kill—stepped into the room and adjusted his blindfold. It slipped down his broad nose. Emerald pulled out the chair next to her.

"It's been three days," Amethyst said. "What happened?"

"Hilarious." He folded his long legs into the chair. "That will only work once. Tea, please."

Emerald poured him a cup, stirred three spoonfuls of honey in it, and set it next to his right hand. They'd the same disgusting tea habits.

"That one? Really?" I gestured at Roland and frowned. "Why's he working the city gates if he's such a good scout?"

Roland grinned. "Oh, that voice. You're Opal?"

He was good looking in a happy way—a wide smile with slightly crooked teeth, huge brown eyes beneath straight brows and a crisp, newly done line up. And like Four had, he knew it.

No one smiled like that and didn't know it.

"Not a word," Emerald said. "Ham's on your left and hash is next to it."

"Thank you." His mouth went even wider, teeth too big and making the smile all that much worse. "Gate duty's usually a nice vacation, but auditions upped the intensity. You have a mean fighting style, knives and a hand."

"My name's Opal."

He laughed, shaking his head. "Sure."

"You're lucky I didn't kill you." I snatched up a piece of ham and tore into it. "You were saying 'us,' Emerald?"

"We are similar in a way. Erlend loathes both of us, but the part of me they would disagree with is to do with attraction." She sighed, long and loud and annoyed. "I experience no romantic attraction. The same is not true of sexual. There are others who experience the opposite or the same or both. Some people who grew up with primarily Erlend ideas have a hard enough time separating sex, romance, and love for me to even finish talking about it."

"And you do hate being interrupted." Roland raised his glass.

Emerald tapped her knuckles against the rim and smiled.

People did get all up in knots over sex and love and romance all the time. Alonians less so, but the farther north you went, the worse it got. Same went for gender.

It wasn't about the clothes or their silly notions about how men and women acted. My life was about me and no one else, but they'd hurt me time and time again—asking me what was under my clothes, assuming I was a girl or boy as if those were the only possibilities and always separate, saying it was hard for them to remember how to refer to me but never asking. It was always about them. Their comfort was more important than my existence.

I was fluid. They were selfish.

That's what it was—they didn't see me as important enough to bother.

"You're not alone here." Emerald blew the steam from her new cup of tea. "Most of us supported Our Queen because we were the ones Erlend wanted dead the most." She nodded to Amethyst. "Or the ones willing to fight even though Erlend wasn't going after them."

Amethyst tapped her soft-boiled egg against Emerald's empty cup. "I won't stop fighting till my corpse is on a pyre."

Least that part of my admiration was warranted.

"About that." Roland gestured to me. "I grew up on the border, before the war, you know, and my parents assumed I was a girl. I assumed, after a while, they were all fools. Not that it's the same, but talking's nicer when it's with someone who understands. Lark and I get together with some other folks occasionally. You should come."

I held out my hand in agreement and tapped the table near his, wanting sealed and sure. Wanting to make sure he was real.

It was different seeing older folks. The ones who'd thrived despite Erlend trying to drag them down.

"I'd like that," I said, fingers closing around his hand when he found mine. "I won't even try to kill you this time."

Lady, let him come back alive. I wanted that talk. And he was older than me. He'd years of living. I wanted that knowledge.

"You could try. I like a fun sparring partner." Roland laughed. "But who knows how alive we'll all be next meeting time?"

Emerald shrugged. "I'm fine with dying so long as the world I leave's safer for it. We have to protect each other, the future included."

"I understand," I said. "No one else innocent dies. No more pyres built for friends. I'm ready to end this."

"Good," Emerald said. "Roland, tell them about Caden de Bain and his rangers."

And much later, once I was fed and watered and packed, Emerald took my face in her hands and kissed my temple. "Step lightly."

"Hit hard." Amethyst took her place and kissed me too. "And come back alive."

Their lips to the Lady's ears.

# CHAPTER
## SEVEN

I rented a carriage for the first leg of the trip. I was terrible at riding horses, always going sideways or getting thrown or both. People and livestock crowded the roads, trying to carry on with their normal lives or fleeing farther south, and I'd no desire to stampede through them just to get there a bit faster. The border was already chaotic enough, and not everyone could just up and leave. I had to take care of Caden de Bain and his rangers quick.

These kids could be their next corpses.

The carriage I was in was boring enough to be any moneyed traveler with a taste for solitude. It was the sort Rath and I used to target most often, the outside gilded but not too fancy and the inside built for four people to share. The cost was more than normal folks could afford unless you were sharing with a wealthier friend, and people out to save a pearl or two from going toward the price never paid for extra guards. I hadn't either, but I was me.

Good evening for it though. The clear sky was only just starting to bruise, and the curtained window let in the dying scent of the last summer blooms. I tilted my head back till the memories of Rath's voice in the dark, the tang of his breath, and the rustle of his hand against his hair overpowered the crickets and clomping hooves. A long, low whistle like a loon's echoed outside.

I opened my eyes and peeked out of the carriage. No one else on the road. I pulled out my knife.

My driver shrieked and yanked the carriage to a stop.

A thief, thin and young as I'd been my first run, flew through my window feet first. They stumbled and spun as the carriage lurched. I didn't know them. Rath must've gotten some new kids.

Six out of ten. Their feet were too close and their balance off. "You're—"

I kicked the thief in the chest. They gasped, stumbling into the seat opposite me. I lurched forward, slammed my hand over their mouth, and pressed a knife into their cheek. They stilled, eyes wide. Too slow.

I patted their cheek. "This is fixing to be a real bad night for you."

Their bushy brows slammed together. A muffled curse.

"Don't worry," I said. "You'll live through it, but I'm not too thrilled about you all taking advantage of the panic."

I'd have done, but I wasn't the decent sort of thief.

Outside, the hushed voice of my driver and a handful of other folks quieted down. They'd be expecting their friend soon.

"Now." I laid my knife against their cheek and smiled. "I'm going to move my hand. You're going to tell me who's outside running this mess, and I'll be out of your life faster than you can blink. Nod if you got it."

They nodded.

I took my hand from their mouth.

"Rath!" They said it so quickly they choked, and I froze. "Rath da Oretta. It's Rath. We're not robbing, you. I swear. He figured you'd not want people seeing's all."

I sheathed my knife and took a deep breath.

Rath, too-kind-to-kill-wasps Rath, who shuddered when thinking about Opal, had come all the way up here, dragging the kids he loved more than life itself this close to the border, to find me. I was traveling without a mask to keep people from thinking Opal was on the move.

How many damned kids had Rath told? He collected them as quick as he collected coins, giving away food and clothes and love till they kept coming back. He was too softhearted, too easy to be taken advantage of. I'd been watching the warrants coming out of Kursk. None of our old gang had any, but Nicolas said the guards down there were living well off of bribes. Had to be him.

He'd pay his way into debt to keep everyone safe. Least until they'd enough money to do something legal.

"Get up." I tapped their knees and nodded to the door. "And next time keep your balance lower."

They tripped out of the carriage and sprinted away. The noise outside died.

"You get lost?" I shouted.

Rath, ever the charmer, shouted back, "Not as much as you."

"Get in here." I kicked the door open and waited, not wanting to see who else he'd brought up here. A series of whispers. "You could've gotten them all killed, you know?"

"They're already getting killed, and I'm more scared of the shadows than I am of you." Rath, familiar face framed by short, black hair twisted out and a new pair of earrings, stepped into the carriage, and the lamplight caught his eyes—brighter and wearier than I remembered. The salted flecks were as ghost pale as the chalky sheen across his dark skin. He'd not been sleeping. "I told your driver to keep going. My lot are running back. We need to talk."

Lady save me. This couldn't be good.

I sat down. "Talk."

"Good." He shut the door and stumbled as the carriage picked up speed, and I waited for him to start.

He didn't.

"You're not one to mull," I finally said. I figured he'd at least hug me, but he was only fiddling with his rings. Stung a bit. "What's going on?"

He ran a hand over his face and shuddered. "Sorry. Lords, Sal, it's all rubbish."

I moved to sit next to him, and he threw himself on me, arms hooking under mine and nose bumping my cheek. I hugged him back tight around his shoulders and got a nose-full of sweat and ink, rotten leaves and old, dry wine. Rath, pure and filthy, eternally too busy with new ideas to bathe till he looked in a mirror. He crumpled in my arms, too heavy for me to hold up. I leaned back.

"I was furious." He pulled back, face slack. Tiredness stuck to his skin like dust. Half circles of puffy skin hung beneath each eye. "You running off to die and leaving me to deal with everything. You were so content to never see me again."

I shifted. "I wasn't thinking of it like that."

"Course you were," he said. "You never think through anything."

That was always his job. He untangled his arms from mine, the relief at having him close dimming. He laced our fingers.

"I'm glad you're Opal." He sniffed. "Not just because I need help. I'm glad you're alive. I'm glad you're getting what you want. Odd to think of you as a court member though."

"Don't worry." I slipped his purse from his pocket, waited to see if he'd notice—not a bit—and held it out to him. "Still some Sal in here."

"Course there is." He snatched the purse. Grinning. "I liked you better when I thought you were dead."

"Usually how missing dead folks goes."

Dealing with Rath was effortless—jokes, joy, and a bit of ribbing without the threat of murder. Court was well and good, better in a dozen ways, but it didn't erase the near decade I'd spent running with Rath through the wilds of southern Igna. He was familiar in a way I couldn't put into words, only memories of shaking hands stitching up my calf and late-night laughter strengthened by a stolen supper.

Comfortable if not quite content. The always-there feel of friendship.

"I can't believe you…" He trailed off, gaze dropping to my hands and darting to the sheaths on my belt.

"Don't think about me killing," I said softly. "Not all necessary ends come from kind beginnings."

"No, I need Opal's help. I need you, necessary ends and all."
He spread his hands out between us, fingers open and palms
faceup. Our signal that we weren't being watched or forced to
talk. "There are kids missing. First, it was just stories from the
north. Figured they were tales to make kids obey, but then one
of the new ones, Cam, he didn't come back one night."

I cracked my knuckles one by one. More missing kids. More
nonsense I didn't know what to do with. "Sure he didn't run?"

"Wouldn't." Rath shook his head. "He's not like the runners.
He's like us."

Nowhere to go. No one to run to. We'd made a family down
south after the war had taken our original ones. Rath was more
insistent on it than me. He liked caring for people, for kids,
making sure they didn't turn out like us.

"What's his full name?" I asked. "I can get guards to look for
him but—"

"No." Rolling his lips together, Rath leaned against the cushion behind him and slumped over. "It was guards took him."

"You sure?" I knocked him with a shoulder. "If Igna guards
are snatching kids, I need to know."

Those guards and whoever was ordering them about need to
die. Now.

Children had no place in this. They already had to inherit
our mess of a world, and these kids had no one who would
come looking for them or could afford to if they wanted. They'd
slipped through the cracks and paid for our mistakes.

We'd take care of these kids. We'd fill in the cracks.

What was the point in stopping a war if the future was dead?

"You know all those people who buy up old soldier uniforms

and then go begging for free drinks by talking about their past?" he asked. "Kids that saw him get snatched say they looked like that—old uniforms missing the new little hems guards got these days. And they were heading north. No town guards are heading north yet."

Rangers. It had to be. "What do you want me to do?"

I was stalling. Opal couldn't agree immediately, but Sal was doing whatever Rath asked. I had left him.

He deserved better.

"Find him. He's my responsibility, and I know you're doing something important, but these are our kids, Sal. This is us. How much better off would we have been if we'd someone come save us? Children have no place in our messes, and I'd rather build my own pyre than build one for Cam. I'm not letting him or any of them die." He twisted so we were fully looking at each other, not just stealing glances, and grabbed my knees. The full weight of him bore down on my legs. "It's was Erlends, right? Those rangers Weylin's got?"

"Maybe." Probably. There'd been no children found near the border, dead or alive, but if it was the rangers, what were they doing with them? The clammy memory of the severed, runed ear from Caldera's desk tingled against my hand. Lady, don't let them be related. "Why Cam?"

Rath shrugged. "There were four other kids there. They ran straight up to him, picked him up, and took off. No one got a word out of them, and by the time the remaining kids found me, Cam was gone."

*Be wary.*

"Fine. I'll help. You can come with me. We'll find Cam or

close as I can get to finding him without starting a war." I couldn't tell Rath I was out solely to kill rangers, but I could poke around. He was good at spying on people so long as no one asked him to pickpocket them. "But if I tell you to do something, you do it. This isn't another normal night, the two of us together again. This is death we're walking into—theirs or ours—and you can't turn away from that."

He nodded.

"Good," I said. "I've not heard much about kids missing, but I know about some missing adults. We'll start their first."

And there was no part of me ever telling Rath I'd found a kid's severed ear runed to shreds and tucked away like a trophy.

# CHAPTER
# EIGHT

Rath and I left the carriage behind a day from the border. We traveled at night when the roads were near empty and most folks asleep. These lands had been Igna before, but the people were still Erlends. Borders didn't change culture or traditions, and while Igna was trying to make the world a safer place for the people Erlend dismissed, I was thrilled about moving through recently reclaimed Erlend lands. Erlend culture was built on the idea that men and women were the only genders and that men were inherently better. People like Elise—a young woman, not solely attracted to men, and born to an Alonian mother—were doomed three times over. As for me…

"I don't like it," Rath said once we were firmly encased among the limbs of a leafy oak and settled in for a night of watching a small homestead. It felt like a good place to be—open fields but still plenty of cover, lots of woods near enough to drinking water, and places for camping where no one could see unless they were standing on you. I opened my mouth to agree, but

Rath continued, "It's cold, and Cam wasn't wearing a sweater when they grabbed him."

I glanced at Rath, grinning. The best parts of him kept getting better. "They took him for a reason. They'll make sure he's all right or else they'd grab any kid."

"I hope so."

"Cam got sweaters back home?" I asked, knowing the answer but wanting to hear it.

"Course." Rath scoffed. "I'm not hiring kids to work outside and not making sure they got sweaters."

I laughed. "You sew them?"

He would if he could, but I'd never seen him darn more than socks.

"Tried." He laughed too and knocked my shoulder with his. "It's real calming though. I need to practice more. I got patches down. Day's trying to teach me embroidery. You remember his coat?"

I nodded.

"It's even more elaborate than the last time you saw it." Rath's smile slipped. He ducked. "I didn't get it back then. How much that coat meant to him. Day always said he wasn't allowed to sew when he lived up here." He raised his head and met my eyes. "I didn't connect it to you hating being close to Erlend. To all the ways they tried to make you feel lesser." He paused, then added, "Makes sense now."

I nodded. The homestead wasn't fun to watch for me, seeing all the little ways adults crushed the spirits and selves of children like me and Elise and Day.

Maybe Rath and I would have time to help with that too.

An owl call, too high to be real, whistled through the night. Rath and I froze.

Rangers? But if they were as good as everyone said, they'd have better calls.

Rath touched my chin and turned my head east, toward a wall of trees thick as night. A small glint of metal flickered in the dark like a distant star, but the two of us knew—a signal. I pulled a black cloth mask, courtesy of Rath, from my pocket. Rath pulled his on too.

No one moved in the tree line. We crept around the edges of the homestead, bodies low and feet quiet. Rath'd gotten better at it, a feat he'd been quick to tell me about on our journey, but I kept him a good few steps behind me in case. A little thicket of broken branches and chewed mint leaves smelled of piss, and I followed a trail of footprints deeper into the woods. Erlend was all trees and fields, endless green. Made it easier to track folks.

A dim light filtered through the trees. I stopped. Rath crept up behind me, and we snuck as close as we could without getting into the light. Four Erlend men—proud of it and taking the piss out of each other for it—sat around a small fire and went over a dirt-scrawled map of the homestead. They all looked about the same, blond hair brown with dirt and white skin the streaked pinks and reds of uneven sunburns. One of them was older than the rest.

"Tomorrow," he said, picking burs out of his socks. "When most of them are away for that draft meeting."

Bandits.

Rath exhaled, fingers digging into the dirt. These men were the worst sort, thieves without practice or trust. They'd leave as many coins behind as they'd leave corpses, and Rath and I had seen plenty of people dead by bandits' hands after a robbery went wrong. They were taking advantage of fear and chaos.

And Erlend would blame any issues on Igna bandits, surely.

A soft, breathless sigh ruffled the leaves to my right. I froze. Held my breath.

A shadow too dark for the blue-green of night slipped into the corner of my sight. The heavy, stifling weight of knowing I wasn't alone pressed into my lungs. I held perfectly still and laid a hand on Rath's knee so he'd know to do the same. There was someone else here, someone else watching. The soft breaths hummed from the right. I didn't turn my head. Only glanced.

An Erlend scout in dark browns and blacks too much for the deep purple of the shadow they were in, stared straight into the bandit camp. They must've just stepped up.

They'd crept in on a breath of air. Stealthy. Near impossible to notice. Rath hadn't heard them at all.

Lady, they were good.

Rath and I stayed perfectly still, breathing with the breeze to cover the sound, and the scout at my side slunk away, vanishing into the thick woods to the right and away from the direction we'd come.

"Is this going to be fun-fun," I asked, "or you-get-us-both-killed fun?"

He shrugged. "Fun."

We circled far around to our little camp, going as slowly as possible and looking out for more scouts. We found nothing, but I kept watch first, staring into the darkness with one hand on Rath and the other on a knife. The sharp, fluttery panic in my chest stayed with me all night. I slept fitfully after Rath took over and woke up on edge.

"Something's wrong," Rath said soon as I opened my eyes. "They should be working, but it's quiet."

"Bandits?"

"No." He shook his head and buried his plum pit.

I started walking, the unease in my stomach burning up my throat. "Come on."

We didn't get far.

The bandits, only three of them, were lined up on the edges of the homestead. They'd been stripped, faces turned to the rising sun. Each one wore a scrap of cloth as a mask—green, purple, white. The sigil of Our Queen of the Eastern Spires and Lady of Lightning Marianna da Ignasi was carved into each and every one of them. As if the Left Hand would kill like that.

We were assassins, not torturers.

Rath vomited behind me. I tossed him a handkerchief.

"Least we know there's more than one scout," I said, voice steadier than my hands. "Guess I know what their game is."

Fear. Intimidation. Propaganda. They were killing their own—the troublemakers, the unwanted, the ones they didn't want to waste time arresting—and using their corpses to make people think Our Queen had released new shadows.

"That's—" Rath gagged again, and I patted his shoulder.

"Shadows." My fingers tightened around his arm. "Not real ones. Erlend scouts are doing it."

The grass beneath the dead was red but not nearly red enough. They'd done this elsewhere and moved them. I grabbed Rath's arm and dragged him north, the direction of the well or river the homesteaders kept returning from with buckets full of water. We'd not needed to check it out, but the scouts would be bloody. They'd need to rinse off.

Not that the blood would bother them. No, trailing blood was as bad as trailing string when you were on the run. The homestead's water source was a river, deep and fast and freezing, and I led Rath farther north, keeping our steps on the rocky shore and out of the mud. Heavy splashing sounds barely louder than the current pulled me down a side creek. Fish swarmed outside the mouth to a cave.

One scout—a boy with the scratched face of someone learning to shave and the determined look of someone trying to prove themselves—lurched from a shallow cave and tossed a bundle of red into the water. Rath stiffened.

Didn't need him being sick again.

"I'll handle it." I pulled out my knife. "Wait—"

Rath sprinted forward, screamed, and drew the sword he didn't know how to use.

CHAPTER
## NINE

The ranger clotheslined him. Rath went flying back, feet up in the air. I darted forward, knife at the ready, and lunged. The ranger backtracked, empty hands feeling for the sheaths not at his unbelted waist, and I aimed my knife for his neck. His hands came up between us, his left forearm knocking my hand away. He grabbed my collar and twisted. His foot hooked my left ankle.

I crashed into the ground. He fell on top of me, knees on either side of my chest. I yanked my legs up and toward my head, body bent in half, and wrapped one around his neck. He went flying back. I rolled on top of him, leg holding him down across his chest. My knife scratched his throat.

"Stop moving," I said, breathing too fast to say more.

Rath, sword in hand, knelt near the ranger's head. He angled his blade against the ranger's cheek. Blood beaded across his skin.

"That's Cam's." Rath's gaze was stuck on a cheap silver cuff cut to look like leaves curled around the ranger's bloodied ear. "Where is he?"

Nothing.

Rath shuddered, tensed, but couldn't make another cut.

I shifted my grip on the ranger. "I can deal with him."

I was Opal because people like Rath couldn't be. We might not have to kill this boy, but if we had to, if he'd the upper hand, Rath was too kind to do it.

Or he would, and it would kill some beautiful part of him, the gentle part that had brought me tea when I was sick or told me jokes while he stitched me up or gave the younger kids birthday presents even when Grell's quota was bearing down on us.

"Where is he?" Rath didn't move. His eyes were wet and his lips bloody, but his voice didn't waver. He sniffed. "You took a boy named Cam. That's his cuff. Where is he?"

This ranger didn't even blink. I felt my kills. I carried them with me, in my blood and in my fears. This boy felt nothing at all.

No wonder North Star loved his rangers—they were dead and dangerous as the shadows, forcing themselves to feel nothing, to care about no one, to only follow orders.

They were worse than the shadows.

They'd chosen this.

Rath dropped his sword and carefully unhooked the cuff. When our old, dead gang leader Grell had taken Rath's littlest finger, he'd taken the grip of that hand too. Rath couldn't make a fist with that hand. Couldn't hold on to things tightly.

But he could've ripped out the cuff.

And even now, facing Cam's kidnappers, he couldn't commit such harm.

The ranger was young, anyway, barely out of childhood, and Rath was too soft softhearted for pure hate.

We tied up the ranger and gagged him, staking his knotted hands into the ground behind him. He'd not be going anywhere soon, and I rifled through his belongings and pockets while Rath cleaned off Cam's ear cuff. A map, crudely drawn and labeled in Erlenian, was tucked into the ranger's boots. The ranger said nothing no matter how many questions I asked. He'd an old Igna guard coat though. I took the map to Rath.

He pressed the silver edges of the cuff back together where the ranger had stretched them out. "Cam didn't like blood." He traced the pattern of three leaves cut into the cuff. "Didn't want to pierce his ear, so I got him this."

"He'll be happy to have it back when we find him. They definitely took him. They've got Igna uniform pieces." I handed the map to Rath. "Can you read this?"

He nodded. "Just names—Hinter, Norventry, Reeds, Brist."

*I am safe. Do not send help. Be wary.*

"What's the circled one?" They were headed there, probably, and had left this new recruit to clean up.

"Hinter."

Good. Wasn't sending help if I was there for other things.

"What we going to do with him?" Rath nodded to the ranger.

I couldn't look at the red blur in the back of the cave, but Rath had to see if the fourth bandit was alive.

He wasn't.

"I'm going to talk to him," I said. "If he doesn't talk back, you'll figure out what I mean to do."

The ranger had been trying to break free of his bonds. I sat down in front of him and sheathed my knife. He stared through me.

"I'm not going to hurt you," I said to the ranger, mind clear as spring water and just as cold. He was younger than me, and he wasn't shaking, but his blue eyes had that same dead look Five had during the audition. "I'm not even going to kill you."

He said nothing.

"I know you didn't see the shadows because those bandits you flayed look like a poacher did it. The shadows were quick. Quiet. Most didn't even know they were hurt till they looked." I swallowed, knife clacking against my leg in time with my shaking hands. "And what came after was worse...but you've never seen it," I whispered. "You've never heard it."

The wet, sucking gasp of skin sloughing off in the rain.

"You're going to. You're going to understand what you did."

The whispers of carrion beetles crawling through the dirt, of dry skin flaking off in the wind, of souls ripped from their place on this earth and calling out to find it. The only sounds for days.

Death was not quiet, and I could hear it even now.

"Rath." I set the water and rations close enough for the ranger to bend over and eat, and he followed my movement, mouth open, face finally showing something. "I need you to do this for me."

The ranger hadn't been born with this apathetic stoicism, not like some whose faces never revealed what they were thinking. He'd been taught it. All those rangers lined up like soulless knives on a butchers table, but they never stuck around to see what they'd carved. This one though would not be found for days, and he would see it. He would smell it. He would hear it.

*Drip.*

I would make death his everything like Erlend had made it mine.

"You're going to look at your work and know what you've done, not only to the dead but to the rest of them, the ones who saw. The ones who remember, like I do, the true fear Erlend caused. You might get nothing out of it."

He stared beyond me, to the shuffling drip of Rath carrying the dead, and I closed my eyes.

*Drip.*

My too-quick breaths, too short, too shallow, too full of this cave and death and memories, echoed around us.

Rath set the body down. It slipped and squished, and the ranger whimpered.

He said, "Please."

"I hope you get something out of it." I opened my eyes and stared up at the setting sun, rust red behind the thick pine trees. "Or I'll be killing you soon."

*Drip.*

## CHAPTER
# TEN

R ath didn't speak much after we left. I didn't either. The world felt separate, like I was walking down another road than the one I was on, and the corpse was dripping behind me. It was louder in my memories.

I was too alive. Too aware. My skin was too tight and too hot and my ribs too cinched to contain my heart. How could I be too here and so far away at once?

"Sal?" Rath coughed—loud—and waved his hand in front of my face. "You good?"

No.

"Why? What's wrong?" I asked.

"Nothing, you're stumbling." He didn't touch me. He knew not to. "We heard about, you know, the murders. Most folks thought them rumors."

"Wish they were." I sipped from my canteen and swished water between my teeth. I could taste the blood, the rot, the steel of the knives. "I'm here to take care of the rangers doing it."

Caden de Bain—a man who took boys and raised them to be monsters, told them it was for the greater good.

Rath nodded. "Good. They need to be stopped."

The rest of the day was silent. We passed fleeing families and merchants and soldiers on the road but stayed far away from all of them, taking to the woods along the path when anyone neared. There was no time to go back to the homestead and help those kids, but maybe defeating North Star would be all the help they needed. Most of the families heading south hid too. The soldiers didn't hide.

Erlend's military was fueled by a draft, and most of the uniformed travelers looked better suited for farming or book-keeping than war. Some looked uncertain. How much had the lives of all these folks changed between being Erlend and being Igna?

Least Our Queen didn't make them fight her wars. They talked of protecting traditions and Erlend's great history, but tradition wasn't tradition when it erased and killed thousands.

Why go back to the traditions that colored you killers?

Most of the soldiers we saw were young. All were male. Or at least, their leaders referred to them as men.

Lark del Evra had told me once that Erlend's inheritance laws were based on older things, ideas Alona and Nacea didn't share about men and women. It was why Erlend saw Elise's attraction to anyone not male as unseemly. Why Lark del Evra had pledged allegiance to Our Queen as soon as they'd heard about her court's goal to end such violent ideas in all parts of the continent. It was why there were no female soldiers.

What would Erlend have done with Lark? Roland? Me?

Drafted half? Made me serve every other day? Forced me to pick one or the other?

It was always one or the other.

As if Erlend could only count by twos.

We never saw scouts though. Not a sight of them anywhere.

Rath and I reached Hinter at dawn. The city proper was sprawling, buildings and fields splayed out like ribs around the towering spine of Winter's hilltop estate. Snowcapped mountains on the horizon crowned the castle roofs with spiked shadows, and what little warmth I'd gathered in my shaking hands, that *drip* still trailing behind me, escaped with every movement. A river spilling down from the mountains had been redirected through the city into four shallow trenches, splitting the land into curving pieces, and the shops and houses closest to the stone wall separating Winter and Elise from the common folk were crowded together like crooked teeth in a too-small mouth. They spread out the farther from the wall they got, and the roads got wider. Carts and crowds were lining up near the wall.

"They're rationing." Rath pointed to a group of people pressed against a gate in the wall, their hands pounding against the wooden door. "We used to do the same when they were late passing out rations at the end of the war."

"Shouldn't be rationing yet," I said. "They've got plenty of land and food."

Where was it going if not to the people?

Rath and I picked our way over the hills, peeking into barns and homes. Rath pulled a poster from a gnathic's door and mumbled to himself before shoving the paper at me. A blond soldier with a square jaw and broad shoulders carried a kid to safety across a river. I shrugged.

"You read what it says?" I asked him.

Rath waved one hand. "Fuel the war. Fuel your saviors. Something like that. 'Saving children, not a child army.'"

So Erlend was telling people Igna was stealing kids.

Why'd Erlend need children though? And what were they doing with ears? They had to be related, but even in the darkest days of the war ten years ago, no one had stooped so low as to hurt children. Erlend would not suddenly start kidnapping children and cutting off their ears for no reason. They'd never avoided hurting children, but they'd not cross that line twice. The ear had to belong to a missing kid.

But I could barely stomach the thought.

"Least we know why Hinter's distributing rations if nothing else." Winter must've been sending all the high-value food north and keeping Hinter on a strict regimen. "Saves money too."

And if your civilians were scared of the shadows creeping closer, they'd be desperate to help the army that protected them.

"I think it's telling people who can't supply the required amount to see Lady Elise de Farone. Looks like 'donations,' except those aren't usually required." He glanced at me. "Someone added that bit after. It's not printed."

I nodded. Elise would handwrite a hundred pleas for those who needed help to come to her.

Like I was coming for her now.

I needed her calmness, her cleverness, her confidence. I knew she was alive, but I'd lost so many the thought of losing her too froze me. She might not be dead yet, but the world was changing. I couldn't let my last memory of her be so bloody.

"Reports of deserters will be rewarded," Rath whispered. "I don't see what any of this has got with Cam."

"Nothing, hopefully." I'd have stuck out if I went strolling through town, so I pulled Rath toward the wall till we hit the gap where the river ran through it. "The other rangers might be here though, and we need to know where they're heading. I'll find them if you keep a look out for Cam or any other kids that look like they're from the Alona bits of Igna."

"Deal." He glanced around. "What we doing out here?"

"Finding a way in." I nodded to the waterway and pulled out a set of lock picks. "No guards, cheap gate. It'll be easy."

Rath held up one hand, walked toward the woods, and rolled an old tree trunk near the edge. "You'll be shaking too much." I gave him a look. "From the cold," he said. "Just ram it."

He meant from fear. I'd had bouts of it all night and day, the odd, breathless, little moments when a bird called too loud too close or the surprise of a fallen leaf brushing down the back of my arm.

"Coastal cities got gates on their waterways too" he continued, "but they're usually pretty flimsy. Not many fish going to bother to pick or break a lock."

"I've met some rowdy fish." I grinned. Rath lived for swimming in the ocean.

He touched his chest, hand fluttering over his heart. "I am, at the very least, a shark."

"Whale shark." I opened my arms wide and mimed the big creatures' bobbing float. "The meekest of predators."

The nicest of thieves.

He helped me onto the tree trunk, pushed me down the channel, and waved. "I hope river sharks eat your toes."

The cold didn't hit till I took a breath. It splashed up my thighs and shivered into my chest, and a teeth-clattering whine kept me from shouting as the log carried me into the tunnel and rammed me into the gate. I lurched forward, nose nearly hitting the bark. The grate door creaked.

I scooted along the log and grasped the bars. Rath was right. Between my fear and the cold, I was shaking too badly to do anything delicate. I pushed the log back and jammed it into the locking mechanism. It cracked and broke open. I drifted through the tunnel.

The other side was deserted, and I climbed up the slick stone walls of the channel to a grassy corner. It took a while to dry my legs and scrape the river gunk from my boots. It wasn't the worst I'd ever looked.

Which made me feel worse.

The area inside the wall was taller than it was wide. The castle had been built decades before and had nothing on the palace. Gray stone and mahogany wood buildings in sharply angled straight walls made up the bulk of the building, and the stout bottom floors supported four corner towers and a wide center spire. The wind cut between them with a low whistle, rattling the thick shutters on each high window. Winter would place himself at the center of everything.

I crept around the outskirts of the area. Guards and servants wandered the paths. The only proper gate inside was facing the town and wide open, letting through civilians come to talk and tradesmen doing business. If I were robbing the place, I'd have followed them and found the reserves, but Elise's quarters would be separated from the common folk. She was a lady in a land obsessed with nobility.

I snuck my way around the area until I found a window on the center tower only a little ways off the ground, second story at most, and waited till the paths were clear. Scaling it was easy.

Getting inside was too.

I wasn't the army he'd spent decades preparing for.

I darted between closets and rafters until a laundress passed with an armful of dresses about the same height as Elise. They were clean and left the scent of washing powder in their wake. I followed.

She knocked on a door several stories up and went in. I found a servants' closet nearby that had a window and made my way from it toward the room. If it wasn't Elise's, I was at least a step closer to her.

And if it was Winter's, I'd a few things to say to him.

My fingers skimmed an open shutter. I pulled myself up, legs shivering. No one screamed as I made my way into the opening, and I sat half in the window. Elise sat in profile on the bed at the far side of the room.

The blue silk scarf wrapped around her hair was the brightest spot of color in her room. Braids fell over each shoulder, peeking out from under the scarf, and her dark skin was speckled with black, fading ink. Pages upon pages fanned out across her legs like a makeshift skirt. She chewed on the end of a wooden brush pen.

I grinned.

Of course all her bad habits were rolled into writing—she always had ink on her nose and teeth marks on her pens. The tight, little flicker of worry I'd carried in my chest since the last time I saw her loosened. A pleasant, content ease settled over my skin.

She was alive. She was fine. She was still surely, solidly Elise from the tip of her bare toes to the spectacles slipping down her nose.

I opened my mouth to talk, but the sound got lost in my throat. Didn't matter. She was so into her reading, she didn't even look up when the window creaked. I tried again.

"You don't chew on charcoal sticks, do you?" I asked.

Elise shrieked. Her papers scattered. She lunged off the bed and spun to me. The wooden beads at the end of each braid clacked together.

She stared, mouth open. Her hands clenched into fists at her sides. "Sal?"

I bowed.

"How?" She stuttered. Her chest rose and fell faster and faster. "What are you doing here?"

"My lady," I said, rising from my bow and sliding from the window. "You missed our last tutoring session. What was I supposed to do?"

And with another soft, gasping shriek, Elise threw her arms around my neck and sobbed.

## CHAPTER
# ELEVEN

E lise's nose pressed into the curve of my neck and shoulder.
A wet spot seeped into my shirt, and I wrapped my arms
around her, fingers sliding up her back till I found the bare skin
of her neck. Her spectacles pinched.

"Hold on." I pulled back and very slowly took her spectacles
off. "Don't want to break them."

She sniffed and rested her forehead against mine. "I have
another pair. I don't have another you."

The words hit my lips, and she tightened her grip on me,
nails digging through my clothes and into my skin. Her eyelashes
brushed my cheeks.

"I had hoped we would meet sooner rather than later," she
whispered, her lips catching mine.

I pressed forward. Elise sighed and kissed me back, and her
tongue parted my lips, barely, quickly, only enough of a taste to
be a promise. I swallowed and pulled back

Being with her was already tempting enough, but being with

her like this would make it impossible to leave. And I'd have to leave eventually.

She kissed me quickly again. "I hadn't hoped for this smell, though."

"That's your river's fault," I said. "Not mine."

She brought up one of her hands to flick my nose and hit my cheek instead. "You leave my river out of this. I've been trying to get those waterways fixed up for ages."

"And why listen to the smartest person in Hinter?" I paused. Swallowed. "Elise, if I could get you out of here—"

"No." She shook her head, braids slapping against my arms, and narrowed her eyes. "Did you get my note?"

I nodded.

"Then you shouldn't ask me that," she said. "I'm not leaving. I can do more good for the people of Hinter and for Igna here." She stiffened and rolled back her shoulders. "And if you are here to take me home, you can swim out the way you came because you do not understand as well as I thought you did."

"I'm not. Don't worry." I tightened my grip on her and laid my cheek against her shoulder. "Just wanted to check. I'm here for those Erlend rangers stealing Igna kids. Thought you might know more about them."

Elise had her own life to live like I had mine. I had to let her live it as she wanted.

"Good." She tugged my wet sleeves. "Spectacles, please."

I chuckled. It was nice to see her fully, without my mask blocking her arms or sides of her face. I settled the spectacles on her nose and slipped the arms behind her ears, shifting the braids aside with careful hands. They clinked as they moved.

A steady sound, quickly familiar and quietly comfortable.

I traced the shell of her ear from top to bottom and trailed my fingers along the round edge of her jaw until I hit the peak of her chin, then the soft dip of her bottom lip and little valley between her nose and mouth, and finally the far corner of her right eye. I straightened her spectacles and kissed her freckled nose. Elise smiled.

"Good to see you're as charming as ever." She pulled me toward the bed and squeezed my damp sleeve. "How are only your arms and legs wet?"

"Thief secrets." I winked. "How'd you know I'd take the tunnel?"

She pushed me into a chair. "The guards marked the three grates as in need of repairs or extra guards, so I marked them all as fixed on the paperwork. It's the easiest way for me to get Alonian-born Erlends away from the rangers and south to safety."

Her nails drifted to my neck, catching on my collar, and I shuddered.

I'd missed her cleverness and touch and the slight sting of the lemon cleaning tonic that clung to her skin.

"You all right though?" The little rumble of panic I'd carried in my heart for Elise since her abduction was fading. "What's happening here? Looked like rations getting handed out, but Erlend can't be in need of that yet. And I've got rangers flaying folks along the border, missing kids, severed ears."

"I'm all right. I am certainly better off than most of Hinter will be soon." She raised a hand to her mouth, rubbing her chapped bottom lip with a thumb. Old bruises and healed cuts marred her hands. She kept her other hand angled away from me. "My father made a mistake and showed Weylin's hand too soon. Weylin was not fully prepared for war, and he's making my father pay for it. I managed to convince him to directly pay half of his debt, but the rest he is repaying in the form of supplies and food for the army."

I held out my hand to her. "The Erlend army can't already be out of supplies."

"It is much worse than you think and the army much larger than any of us knew. I haven't had a chance to get out another note, but Weylin has collected nearly every Erlend boy to fight, and they are very happy to go to war against the shadows of Igna that killed their parents or uncles or friends ten years ago."

"Course they are," I said. "Erlend rangers are leaving flayed folks all up and down the border. How they going to feel when they find out it was their king killing them this whole time?"

"The people of Hinter are my responsibility no matter where their parents were from—Erlend or Alona or if they still quietly claim Igna citizenship—and if I leave, my father will not look after them as he should. He sees them as pieces, not people. They are his to use to meet whatever ends he seeks." Scowling, she showed me her hand. "He has not apologized. It was my fault for fighting, so he says."

She was missing three nails—first, second, and forth. Her thumbnail had been torn in half. Scabs speckled the nail beds.

I winced. "He's not—"

"No," she said quickly. "Erlend tracks inheritance by bloodlines, not family name. If he loses me, his family dies out."

"Like that's the worst outcome of you dying or getting hurt."

I kissed her knuckles and stroked her wrist. "How they ever going to believe someone like you is on their side?"

"Not easily." She stayed standing before me, gently pressing my hand to her side. Her hips were still round, my fingers barely spanning from hip to rib, but I could feel the lack of her, the weight worry and work had taken away. "He's holding out hope that he can save me from my disastrous ways since Lena managed to rein me in as a child. I'm pretending it's working."

"I've met your Lena."

Elise grinned. "Really? Is she safe? Is she with Our Queen?" I opened my mouth to answer but Elise rambled on, gesturing wildly. "Of course she is! She's very clever, and she was always furious with Weylin. He gifted her her land, you know, but only after she showed him that she'd been running it behind her father's back for years. If Hinter and my father hadn't joined Igna, I'd not be able to inherit. Lena told me all about it, how to play Weylin and all his lords at their own game."

"I'm glad you had her."

Mostly. She was getting under my skin.

"Me too." She sighed and pulled away, drifting to the pile of papers on her bed. "You mentioned children and rangers. I'm not surprised by their involvement in the murders, but I had noticed several children gone. Until now, I had assumed they'd run to Igna."

I shrugged and stood. "They might've, but the group I used to run with had a kid get snatched, and we found some of his things on a ranger."

"If I thought Weylin needed it, I would say he's collecting children for work, but he's got civilians for that, the ones who couldn't be drafted." She beckoned me to the bed. "I've only seen one group of rangers, and they were missing a member."

"That's the group I'm after then." I tripped over a book in the middle of the floor and stumbled.

Elise let out a breathy laugh. "They scare me. I didn't meet with them, but I've seen them. It was one of the older groups under Caden de Bain. My father hates him. Says he's so far gone into his violence that most of his blood probably isn't his anymore, and his underlings are much the same, taking joy in their jobs. The only useful thing I know isn't even that useful—they brought news of a spy in Our Queen's estate. A servant. Said they had fulfilled their 'end of her deal,' whatever that may be. It's the first I've heard of it, and I have trouble believing Weylin would hire a woman. He hates us so."

A servant spy. It'd be good cover and enough freedom to work. And it was the opposite of what everyone expected.

I'd have to tell Nicolas.

"How you know the rangers take joy in it?" I asked.

She shuddered. "They make a game of it, I think, if what I heard was them discussing children. A drinking game."

Disgusting.

"But Caden de Bain was here?" I moved the stacks of research between us aside and scooted closer, my thigh flush to hers. "And his rangers?"

"Four of them and Bain." She nodded. "If my father didn't hate Bain so much, he'd have tried to set me up with one of the rangers. He's lying to himself and assuming I'm attracted to dangerous men, not dashing people of relative good looks and comparable morals."

Relative good looks. If half our conversation weren't sad, I'd be howling

"You meet a lot of those here?" I grinned and leaned in close. "Get robbed by anyone with manners as monstrous as their complexions?"

"No robberies recently." She kissed the tip of my nose. "Only a few wet rats sneaking in through the window."

I scowled, exaggerating the expression till she laughed, and leaned against her shoulder. "And people think you're an upstanding, nice young lady."

"Oh, many do not." She whistled and rolled her eyes. "My mother was Alonian, which is clearly the seat of all my troubles."

"Clearly." A locket I'd not stolen, one from the night we'd first met, still hung from her neck. "The problem isn't them having nonsense ideas about what 'lady' means."

"Absolutely not." Elise touched my arm, sliding toward the head of the bed with an expectant look.

I swallowed. My nerves hung in the back of my throat, heavy and uncertain and blocking any words I might've said, and Elise only grinned, a soft, ruddy red rising in her cheeks.

"I know you can't stay for long," she muttered. "We should make the most of it."

I glanced at the notebook in her hands. "You mean reading, don't you?"

"Hush." The blush on her cheeks darkened, hiding her freckles. "We can do two things, and if we're going to talk about bad things, we should be experiencing pleasant things, don't you think?"

"Course, my lady." I bowed at the waist. "What do you want?"

She scowled and laughed so hard her spectacles slipped off. "Just come here."

I did. She pulled me into the space between her legs until my back was against her chest and her arms were around my waist, the book she was holding out in front of us. It was a map of the world, and she pointed to a continent far to the east, over the mountains shadowing Hinter, across the large expanse of Berengard, and over the Shattered Sea.

"Eredan and its Conquered States," she said. "My father's family lived there over five hundred years ago. It was ruled by a king and his court that traced the power of nobility, magic, and inheritance through the bloodlines of noblemen, each one a descendant of their first king."

Nacea had honored blood. It was the seat of the soul, and all souls had a right to live as they needed, an innate right to preserve the sanctity of their selves. We thought it important. Cherished. We'd not valued one type over the other. It was all the same. Everyone bled. Everyone deserved to live.

"Please don't call me by my title when we're together like this." Her spectacles bumped my ear. "I know you're joking, but I don't want to take advantage of you. When we met, I was noble and you weren't."

"I won't anymore," I said, even though I was certain she didn't know the meaning of the words. Not really. "I liked you because you didn't use it against me. You played with it, but not a lot. And I'm Opal now. I outrank you."

She rested her chin on my shoulder. "I'm not going to be scared of someone who couldn't even rob me."

"You keep bringing that up." I took a breath and got a nose

full of grape oil and lemon. "Didn't happen that often. You being pretty and talkative caught me off guard. I was a very fearsome thief."

"And you are a very fearsome Opal. Yet I am fairly certain I could explain each of your kills as justified." She sighed. "We're very similar, only different sides of the same moral choices."

Elise's side of moral choices was somewhere left of just and right of nice-enough-to-trust-assassins.

"You don't know what I've done."

How many deaths I'd taken joy in.

"You killed Horatio del Seve for pleasure, yes, and you were going to kill my father." She paused, took a breath, and softly said, "He deserved it though, and you showed mercy when I asked for it. I'm inclined, knowing the rest, that Horatio deserved it too. They would have killed many, many people. But did you kill him to save others or to take joy in it?"

"Bit of both, if you want me to be honest." I stiffened.

She tightened her grip on me. "I like you honest. I like you as you. I'm not as innocent as you think."

"I know." I leaned my head back against her shoulder till I could kiss the hollow behind her ear. "You're still a better person than most."

"If you say so." She shivered. "I'm going to learn everything I can about Erlend and Eredan and Gaspar del Weylin's odd, old traditions, and I am going to use that to tear them down. We do not deserve the power entrusted to us any longer."

She did, and there were sure to be others, the noble children who'd grown up under Our Queen's rule before their parents seceded, the ones who felt stifled and erased and cast aside by

Erlend's strict rules and ideas. The ones whose selves weren't being honored. The ones like Elise.

"Teach me too," I whispered. "Let's tear them down."

# CHAPTER
# TWELVE

We sat like that for a long while, my heart slowing and the fluttering panic in my veins settling with each of Elise's low laughs and breaths against my ear as we talked about Erlend and Igna and the century-long list of Erlend being an ass. The rangers too were Our Queen's oldest problem. They'd been killing people for as long as she'd been queen. They were why the Left Hand existed.

Caden de Bain was the founder and only survivor of the originals.

And Elise told me he was taking his rangers due west.

"It's a clear setup to blame the war on Igna and absolve Weylin of guilt," she said. "It will make him look like the measured hero."

"I know you're not leaving." Elise would keep the Erlends who'd no place in Weylin's war safe and sneak as much information as she could to Igna. I respected that. But I still worried. "Just please stay safe."

"I will." She held me close. "Don't lose yourself. Don't give in to the power being Opal gives. Stay Sal. The rangers don't stay themselves. They think they're better than all the people they kill. They don't regret it."

We were standing now, face to face, arms curled around each other. The slow rise and fall of Elise's chest echoed in mine. A warm trail of contact and contentment ran from forehead to nose to shoulders to stomach to knees. I pulled her closer.

"Don't worry about me." I kissed her again, lips lingering against hers. "I know what I want. They don't want anything except the thrill of killing."

Losing Nacea—

No, having Nacea ripped from me, had forced me to be many things, many people. Being Opal, getting revenge, might've been personal, but at least my vengeance left the world a better place.

Wasn't I paying back my debt, then? Getting Caden de Bain out of the way was sure to improve the whole continent. I was damn sure it'd improve my life.

"You're not immortal," she said.

I pulled one of her hands from my waist and kissed her palm, tasted sweat and lemon and the sting of whatever solvent she used to rid the ink from her fingers. All the little words we'd traded were long gone, and we weren't the same. Wouldn't ever be again.

"No." I kissed her wrist, her elbow, her hand again. "But neither's anyone else."

I was Opal, but I still stuttered at the brush of her mouth over mine as she untangled our arms and pushed me away.

"I'll be following those rangers," I said quickly. "If you do need help, get word to me. I'll be closest."

"I will."

But we both knew she wouldn't.

She kissed me once again—quick, soft, chapped lips scratching mine—and opened the door. "All clear."

I fled the way I had come, out the window and back into the hall full of hiding places to stay out of sight. The river was cold as I'd left it, and this time I had to wade against the current and back beyond the wall. The chill sunk into my bones even with the sun burning through the back of my neck. I trudged to the edge of Hinter and sat down to dry. Rath showed up near dusk.

He was dusty and tired eyed, and he laughed when he looked me over. "Why are you so happy?"

"What?" I shook out my boots and pants. Seeing Elise had made the knowledge she was safe feel real and settled the panic her abduction had left. And now I knew where Caden de Bain was heading. "I can't be happy?"

"You? Not usually." He sat down next to me and huffed. "You know where the rangers are, don't you?"

I nodded.

For once, I'd a collection of memories bright and lovely and burning within me, and while I knew Elise wasn't mine, I still didn't want to share her—or my time with her. My childhood had been nothing but sharing. Clothes and beds and food and punishment. This time, I wanted something for myself.

"West. Got descriptions too."

Elise had said they were young but looked much older, a bit like me. Deader behind the eyes.

Caden de Bain broke boys and made them monsters, not men.

"Blond, tall, wearing normal green uniforms with not normal paring knives strapped to their sides instead of daggers, and dragging a boy about town?" Rath asked.

I nodded.

"They were here. I watched them for a while." He pulled out a small looking glass and rubbed his face. "Boy's not Cam, but he sure as the Triad's not theirs. They'd bandaged his head up. None of them looked special, just mean."

About right.

Couldn't tell Rath about the ears though. Not yet.

"Let's go." I grabbed my pack and laced up my boots. "I'm tired of them existing."

We headed west. Homesteads and farmlands nearer the border were already abandoned and quartering soldiers. We stayed for a bit at those, peeking through Rath's spyglass to see if the rangers were there, but it was only soldiers. We moved on, deeper into the wilds and closer to the border between Igna and Erlend, and in the dark of an abandoned farm, I caught the flicker of metal in moonlight. I froze.

Rath stopped, looking round. I tilted my head toward where I'd seen the glint.

It was a ranger with a spyglass pointed southeast, and their attention was focused on a small, distant circle. We watched him for ages, waiting for him to move, but he never did. Not until another ranger exited the barn to replace him, flashing us a shot of the four other people inside, one much smaller than the others. Only one lookout.

They'd rigged the place with traps, surely, else they'd have at least one other person watching the edges.

Least their watches were long.

I touched Rath's arm, held a hand over my mouth, and laid my hand flat against the earth. He nodded.

This ranger was mine.

Time to get to work.

# CHAPTER
# THIRTEEN

The ranger was older than me but not by much. He didn't stand like soldiers did when keeping watch, back straight and hands on their spear. His mottled green and brown clothes were dust streaked and sweat stained, and the weapons he carried were more like a poacher's kit than a soldier's fare. I pulled out Rath's spyglass, covering the reflective metal, and looked where he stared. A camp of young boys crowded around a low fire, and the ranger watched them. I crept up behind him.

He noticed. His knife tore for my throat, and I ducked. My fist slammed into his stomach. He doubled over. Gagged.

I grabbed his hair, bent him over, and stabbed my knife into the back of his neck. He stilled.

Rath didn't come to check on me, but I felt his eyes on my back as I walked toward the barn, following the same path the last ranger had taken and stopping to show the tripwires to Rath. He'd have to follow my path exactly.

Caden de Bain. Three rangers. One boy.

Too many to fight at once.

I stopped a little ways out from the door. It had shut behind that last ranger without them bothering to push it and would probably do the same again. Across the path I'd taken, I strung an extra bowstring at ankle height. I waved Rath over and gestured at the ground. He'd have seen what I was doing. It was an old trick we used to get into locked places.

He'd trip one of their wires when I gave the signal, one of them would come running out, and they'd trip over my wire. Wasn't fancy, but it worked.

I scaled the boarded-up backside of the barn and peeked between the old, splintered boards. In the light of their low fire, they looked ghostly, the moss greens and dead-leaf browns of their uniforms blending together into blurs among the shadows. None of them had coats or medals or sigils, but each carried a bow or crossbow and a hunting knife with a gut hook. Two had bird beak paring knives on their belts. Just like Five had carried.

Just like Five had used to strip the skin from Three's body during auditions.

Two of the three rangers were the same weathered tan of long treks, and the other was the smeared pink of sunburned white skin. Their shaved, blond hair was nothing more than a prickle of pale yellow.

The one who'd finished watching was asleep before the fire. He snored with every breath and had stretched out on the old floorboards. The other two were playing a game of five-finger fillet. They'd each spread out a hand against the floor and were jabbing worn knives into the spaces between each finger, never taking their eyes off each other. One was bleeding, the cut on his hand shallow but long. The boy was staring at the blood.

They'd made him play too, but his moves were slower and shakier. He'd a bandage around his head. Blood seeped through one side where his ear would be.

Lady, what were they doing with children's ears?

The boy nicked his fingered and whimpered. Caden de Bain ripped the knife from his hand and stabbed it into the shuddering space between his fingers.

"Again," Caden de Bain said. He tilted his head up, and the shadows hollowed it out. He was hard and jagged, like shoreline stones eaten away by the tide, and his white skin, stretched too tight across muscles built for show, was the muddied brown of winter slush. The downward hook of his nose was more likely gotten from a spear butt than a birthright. He leaned forward. "No stopping. No crying."

He was the opposite of Emerald. The two of them might've been the longest surviving of their groups, but he was cruel where she'd be sarcastic, vicious where she'd be cutting, and stoic where she'd be unamused. Caden de Bain had cut away his emotions like he'd stripped away skin, and Emerald wore her battered, armored heart in a secret pocket of her sleeve. She wasn't cold.

When she looked at me, I didn't feel lesser.

But when Caden de Bain looked at that boy, I was scared. He wanted to see the boy bleed. Wanted to see him hurt. Wanted to break him.

Emerald was Emerald out of love.

Caden de Bain was a ranger out of love for hurting people.

I pulled on my Opal mask, the deep dark one of midnight

which served as mask and helm, and pulled the bow from my back. I didn't need to kill with this shot, only wound. I signaled Rath.

He plucked the tripwire. One of the rangers took off running, knife in one hand and sword in the other. Rath ducked into the tall grass, and the ranger sprinted over the wire, foot catching. He tripped, tumbled, and rolled over his shoulder at the last minute. He bounced to his feet.

Rath tackled him.

Lady, let him finally land a punch.

I shot an arrow at the sleeping ranger. It struck his shoulder, burrowing deep. Caden de Bain leapt to his feet, and the other ranger shoved the boy aside—I'd figured they'd use him as a shield. The two of them stood back to back. Waiting.

Content to let their fellows die.

I fired another shot and dropped to the ground. A solid smack of metal on wood meant I'd hit nothing. Rath tumbled round the dirt with his ranger, and I kicked open the door to deal with mine.

Caden de Bain looked me over. The ranger didn't stop to look. He came at me like a boxer, a proper one. He'd been trained to fight.

He slashed. I ducked, clamping my teeth together to keep from biting my tongue. Other hand empty, he jabbed, and I took the blow in my forearm. I lunged, knives barely missing his chest, and he leaned back. His balance shifted to his left leg, and he struck out, right foot slamming into my chest. I stumbled back. My knees buckled.

In Kursk, in the fights I did while working for Grell, it was easy to know who'd been around the rings a few times. It was in the balance, the efficiency, how smoothly they shifted from one strike to the next like they had seen every movement and practiced every stance until it was so deep in their bones their kids would remember it. They knew fighting. They knew winning.

And in the late-night fights, once the legal ones were done and I took to the ring so the folks with too much coin and a taste for blood could bet on dirtier fights with bigger payouts, the kids who'd more desperation in their fists than most folks had in their whole body fought and fought and fought until only a few were left standing. The unconscious won nothing.

Grell didn't like me unconscious.

He wouldn't have liked this ranger who couldn't shake the proper training from his bones.

Three moves and he'd be dead.

I let him lunge, let him get in close, and slammed my fist into his stomach. He gagged and faltered, and I grabbed his collar. The blade at my side sliced through shirt and skin, but I tightened my grip and yanked him left while my foot swept his legs right. He went down, taking a good measure of my blood with him. I buried my knife into his neck.

"You're the new one." Caden de Bain shifted his grip on his sword and widened his stance. "I've not had the pleasure of scarring you yet."

"It won't be a pleasure." Gasping against the sharp sting across my ribs, I stood and readied my knives. He'd the reach, but I'd the speed. "Hard to enjoy something when you're dead."

He clucked his tongue three times. "You look like you've got a score to settle."

This would be easy.

Just like his rangers.

"And you've got debts to pay."

# CHAPTER
# FOURTEEN

He hoisted me up by my shirt and slammed me into the wall, not even bothering with his sword. I must've been less than a traveling pack to him. I jerked from his grasp and fell to the floor, and he stretched his arms out while I crawled away. A howl, not Rath's, was cut off outside.

Least Rath had landed something.

"It's not that easy." Caden de Bain grabbed my foot and yanked me back to him. "Those were my newest trainees, and there's no fun in training. You owe me for making me suffer through it again."

He pulled up till my fingers were scrambling for purchase on the ground and he'd the whole of my stomach before him to stab, but he only pressed his blade to my wounded side. I shrieked and twisted. He dropped me.

I hit the ground with a rib-cracking thwack and muttered, "Only thing I owe you is a slow death."

"You're too rash for that." He stood over me, one hand

tightening around his sword and the other flexing. "Get up. Raise your hands."

I laughed and spat out a glob of blood. "You all right with me killing all your rangers?"

"I've got hundreds of boys dreaming of being rangers." He raised his sword. "You can't kill all of them too."

I didn't need to.

"No, I'm just going to kill you." I lunged.

He dodged. His blade swept across my side, skimming my shirt. I groaned and fell as if he'd hurt me. He grabbed my arm and lifted me up. I let him move in for the kill. Let him think I was done for.

"You're all talk," he said. "All full of nothing, fallow through and through."

He dropped me and raised his blade. I rammed my heels into his unprotected ankles. He toppled, head bouncing off the floor, and I leapt onto his chest. My knees dug into the soft spots where his arms met his sides.

I felt him tense. His sword nicked my thigh.

"Stop moving." Rath—nose bleeding and lip split, a sword not his own trembling in his hand—stared down at Caden de Bain and pressed his stolen sword to the ranger's throat. "You're going to tell me where you got that boy and where you've been taking them, or I'm going to peel you apart like an orange."

Bain moved to stab me, and I slammed my fist into his temple. His hand fell.

"You all right?" Rath tossed the sword aside and wiped his hands clean. He'd a solid cuff of bruises around his wrist.

I kicked Bain's sword away. "Don't throw away better weapons."

"Fine." He helped me tie up Bain and grabbed the sword, holding it like a hairbrush. "The ranger outside's getting bitey."

Nothing out of ten. I was worse at fencing just for looking at him.

"Bitey?"

Rath held up a damp sleeve. "He didn't like being hog-tied."

I dealt with the rangers. Rath handled the boy. He was better with kids, gentler and more patient. I'd never understood child-hood like Rath.

How easily the boy laughed as soon as Rath showed him how to make a coin dance across his knuckles. Not a lick of sense.

"Rath," I said once I'd lined up the three captives. "Don't look."

It was the boy I was worried about. Rath had been shaking though.

I was Opal for this—to bear the weight of death so they didn't have to.

"Now." I pulled one of the paring knives from a ranger's belt and ran my thumb down the blade. Red bubbled over the steel. "Which one of you all's going to talk?"

I started with the hog-tied ranger. Laid my knife against his nose.

He said nothing.

"Why are you stealing children?" I asked.

Nothing.

"Why are you inking runes in their ears?"

Nothing.

I sighed. "They only way you walk out of here alive is if you're more valuable alive than dead."

"Kill me." He spat at my feet, pink dripping down his chin.

I slit his throat. "Deal."

I turned to the ranger I'd shot, not bothering to clean the knife, and pressed it to his neck. Blood dripped down his chest. That shook him awake. His eyes refocused. The arrow in his shoulder shook.

"You going to talk to me?" Probably not, but Rath had asked me to find Cam and these rangers were our best hope. "Or you want to die too?"

His head lolled to the side. He was the off-white pale of buttermilk, blood leaking through the twin holes of his wound. He stared at his dead partner.

I patted his cheek. "What you doing with the kids?"

"Briar?" the ranger muttered, gaze still stuck on the other dead ranger.

"What?" I tapped his face. "Briar what?"

"They got nicknames," the boy said. He waited for me to turn and peeked out from behind Rath. "That one's Vine."

"They can regrow us," Vine said. His eyes were unfocused. His lips tinted blue. "They can always pick another."

Of course Erlend ruined even its rangers. Bain burned their real selves down and regrew them from the ashes, a forest fire of a person.

"Wouldn't that get confusing?" Rath asked. "All having the same name?"

I glanced back at him. "I know you've met least three people with your name. You get confused?"

He rolled his eyes.

"Vine, eyes here." I flicked the ranger's nose and held two fingers up to my face. "Why you stealing kids?"

"I don't know." He coughed, blood bubbling between his teeth. "Orders."

Orders.

North Star, Deadfall, Riparian, Caldera, and Winter had given orders, soldiers had obeyed, and my entire country had been slaughtered. Orders were the last defense of ethically corrupt.

"Where you taking them?" I took his chin in my hand and lifted it, letting the blood drain back down his throat and buying him a few more words. "How do you know which kids?"

Bain clacked his teeth together, like cracking a pumpkin seed. He'd given in too quietly. I pointed the knife at him. He stilled.

Vine coughed again. "Lynd. They're the ones don't bleed less you cut them."

"What you mean?" I asked.

"We got an example—"

Bain spat. A white blur shot out of his mouth and lodged in the back of Vine's throat. I shoved Bain aside, and Vine, gasping and hacking up blood, collapsed. My hands held his throat.

No pulse.

"Rath," I said quickly. "Search him."

I held two knives to Bain's neck while Rath went through his pockets. It was typical, really. Erlend stealing kids from other countries and using them for their own means. They stole land, titles, lives. What were a few children on top of that?

"Sal." Rath's soft voice barely reached me over the crackling fire. "Why's he got an ear?"

Rath held an ear in his palm, a tiny one with wrinkled, brown skin and a piercing in the lobe. Runes, black and solid, lined the upper shell.

Magic had no place in mortal skin even when it was allowed, but to carve runes into a child when magic didn't even work, when nothing but blood would come of it, was a level few mages had ever lowered themselves to.

I shuddered.

"What's this mean?" Rath shoved the ear under Bain's nose. "Who'd you take this from?"

"Can't be Cam. Don't worry." I pulled it from him, a memory itching in the back of my head, and turned it over in my hands. "Looks familiar."

Bain turned fully to me, eyes widening.

I traced the runes. Turned the ear sideways.

"It's not runes," I said softly. It was a word. "Eat."

A Nacean word. Sliced into dead flesh. The bone-shivering word settled over me, too soft, too long in my mouth for the sharp pain it caused.

"That one didn't work, like most things in the Fallow." Caden de Bain chuckled. "North Star will tear you apart just like he did all your others a decade ago."

I froze, then whispered, "Fallow. You keeping mentioning 'fallow.' And you called Weylin 'North Star.'"

No Erlend had ever called Gaspar del Weylin that. None would know it unless they'd a secret name too.

Caden de Bain did not move, did not speak, did not do much of anything, and I flipped the knife to a forward grip. The blade stood upright between us.

"Which one are you?" I asked him. "Deadfall or Riparian?"

He laughed.

I knew the answer. I knew him now better than I knew myself.

Because of him, I knew him better than I knew Nacea. Riparian was too gentle a name, too much like the rivers it described.

I'd not even had to go looking.

He was practically Lady sent.

*Deadfall.*

I slammed the hilt of my knife into the back of his hand.

"You'll have to hit harder than that." He laughed. "You're much too scared to make a shadow of me." He leaned in close.

I turned the knife over. Pinned his hand to the floor.

"I'll never tell you what we did with those kids," Deadfall said, "but want to know what I did to you?"

Rath sniffed. "So you know where they are?"

"Your country had three queens or whatever you called them, and I used to watch them." His head tilted, his gaze slipping from my face to the knife and back to me. "Namrantha, up north, was my favorite, but I got sent down south. That one started forcing soldiers off the land, making trouble, talking to Alona, and Gaspar asked me to take care of it. So I snuck in a mage and we did. We created the first shadow in Nacea. She didn't scream. Most of them did, but she never uttered a word."

The Stars of Nacea, one of each of the Lady's stars, were the last living descendants of her. They were perfect. They were sacred.

They were dead.

"She didn't talk till the end. Sounded like wind or breathing. We didn't leave her tongue, but she talked. Always wondered how they did that. Pulled her teeth out too." He shook his head, blood dripping down the wall behind him. "Wouldn't have known though, if you'd seen her gnaw her sister's face off."

Drip. "Soon she was busy with the other soon-to-be corpses we gave her."

I was back in Nacea. The fire at my back dimmed. My vision tightened to one pinprick of light. The shadows at the corners twisted and spread. Blood, like salt in the air, burned in my nose, and the creak of the firewood became the skittering of beetle legs on bone. A shadow peeled itself from between the rangers. Their blood seeped into its nothing mouth.

"We didn't bring shadows to Nacea." Deadfall leaned in close. Grinned. "We made them there."

I jammed the knife into his throat.

# CHAPTER
# FIFTEEN

Deadfall died laughing.

His blood soaked my hands. It dripped in the quiet rushing of my mind, slowing with each of my breaths. My heartbeat, too fast and flighty, fluttered in my head, and the howling nothing in my ears grew. I turned over my red, warm hands.

Coachwhip. Caldera. Deadfall.

My right ear ached. Rath's voice, far, far away.

Dead. Dead. Dead.

Like my parents. Like my siblings. Like Nacea.

But I didn't feel better.

The ache again. Rath's voice echoed in my head. The words didn't make sense. I twisted to him.

He punched me.

I blinked, facedown on the floor, and lifted my head. It was like wading, like the air was water and my ears were full of it. It muffled Rath and held me down. He sneered over me.

It was like watching someone else. Like being someone else. No, I was me, but I wasn't the Sal here now. This was happening to someone else.

I touched my stinging cheek, my wounded side, and came away with nothing but the throbbing sting of new pain.

Rath screamed and snatched my arm.

"He was goading you." Rath's fingers dug into my arm as his voice wobbled and slowed. The rushing in my ears dulled. "He wanted you to kill him so he'd not have to tell us."

"Good," the Sal who couldn't be me said. "He deserved it."

Rath threw his pack at me. "Does Cam?"

I couldn't get my mouth to move.

"You ass!" Rath stumbled back, raking his hands across his face. "He knew where Cam was. We had him. He could've taken us to him."

"He'd have never told us anything unless it hurt us." Deadfall—Caden de Bain—was made of hurts. He'd have fed us lies till we were sick. It was all he was and all he had.

Rath leaned over me, salted eyes narrow. "You don't know that."

"I do." Bain hadn't flinched as I killed his rangers, and he'd not moved when I stabbed his hand. There was nothing we could've said, no goodness we could've appealed to, to get the truth from him. He'd sooner have died than give anyone but him satisfaction. "He'd have led us round in circles till Cam was dead or led us to a grave or a different boy or a soldier camp. He'd have done anything to hurt us and nothing to help no matter what."

Wouldn't he have?

*We made them there.*

I shuddered and swallowed back the sick creeping up my throat. "I was sent here to kill him, and he was—"

"Damn your orders." Rath crouched and took my face in his hands. "Lords, Sal, you going to pull rank and jobs on me? Over family? Over helping kids? They come first. What's the point in protecting Igna if we've got no future to live in it?"

His touch prickled across my skin. Too much.

I pulled away.

"Sal?" he asked. "You really that heartless? You really going to leave Cam?"

Rath didn't believe in leaving kids behind. They deserved coddling and chances and all the things Rath and I hadn't had.

"You wouldn't understand."

Rath was too kind. He was full of softness and truth and all the pretty things in the world. He hand-fed sick starlings at our window no matter how long they kept us awake with their cawing. He bought the extra-fancy, double-the-price tonics and syrups for the young members of Grell's gang when they were sick just because the cheap ones tasted like feet. He was the opposite of suffering and death.

The opposite of Deadfall.

"If I'd left him alive," I said slowly, "he'd have led us to some other death. He'd never have told us. Never."

And now he was dead, but so was everyone else still. I didn't feel better no matter what I was telling Rath. I felt nothing. Felt everything. My body was too small, too tight. An uncomfortable reminder of still being here.

"Think I've had more meetings with grief and death than

you." I sniffed, nose burning. "I get it. I'm sorry I killed him before you were satisfied."

Rath scowled. "And now Cam can join your useless, dead family, all thanks to you."

A quick, sharp pain shot through me. In all our years together, he'd never spoken of my family. He'd never pushed me to explain beyond what I was comfortable saying. He'd never asked me for proof. He'd never doubted my pain.

We could get Cam back. I only had to think. Move. "Help me up. We can find him."

If they were taking kids from the south and shipping them up north to Lynd, Cam still had a few days before he got here.

Unless the ears were part of something more harmful than dead runes and severed ears.

"Help yourself." Rath spun away from me and made a choking, disgusted sound in the back of his throat, then knelt before the boy. "You want me to take you home?"

The boy nodded.

"Come on." Rath pulled him into a hug. They boy was hardly seven and small enough for Rath to carry. "Let's get you back to your family and then I can find mine."

I sat back against the wall, chest aching.

Rath's family didn't include me anymore.

"We could do it, you know," I said. "Find him. I can—"

"Don't worry about it. Just do your job, Opal." Rath stopped in the doorway to the barn. "I don't know which 'we' you're talking about."

"Us," I said quickly. The empty space where he had been widened and pressed in. I scratched my arms. "Always us."

It had always been us, against everyone and everything.

"There's no 'us.'" Rath didn't look at me. "Not anymore. I can't tell if I'm talking to Sal or Opal half the time, and that's too much Opal for me. You go do your job. I'll find Cam. If you want to help, hunt me down. I'll be in Mossvale."

I stumbled to my feet, but Rath walked away.

He was right.

I was Opal. I wasn't Sal, not anymore, but Sal and Opal understood Deadfall better than he ever could. Viciousness for the sake of viciousness escaped Rath. I'd been molded by it.

I sunk back to the floor.

I didn't sleep. An uneasy heat stuck to my skin, itching each time I breathed. The blood washed off easy, and the fire died. In the dark of the barn with nothing but corpses for company, the shadows returned, and I curled up in the corner with my eyes on the door and my back to a wall. They slithered in the edges of my sight, always just out of reach, vanishing when I turned to look. It was only the shadow of a bird outside. Only the shadow of my hands.

I waited and watched. A shadow slipped through the cracks in the walls, oozing over the floor and swallowing up Deadfall in a puddle of dark. Not black.

Black was a color.

Shadows had no substance.

Not real.

It peered at me, the blurred edges of its face too black against the night.

Not real.

It touched my bleeding side. "Is this you?"

My blood dripped from the nothing where its fingers should've been.

I couldn't speak. I was on my back and couldn't move. The shadow slunk away in the silence, blood splattering across the floor. A low rumble rose in the distance. I jerked up.

Awake. Up. Awake.

Had I been asleep?

My eyes weren't stuck together, and I couldn't remember closing or opening them. I struggled to stand and pulled myself to my feet. Deadfall and the rangers were still there, no shadows, only flies freckling their pale skin. Rath and the boy were truly gone. It was light out. They'd be a good ways away now.

I groaned and stretched.

The squish of carriage wheels in wet grass came from outside. New, louder sounds rattled through the barn and in my head. It wasn't as bad now, the water and the wading and the roar.

I picked up Deadfall's sword and pulled out my knife.

Time to be Opal again.

# CHAPTER
# SIXTEEN

The barn was all right cover, and I sat in wait behind the uneven slats. A plain carriage, the cheap kind with no extras or guards, rolled into view, and the driver pulled back at sight of the barn. She shouted something to the occupants.

Five guards, armored but not adorned in any colors that would betray their loyalties, darted out of the carriage and started searching the area. Two headed for the barn.

I sighed, raised my weapons, and pulled on the dark midnight mask.

I wouldn't look like Opal, but I'd look like a member of Our Queen's Left Hand, and maybe that would be threatening enough.

"Barn's occupied." I stepped out of it, shoulders rolled back. The blood on my clothes would have to stay. Maybe, like the scars, it'd make me look dashing instead of like a mess. "So you should move along."

The guards all stilled, arms pulled back to throw a spear or fire a bolt, and I tapped my mask with my knife.

"There's four dead rangers in there," I said, putting all the loathing and bite Emerald would into the words. "What's four normal soldiers going to be to me?"

"Opal?" a voice called from the carriage.

I nodded. "And you are?"

Lena de Arian stepped from the carriage. She was wearing a dress of silver so pale it looked white, and the simple design couldn't hide the expensive wool or stitching. The key necklace dangled freely from her neck. No blue, no green. Traveling without loyalties.

"Excellent." She swept a few strands of light hair from her face and grinned. "It's good to see you."

Her guards stood down.

"What are you doing here?" I lowered my knife and sword and stepped forward, the unsettling prickle of being watched fading. "You're across the border."

She sniffed, face pulling up into the sneer Elise must've learned from her. "Hardly. My lands are a day's ride east of here, and it was safer to cross here than try to get through Mattin's chaotic mess. My lands are between the old Alona and Erlend border, and I've no intention of letting Erlend move in simply because I've been at court."

"Well, the rangers here won't bother you anymore." I nodded to the barn. "You need an escort?"

"No," she said, gesturing back to the carriage. "I think we're prepared."

And then, from the dark within the carriage, a familiar, calloused hand reached out and grasped the door for support. Maud stepped out.

"If you don't mind, I'd prefer to offer my brief resignation from my duties in person." Maud bowed to Lena and then to me. "Opal."

I inclined my head. "Maud."

"I'm sorry for doing this while you were gone, but Lena has offered me a very good opportunity to see where I was born and perhaps reclaim my mother's home, and I couldn't pass it up." Maud flipped her braid over her shoulder, the emerald hairpin glittering behind her ear. She wasn't in gray, and it didn't look right. Her leggings were the thick, deep bronze of age-old weapons, and her flowing blouse and sweater were a dark, nearly black green. She looked sharp. Flowy. Nothing like the Maud I knew who wore and cared for her uniform like it was the best thing in the world. "I'm going with her to Aren while I still can. My siblings have family there. They might not have taken them in, but war changes people. I want to see what they have to say now. I can't deny them that."

I swallowed. A yawning, bitter pit opened in the back of my throat and swallowed all my words. Maud too then.

No Rath. No Elise. No Maud.

The best parts of my world were scattering.

"All right." If that was what Maud wanted, I'd no business stopping her. "You need me to do anything?"

"No." She shook her head and crinkled her nose. Not the good kind. "No, thank you. Lena has more than taken care of everything."

Something about Maud—her tone, her posture, her still-wrinkled nose—was off, but I couldn't put my finger on it.

"You all right, though?" I leaned in close and whispered loud enough for Lena to hear, "You mad at me?"

If something odd was going on, let Maud be able to tell me.

Let Maud trust me as I trusted her. I couldn't lose two in one day.

Not Maud too.

"Anything you want—hairpins, a pet, a new employer." I touched her arm and pulled her close, the possibilities of what was wrong endless. "I don't want you to leave."

Her mouth opened. The little muscles at the corners of her mouth pulled taut, and she laid her hand over mine. Her shoulders tensed. "I'm not mad at you. Not at all. Please, don't worry. I haven't been home in ages, and I want to see it now in case anything happens."

"Nothing's ever happening to you." I pulled her into a hug, the baby hairs around her ears tickling the skin between my mask and scalp, and as soft as I could, asked, "What's wrong?"

No one could see my mouth move. Only Maud would know I'd spoken.

"Go home," she whispered back, lips hidden from view behind my arm. "Trust me."

I squeezed her once, let her go, and nodded to Lena. "You owe me a servant."

"Of course." She smiled. "I believe Maud selected a temporary replacement?"

Maud laughed. "Oh yes, someone has to clean up Opal's messes."

I laughed too.

Something was definitely wrong. Maud always used my full title when making fun of me, and I'd heard her style of jokes often enough to know one. This wasn't one.

But she'd told me to go home, not help.

It wasn't like she was with someone terrifying. Lena had sent me after Caldera and been vital to Our Queen. Something else was wrong.

I ducked—Lady bless, I was covered in blood and Maud hated it—and bowed a little lower and longer than would've been necessary. "Unless you would like an escort, I'll leave you."

The Left Hand served as court bodyguards sometimes, and maybe I'd be able to figure out what was eating Maud.

I shuddered.

Eat.

My circle of family was ever shrinking and now it began and ended with Maud.

Was there some other Nacean out there? An Erlend Sal as lonely and cut off as I felt? Or maybe they'd willingly given up being Nacean and not had it ripped from them? It hurt to hope, to think I'd even one person to share my life with.

"We're well." Maud's eyebrows wrinkled together. "I am to assume the barn is not a comfortable resting place?"

"No," I said, thoughts stuck on the Nacean-runed ear. "I wouldn't recommend it."

Maud stepped back into the carriage, not even glancing at me. Was she hiding something, or did she truly not care?

Lena joined Maud, but she stopped on the steps and stared at me.

"Will you tell Our Queen I've seen no sign of Hinter guards?" she asked. "I know you are not a messenger, but Lord Nevierno del Farone has been expanding since Lord Mattin del Aer's death. I would like to reassure her of our success."

"I will." I did not tell her I had spoken to Elise. That information was mine and mine alone, tucked away to keep me going. "Sure you got enough guards?"

"There are more ahead and behind." She smiled and ducked into the carriage. "Please do not kill them. Though I am sure Lady Emerald would take offense at the idea of anyone killing her. She's traveled near us for some time."

I bowed, side burning, and waved her farewell.

Once the carriage left, I started walking south. There was nothing left for me here. I'd days to travel before I made it back to Willowknot, and even then, I'd have to leave soon enough to begin the hunt for Cam and Rath. I needed to ask a mage about the ears too.

Why'd they mistake the Nacean language for runes?

Course, I had too, but my memories of Nacean were little more than fog. The Nacean books I'd been gifted hadn't helped much. The writing and printing looked nothing like my father's careful handwriting. Didn't even sound the same when I said them.

An Erlend soldier, no ranger but just as annoying, rose up from the underbrush and aimed his crossbow at me. I stopped.

Two out of ten. I could take him, but I should never have been caught.

"Hands out, little traveler." The soldier whistled with the blade of grass between his lips and an arrow ripped through his throat.

# CHAPTER
# SEVENTEEN

The soldier clawed at his neck, dropping his crossbow. I lurched away, knives drawn and looking around, but nothing else came flying. His fingers tugged at the turkey feather fletching. Same kind rangers used.

He gurgled and collapsed. I ducked.

"I'm curious if your survival until this point has been due to luck or skill." Emerald—clad in dark blues and greens, wearing a faceless midnight mask, and carrying a long bow with three more arrows clasped between her fingers and ready to shoot—crept out of the shadows. "You looked like you needed help."

I groaned. "Depends. How much lecturing am I about to get?"

"Well, it is several days back to Willowknot." The skin above her ear tightened, and I knew she was raising one perfectly arched eyebrow at me. "I take it the rangers are dead?"

"Very. Caden de Bain too." I glanced at the empty, little clearing ahead of us. "What are you doing here?"

She held up her bow. "One of the assassins Weylin sent after

Our Queen years ago abandoned his post and lived a normal life in Willowknot until three days ago. I'm hunting him." She gestured me forward.

I hesitated.

"Don't worry," Emerald said, tapping the empty quiver at her hip. "The soldiers who were camped out this way were very terrible people and are now very dead."

We started walking. Emerald didn't say much for the first bit. I'd plenty to tell her, but my mind kept shoving all my news into my mouth, making it impossible to get any of it out—until we started running. Then, no words came at all. Only the empty rhythm of nothing rang in my head.

The moment we stopped, I said, "It's Nacean."

"What?" Arms resting on her head, Emerald huffed—she'd taken her mask off without mentioning it to me and only suggested I do the same once I was gasping. "Finish your thought."

"The runes on the ears aren't runes." I pulled out the ear Deadfall had been carrying and showed it to her. "That's Nacean."

"Eat." She stared at the black lines, tracing them. "This is odd."

"Who's writing Nacean words on Igna ears?" I asked. "And why did you all mistake it for runes?"

"Runes could be anything. That's nothing." Emerald waved her hand and kept walking, gaze fixed on the ear. She turned it over. Studied the cut. Picked at the inked bit. "What I'm wondering is why?"

I shrugged. "Make it look like magic's back and shadows are possible."

"Maybe." She tapped the runes on her eyelid and stylized tulips on her eye patch—the emerald eye was too telling, she said, for public—and then drew the first letter of the Erlenian and Alonian alphabet in the air. "The runes knew no language or geographic boundaries and answered to any who called upon them. It was a Triad-sent gift that countered our monarchy, improved the lives of many, and ruined an equal number. It granted power to those who sought it. We had to regulate it."

"Language boundaries?" I glanced at her. "I thought they were their own language."

"There was no one language of runes but many. Runes were whatever you needed them to be—Erlenian, Alonian, Nacean. It's why Mizuho's magic is completely different from ours." Mizuho was a country across the wide ocean to our west, and even though they'd supported Our Queen during the war, few had traveled here after the loss of magic. Kita Nanami was the only person from there I'd ever properly met. "Magic doesn't even require runes in Mizuho, and Nanami says only specific royals are allowed to use it anyway." Emerald drew a symbol on the back of her hand. "They weren't always necessary here either. We used runes to help focus the magic into a medium. They strengthened our control over it like a handmade river lined with stones instead of dirt. The only difference between a word and a rune was intention."

"Seems dicey."

Emerald grinned. "I believe Naceans referred to it as the Lady being fickle with who she blessed."

I laughed.

"It was mostly Erlend mages who tried to set up a standard," Emerald said. "Poor Nicolas was sent to the Thrice-Blessed School thinking magic could only be done in old Erlenian and that Naceans couldn't do magic, not that they chose not to. Some did, the physicians. Much like us, they took up an occupation so that others wouldn't have to."

I'd spent my life not thinking about magic. It was one of the only Nacean things I knew for sure—we did not meddle in magic—but that wasn't true. There'd been Nacean physicians. Naceans had attended the Thrice-Blessed School. The world I'd built was falling out from under me.

"If I'd wanted to be a mage," I asked, "how'd it have worked?"

She glanced at me, canteen half raised to her mouth. "Really?"

I nodded. "The Lady knows what they're doing with those ears, but there were Nacean words on them that you're saying were runes. So how'd magic work? Some Nacean is out there somewhere thinking they're doing magic. Or trying to pretend they are. So why the runes?"

Plenty of people had needed magic to live comfortably or to live at all, and it was a necessity to them. It hadn't always been a weapon, not till Erlend's taste for power was thrown into the mix.

"Being good at magic wasn't dependent on noble rank or wealth. You could study all you wanted, but to use magic, you had to *want* it. You had to know exactly what you wanted and what you were giving up, or else, no matter how many runes you drew or blood to lost, you would not accomplish what you set out to." She bushed aside a branch, letting it swing back to hit me, and chuckled when I snapped it. "You would have been good at it. The most stubborn were. Magic wasn't innate. It was like wind or light or gravity. It was without us—always there in our world but not how we think of things. Like how shadows, normal shadows, exist but are not real. It's power. Just as light-ning harms what it strikes, great magnitudes of magic harmed the mage. That's why runes were used. They tied the magic to this earth and forced the power to use up the medium and not the magic."

I reached out and touched her shoulder. She'd a rune under her shirt, an old one with a series of jagged lines I couldn't deci-pher. "If it uses up the medium and you don't want to get used up, why the ink?"

"Because the stronger the medium's tie to this earth, the greater control you had. Blood beats paper any day, and bone is better than most." She paused, chuckling. "Was. It's why we priests were the only ones allowed to use blood. All energy must be derived from somewhere, and we had enough control to keep from using too much. It's why we never used soft tissues except for the most delicate and necessary of workings. Only the most important ones were placed in flesh."

Like the ones along her eyelid or around Isidora's wrists. But Lady's sake, they'd misjudged everything about the shadows, letting the magic devour their whole body and mind, somehow thinking they were the exception, the soul strong enough to keep their self intact.

I scratched at the scabs on my arms, skin prickling at the thought of that child's ear I'd found in Caldera's study and whatever was happening to them now. I might've made that Cam's fate.

"We never put runes on ears," she said softly. "They're like your nose. They wouldn't grow back."

"What about—"

She shushed me. I scowled.

"One question each day," Emerald said softly. "Every time we stop to rest, you may ask a question and I will give an answer."

That was fair.

"You done talking, or should I tell you about how I went to see Elise?" I asked after a long, long silence.

Emerald spun to me. "Is this really the time for petty?"

"I'm just asking." I liked riling her up. She was wonderful, beautiful, brilliant, but she'd been one of the court members who let Nacea's slaughter fall by the wayside. She'd helped erase it and erase Erlend's guilt. "The rangers went to Hinter, so I talked to her. She's not coming back, but she'll try to send us news."

"Good. I did not expect her to return even if we sent the whole army to save her." Emerald turned from me and kept walking. "What did she say?"

Sharing her words hurt, but I had to.

"A girl, making a real difference," I finished. "Seems like all you were wrong about Weylin."

She hummed. "And here I thought him incapable of conceiving a woman's work as outside of the home."

We didn't speak again till we'd settled in for the night, deep in the woods and far away from travelers and rangers. Not that either of us slept much, but we pretended to. I sat with my back against a rough trunk and stared through the gaps between trees. She twirled an arrow in her hands.

"Can I ask my question?"

"Tomorrow," she said, exhaling through her nose. "Shush."

I glanced round. "You think the trees are spying on us?"

"No." She pushed her hood back and drew her small, hazel bow. "But I can at least imagine this is restful if it's quiet."

A rustle in the bushes drew her attention, and head turning toward the sound, she drew back her bow. The arrow sliced through the branches, and something small let out a last chattering breath. Emerald pulled her prey from the underbrush.

She'd hit the squirrel clean through the skull.

And I had my next question.

CHAPTER
EIGHTEEN

W e walked from before dawn till after dusk, clothes drenched in sweat even in the dim, frosted light of early morning, and by noon the sun was bearing down on us with streaks of fire-hot light burning through the backs of our necks. I'd a layer of sweat and dirt thicker than my clothes and my over-worked ribs ached with each shallow breath.

We didn't stop until the sun had long since disappeared under the horizon. Emerald paused in a clearing, stared to the east, and nodded. I collapsed.

"I've got a question," I said after downing an entire mug of boiled water. Scalded my tongue but it was worth it. "It's about your eyesight and archery, but I won't ask if you don't want me to."

She turned to face me, fully, and the weight of her stare pushed me back. "Ask, and I will decide if I answer."

"I get worse if I shut one eye." I pulled out my pack of dried turkey and offered her some. "How do you aim? Or how'd you learn?"

"Easily. My eye was removed when I was very young, and I had plenty of time to practice." She pulled a strip of turkey from the pack. "I found it calming, as a child, to have consistent movement. I juggled first though. The physician asked other patients what had most helped them, and they told me to juggle to learn how to judge depth. But you are not me. Do what's best for you and practice."

She tore into her turkey.

I laughed. "You juggle?"

"Oh, yes." She tossed a rock at me. "And I am very good at it."

Course. She was good at most things. "If I let you throw two more rocks at me, will you juggle them?"

"All the way back to Willowknot after leaving you here."

I laughed, and she smiled, the strain on her face easing.

In the dark, as Opal and Emerald's peer in rank if not in years or experience, the words came easily.

"Caden de Bain was on my list," I whispered. "Deadfall."

"Good."

---

The next night, after a day of hiking up and down the grassy hills of southern Erlend, we crossed over into northern Igna. We were probably in safe territory, but the overlap between the two had become a festering mess of soldiers, rangers, scouts, spies, and civilians all tripping over each other in their frantic movements. We camped at the base of a ridge in the safety of a narrow cave. Emerald waited for me to ask.

I closed my eyes. "Why'd you let history sweep Nacea out to sea and swallow it?"

A lost, sunken ship with the survivors set adrift in a confusing, endless sea.

Metal dragged across skin, catching on the short ends of shaved hair. "You didn't go to school. You would have—"

"Don't lay this at my feet." I snapped a twig in my hands. "We were already dead and you needed to save the living, nonsense, nonsense, nonsense. I get it. I don't want to, but I do, and I hate you all for that. But telling me stories like that does nothing but soothe your guilt."

I'd heard some of the stuff schools taught, and I'd heard the same explanation before.

Their actions had severed me from Nacea, and now they wanted me to learn about Nacea from the people who'd made its destruction possible.

"Are you looking for real answers?" She tapped her cheek, fingers slow. "Or are you trying to hate us less?"

I closed my eyes. I didn't know what I wanted. I'd wanted to be Opal and hunt down my Erlend lords, but now, with Rath running after Cam and a heavy chunk of guilt sitting in the back of my throat, the truth of being Opal was lonely. There were so many things I needed to do.

So many wrongs I had to answer for.

"It's hard to stop hating people you're meant to trust when they keep lying to you." I peeked at her with one half-open eye.

She shook her head. "You used to look at Our Queen with stars in your eyes."

"Did you think twice about it?" I opened both eyes, not wanting to see her face but needing to put an expression to the answer. It was another question, but if she refused, she was crueler than I thought. "Did you want to avoid it?"

Guilt was what set us apart from the Erlends. Guilt and regret, empathy and grief, the way joy felt after dealing with them.

"We regretted it constantly." She held up her hand and shook her head. "I regretted it. I will not answer for others. And that means nothing to anyone but me, does it?"

"It makes it so much worse," I whispered. "I've got no one to talk to about Nacea, not really, and when I tell them what happened to me, it's all they can do not to say something starting with 'from what I heard.' Then there are those young kids who've never heard of Nacea. How was I supposed to be Sallot Leon when all my choices on how to be Sallot were taken?"

She didn't answer.

Probably best.

There were no words she could offer up to match this feeling, this hole that had replaced my heart, eating everything I'd laid down in it—old memories of my mother's face, new knowledge of Nacean history, the true sound of my sister's voice. It ached like hunger and stuck to my ribs, the pull so tight I wanted to curl up most times. It wasn't fair.

"It was easy to see when you started hating us," Emerald said much, much later.

I shrugged. "Maybe you all just aren't that great."

"Sal." She exhaled and shook her head. "Why'd you become Opal?"

"Revenge, better life, the usual." Rage and nothing and a flicker of want pulsed within me every moment of every day Erlend wasn't held accountable, and I didn't know what else to do. I wanted to hate them. I wanted to treasure them. I wanted to learn from them. I wanted to be better than them.

I wanted to be free of the emotions thrust upon me by their actions, but I didn't want to say it aloud.

"Why'd you become Emerald?" A second question, but she'd not stop a conversation.

She glanced at the sky. "Two questions?"

"Fine." I wrapped my coat around my shoulders and turned away. "But don't think of a way out of it."

"I intend for no one to ever hold the position of Emerald but me. No one should know the weight of what killing means. I can handle it. Some couldn't. I know how far I am willing to go to make sure the people of Igna and Our Queen can live safely. I know how far I can go and still return as myself. My answer to this will always be the same—I love the people that depend on me far too much to let them die or let them know what killing's like."

We did not speak at all after that. We walked for another full day, me slightly behind her. Looking for anything suspicious, I wove through a caravan of people trying to cross into Igna and bartering lunch, and when it came time to cross the line of Erlend soldiers proper, Emerald and I slipped in with their group to keep our movements quiet. No one needed to know where Emerald and Opal had been.

"One of the kids Erlend took north is from my old gang," I said softly. "If Our Queen's got nothing else for me to do, I could go get him and figure out what they're doing."

"No." She glanced at me from over the corpse of an Erlend soldier, who'd been too eagerly hunting draft dodgers to kill for us to arrest alive. "You will do what Igna needs done. There are rangers out now looking for those children."

I didn't speak again until we were camped out near the caravan, a day's walk from Willowknot.

"Why do you shave your head every new moon?"

Emerald laughed, the upturned corners of her eyes scrunching together. "That's your last question?"

"It makes you happy." I nodded. "I want to know how to be happy."

"It's not a happy story." She took a deep breath and tilted her head back till the moonlight shimmered across her skin and caught in her eye. "When Marianna and I were at the Thrice-Blessed School, we taught a non-runed alchemy course with a physician named Gaila. Marianna made chalk that she could run through her curls to color. It made her students interested in alchemy and made them think about what they could do. She loved making sure they were happy, not just learning."

Sounded good.

Her metallic nails traced runes on her arms. "It wasn't just that though. Hair's its own culture, isn't it? Another thing she lost. She felt so apart from the Sun-Drenched Coast after—"

"You're skipping ahead." I was grinning. I didn't want to be, but it was hard to hate the memories of someone being nice.

Emerald licked her lips and covered her eyes with one hand. "Our Queen Marianna da Ignasi died the night she banished magic. Her heart stopped, and the night sky went completely dark. She was ill for a very long time, and she started losing her hair. So we made a party of it, shaving our heads. It stuck. It's tradition now."

I sniffed. "That's nice of you."

"It's a good excuse to pretend we're back in school and our problems are someone else's." She studied her hands, turning them over in the thin streaks of light hitting us, and shook her head. "There were twenty attempts on Marianna's life within the first three months of founding Igna. More followed. Gaspar del Weylin sent person after person, not caring if they lived, not caring if they were good. He wanted her dead in any way possible. There were others too, who just wanted her dead—for banishing magic, for being a mage, for the war, for not surrendering the school. So then the whole of us, the court back then, decided it would be better if we went after the people hiring the contractors and the killers they hired before they came for us. We went after the mages too, who were trying to bring back magic and create new shadows. It was a mess, but Weylin was intent on destroying us. There were no words or calm discussions to be had. His entire ideology is built on our eradication. You cannot reason with that. We tried, failed, got killed, and decided no one else was dying. That is why I am Emerald. That is why Our Queen has a Left Hand. That is why you are Opal. You're out to kill them so they don't do what they did to Nacea ever again. Hold on to that."

In the dark quiet a few breaths later, without any of the bite her voice usually held, Emerald said, "We're not perfect. We're not good. If we went back, I doubt we'd make the same decisions, but that's why we're making sure people like you and Elise de Farone and all the others out there have what they need to make the world better than we ever could."

I glanced up at the Lady's stars. Only one of the three was visible, a flicker of silver between the leaves.

I pried up one of the scabs on my arm, finger sticking to the tacky blood. I'd killed Deadfall. I'd bled for him and the other rangers.

Least I was in charge of who hurt me now.

Sometimes I swore the Lady's stars flickered in time to my prayers, blinking to black with each of my pleas.

*North Star. Let me find the other Naceans. Deadfall. Let me kill the people who took them from me. Riparian. Let me sleep through the night without my family's faces peering out from the dark at me. Winter. Let me rest.*

It worked half the time, which meant it wasn't working at all. Rath called it gambler's luck.

CHAPTER

# NINETEEN

W e walked for one more day and wandered into Willowknot with masks blazing in the sun and skin clean as Emerald could make it. She'd insisted we put our masks on before getting to the capital and dust off the days' worth of dirt before being seen by people—an image to keep up now, so much of politics was image—and she led through the crowds and paths and gates till we reached the common quarters of the Left Hand. The buildings and paths were quiet, a forest hushed before a storm. She squeezed my arm.

"Sleep." Her mask came away, and she nudged me to my room. "Amethyst is guarding Our Queen, and I will send her to speak to you when you wake."

I nodded. "All right."

For all the odd feelings between us, it was still best to do as she said, and some small part of me was still thrilled by her acknowledgment.

I stumbled into my rooms. They were spotless, as if Maud

would leave them as anything else. She'd laid out enough clean clothes for me to pick from as I wished—picking out what went together instead of leaving it up to me—and packed me two more bags in case I needed to leave again. I touched the bags, the clothes, and fell into bed. The ache in my chest was only half the rangers' fault.

I hurt now, but it was worth it. It made the love real, made my feelings real. No one—not even Rath—could call me heart-less when such a small absence hurt so much.

"Keep them safe," I muttered to the ceiling, where I'd painted the Lady's stars. "Elise, Maud, and Rath. Cam too. Not for me."

They'd so many things left they deserved to do. I wanted to see them through.

I slept for a full day, waking only to remember Maud was gone and days away. Ruby's old servant had been brought back to take her place until she returned, but having him in my space made me think of nothing but being watched. I didn't give him a key to the rooms.

Maud's was on the table by the door.

I'd not moved it.

Emerald was stretched out on one of the couches in the common room, a plate of dried fruit balanced on her stomach and using a bundled-up quilt as a pillow. I poured myself some water and sat in a chair near her.

"I had considered waking you up for a nice round of target practice." Her eye was closed. She'd a piece of damp cloth draped over her forehead. "You're welcome."

"You're too kind." I sipped my water. "Anything happen?"

Attacks? Assassinations? Spies? Deaths? News?

"Nothing." She turned her head and opened her eye. "However, I think it's important for you to think about why you're Opal."

I huffed and flopped back in the chair, arms covering my face. "You making this a daily thing?"

"Maybe," she said. "How fulfilling has killing them been?"

Not at all. Nothing like I thought. Not enough for what I was doing.

She nodded. "Killing for revenge is all well and good until they're dead and you're left with nothing to do."

"Who are we killing?" Amethyst poked her head through her door, hair damp and the pale spaces of her face red from heat. "Because I'm looking forward to this day off."

"You can't call it that if you're awake longer than you're asleep," Emerald muttered. "You need better reasons than revenge to commit to this if you don't want to lose your entire self to it."

"Well, Erlend's got plenty of faults." I rose and got myself one of the soft, brown rolls from the table. "I'm sure I can find one."

Or one hundred.

"I imagine Eredan heritage will be an excellent starting point. It seems to be the root of all their issues." Amethyst scoffed, setting down her cup with as much care as she handled spears. She controlled everything around her. "Or perhaps you can focus on their insistence that if it's not affecting them, it isn't that bad."

"Our discomfort and death is a small price for them to pay for their comfort." Emerald took the plate from her. "We fought back and formed Igna because they valued their mindsets over lives and were happy to let us die. They're not doing it again."

From her lips to the Lady's ears.

Amethyst spread her arms wide. "And now they've returned to crush us and retake their seats above us. They don't know how to function without a scapegoat."

I was as I was, and the rest of the world had to deal with it. I wasn't alive for them. I wasn't their scapegoat.

All this explained why south Igna—old Alona, the cities of the Sun-Drenched Coast—felt safest to me. Erlend's ideas hadn't seeped into the coast yet. Not everyone down there viewed it as a strict divide between two.

"Speaking of scapegoats, we have a court meeting soon." Emerald pointed at me. "We'll be discussing the spy situation. We've been bleeding out information, and it's most certainly a servant. Nicolas narrowed it down to the domestic spaces."

Good.

"I'm off until dawn." Amethyst pulled a plate a food toward herself. "And I intend to spend it sleeping. Let me know if we've whittled it down by then."

"Yes, yes." Emerald pulled on her mask and tied the ribbons back. "Mask on, weapons ready."

A guard that Emerald forced to stand on her blind side escorted us to a small room I'd never been to before. Part of the palace's safety was its maze of hallways and minimal exterior doors, and until we passed a window, I'd no idea which direction we were facing. The door was a thick, solid oak and had two guards standing on either side of it. It locked behind us.

Our Queen nodded when we entered. Nicolas rose from his chair, his knee-length coat swishing about his knees. He was in cheap, layered clothes not tailored to fit him or accommodate his missing arm. He was normally so particular about clothes.

"Who you been spying on?" I asked.

He blinked, the runes running across his eyelid covered by cosmetics. "I was out for a drink, not spying."

"It doesn't make you sound more interesting or less like a spy, only insufferable, dear," Emerald said. "What's happened?"

"The spy isn't a woman." He tossed a ripped letter to her and shrugged off his coat. The two sheaths on his belt tapped against his boots. "A woman recruited and sent them here."

Emerald held up the note to one of the lamps. "Who wrote this?"

"An Erlend spy who gave up his life of spying to live his life in Igna." Nicolas sat back down and bowed his head to Emerald. "The one you killed was still active. This one wasn't. He liked Igna, quite a bit to hear him tell it, and I tracked him down from some old census records. He agreed to talk and is staying in the Gray Rooms."

It was a pleasant name for the barely furnished, over-guarded blocks where we housed noncriminal prisoners who needed watching on palace grounds.

Politically better sounding, Nicolas had told me.

Which more and more meant disguising the truth.

Emerald scowled so hard her mask moved. "Do you think this means they were the only ones left here, or the rest remained loyal and none of them tried to leave Willowknot?"

Emerald had been sent to kill a spy running for Erlend after a decade of spying on us, and the idea of more of them still here, still spying, still reporting to Erlend, made me shudder. At least some had defected.

She handed me the note. It had been torn down the middle, making most of the words impossible to read.

"I think it is safest if we assume the others remained loyal to Erlend and are still out to assassinate Our Queen or one of us." Nicolas rested his elbow on his knee and leaned his chin on it. His tall torso still barely fit in the chair. "It is certainly a domestic servant and someone now of age. The one I found is desperate to prove his loyalty but unable to name any others but two—both dead."

Our Queen laughed so softly I almost missed it. "Weylin has been exaggerating the greatness of his Erlend pieces and the weaknesses of Igna for so long, but it seems many have finally seen the truth."

He couldn't operate without all his lies and propaganda. But not everyone bought into it.

"Opal." Emerald turned to me. "If you were sent to kill Our Queen, how would you do it?"

I laughed.

Our Queen didn't.

"Knowing what I do about this place?" I asked, and Emerald nodded. "Lock the doors to a court meeting in one of these weird, escape-proof rooms and set the place on fire."

Emerald snorted. "We do need to change those up."

"We can tomorrow, and we'll have an idea of who we're looking for by then. The records from longer than five years ago, around when we gained most of the domestic servant staff, are incomplete and not standardized." Nicolas glanced at the door. "Lena and I tried to go through them, but it was staggering how ill equipped our accounting was back then. We vetted several servants—each Left Hand servant; Dimas, since he's been keeping the records for the visiting and military boarding since; and a few others. They're sending up the list of names within my guidelines any moment. Our other pressing matter is the missing children."

I shifted and moved behind one of the chairs. Itching unease crept down my back and arms, and I gripped the chair back. Cam could be dead.

I was certainly dead to Rath, regardless of the outcome.

"Some of the writing in the letter you found was Nacean, wasn't it?" Emerald asked.

There was no remnant of Nacea that would work with Erlend. Not willingly. Not that we wouldn't know about.

"Location names, yes, but there are still several towns around the old borders bearing Nacean names." Nicolas's eyes flicked to me. He stiffened. "I doubt the spy is Nacean and especially doubt they would willingly work for Lord del Weylin if they were."

*Her hands were too busy with the other soon-to-be corpses we gave her.*

"Deadfall made the shadows in Nacea," I said, but it barely escaped my mask. "The first shadow in Nacea was the First Star. He told me that."

Our Queen ground her teeth together, locking her fingers together. "I am glad you had a chance to meet another on your list."

I'd a mind to respond rudely, but someone knocked on the door. Emerald opened it, short sword out. It was Dimas.

"Apologies for my lateness." He bowed spectacularly deep for all of us, and his braid of black hair tumbled over his shoulder.

The cuff on his ear sparkled in the lights. "I have the records you requested, though I recommend reading the transcriptions first, as the originals are quite worn."

"Thank you, Dimas." Nicolas waved him to the empty chair.

"I'm sorry." Dimas set the box down on the chair. "Really."

He ripped a stiletto knife from the papery depths, ink splattering across the floor, and brought it down toward Our Queen's heart.

# CHAPTER
# TWENTY

Nicolas pushed her out of the way. She went flying into the wall, and I went flying for Dimas. He spun, blade slicing through the air, and I ducked. Nicolas, off balance, caught the knife in his chest. Dimas ripped it out. A blur of green dove past my head as I tackled him.

Dimas shrieked, hitting the ground back first. I rose to my knees and punched him. Blood splattered across my hands and the stones, and Dimas slapped my shoulder. I toppled over.

An ear-ringing pain shot through my head, and I slashed at Dimas's arms. Nothing.

Lady, how'd he hit me so hard?

Dimas, weaponless and listing, used the far wall to stand. A jagged streak of red dripped down the back of his hand. He turned to run, but an arrow pinned his hand to the wall. He screamed, nearly tearing it free in his panic. I crawled to my feet, stumbling, and turned. Emerald lowered her bow.

"Stay," she said. She did not move, but I knew she looked

at me. "Opal, keep him there. Pin him somewhere else if you must, but he does not leave."

"Not alive at least," I said.

"Keep him alive." Nicolas coughed and rolled over, blood pooling beneath his shoulder. His old mage's sword fell from its sheath. "He was kind enough to apologize. Perhaps he'll be kind enough to tell us everything he knows."

Our Queen knelt before Nicolas and peeled back his torn shirt from the wound. "Clean strike at least. No lung damage. Come, before you bleed to death. Emerald?"

"On it." Emerald threw open the door and took the nearest guard by their collar. "You're staying here, both of you, and no one except the Left Hand walks through that door once the three of us leave. Understand?"

One guard bowed. The one she was holding nodded.

"You all right to walk or—"

"Walk. Help me up." Nicolas held out his hand to Emerald. His eyes were squeezed shut and his chest heaving. "Dimas, I hired you. You were nine. You had no ties to Weylin. He orphaned you, for Triad's sake. Why?"

Nothing.

I rounded on Dimas. "Least you justified my dislike of you."

He wheezed but said nothing.

Emerald hauled Nicolas to his feet and hooked an arm around his waist. Our Queen followed them out. The door clicked shut.

"Well, you failed, which, considering you attacked her with Emerald in the room, isn't surprising." I dragged a chair so that I could sit before him. "Bit of a disappointment, aren't you?"

"You know nothing about me. No one here does, only the Lady, and you have no idea—"

"Which lady?" I asked. "The Erlend one who recruited you? Who you think is going to save you?"

He stayed silent.

"You dye your hair black," I said. I'd not pegged him for the sneering Erlend type, but I could play that game, and I could play it well. "You paint your nails to keep from biting them, and you'd never touched a knife until today. Except in the kitchen. You've cooked. You held that stiletto like you were going to chop onions." I glanced at his bleeding hand and his disgusted sneer. "And you're not used to seeing your own blood. It's unfair, really, being all right with spilling other's but not all right with spilling yours. You have to give some to take it."

Erlend might've laughed at the Lady or called her old fashioned, but she was there, staring down on us.

Judging us.

"Every Erlend I've ever killed for prizing their power and their nation over the lives of Igna's people was just like you—concerned with looking good, looking powerful…and dead days after I met them. I met Caden de Bain. Man was a monster, but at least he was willing to bleed to get what he wanted."

Dimas shuddered. "I am nothing like him or any of those others."

He was hunched and on his knees, right hand pinned to the wall. Blood dripped down his elbow and splattered against the floor. I laid my knife across my knee. He shuddered.

"Well, Our Queen's not dead and Nicolas's isn't either, so you're at least as disappointing a person as they are."

He opened his mouth, crying too hard to speak, and stopped. A shiver ran through him. His gaze went through me, unseeing.

"I failed," he muttered. He laughed, then sobbed, then threw his head back against the wall. The sobs shook out of him, choking him till he was nearly sick. His pinned hand tore with a sickening squelch. "Lady, forgive me. I killed them. I killed them."

"What?"

I'd never heard anyone but me use that phrase with such care, and my ears were singing from the way he said it, with an emphasis just like mine.

He didn't like spilling blood. Even now, still rambling and shaking with grief, he didn't make the sign of the Triad.

My knife clattered against the floor. "What did you say?"

He sobbed into the crook of this red-soaked, dripping elbow, the other hand wrapped around his knees.

"Dimas!" I picked up Nicolas's mage sword. It was only a hilt with a sawtooth inlay on the grip—mages had no need for a blade when they'd plenty of blood and runes to spare—and chucked it at Dimas. It bounced off his shoulder. "What did you just say about the Lady?"

I'd thought he meant "a lady," not mine.

He turned to me, the red lines crowded the whites of his eyes too bright in the dim light. Not dark like the smear of him dripping down the wall. "No."

"Fine." I rose from the chair and sat down on the floor across from him. If I reached out, my fingers would have brushed his boots. But I didn't. My hands were shaking. A cold, heavy sweat coated my skin. Let me be wrong. "What was your mother's name?"

His hand twitched, long fingers clenching together. More blood dripped.

"I already didn't like you, and I'm not inclined to like you since you upset Maud," I said. "You're not really helping your case."

His brows drew together. "Is she all right?"

"Don't worry about her. She wouldn't want you to think about her at all in any way." I leaned forward. "Is your real name Dimas Gaila?"

Let Gaila not be his mother's name. Let him not have changed his name. Let him deny. Let me be wrong. Let me not meet someone from Nacea in this damned, bloody place.

He shook his head. "I can't. I'm not supposed to." He swallowed and shook his head. "It was the last thing she said to me—do not tell them your real name."

A tight, shuddering breath sat hot and heavy in my lungs.

Dimas Gaila.

His mother's name.

A Nacean name.

"Dimas Gaila?" I reached out and touched his foot, my fingers brushing the solid, real heel of his shoes. I closed my eyes, sure I'd pass straight through despite how mortal weapons pinned him now, and sighed. "Are you lying?"

He shook his head, gaze stuck on the tips of my fingers on his shoes. His fingers, ink stained and bloody, trembled against his mouth as if trying to catch the words before they left. "They had my mother's silver cuffs and knew my sister's name. I thought they were dead. They should be dead. Everyone is."

He was Nacean.

He was Nacean sure as I was.

"We're not," I said in Nacean. "We're not dead no matter if Nacea remains or not."

He froze. Shuddered.

"I want to hear about your mother and sister and who has them, but I'm more interested in hearing about Nacea now." I gripped his hand in mine. Too tight to be pleasant. "And if you tell me, maybe you won't die for trying to kill Our Queen."

A lie. I could not kill him—I could not bring myself to think of it now. Hard as it was to comprehend, I couldn't stand him, but I needed him. I needed Nacea.

But Our Queen might kill him.

"You're Nacean." His voice was soft, the Nacean from his mouth rounder and slower than I remembered. It went up at the ends. He laughed, and it dragged up more tears. "You sound like my second mother. She was from Salt Lick, on the southwestern coast. She's dead."

Accents. Cities. Memories.

I couldn't smile. The world was clear and sharp, like staring through the cold, still air of a winter day. My throat burned. My chest ached. Each breath came faster and faster and shorter and shorter.

"You're really Nacean." He laughed again, louder this time, and unfolded his legs. "Do you... Have you ever met anyone else?"

I shook my head. Heat burned in my stomach.

"Because I haven't," he said. "And I stopped looking until they said my first mother and sister lived, and then home was alive again, and I had to—"

My memories of Nacea tasted like bile and blood, the wet, dripping touch of spit pooling in the back of my throat.

"I had to do it," he whispered. "She'd understand, wouldn't she? Erlend found my mother and my sister and said they'd die if I didn't help kill Our Queen."

Nacean prayers. Nacean words. The same rushing, writhing sound of nothing filled my ears. I pressed my palms into my eyes.

"Dimas Gaila."

"But you're Our Honorable Opal." Dimas, wide eyed and desperate, reached for me. "How? How do you do it?"

"Sallot." I looked up. "My name is Sallot."

I could not give him my mother's name. He didn't deserve it.

I wanted to, but the drip of his blood down the stones and the memory of Nicolas's red-stained skin clung to me.

"Sallot," he said, drawing out the end in the soft sound of my name said properly.

I laughed. "No one ever gets that right on the first try."

I wanted to touch him and know he was there, but the rest of me recoiled at the idea, winced as the image of him, knife in hand, stuck in my mind.

I sniffed and wiped my nose instead. "I feel like I'm going to be sick."

"Me too." He dragged himself closer, till I could see the peppering of scars along his jaw. "What happened? I always thought the south was lost. We only barely made it to Lyncester."

I leaned forward and swallowed. My throat burned. "You ran to Weylin?"

"We ran to safety," he said quickly. "Erlend cities were supposed to quarter Nacean citizens in times of strife. The shadows were coming from the south, so we ran north. But we didn't make it."

I grabbed his foot. A single point of contact.

He was shaking.

"But you ran north with folk?" My breath stuck in my throat. I choked. "Did they live? Are there more?"

He shook his head, and it was like falling into the Caracol all over again.

"I remember snow," he said softly, hand fluttering around his face like a hatchling. He was careful and controlled, like Maud had said, and he ignored the bleeding hole in his hand. "The sky was gray and the ground was white—blinding and brutally cold, yet I still got a sunburn. All I wanted to do was stop walking, but we never stopped. There were shadows on the horizon, and we didn't have time for pyres. We ran into soldiers the last night I remember. And then my mother paid a man to take me away. I was bleeding. I don't..."

He stopped, swallowing.

"You don't remember?" I asked.

There were days when I was running, when my feet were blistered and my lungs full of rot, that I didn't remember. I remembered panic and fear and corpses soft with heat beneath me, but the spaces between running and sleeping were nothing. I liked running at night.

I couldn't see what I was running on then.

"It's not like normal bad stuff," he said quickly. "It's not like that at all. It's fuzzy. Like poppy tincture—you remember before and after but the in-between is gone and the edges blurry. My parents were a fisher and a midwife, and we always had a steady supply of scrapes and tinctures. I know that feeling. I was drugged."

"Why?"

"I don't know." He shrugged, fingers tapping against the floor and smearing blood across the stones. "My mother told me to never say I was Nacean. She never said why. She kissed me. I don't know what happened to my second mother. She would've said goodbye. She only wouldn't if—"

A shiver so violent it rattled his teeth ripped through him, and I grasped his arm. Speaking things made them real. Brought back the fear.

"I thought they were all dead, to bandits or shadows or soldiers, but then I got a letter." He glanced at me, dark gaze fixed on mine. "I tried to take it to Amethyst, but a guard I didn't know was outside my door. They know things only my mother could know. They told me about her and my sister, and they told me how they'd kill both. And then there were always guards I didn't know following me. I don't think they ever left after the war. They've been here the whole time, waiting." He took a breath. Shuddered. Closed his eyes. "I tried to get Fernando de Lex—Five—out of auditions, and that night the guards were in my room when I woke up"

"What did they do?" I asked, too shocked and sad and furious to ask anything else. Four Naceans alive, and two had been used to extort the third.

But all the anger in me was dying. I'd have done the same as Dimas. I might've done worse than Dimas.

There was nothing I wouldn't do to see my family again.

"My mother was a midwife. She had one rune on her arm to help with healing. They carved out that patch of skin, rune and scars and all, and laid it on my bed." He shuddered and gagged. "I did what they wanted after that."

He closed his eyes, breaths unsteady. "I can still remember the way out of the corn mazes I used to make with my sister and how my mothers took their tea and how it felt when I knew they were dead. All of them. Forever. I was adrift. And suddenly I was saying my sister's name for the first time in years and holding a piece of my mother's flesh, and I knew it was real. They were alive. I couldn't let them die. I couldn't let Erlend hurt them. I would've died before betraying Our Queen, but I can't let my family die. Not again."

I licked my lips, mouth dry and words failing. "I'm sorry."

"Me too." He looked up at me, tears dripping down his face, pooling in the crook of his chin, splattering against the floor. A steady drip. "I didn't want to do this. You're Nacean. We could've been talking."

I leaned back, the deep need of *me* tugging at my heart. "Do you think we count?"

Was I Nacean if I barely remembered the sound of my name on my siblings' fumbling lips or the taste of my father's favorite spiced, soft-boiled eggs? Erlend had taken Nacea, my family, my words, my sense of safety, the comforting rise and fall of my mother's songs on the evening wind as she taught my sister the name of each of our barn cats. Was there anything left of me they hadn't ruined?

I wanted to talk about all those things. Make them real again. But the words never came.

What if my accent was off or my words all wrong? Dimas was older than me, had been old enough to remember what Nacea was like, to remember what being Nacean meant. What if I was all wrong?

"I think we do. A Nacean is always a Nacean. It knows no bounds or rules. It's feeling and soul." He wiped his face and smeared red across one cheek. "My mother used to say that—Nacea is home and home is a feeling."

He paused, his hand leaving jagged lines of spiderwebbed blood across the floor. "I used to think I wasn't, not when I was keeping it a secret, when I changed my name, when I pretended I was Erlend, but it didn't last. All the little pieces bubbled up—the words I didn't know the translations for, the food I didn't like, the pointing and bowing and hierarchy. We never bowed to the stars. They were just the folks who counted votes and broke ties. Everything was different. I felt different. And then I didn't want to lose it. I was as I was, and all I could remember was my mother's face as she told me to never tell. I thought it would get better, that I'd not feel sad so often the further from my old life I got—cleaning and mathematics and making sure everything and everyone has a place; it's as different from fishing and physician work as I could get—but it didn't work."

It gave him a place but didn't take away the little thread of grief that knotted up everything.

"Sometimes I feel empty," I said slowly. "Like being hungry but it's in my bones, aching and burning all the way up to my head. I cried, once, when I saw a kid who looked like my sister laughing. I couldn't remember how my sister sounded."

There were a dozen words and feelings and pieces of me I wanted to know and hold, to gather up in my arms and cradle so tight against my chest that they melted into me and took hold like ice on frosted mornings. But each time I tried to pull myself together, the dregs of my Nacean memories slipped through my fingers like water.

Split. Spilled. Broken.

I wasn't those things, but I felt them. It wasn't fair.

"What was her name?" he asked.

"Shea."

He smiled. "Were you the oldest?"

"Yes."

I had been and would always be older than my sister, Shea, and my brother, Hia,even if Erlend killed me tomorrow.

"You were old enough to pick your name." He sniffed. "You were five, at least. You don't remember your childhood name?"

Sallot had always been my name. I thought it had been. But my memories were a blur, a smear of senses and details I couldn't connect, the taste of honey and smoke as my mother lit a candle and heated a needle to red hot. I'd written "Sallot" in blood and burned it.

A prayer for protection.

*"There," my mother whispered. "She knows you now, and you'll always be in her sight. And if you decide you want a change, you know how to tell her."*

"Do you burn it?" I asked. "The new name you pick?"

"So the Lady knows the new one." He held his hands out, palms flat and up, and a little burn scar had regrown over the whorls of his thumbprint. "I grabbed the candle flame by accident when doing mine."

I laughed, and my tongue still tasted vile, but I felt light. Empty. A better kind of nothing than I'd ever felt before. Like picking off a scab you didn't need.

"It's a wound." Dimas smiled. "One of those that never really heals."

I knew this smile. The tight stretch. The sharp pain at the back of my jaw. The ache behind my eyes. That pitiful, little grin we offered up to others who shared our secret pains even as happiness crept in.

Sallot. Dimas.

Two sides of a bloody, stolen coin.

"I'm killing them," I said, quietly, slowly, drawing the edge from my voice like venom from a bite. "The lords who let their soldiers leave Nacea. The ones who didn't warn us the shadows were loose. I'm going to kill them all for leaving us to die. They'd do it again if they could, and I can't let them do that. Not to anyone else."

So long as they lived, the Erlends entrenched in North Star's ideals would be a threat to lives everywhere.

Killing them was a mercy. A handful of deaths to save thousands.

A muscle beneath his eye twitched. "I shouldn't feel glad for that. You are as you are."

I was as I was, and they'd be dead.

As the guilty should be.

"I'm sorry you have to do that." He drew one lone line of red between us. "And I'm sorry for what I have to do."

The room exploded.

# CHAPTER
# TWENTY-ONE

A dull, distant echo thrummed in and out, the push and pull of tidewaters in my ears. I was staring at the night sky, the deep nothing and flicker of stars. Heat lapped at my feet and arms and face. A damp chill seeped down my stomach.

I coughed, choked, and let my face fall to the side.

"Be alive." A hand touched my arm. "Please, please, please. I didn't think it would be that big. I'm sorry."

Dimas.

I wrenched open my eyes, the sticky sting of light and pain forcing them back together. Again.

My vision was a blur. The smear that was Dimas stood and turned away. A spot of silver rested near my head, and I grabbed it, arm aching. Had to get up, I had to move. Dimas was Nacean. Dimas was a traitor.

Dimas was escaping.

I pushed myself up and grabbed the silver. Pain and pain and pain and then the steady heat of rage.

He'd tried to kill Our Queen and nearly killed me? After all that? After Nacea?

I fixed my grip on the silver—the pain giving way to the blood-singing joy of knowing what to do, the hairs on my arm rising, the shudder running through me stopping dead—and threw it at Dimas.

It sailed through the edges of his blur.

"Lady." It died on my lips. The little spark of awareness I'd had faded, and I collapsed. My head hit the stones. I couldn't move, not easily. My vision cleared, but the rumble in my ears remained. I stayed there, twitching and staring and coughing. The room was ruined. The wall Dimas had been pinned to was only a small series of bricks a bit shorter than me, and sunlight was streaming in. He'd escaped into the evergreen sea circling the palace grounds.

And if he got stopped, how many more whatever-did-this did he have? It had to be alchemy. Explosives were easy enough to make so long as you'd the right things and steady hands.

I willed my hands to move, and they shook. My head rolled back to stare into the daylight. I blinked.

Scrawled across the stones still standing was a single line in burned-black blood.

*Lady, let me out.*

A crashed sounded behind me, a shout that might've been my title came, but I could only think, *Had she?*

The turtle green of a physician's cloak loomed in the corner of my sight. Hands grabbed my shoulders. I flinched.

"Isidora." I coughed, chest aching. "I want Isidora."

She was too important to deal with me, but I wasn't dying,

and I wanted familiar eyes and hands on me. She was clever and kind, and she'd always been nice to me even in the throes of grief. She'd understand me now.

The pair of hands gently cupped my face but didn't move me. "It's me. It's all right. Move your feet for me."

I did.

"Good, good. Now look at me." Her face came into focus, thin lips drawn and freckles outnumbered by flecks of dust and ash. She pushed her bulky sleeves up past her elbows. "Can you tell me what happened?"

"Dimas." I coughed again, spit and snot dripping down the back of my throat. "Did something. He said they, Erlend, had his mother. Erlend's got his family. He kept apologizing, and then I was on my back."

"That's all right. I'll tell Emerald. Just rest." Her words dripped over me, hitting my ears in wavering, wobbling sounds. A panic I couldn't place took hold of my heart. "Your hand is the worst bit. I won't have to stitch it up, but it looks like a saw-toothed hilt?"

I held up my hand to the light. "I threw Nicolas's sword at Dimas."

I shouldn't have looked at my hand.

The wound was familiar, deep and dark, blood pooling in the holes where the hilt had been. I'd seen wounds like this before on corpses' skin. In festering skin.

Little heads like grains of rice poked through the gaps of what was left of my brother Hia's skin. Holes no bigger than my littlest nail filled with blood that sloshed and spilled as blowflies probed the jagged edges. A creeping itch gnawed at my hand.

I shuddered and closed my eyes.

Hia, dead for a day and torn flesh moving, overflowing with other creeping, gnawing lives.

Life dripping from his wounds.

"It's not too deep. That's good." Isidora pulled a bag from her pocket and cleaned out the holes, wet cloth burning against my skin. In my skin. Beneath it. "I'll have to stitch it up, and Nicolas certainly owes you something nice for this."

"How is he?" I choked on the last word, and she helped me sit up. Even turned away to let me spit a blob of snot pricked with red across the room. I took a deep breath. "He got stabbed."

She swallowed, lips pursing. "Yes, but he'll be fine so long as we keep an eye on it. No lasting damage."

The burn in me went deep, seeping into the wrinkles of my palm and down into the bones where I swear the cloth slipped under my skin easy as a shadow and drank up the blood the hilt had left behind. I felt it moving.

"Could you just bandage it up?" I asked. "I don't like stitches."

Didn't like feeling them. Looking at them.

She eyed me. "All right. If it starts hurting or looking inflamed—"

"It's infected. I got it." I pulled my hand away once she was done with the bandage. "Thank you. Really. It's easier this way."

The room was blown to nothing. Only the door still stood. The two guards who'd been next to it were clearing rubble from the hallway. Isidora touched my shoulder. The astringent from her rag dripped onto my shoulder, and I shuddered.

"Let me take you to your room," she said. "I want to make sure there's nothing there that will exacerbate your injury, and since Maud de Pavo left, I doubt you want anyone else looking you over in your quarters."

I nodded. "I'll need help standing."

"Serra?" She turned to one of the guards. "Help Honorable Opal and I up, please?"

The guard sprinted to us and held out her hands. She walked us to the door to the Left Hand private quarters too, and Isidora dismissed her with a nod.

"I used to visit Ruby," Isidora muttered as I hesitated at the door. "Let me check you once you're settled, mask on, and then I'll wear a blindfold. Amethyst and Emerald are with Our Queen."

I shook my head and opened the door.

"You're quite well for such a large explosion so close to you." She set her bag of supplies on the dining table. "Sit somewhere comfortable, and I'll clean the rest of those."

I raised my arms. Dozens of little splinters and scratches lined my arms and chest. I pulled one out, the pain peaking. Isidora sucked in a breath.

"Let me." She doused a cloth in astringent. "Here."

*Drip.*

I sat still, ears ringing.

"I've been meaning to speak with you." Isidora's voice drooped at the end but her stare stayed steady. She wiped the blood from my mask. "Are you sure you feel all right?" She pressed her fingers to the pulse point of my throat, other hand holding the rag over the wounds. "It's a bit fast."

"Is it?" I felt apart. Blurry. Like I was half-in and half-out of myself, like that cloth or the hilt or a maggot. "I did get blown up."

I'd seen my muscles gleaming, red and bright, beneath my skin.

"I'm not surprised." She pulled my boots off and rolled up my trousers. "You're a very strong person."

People at court had started using words for me that carried no gender when they weren't sure, like "person." It was nice. I wanted it all the time. I wanted it to feel nice now.

I couldn't feel anything.

"This will be cold." Isidora poured a small bowl of water down my legs.

The sound echoed. I shuddered.

"Anything hurt?" she asked.

I shook my head.

*Drip.*

She swung the cloth around to soak it again, flinging the last droplets from it.

*Drip.*

"I feel panicky." I scratched at my bandaged hand, the itching unbearable. The pool of water between us rippled. "Nothing really hurts more than anything else."

My world was a dull, constant ache.

"You're injured and were recently in a sudden trauma." Isidora rung out the cloth over the hand-washing basin in the corner, her bottom lip caught between her teeth. Little indents appeared in her reddened flesh. I blinked, but the indents spread, leaving a bloody trail Isidora didn't notice. I tried to shake loose the vision, but pain shot through my head.

It wasn't real. It wasn't real.

*Drip.*

Was it?

"Stop."

Isidora froze. "What?"

"The water." I flinched. "You're dripping everywhere."

"Yes," she said, jaw tensing. The veins beneath her skin darkened. Rose. Poked out of her skin, heads black above the muddy red. "Opal? What's wrong?"

I took a deep breath but it didn't help. The panic stayed. My heart sped up. My lungs were too small, too tight, and the moment stretched out forever, the terrifying space between the sounds filling my head. Nothing but death. Nothing but shadows. Nothing at all getting closer and closer, blood and flesh dripping from it. I blinked.

Nothing was happening to Isidora's veins.

*Drip.*

I leapt to my feet. I had to run. I had to do something. My heart was loud between my ears, in the back of my eyes, and my breaths were too shallow, too short. This was wrong.

What was wrong?

*Drip.*

I ripped the cloth from her hands. They were red, dripping, skin speckled with holes, bone-white mouths boring through the flesh. She flinched, stumbling back. A dull, low gnawing filled my ears. Like gnashing mouths. Like pumping blood.

Isidora's mouth moved, but I didn't hear anything. Nothing.

*Drip.*

The dark water between us writhed and twitched. Shadows dripped across her feet.

I ran.

I tripped over my chair and kept going, slamming into the

side of the table. High ground. Safety. I grabbed the edge of the table and hoisted myself on top of it. My face was numb, my skin too tight, and my hands moved without me, clawing at the edge of the wardrobe. I crawled onto the top of it, behind the elaborate whorls of wood, and curled up with my back to the wall. My hands shook. The drip remained.

The panic stretched on forever.

I breathed in and out, dust clouds bursting from the top of the wardrobe with each breath. My eyes burned like I'd been crying. I'd dealt with grief before. I'd shaken myself awake from plenty of monstrous dreams, but I was awake.

"Opal?"

I winced.

"Panic attack?" And Isidora, whose late-night screams of pain and grief I knew as well as I knew my own, reached a hand to the top of the wardrobe, fingers barely skimming the edge. "I thought this might happen."

"What?"

She sighed. "It happens to many of us, panicking with no obvious reason, but there are small things, reminders, that set it off. It was the sound, wasn't it?"

I sunk into my spot. "It happens to others?"

"Oh yes," she said. "It's why Rodolfo—Ruby—slept with a lamp."

Her voice hitched, and I reached over the edge to touch her fingers.

"I'm Opal." The world cleared slowly, like a clean streak through rain on glass windows. "I shouldn't be scared of anything, especially when nothing bad is happening."

"Says who?" Isidora laughed, harsher than I'd ever heard

her. "You're Opal. You can feel however you like and anyone who disagrees can take their opinions elsewhere."

She waited for me to climb down and settle on one of the couches, my back to a wall and a thick pillow in my lap. She sat next to me, legs crossed and sweater bulging. She rested a hand against her stomach. "I typically do not push it, but I think you might need it—the sound and your hand are what pushed it over? You've seen wounds like that before?"

I swallowed. "Is it still a wound if they're already dead?"

"I know what the dead look like." She rested her chin on her palm, fingers curled around her face. Dark brown scars covered the backs of her hands like lacework gloves, and she tapped her cheek. "It didn't occur to me why you were flinching, but it was your hand, wasn't it? There's nothing wrong with that."

"It's just holes." I shivered, the memory of it scratching up my spine. "How can I be scared of that?"

"Because you saw them first during the most terrifying time of your life," Isidora said. "So now they are a part of that terror.

"We'd no time to preserve the dead during the war and eventually no magic to preserve the living." She shifted, drawing a line from her wrist to her elbow. "A shadow flayed Nicolas's arm, and Our Queen banished magic. I could do nothing for him. Rot set in."

She closed her mouth, swallowed, and shook her head. I knew what she was feeling. I did it all the time too.

"Nicolas and I don't each much meat now," she said, voice hushed. "A fear wrought of war."

I swallowed, skin itching and hot. "You said Ruby slept with a lantern."

"Oh, yes. Always. And sometimes, all of us, each and every one of us, wakes up from a dream or a nap or even just blinks, and we're back there—shadows slipping through hands like wind through window cracks and Erlend swords bearing down upon us." Her fingers hovered over my arm. "You're not alone. You're not odd. Your mind is just trying to protect you from what it grew up thinking was a threat."

"It was safe in the trees or roofs or rafters," I whispered. "They never looked up."

"May I touch you?"

I nodded.

She pulled me in close, her forehead to mine, and said, "When I am very stressed, when my mind is pulled in many directions, I can't even stand the sound of spoons scraping copper mugs or knives dragging against plates."

"They were wet." The words spilled from me. People were wet. "The smell came first and then the dripping as they stood still, waiting to find a new face."

*Drip.*

They were nothing but the rustling of pine needles and blowflies on those days.

*Drip.*

Waiting. Stitching. Circling the base of my tree.

"Opal?" Isidora's low voice rumbled in my head. Her fingers clasped my arms. "You're safe."

I pressed myself into the tree. No. No. No.

"You're remembering what happened," she said softly. "It's not real. It's a memory."

A shadow, long and lean and bare, no skin claimed and no

stolen face, rose from the dark cracks between the fallen leaves. White heads poked through its nothing flesh.

"There are no shadows now. You're safe. You're here. No magic, no shadows. That was then. This is now."

I closed my eyes. "I see them."

"They can't touch you now. It's perfectly safe." Her breath warmed my shoulder. "Do you understand?"

"I hear them first," I said, "and then they're here."

"Does it smell?"

"No."

Not real. They always smelled.

Always.

I opened my eyes. Isidora's face, so close to mine, was pale and drawn, her freckles a rusty shade of red and the lines around her mouth deep. I rubbed my face.

"Can I touch you?" she asked again.

I nodded. "I don't like being scared of nothing."

"It's not nothing. You're just a bit too good at survival right now." She checked my pulse, my eyes. "You need to talk to a physician. Properly. They can help you pinpoint how to make sure you're safe when this happens. I would say you need them now, but..."

But the world was falling apart as fast as me.

Her fingers closed around my hand. I stared, head tilted, breathing fast.

How could she touch me? How could her runes stand to be next to my bloodied skin?

The Lady had gifted her those. Had seen her fit to wield such power and know how to use it.

And I was spilling blood. All the blood that she'd help save.

I thought the Lady might forgive me, understand me, but maybe my existence was punishment enough for her. Her way of seeing me repent.

"The ways you've been coping with it aren't healthy no matter how much you believe they work." She very gently touched my hand, prying it from my thigh.

"I killed them. How would you cope with that?"

"I've had many, many people die when their lives were in my hands because my understanding of medicine wasn't enough. Was that my fault?"

"You're good. You're nice. You don't hurt anyone." I flipped my hand over and touched one of her turtles. "You weren't even allowed to."

"Good is relative. I hurt all the loved ones of the people I failed to save," she said. "And not all of the ways I coped were good for me or the people around me. Try to stop—you won't always succeed. You just need to try, or else you'll go too far. You don't deserve pain. You can control other things. The world is not out of your hands, and you don't have to deal with everything alone."

How Nacean was I when my entire life went against the only Nacean trait I remembered? If I spilled my blood and the blood of others?

Could I trust Dimas's comments on being Nacean when he left me like that?

"You can always take off the mask."

"I can't bring folks back to life."

I couldn't undo what I'd done, and I could never repay

enough in my blood to make up for it. Lives weren't exchange-able. Even if they did deserve to die.

She rose to her feet, as graceful as Ruby—they moved the same, slow and calculated till they made up their minds—and helped me up. A warm piece of metal slid from her palm into mine. I let go and looked at it.

It was a ring—plain silver with a slightly raised band that spun when I ran my nail across it.

"Spin it when you're nervous." She smiled. "Emerald made it. We had better ones when magic was around, but she's been trying to figure out those for a few months, and I didn't have the heart to import a runed one from elsewhere. All of this," Isidora said, touching my arm, "rarely starts out bad, but it goes bad quickly."

With Weylin and this secret keepers dead set on ruling these lands no matter how much they ruined it, the rangers stealing kids, doing Lady knew what with their ears and picking up the ones who could fight to use as soldiers, and Elise determined on fixing Hinter no matter what happened, the world would need a way to cope in the coming days.

I would need a way to cope.

I whispered, "A runed one from elsewhere? What do you mean by that?"

"Mizuho and the Free Nations still have magic. Berengard probably still does if they're alive. It's just us that's been cut off." Her fingers tapped the runes in her wrists. "Probably for the best, wouldn't you say?"

I laughed. "Should've done it sooner."

"I have another, older gift for you, but first." Isidora gently gripped my wrist, fingers barely closed over my forearm. "You're with me, and you're Opal. It's a high crime to hurt a physician, a crime to hurt a member of court, and I'm terrifying enough for the two of us. Nothing can hurt you now."

I grinned.

I only had to hold that close. I was Opal. I was safe.

As Isidora gently tended the rest of my wounds, I repeated the still-living names from my list: North Star, Riparian, Winter. I would kill them, and the world would be all the safer for it.

CHAPTER
# TWENTY-TWO

T he gift was a small, leather-bound journal, the sort merchants used to keep track of accounting, and the numbers
and names were written in Nacean. There were nine thousand
people listed, nine thousand Nacean neighbors I'd never known
and never would. Nicolas had found it in his library, Isidora had
said, and he thought I was from southern Nacea. The first victims of the shadows.

"Three-fourths of the way through," Isidora had said. "We
think that's them."

I'd flipped through the pages—racing past sharp scribbles
that looked like names and numbers, maps of roads and rivers
cutting through endless fields: sigils for Nacean things I didn't
know and letters I barely remembered.

The writing itself was easier to recognize, to remember.
It was all hills and mountain peaks, lines and angles instead of
Alonian's and Erlenian's round, soft symbols. I didn't have the

patience to read the notes, but I knew my name. I knew the names of my family.

The writing blurred, and I shook my head.

*"It's important to know your past."* My father, sitting in the dim light every morning when Shea and Hia were still asleep, measured tea leaves with one hand and drew letters on my palm with the other while he taught me to read. Easier to learn the feel of them. *"If you do, you will understand the present and the future. We invented printing presses to maintain our histories, to ensure our pasts were available for all. You're part of those histories now and forever."*

Now and forever. From Nacean memories to Nacean hands to Nacean pages to me. These weren't myths or stories, not laws lived here.

But these names were history. Nine thousand histories that had to matter now.

*Leon Margo. Perrin Cal. Sallot Leon. Shea Leon. Hia Leon.*

I would make them matter.

I'd tucked the book into my chest pocket, better to feel their histories against my heart, and straightened my shoulders before entering Our Queen's new safe room.

I was Opal, deadly and still alive. Mostly.

I'd no reason to fear this room or these people.

Isidora entered before me, bowed, and moved aside, and I followed, eyes rising to Our Queen and the rest of the room. Nicolas laid on a couch, propped up by pillows and poppy by the looks of his eyes. Isidora sat near his feet and curled one hand around his bare ankle. Amethyst and Emerald, hands empty but stances ready, stood on either side of Our Queen. I bowed.

"Our Queen?" I waited for her to speak.

She rose instead and touched my bandaged hand. "I would comment on Dimas's escape, but I fear we're all quite baffled."

"All" was an understatement.

"I don't know what he did." I straightened up and shook my head. "He was talking one moment, and then everything exploded."

Emerald hummed. "I don't recall him studying alchemy."

"There are many cleaning solutions and healer's kits that come with easily combustible ingredients." Isidora took a deep breath and shrugged. "I cannot be sure what he used, but it worked on solid stone three different times. He must have had quite a lot of it."

"He used it three times?" I asked.

"He blew holes in anything in his way." Amethyst held up her own bandaged hand. "He escaped in the chaos. Willowknot is on lockdown. There's a hole the size of a house in the wall."

Maybe The Lady had taken a liking to him, but why?

Was she watching me? Had I been found wanting?

"He said Erlend has his mother and sister hostage." I used my uninjured hand to make a "maybe" gesture. "Sounded real, but course, I didn't see the explosion coming, so I don't know."

"Weylin's reign—politically, ideologically, morally—ends with us." Our Queen took a breath and held it, steadying herself. "We have been fighting against him for too long. He has peddled his ideas of power to anyone disenfranchised, and he has encouraged his citizens to view life as expendable, to view all resources and rights as finite. We have limited years left. We cannot waste them fixing his mistakes. This is the last war with Erlend or the last stand of Igna. Opal?"

I stepped forward, mind shuffling through her speech. She was, at least, determined to leave the world in better hands once she died. Not her family's hands, not her friends' hands. Better ones that would do right by us. "Yes, Our Queen?"

"How is your list?"

"Shorter than it was." I could not hate her here, not with all them watching. She was, for all her faults, trying. "Riparian is the only unknown now."

"Good," she said, voice rough, throat tense around the words. Her nails scraped up the arm of her chair. "Kill them. I do not care how, I do not care who sees. Kill them all. Bring Erlend's supremacist traditions to an end. Give peace a chance to return. You will go after Dimas, as well. No one tries to kill me and gets away."

I bowed—deep, slow, the back of my neck exposed to everyone in the room—even though she could only hear the swishing of my coat and closeness of my breaths. "They'll be dead, or I'll die trying."

"Good." She inclined her head to me. "Leave tomorrow morning once you've rested and prepared. Get Dimas first."

I could go after Rath, then. Least I could make something right.

Emerald stayed with Our Queen. Amethyst and I went back to the Left Hand quarters. My rooms were a mess—no Maud, no order—and I'd no energy left to leave my clothes anywhere but the floor. I sunk into a bath and crawled into bed. A piece of paper crinkled. I pulled the note from under my pillow.

Opal,

*I believe in you. I am certain you'll pass out the moment you return, and I won't get a chance to talk to you, but I do worry when you leave. It is nice to have a friend who trusts me, and I do trust you whether you believe it or not. We are kindred souls, I think, too ambitious to let others in. Perhaps ambition will be our downfall, but I think it will be the start of our success.*

*Regardless, when you wake up and read this, please remember to unlock the door so I can enter.*

*Also, you have terrible taste in jewelry. Pease stop offering to buy me some. Your company is enough.*

*My paycheck, of course, is an integral part of your company.*

*Yours,*

*Maud*

*I know you'll have to ask Amethyst or Emerald to read this. Please accept having to get out of bed and knock on their door as punishment for tearing holes in the heels of all your socks.*

*I darned your socks. You're welcome.*

Amethyst had laughed when reading that last bit. I'd thanked her—quietly—and snatched the note back. After she left, I tucked the note into my pocket with the book and curled up beneath the blankets, restless and sobbing until sleep claimed me. It did not come quickly.

I left a lamp burning.

And the next morning, when I pulled on my socks and started crying, I wiped my face on the long sleeve of my dress. Three scattered dots of white thread had been sewn into the black cloth.

The Lady's stars, close enough to touch.

Emerald didn't see me off, but Amethyst did. She was dressed to travel too, and a huge painted mare snuffled at her pockets. We were alone at the back gates, our masks bright in the dawn light.

"Aim to kill," she said. "Don't hesitate. We're beyond that now. Dimas went northeast."

I nodded. "Thank you."

"Stay alive." She rested her hands on my shoulders. "And if that fails, do what you normally do."

A snort came from behind me, and I turned.

Emerald shook her head, light bouncing off her expression-less face. "Do better than you normally do."

"All right." I glanced between the two. "Is that all in order of importance?"

"Stop." Emerald held up her hand, palm facing me. "Stay alive and end this. Order of importance."

I smiled.

Bowing her head to me, she said, "Those with privilege always allow responsibility to trickle down, but while you kill them, we'll take care of the rest. This isn't a one-person job. Be safe. I can't come save you this time."

CHAPTER
# TWENTY-THREE

I was too weak to go after Dimas immediately. Instead, I went east and followed the leftover posters and rumors littering every southeastern town.

The Carnival of Cheats was making its rounds with a whole new set of cheaters—they'd lost at least three of their performers during auditions, and they were advertising flesh blood in order to draw a crowd.

It took me two days on the back of a wagon to make it to Felmark, and the tickets were already sold out. Getting tickets was hard enough when they were actually selling them. I'd have to cheat my way into a show full of folks as observant as me.

I hoped Two was still working here. I'd never gotten her real name, but she had to be.

If Rath had been here, he'd have told me I'd more confidence than blood. That I trusted my way to be right too often for no reason.

She might not even agree to my idea. Two and I weren't

friends. There was a chance she wasn't even here or wanted nothing to do with me. She might've given up her life of deadly feats and knife throwing to live as a pastry chef for all I knew.

I wandered the streets as a normal person. Not Opal and not quite Sal. The world looked different.

The town proper was well within the shadows of the south-ernmost tip of the Snake Spine Range, their dark crags blocking the eastern horizon. The main market, an open-air circle sur-rounded by a crescent of tall apartments atop street-front stores, was wreathed in flags of red and gold. They flickered like flames in the wind.

I dove into the crowd. It was the evening after Tulen, the har-vest moon hanging low and heavy in the sky. A fire burned in the heart of the market, warm and bright atop a public fountain more pond than architecture. The flames crept toward the carnival cheaters preforming high overhead. People trying their hardest to ignore the scrape of bare feet on the ropes above reached into their pockets for purses and pulled out tickets instead. That was how it usually worked—an invitation whether you wanted it or not.

The brave ones who did want it went to the source and ducked under an arch of knives juggled by two cheaters so far into the dark they were nothing but the sounds of hilts hitting hands. They only accepted the tickets and payments from the people that didn't flinch, gossips said.

But I ducked under them without flinching and got nothing. Liars.

I paced between town and carnival, waiting for a hand to make its way into my pocket. Shouldn't have been this hard to get robbed.

None of the ones I picked had tickets. Only coins and hand-kerchiefs and canteens of mulled wine that coated my tongue in uncomfortable sweetness. I spat a mouthful of it out in an alley.

A voice from above said, "You're supposed to dilute it with water."

"Doubt it's drinkable either way." I looked up at the familiar voice of auditioner Two and grinned. "You been watching me?"

"You could've asked for tickets." She wore no mask, and her upside-down smile—she'd dimples, I'd never pictured dimples on an assassin—was a touch too wide to be sincere. A thin scar split the cleft of her chin. "But I liked the show. You've got light hands."

"And you've got strong feet." I tilted my head back till the web of wires and ropes she'd hooked her feet over was visible. "How long you been up there?"

"I could go days without touching the ground," she said. "Pleasure to meet you face to face."

She held out her hand. I took it, how Ruby had taught the both of us.

"Nice to meet you." I shrugged. "Again."

"Adella," she said quickly, springy, black curls bouncing round her face as her rope jiggled. "No more numbers. I'm Adella da Zito till I die."

"Hello, Adella." Grinning, I gave her my real name. "You can call me Sal."

She laughed, a bit too hard to be happy, and pulled herself onto the rope, sitting like it was a chair. "What do you want, Sal?"

*Sal, Sal, Sal.*

"Help," I said. "I've got to do something as Opal, but I'm

———— ❧ 178 ❧ ————

afraid others might get hurt during it, and I'd like you to make sure that doesn't happen."

I needed a buffer between me and my anger, between me and Rath. Cam and those kids needed saving no matter what, and I'd a duty to do everything I could to ensure that.

"Meet me by the main tent." She stood atop the rope and started walking away. "I need to tell my apprentice it's her lucky night."

The main tent was a monstrous thing as tall as castle walls. I bought a stick of sugar-coated fruit, crunching through it as I waited. The thick canvas behind us trapped the heat inside, filling the air with the scents of roasted corn and warm skin sweating in wool each time the flaps parted. Kids, each marked with the carnival's flames from the leather bands holding up their hair to the cosmetics melting down their cheeks, peeked out at us from under the tent. I grinned.

"Don't you all have a show to do?" I asked.

They giggled.

"They're much too silly for shows." Adella, dressed in plain traveling clothes and carrying a pack stuffed to the brim, shoved her way from the tent. "You ready?"

"Yes." I bit into a small, tart fruit. "You don't even know what we're doing exactly."

"I don't care." She looked me over, face blank. In the bright, white lights of the carnival lamps, her dark brown skin was scarred. She'd tattooed a 3 and 4 behind each ear. "I want to figure out why a thief from nowhere survived while the two best people I knew died."

I tossed the kids the rest of my fruit. "I wasn't just a thief."

"Point still stands." Her eyes were ringed in the reddish-brown smear of sleepless nights. "I thought I would die. I didn't expect to almost die and get stuck here without them. I thought Theo would be Opal. He wanted it the most."

"Your job is almost dying."

She rolled her eyes. "The trick between fun and dying is almost. Back when magic was still around, my parents held beating hearts in their hands every other night. That would've been a good job. This is boring."

I winced. "I like my bits inside me, thank you."

"Your loss." Adella smiled. It wasn't pleasant. It was cornered foxes snarling at nearing hunters. "Let's see what you can do, Sal, Sal, Sal."

I told Adella everything that night. We were heading to Mossvale first, hunting down Rath and seeing where his search for Cam took him. It was in Lena's lands, a skip over a sliver of Erlend land, and we'd be on the lookout for Lena and Maud too. "Testing her security," I called it.

Adella had laughed. "I'm glad it wasn't me." She kept her bow and three arrows in hand as we walked, and her mood worsened the farther north we got. "Are you glad it was you?"

I shrugged. "It's what I wanted."

I had wanted to be Opal forever.

"Yes," Adella said. "That's why I'm asking. I've known cheaters with less of a death wish than you, and I've been with the carnival for my whole eighteen years."

"I thought you were older." I rubbed my ears, tips cold in the wind, and breathed into my hands.

She grinned her crooked, close-mouthed grin and laughed.

LINSEY MILLER

"And I thought you'd be better looking under that mask but here we are."

"Fair." I nudged her arm with my elbow as we picked our way down a hill. "Can I ask you something?"

"Depends." She ran a chain through her fingers, a simple thing of sturdy loops and polished steel, and let it pool in her palm. Three interlocking circles hung from it. "Is it about Myra and Theo?"

I nodded. "Was his name really Theo?"

Wasn't a name I'd have picked for him.

"It's too round for him, isn't it?" She froze. "Doesn't matter now." She twisted the necklace so tight the red dents in her skin broke open. "Death always happened to other people. Never them."

I winced. "Sorry. I liked them."

"Yes," she said softly. "I'm sorry too."

"You sure you're up to this?" I offered her a canteen full of tea and an out. "I know I'm Opal, but there's really no mystery to it. Five was an Erlend spy and you were the one I thought they'd pick, but apparently my thieving was what they wanted."

"Don't celebrate too much." Adella glanced at me, the whole of her hair pulled into a single wobbling puff atop her head, and touched her three fingers to her lips to send a prayer to the Triad. "I told them I didn't want it. Think they were going to pick you regardless, but it's not like you'd any competition."

Great.

We traveled for four whole days, only stopping to sleep in shifts. Adella and I talked of childhoods and friends, Theo and Myra and Rath mostly. Four, Theo, had been with the carnival for near his whole life. Myra had been the oldest, twenty-two and on top of the world, the lead act and everything. And sick.

Myra da Barre, Three to me and the face that haunted my nightmares, had been dying long before heading to auditions, something to do with blood and bone growing too much. Without magic, no physician could track how long she had or ease the random bouts of excruciating pain. But she was still the best fighter out of the three of them—Two, Three, and Four.

And they'd expected her to be Opal.

"I'd never gone more than a few days without seeing them," Adella whispered one night. "And now I can't even remember what shape the scar on Theo's arm was. How Myra looked in the morning. What our last words were. It was too hectic. I didn't think I'd need to remember."

Adella and Theo had figured they'd die, or the three of them would work together to make sure Myra got to the end of the audition. Then, Adella and Theo would get disqualified or quit.

Myra had wanted something new. They'd all wanted that newness together.

"I'm all that's left."

I'd not said anything to that. Wasn't the same, but she'd a right to her grief and, Lady, if it wasn't full of pain.

We didn't talk about the auditions after that.

Days later, long after we'd crossed the border, we stumbled onto the outskirts of Mossvale. It was a small, scattered town, and there wasn't a hint of Rath in sight. Adella snapped her teeth together.

"You sure he's here?" she asked. "Doesn't look like anyone new has been here in a while."

Footsteps crept up behind us, crinkling leaves in the under-brush. We both turned.

Rath, dirt-streaked but alive, froze in place. "Sal."

He was such a terrible thief.

"Rath." I itched to grab him, hug him, hold on to some part of our childhood and tell him I'd make this right, but I only nodded to Adella. "This is Adella. The only other surviving auditioner."

I'd a hard time imagining the disqualified two were still alive. Not with the way they lived.

He narrowed his eyes. "I found the rangers taking the kids."

"Good." An awkward, stilted tension hung in the air. "Let's get them."

Adella glanced between us. Rath huffed.

"Come on." He turned and led us around Mossvale and far-ther north. "They've got two other kids now. I've been watching them for a while."

And that was that. I swallowed down my disappointment and followed.

It was getting dark when Rath stopped walking and held a hand to his mouth. Adella and I crept after him, and in the clear-ing beyond sat four rangers and two kids. Two of the rangers were sleeping and two were talking around their small fire, toss-ing the kids food every now and then. The kids were shackled and gagged, metal bars connecting the cuffs instead of chains so that no matter how they moved, the kids couldn't use their hands or bring them together.

"There's a lady that's been visiting too," Rath whispered. "Short, dark, braided hair, button nose. I don't know her. She's nice to the kids though. Small miracle, considering."

"We're on Igna land, technically." I glanced up. "Little more north and we won't be, but Lady de Arian rules all of Aren, and she's siding with Our Queen."

Rath nodded. "Good. She can help relocate these kids and find Cam."

The kids were hooked together by a single chain looped in a circle through each of their arm bars. I secured my mask.

"The sleeping ones'll be easy." I'd a length of metal wire in my pack courtesy of Isidora's alchemy research, and they'd settled down against separate tree trunks on either side of camp. I could tie them up to buy us time. "We can each take one, and I'll get the one patrolling too."

Rath tapped his teeth together, gaze going blank as he stared at the little camp. "They'll just get other kids."

"They might." I nudged him. "What you thinking?"

"They don't get these kids, they'll just take others. Same outcome, different kids. How's that fair?"

It wasn't, but it was as it was.

"What if you—" Rath drew a finger across his throat, face the hardest I'd ever seen it. He couldn't even say it.

"You sure?" He was right, of course, but this was Rath. He rescued stray dogs and refused to kill spiders unless they bit him. He'd feared me, and I'd sooner walk into the Blue Silk Sea than hurt him. Erlend would crush and devour nation after nation until the world was ruined at its feet. It wouldn't leave us alone and alive until we bowed to it. Why should we let it live, spreading its damage across the world? "I can tie them up or something."

He took my face in his hands. "They're kidnapping kids, Sal, and Triad knows what they're doing with them. I got a feeling it's worse than what Grell did to us."

Rath was too kind, too clever, and should never have been stuck with me as a found sibling.

"All right." I patted his hand—he smelled of rain and mold and day-old tea—and nodded. "You get the kids. Adella and I'll get the guards. I'll whistle when I'm ready for you to go."

He snatched my hand and pulled me close. "I am furious at you, but stop staring at me like I stabbed you. We'll always be family."

Adella pinched her nose and turned away, a shiver running down her back.

"I'm sorry." I squeezed his hand. "I am, and I'm ready to help you now."

Family for life.

## CHAPTER
# TWENTY-FIVE

I slunk into the woods, hiding my smile behind my mask. The two awake and gambling weren't paying attention to their partners. I crept my way into the bushes behind the sleeper closest to the kids. He snored and shifted. I pulled out a knife.

Killing folks quiet was harder than picking their pocket. You had to get it right the first time, and there was no running away to try again here. I'd one chance.

I covered his mouth with one hand, slid my knife through the side of his neck—one smooth motion like Amethyst had taught me—with the other, and waited. He gasped and bit, but blood pumped through the gap between blade and skin. He wasn't awake when he died, and it came quick. I pulled my blade out after to keep from making a mess. In the night, against the dark greens of his clothes, the blood looked more shadow than stain. I covered his throat with his collar.

The second one died the same—one gasp, one hand to his

sword, and a slouching death rattle bubbling through the holes of his neck. There were no funeral rites.

The Lady could have my life and soul if she thought they were worthy of them, but nothing struck me down.

I looked up. Across the way, Adella was poised to shoot and waiting for my signal. I let out the low birdcall I'd been whistling at Rath since I was ten. A branch cracked behind me.

Shit.

I spun. A spear clipped the bottom of my face, clacking against my mask.

"No fussing, Lady Opal." The guard pushed the spear into my throat until I couldn't speak for fear of slitting it. "Lady de Arian's been waiting for you, and we've got others collecting your associates. Move and they die."

The female spy wasn't a servant. It was Lena.

They dragged the three of us to a barn. The guard at my back tied my hands—no locks—and pulled every bit of help from my body. I'd no weapons, no lock picks, and no jewelry left. Just clothes.

This was what I got for not scouting out Rath's plan.

My guard knocked on the door. "Lady de Arian? We have Opal, the boy, and another girl."

Lena had betrayed Elise, she'd betrayed me, she'd betrayed Igna. We'd had her in every meeting, every talk, and she was working for Weylin the whole damned time?

"Good." The door muffled her voice, but it was soft and calm, more like "Bring them in."

The guard opened the door, let my guard go first, and then pulled me into the room, forcing me to my knees soon as I passed the threshold. I didn't bow my head.

I was too angry to move. She'd been talking aid and help and saving people's lives, and here she was. She wasn't interested in saving everyone, just saving her own lands and self.

I should've known.

"Lady Opal," she said—I was but I didn't like the way she said it, like she'd say it no matter what—and smiled. "What a pleasure it is to see you."

"Honorable Opal." See how she liked being countered. "I've had worse welcomes."

She only just held back her sneer. "A pity you insist."

"I insist," I said. "And I don't care about your opinions on it."

Lena de Arian had outfitted the barn like a study—a large, warm rug of deep-brown fur spread out over the center of the boards, a kneeling desk held her papers and ink pot, and she sat behind it like she held nighttime meetings in barns every day. She even had a servant at her side pouring tea.

Maud.

A final, little twist of the knife. I'd have rather been stabbed in the back for real. Least then I'd have a knife.

"Nice to see you again, Maud." I ground my teeth together. Prisoner or participant?

Lena laughed and covered her mouth with one hand. No rings. No jewelry at all. The only bit of sparkle was the gold and emerald sigil pinned over her heart.

"I can only imagine." She brushed a strand of stray hair from her face, patting it back down onto the back-combed bun at her crown, and picked up a small book from her desk. "Now, your friend has been circling around my rangers for a while. Thank you, of course, for taking care of those two others. They were," she said and paused, sipping her tea and weighing her options. "Disappointing. They were not worth their severance pay, you understand."

I didn't. She spoke of folks in terms of pay—worth—and must've thought of them as little more than lines in an accounting book. It was so easy to kill people when they were only numbers. I would know.

I shuddered, and the terrible missing pieces fell into place.

"You're Riparian." I twisted my hands in the shackles, disgust prickling up my arms. I'd touched her. Talked to her. Let her comfort me and comforted her in return. I'd felt sorry for her, coming from a country where folks discounted her for simply being her.

And she'd had a hand in my family's murder. In Nacea's slaughter.

She smiled wider. "Yes. Gaspar del Weylin gifted me that name when he named me the inheritor of my father's estates and welcomed me into his court—the first Erlend woman to inherit. As though I would give up all of my hard work for a nation determined to handout success for free the moment people call foul."

I lurched forward, too angry to think, and my guard jerked me back. Their hand closed around the back of my neck, and their fingers curled into my throat. A sharp, choking pain kept me quiet.

She was angry Erlend had made her run an obstacle course to succeed and couldn't even see that some folks didn't even have the option of the course.

"That's nonsense." Adella huffed and yanked away from her guard. "Not everyone's got the same chances as you."

Even with her outfitted barn, Riparian's pale skin was red in the cold night air, but it did nothing to hide the furious flush that rose in her round cheeks. Maud, the same as ever except for her green and gold uniform and bowed head, backed away.

"Oh yes, such sage words from a failed member of the Carnival of Cheats," Riparian said, taking a slow breath. "Save her for testing. Perhaps she'll finally be useful."

A guard yanked a bag over Adella's head. She flailed and panicked, and they pulled the drawstring tight around her neck. She stopped, and Dimas entered through the back door of the barn. He was dressed like Maud, but the silver cuff that used to adorn his ear was gone. His hand was wrapped in bandages.

Rath and I tried to move to Adella, but my guard gripped my neck tighter, cutting off all my air, and Rath's slammed him into the dirt.

"Put her in the third trunk," Dimas muttered. "I'll test her after this."

Rising to her feet in one smooth motion, Lena glided—there was no other word for how she moved, so graceful and silent in the quiet night—to us. She was wearing Erlend colors now, pale brown wool so bleached it was almost white, and her face was paler, patted with white cosmetic powder and glowing in the light. She looked as unassuming as ever.

Calculated meekness. Strong enough to be an asset to Our Queen and weak enough to never be suspected of betraying her.

Did Our Queen even know now what Riparian had done?

"Now, who are you?" She peered at Rath. "I know you're looking for one of the children, but they're quite occupied. They're much more useful this way."

He spat in her face.

Riparian didn't even blink. Maud rushed forward, pulled a handkerchief from her pocket, and wiped the glob of spit from Riparian's cheek. She didn't move while Maud worked, only stared down at Rath. Her gaze moved from his eyes to his hands to his ear.

"Useless," Riparian said, "but at least I won't need to record your name."

She pulled a knife from beneath her coat. I fell forward, legs kicking back, and my guard let me go. I crawled to Rath. The knife slipped between his ribs, and he let out a soft gasp. A boot slammed into my spine. My face hit the dirt.

A gurgling cough hit my ears. Blood splattered across the floor before me and dripped into my hair. Rath fell to his knees.

He collapsed, mouth moving and eyes focused on me. I crawled to him. Tried to reach him. My guard pulled me back.

This wasn't real.

This was another nightmare.

"Cam," Rath said, blood dripping from his lips. His eyes lost their focus, staring unseeing into mine.

The world broke. Riparian's mouth moved. I heard nothing. The guards holding me down yanked me up, but it didn't hurt. Nothing could hurt ever again.

Why would it?

Rath was dead.

A guard kicked me over. A knife pricked my throat.

"No, no." Riparian's words barely made it through to me.

Nothing sounded right. Nothing felt right. The dirt was too coarse. The air too thick. This wasn't real.

"No." Riparian tilted her head to the side and held out a hand to Maud. "I want Maud to do it." She leaned in close to me, gaze searching, and smiled. "Your queen Marianna didn't send you at all, did she?"

I laughed, dirt coating my lips. "I wasn't here for Igna."

"Maud, how would you like to do this?"

"Yes, Maud." I cackled, mind too full to even look at her. "How would you like to kill me?"

"I really am not good with blood, my lady." Maud's soft voice was almost comforting. Familiar. And all familiar things were lost to me in the end. "Would drowning be all right?"

I laughed and laughed and couldn't stop laughing even when they dragged me to a bridge and Maud filled my pockets with stones while muttering to Riparian, "She can't swim. Southerners, you know?"

Lady, is this what I deserved?

Maybe I should've died. Rocks clacked into my pockets. My ribs ached with the weight of them, one after another dragging me down. I slouched, tried to act heavier than I was, and they shoved me against a railing—a bridge, we had to be on a bridge. Water rippled beneath us, gurgling. Choking.

Like Rath.

They removed my shackles but not the knife at my throat, and Maud tied a rope around my wrists in a tight, complicated little knot.

Behind me, one of the guards said, "Grab his feet."

The bridge rattled. Weight struck the boards. Rath.

"One."

Air blew past me, thick with blood and sweat.

"Two."

I gagged.

"Three."

Rath hit the water with a spine-shattering crack.

The same river. At least we'd have that.

Maud stepped in front of me. Her lips were drawn tight and half-circles of dark, deep purple marred the skin beneath her eyes. She touched my bound hands.

"Get it over with." I let my head loll forward and stared at her calloused fingers checking the knot.

A quick release knot.

"Please," Maud said finally, no trace of a hitch or hesitation in her voice, "consider this my official resignation."

And pushed me off the bridge.

I hit the water feetfirst. My lungs stopped working. The cold devoured me, going bone deep before I could move. My vision blurred and blackened, and I twisted till my arms were free of my coat and the rocks weighing me down. Stabbing, burning pins and needles pricked at every bit of me, and I kicked forward. The knots binding my hands together fell away easy. I slammed into a rock.

Stay under. Stay under. I had to stay under. They had to think me dead. But Rath was in here, weighed down and sinking, and he'd no business staying here. I reached out a hand, brushed cloth.

The rocks in my dress pockets weighed me down, dragging me deeper and deeper toward the riverbed, ramming me into fallen logs and jagged rocks.

My chest burned. This had to be long enough. I was drifting, dragging through rotten branches and fish bones, my nails scraping over rocks. I rolled and tore at the handful of dress tangled in my arm. The rocks tumbled through the hole.

And the only thought rising up within me was that Maud knew damn well I could swim.

I burst to the surface. The cold air burned, stinging through my nose and mouth. I coughed and paddled toward the shore, crumbling at the base of a rocky ledge.

I glanced back, vision blurred and speckled with black, and the bridge was well out of sight beyond the bend.

I pressed my back to the stone and screamed into my shirt, muffling the sound. Washing it away. I looked for any sign of Rath, but the dark was thick. I wanted Rath. I wanted to carry him home one last time, but now I was stuck, cold and dying, in the lands of the woman who'd killed my family.

I sat at the water's edge, teeth chattering, and watched the current sweep Rath farther and farther from me, into the depths where I couldn't follow.

I woke to pain. I was alone. The numb tingling of sleeping limbs covered me. I opened my eyes slowly. Moonlight filtered through the trees. Not bright enough to help me see.

I sat up. Nothing snapped. No broken bones.

There was nothing left for Erlend to take from me—family, home, innocence, friends.

They were thieves.

And I was the shadow they'd made, ripped from my life and left to wander, trying to piece together the fragments of the life Erlend had left me. I buried my face in my hands, too cold and empty to cry. They'd stolen *everything*.

I'd have been a farmer or weaver or anything else if they'd never gotten greedy for more land and started the civil war. I'd not have been Opal.

Rath would've been a merchant by now, traveling between here and Mizuho and charming folks left and right. He'd be alive. He'd be warm.

"Cam." The voice wasn't mine. It couldn't be because there was no world where Rath died and I'd lost him in a river, so my voice couldn't crack, and my throat couldn't hurt. I'd touched him. I'd nearly had him. "Adella. Elise. Maud."

The memory *seared*.

When did his body stop being his? To be him? How long till I wouldn't recognize him in death? Wouldn't remember the sound of his laugh or rhythm of his breathing in bed next to me? How long till thinking his name didn't hurt?

I was drowning, choking, the memories of Rath and me a deep well from which I couldn't escape.

I took the long way around, hoping Rath would be caught at the edge of the river. Alive. Dead. Just let me see him again.

And a long time later, I found the clearing where the rangers and the two children had been. I restarted the fire, stripped, and stole the clothes off the dead ranger closest to my size. I curled up next to the fire.

At noon, when I woke up, I built Rath a funeral pyre. It wasn't big, probably not hot enough either, but it was all I could do. At least I could build him a fire even if he wasn't in it.

I picked up my pack, burned the rangers' things I didn't need, and sat before the fire.

"I'll throw you a party when this is over." My nails scraped over the ring, picked at the fresh scabs along my knuckles, and I held my hand above the flames. Not close enough to burn. "I'll find Cam. I'll keep him safe, and I'll take all your kids to see the

Carnival of Cheats. They'll like it, and we'll be even. I hope your Triad's happy to see you."

They would be. Who wouldn't?

I left. I did not cry.

I had nothing left to lose.

*North Star. Riparian. Winter.*

The sun melted away the frost of a wicked Erlend winter but not the seeping chill in my creaking ribs as I started walking north.

To Riparian.

To Maud, who was not a traitor but definitely in danger.

To Adella. Tests and Erlends could only end poorly.

To Elise.

And hopefully to Cam.

With any luck, Riparian would think me truly dead, and I could move through Erlend like a ghost.

The ghost of Nacea hunting its killers. Elise would call it poetic.

But there were no pretty words or turns of phrases that could capture the raging *want* that Nacean memories awoke within me—I wanted to taste the words I didn't know, sink into the splattering sound of warm blood on frozen earth, and memorize the wide, shocked looks on their faces as they realized what they'd created.

I would be a death of their own making.

I went to Hinter first.

The journey to Hinter went faster than it should've. I slept in bushes and trees, beneath the cover of my cloak and pack in the woods off the road. There were soldiers and rangers and farmers chasing cows, and I skirted round the countryside, darting from main road to hunting trails to avoid them. The air bit deeper the farther I went and thickened into frost each morning. I drew my scarf over my face.

"Hello again," I muttered to Hinter from atop the hills just south of it.

The guards patrolling the low walls surrounding the city proper and the fortress at its heart moved slowly among the frantic bustle of the city. I edged closer after each round's schedule became clear. In the hollowed-out stump of an old, wide pine, I half slept till evening.

*North Star. Riparian. Winter.*

Their reign of fear was over.

# CHAPTER
# TWENTY-SEVEN

I climbed over the wall this time. Let them see me, let them catch me. It was dark by the time I'd enough strength to scale the wall, and it wasn't the guards I had to worry about. The wall was slick with cold, my fingers trembling and scrambling for holds against the smooth expanse. I had to make my own, nearly fell twice before reaching the top, and the close calls ripped two fingernails clean off. It should've hurt, but I didn't feel it. I didn't feel anything. Not my wounded hands or scraped up knees or the biting cold.

I'd survived one fall. What did another matter?

Shadows bounced between the hanging lamps dotting the top of the wall. I edged my way between two and sneaked into the main building through the servants' doors. They'd cheaper locks.

Elise wasn't in her room. The bed was made and her night-clothes left across her chair. Only her desk had a touch of her, the papers scattered and stacked in unsteady towers. Charcoal pens used down to the nub and bottles of ink dotted the area.

One brush pen with teeth marks in the tip balanced on the edge of an open drawer. Writing covered every part of the papers.

She was planning something.

I waited on the edge of her chair, too dusty for the bed and too tired for the floor. I'd not get back up if I sat down there.

The door rattled. I darted behind her wardrobe, praying she was alone.

"Wake me up as soon as they get here." Elise paused in the doorway of her room, face turned back to whoever was in the hallway. "Don't bother me until then."

By the look of her trembling hands and slumped shoulders, Elise would be awake until they knocked again.

Elise turned, shutting the door, and leaned back against it with her head tilted up and eyes shut. Time and frustration had taken their toll on her. Her brown skin had paled, darkening the deep shadows beneath her eyes. The whites of her eyes were a pale, pale red, and cracks split her lips, the reddish tint more cold than cosmetic. She glanced up, glasses slipping down her nose, and froze. Her wide eyes settled on me.

"It's Sal," I said. "Don't scream."

"Sal!" The grin stretched to the hollow of each cheek—the outline of her jaw was sharper, more defined, and her smile lacked its usual luster—but it was real. The tension in her shoulders softened. "What are you doing here?"

"I wanted to see you." Everything was different. I wasn't the last Nacean, I wasn't alone in my fear, and I'd only three more names on my list. I felt crowded, from the constant ringing of Isidora's words in my head to my thoughts of Elise and Maud and Dimas and Rath and Adella and the dozen others I'd learned to care about.

I had to hold on to their names, their faces. I needed to know something was the same. "And we need to talk about Erlend."

She'd a better mind for politics than me.

"My least favorite phrase." She locked the door, chin down and eyes narrowed.

I bowed. "My favorite since it means I'm talking to you more often than not."

"It take you long to think of that line?" she asked, pulling the silk scarf from her head. The new copper cuffs she'd added to the braids rattled as she looked me over, and the line between her brows gave her away. "How are you? You look..."

"That bad?" My voice cracked. I didn't want to linger on it, but I needed comfort. Rath was dead. There was nothing good left in the world. Nothing except Elise.

And she knew something was wrong. Or knew the look on my face well enough to know death and grief were clinging to me. Her arms closed around my shoulders and held me tight, folding me in the warm scent of her skin and clothes—dry ink and lemon soap—and I let her hold me up.

"What's happened?" she asked, lips moving against my ear, and the closeness of it, the intimacy, nearly made me sob.

"Too much." A whine whistled from my lips.

Sniffling, I pulled away. She let me go and arched her neck from where it had been bent to let me cry into her shoulder. She stared at me, gaze sliding down to my stolen ranger uniform.

"What's wrong? Really?"

"My friend died." I had to get to Riparian and North Star before they moved. I had to find Cam. If nothing else, Cam. "I just wanted to see you again before moving on."

"I'm so sorry." She took me in her arms, not stiffening when I didn't return the hug. I tucked my face into her shoulder, and she ran her fingers through my matted hair. "I'm glad you're here. I won't be here much longer. Weylin wants us in Lynd."

"What's going on?" I looked up and Elise stepped back, turning her face from me. "Or not?"

"How long can you stay?" she asked.

I kissed her, gently, quickly, savoring the press of her nose and scratch of her lips. She was alive and so was I, and the world couldn't change that. I wouldn't let it.

I had to live, at least for a little bit longer, and I wanted to do part of that living with her.

"Not long." I pulled back. "Why does Weylin want you?"

"To keep an eye on me, I'm sure." Her lips twisted as she said it, and her hands pushed me toward to the bed. "In what I am sure is a terrible shock to my father, Weylin does not believe I am fully dedicated to the Erlend cause, and my father, for all his faults, is loath to renounce me."

I bounced as I sat, and she collapsed next to me. Her thigh, warm and soft, pressed against mine, and I pulled her legs across my lap.

"Why's Weylin still suspicious of you? You've been nothing but loyal to your father, to Erlend, since you've been back," I asked. "I mean, you made it seem like that at least."

For someone as kind as Elise, the lying had to be eating away at her.

She gestured to the whole of herself. "My mother was Alonian by birth and Erlend by marriage before the war, and I am 'a benefit despite my unfortunate inheritance' but still unfortunate."

The worst sort of insult—the kind folks bundled up in nice words and intentions but built on the backs of rudeness, power, and misconception.

It was always the high north Erlends, the ones who made names for themselves and managed to keep them, the ones with their blond hair pulled back in tight, slick knots while they cleaned their nails on silk shirts and covered pale eyes with spectacles of colored glass. The ones who'd all sorts of ideas about what it meant to be properly male or female, able or not, of value or valueless. Never anything else.

North Star's ideal sort.

"I'm a better liar than you'd think, and he thinks I'm still hiding things." Her fingers brushed my back, gliding from shoulder blade to hip and back again. "It's because I worked so closely with the Left Hand and refuse to divulge any secrets."

I slid a hand into the open mouth of her boot and laid my hands against her warm, sock-covered calf. "I thought you were just working with them for auditions?"

She nodded. "My father thinks that too, but Lord Ruby asked me to screen the uninvited."

I stilled. "Screen the uninvited?"

"Yes." Her voice changed, the soft tone slowing. She moved her hand away from my back. "Sal—"

"No, stop."

I'd never considered the coincidence. How she was so certain it was me.

I gently pushed her legs out of my lap.

It didn't have to be me—any of the uninvited might've fit her statement if they were as hesitant as I'd been.

"You were spying on me." I rose from the bed, the awful patter of my heart getting quicker and quicker, stuttering my breaths. "You had a poster. You weren't upset at being robbed. Your guards didn't give chase. You knew me at tutoring. You asked me questions. You pursued me."

We'd been playing each other.

"Well, yes, but no, I wasn't still working for Ruby in tutoring." She shifted, bed creaking. "It was the invitations. They needed to attract specific people, so they had me and several others travel around with decoy purses, and you happened upon me—"

"And you decided I was good enough?" I asked. "That I was worthy?"

Why was it that Erlends always decided my worth in the end?

"Why does that matter?" She threw her hands up and slid off the bed. "You fit their qualifications. I didn't demand you audition. I just supplied the information."

I spun back to her. "Because I'm Opal! Because my whole life depended on how nice you thought me. Was it because we flirted? You liked the sound of my voice so much you thought I'd make a fun auditioner to have around? I didn't get to auditions—you got me there!"

The muscles of her neck tensed. Her nostrils flared. "I gave those flyers to everyone the Left Hand instructed me to: people of skill and some sense of good moral judgment. You met their requirements. And it's not like the whole thing isn't rigged! Half of them were purposefully lured there to be watched or killed. Be glad I thought you should be Opal."

"And none of that seemed important enough to tell me?" I asked. "Or were you just thinking you'd found a rogue who fit your wants and all was working out, so might as well see it through?"

"Why would I invite someone I liked to a competition where the majority of people died?" She drew her hands together in front of her, palms pressed flat and fingers splayed, and she took a deep breath. "I didn't see the issue. I wasn't lying."

"Not sharing the whole truth's a different kind of lie." I tapped one of the books on her desk. "The sort you Erlend historians love to tell."

"Sallot." Elise dropped her hands, fingers curled into fists. "I know you are upset, but this is unfair. My giving you that purse and my affection for you are two different creatures."

A chill crept up my arms. I wrapped them around myself.

"I know, but everyone lies to me. All the time, and I hate it." Elise. Our Queen. Maud. Emerald. Amethyst. Nicolas. All of them had known Erlend had been responsible for Nacea's slaughter. Lena de Arian and Dimas had betrayed me. "Everyone's got their reasons too, but all it means is I'm not in control of my life."

She'd taken away the choice. My auditioning wasn't my own now, it was hers and Ruby's and Our Queen's. It was orchestrated. Opal was a tool, but they'd maneuvered me into being Opal with handmade circumstances.

"Forget it." I held out my hands and shook my head. "We can deal with it later. I need to know what you've found out about the rangers and those ears. Anything?"

She stared at me for a moment before letting the subject change.

"I would think it a hoax if I'd not seen an ear." She shuddered. "They're from the missing children, but there's always

Igna signifiers nearby. It's so clearly planted that I don't know what to do. Why we'd cut off ears just for that?"

"It's probably extra." They were using the ears for something else, they had to be, and they had to have been doing it for a while if Dimas was involved. But what for? Magic was dead unless they were trying to bring it back, and if they were, how long had they been trying? Let it be new, let there not be a decade of missing kids we hadn't found.

"You've gotten no word from anyone?" I asked.

"I did speak with Lena about some things a while ago." Elise sighed, shoulders slumping. "I am concerned about the others in Hinter who don't follow Erlend tradition, the ones like me who are attracted to men and women. It's not smiled upon, and I don't want them to be stuck in a place that denies them like I was before I went to Igna. It's Erlend that's wrong, but I say that, they'll kill me and then there will be no one here."

I winced. Good intentions, bad execution.

Always so focused on man and woman, man or woman.

"I'm not a man or a woman," I said slowly. "My gender doesn't change from day to day. I am fluid. You do not get to define me by your attractions. I understand what you meant and I can't define you, but if you're attracted to me, I'm uncomfortable with that."

She raised a hand to her mouth. "I'm sorry. That's not what I—"

"I know," I said quickly. "Still hurts. Never mind that for now. Tell me more about Lena."

"Lena?" Her voice went up. "What do you want with Lena?"

How did I tell her Lena was wicked and two of her loved ones were on my list?

"She betrayed us." My chest ached with each word, the sounds stone heavy in my mouth. "She was one of the nobles working with your father. She helped destroy Nacea. She's working for Gaspar del Weylin. She always has been."

"No!" Elise laughed, the crackling, snotty sound of disbelief. "That can't be true."

I stilled, a little ember of rage flaring in my chest. "She's the Riparian on my list of Erlend nobles, and she's a monster."

"Lena de Arian has done more for the people of Erlend and Igna alike than most nobles accomplish in their entire life." Elise's face paled. "You're wrong."

"Really?" I raked my hands over my face, too angry, too tired, too *everything*, to deal with this. "You just admitted to lying to me, but I'm the one in the wrong now?"

"I apologize and accept my role in that, but this has nothing to do with auditions." Elise held one hand up as though to wave me away. "She's the reason I can inherit my father's title. I'm a historian because of her. She taught me to read and to write. She helped me find the words to explain myself. To know who I was when everything I learned as a child in Erlend told me I was wrong for being attracted to more than just men. She held my hand at my mother's funeral, and when I went to live with Isidora and Nicolas, she visited whenever she could. She was like a mother to me, and I know her as if she were mine. She's not your Riparian."

"She directed the shadows through Nacea so that they'd kill Naceans—my family—instead of Erlend soldiers." I wanted to be wrong. I didn't want to steal two people from Elise or ruin her childhood hero as Our Queen had been ruined for me. There were no truly good people in this world. There were only people. "She's Riparian."

"No. She's not a monster. Not like my father." Elise's fingers curled into fists. "She's not, and she has done too much for Erlend women for you to slander her."

I spun the ring on my finger, teeth aching from the strength it took not to shout. I took a breath. "She's done a lot for Erlend women? What about the rest of us? How many Alonian women has she helped? How many from Mizuho? Berengard? Nacea? What about me? How worthy am I to her? Or would she only try to help me when I'm following all the made-up rules of what she considers womanly? She admitted her involvement to me. She only helps Erlend women because she's as bad as all those lords throwing people to the shadows to save their own skins. She's just saving all the folks exactly like her too. The ones she thinks are worthy. You don't get to decide what people are worthy, but she thinks she does. She said that to me, near exactly those words."

"Were you armed?" Elise rolled her lips together. "I've been at the deadly end of your knives, and people will say and do many things not to get stabbed."

A cold, sharp sting burned through my chest.

"She murdered my friend," I said. "I watched her stab him, and then I had listen to him die, drowning in his own blood."

She froze. Closed her eyes. A puddle of tears gathered along the rims of her eyes. "Now you're lying."

I gasped and sniffed. "Why would I lie about him being dead?"

"Lena has never used a knife." Elise swallowed, raised her chin, and twisted her face into the stubborn, righteous look of

Erlend. "I might have believed her having someone else do it, but you don't know her at all. Obviously."

"Obviously."

I knew her soul was redder than mine. She'd a world of ghosts within her, every Nacean she'd killed to save Erlend was another life added to her debt. She was worse than me, but I was the enemy here.

I could hold on to nothing. Nothing was in my control. Riparian was killing me slowly from days away.

"I don't know you," I said. "And I don't want to right now."

She was Erlend nobility through and through, and I was a fool.

"You don't know everything. People have dozens of reasons to do what they do, and Lena has supported me and her people at every turn. She sacrificed part of her inheritance so I could rebuild Hinter's schools." Elise swallowed, face hard. Her jaw tightened. "So you will take my father and my idol from me and still expect compassion?"

The words left Elise like water, dripping between us and echoing in the silence. I wanted to listen to her, soak up her every word and let them quench the burning, terrible anger in my chest, but she was wrong. Erlend's legacy was a river of violence.

And for all her good work, she was still drowning in it.

But I was cruel too.

For all our differences, the world and I shared that.

"She is why I am who I am." Elise crossed her arms over her chest. She kept her voice even, but her fingers shook against her arms. "She supported me when not even my father would."

The last bit of care I had snapped, sliding the world into place.

So this was how it would be.

"She's a traitor," I said slowly. "She killed my friend, and when she throws you aside to save her own life, I hope you've got enough sense to trust me and run."

"I'm sorry your friend is dead, but I do not believe she killed him." She rolled her shoulders back. They shook. "And I don't appreciate you lying about that to try and make me believe you about Lena's intentions."

"I'm disappointed in you." I pulled my mask back on. I couldn't let her see me crying. "We only knew each other for half a year, and most of that was lies or cons. Lena de Arian might've helped you, but she ruined Nacea. She killed hundreds of thousands because she thought they weren't worth saving. She forced the only other Nacean I've ever met to kill to save his family. She's got Maud serving her and might kill Maud at any moment. She killed the only person I ever had who was my own, the only living person I called family." I lifted my mask and wiped my face, crying so hard I couldn't stop talking for fear of drowning in my own grief. "She killed Rath da Oretta, she killed my family, she killed Nacea, and there's no coming back from that."

"Sal." Elise reached for me and winced when I pulled away. "You're wrong about her. You have to be."

"I don't care." I shrugged. "If you don't trust me, you don't trust me. So I don't trust you."

Face to the stars and back to Elise, I leapt from her window to the ledge beneath it. I couldn't go back, and she couldn't chase. Couldn't offer excuse after excuse. I should've known.

No more trust.

No more mercy.

Only a prayer to my triad—North Star, Winter, Riparian—and under the pale glow of the moon, running north toward death, alone like always, I broke as ice breaks.

## CHAPTER
# TWENTY-EIGHT

Lena de Arian was going to Lynd.

At least some good had come out of that.

But I'd never cried while running before. It burned deep in my chest and up through the backs of my eyes. Snot dripped into my open mouth, bitter and slick, and I stumbled to a stop a good ways out of Hinter. Elise had been concerned for the missing children. Would she have been less worried if Lena were stealing them?

This was where hope and mercy got me.

Sobbing in the middle of a dark forest, spit all down my shirt and nose stuffed, the dry scents of ink and paper clinging to my hands, the barely-there trails of the rangers ahead of me vanished with each breeze. A cacophony of whippoorwills and mocking-birds drowned out my crying.

"Where's the line?" I asked the stars, my head tilted up to the pine needles casting the forest floor in darkness. Only one glittering light broke through. "Before me or behind me?"

North Star.

I ran north. I stayed as close to the roads as I could, keeping an eye out for Riparian's carriage or guards. I found them on the third night. The guards were spread out, attentive and well trained, and the carriage had glass in the little viewing window. A wagon rolled behind it, stacked half-full with trunks and boxes. Dimas sat atop one, head in his hands. Maud sat next to him.

Of all the things I couldn't think about, her going with Riparian wasn't one of them. It haunted me. I dreamed about it. Why had Maud left with Riparian in the first place?

I followed their procession, watching from afar anytime I could, and kept my eyes on Maud. She did servant things, nothing else. Riparian's interest in her had waned.

I squashed the flare of panic in my chest.

Maud hadn't been found out. She'd have been dead if Riparian knew she'd not killed me and not even tried.

Two nights later, after tracking the guards and late-night movements of their little camps, I waited in the pitch dark of the trees for Maud to take her nightly walk to clear her head. Dimas tried to join her, coming into the conversation with the slump of someone who knew they'd been defeated ages before. Maud laughed and shook her head. He fidgeted.

"You're in danger." He wasn't his normal self—his hair was loose and tangled, his clothes were more dust than wool, and the ink stains on his fingertips had been there for days, building up one after the other. "Do you know how many times I've had to convince her you're serious?"

"Are you threatening me?" Maud rounded on him and slapped his shoulder with her braid.

He backtracked. His face fell. "No! I'm trying to keep you out of danger. This is a disaster."

"I don't want you to do anything for me, Dimas," she said, low and furious, "except leave me alone."

"Please be careful." He slunk away from her.

Finally.

I crept forward to the path I knew Maud would take and crouched in the underbrush. The guards gave her privacy because she spent the first five minutes praying, and personal prayers weren't the place for an audience. They walked away after the first line.

I slid up behind her and clasped a hand over her mouth. "It's me, it's me. It's Opal. It's Sal."

Her sobbing gasp escaped through the cracks of my fingers.

"Sal." She cried into my shoulder, and it killed me—the sound, the shudders, the damp. "I thought I'd killed you. I'm so sorry. I'm sorry."

Maud muttered apologies she didn't owe into my shoulder, and I leaned my cheek against her scalp. The scratch of her hair and digging of her nails sharpened the world. I had no bad memories of her. No last-time hug. No last look before death. Only joy.

"I figured out you weren't serious when you told her I couldn't swim." I squeezed her tight. "Was real confused for a while there."

"It was sudden." She lifted her head and pulled back. "Oh, you're filthy."

"My servant resigned." I let her go and placed my hands on her shoulders. "Maud, what's going on?"

"I knew something was wrong with Lena, and then she

focused on Dimas and me. I liked it at first. It was sort of like having a mother again." Maud shrugged, one shoulder rising, and wiped her face. "But then it was odd. Dimas has always been very particular about what jobs he takes, and this wasn't like him at all. I know him, knew him, better than most. We talked of growing up alone so often, and then suddenly he didn't want to talk about his family ever again."

"He said Erlend had his mother? And sister?"

How much was true and how much was Dimas's wishful thinking overworking so he could play assassin?

Maud nodded. "He told me that too, after he came back. Lena was furious when she found he hadn't killed Our Queen or anyone. If they were alive, I would think they'd be dead now. You've seen what she's capable of."

"I do." I was certain she'd say she didn't need me, didn't need anything from me, but I asked anyway. Maybe I'd get her another hairpin. "You need anything? Is there anything else going on?"

"There is more, but—" She froze. "It might be best if you see it for yourself because I can't explain it. You won't believe me."

I glanced around. Her praying time was about up. "Will it kill me?"

"No, Triad no, I'm not killing you ever again." She straightened my collar and brushed off my shirt, nervous hands too shaky to hold still. "Watch Dimas tonight."

"All right." I nodded and hugged her one last time. "You should go. Stay safe."

I couldn't lose Maud too.

She smiled and kissed my cheek. "Thank you for coming after me."

"Always." I let her go. "We're friends. I've not got enough of them to let one run off to Lynd."

She laughed softly and started stepping back toward camp. "Dimas, tonight, north side of camp. I'll be there. Don't be scared."

And Maud, for the first time I'd ever seen, vanished like a Left Hand into the night.

Full of surprises.

Six days till Lynd.

Six days to figure out how North Star, Riparian, and Winter would die.

# CHAPTER
# TWENTY-NINE

Once Maud left, I snuck to the far side of the camp, as north as north could get, and climbed into the high branches of an old pine drooping beneath the weight of its needles. The uneasy panic settled as I looked down on the world, everything coming into focus. The wagon half-full with trunks was set up under a series of trees, the five trunks locked and punched with holes, and I kept the bile from crawling up my throat by gnawing on too-hard tack. Something was alive in there. Adella?

I'd not seen her at all. Lady, don't let her be dead. Not another death on my soul.

Dimas showed up a long time later, a ring of keys on his wrist. His bandaged hand was strapped to his chest, and the only thing he truly carried was a small pot. Maud, arms full of bandages, came a while later. She didn't look at him, didn't acknowledge him.

But he didn't say anything when she slipped hunks of bread through the holes in the trunks or when she hid the evidence right before Riparian walked into the little moonlit clearing. She set her lantern atop a blue trunk.

I wasn't close enough to hear what they were saying. Riparian instructed Dimas to do something, he bowed, and Maud left only to return shortly with a canteen and quilt. Dimas unlocked an old, brown trunk, and Adella came flying out of it headfirst. Her legs and arms were bound and she was gagged, but she launched herself into Dimas. They collapsed to the ground, and a guard came running forward. Adella elbowed Dimas in the face. The guard kicked her off him.

A warm hate boiled in me, and I leaned closer. Tried to catch a bit of the conversation.

"...can't hurt her," Riparian said, staring down the guard. "There are very few touched just enough to trigger the response."

I shuddered. I had to save Cam.

There was no good outcome with sentences like that.

The guard sat Adella on the trunk and fastened her to the trunk lid. She growled at her.

The snap of her teeth behind the gag echoed louder than anything, and Dimas opened the little bottle. Maud lowered her head.

Dimas dipped a finger into the bottle, skin coming away dark, dark blue. He painted a line down the shell of Adella's ear, and I shuddered, knowing what was coming without being able to see the details. His runes didn't look the same, but I could read the short word scrawled across her ear.

*Eat.*

A prickling, uneasy itch spilled down my arms and over my legs, begging me to run, and I tightened my grip on the tree.

Something twisted in my chest, a panicked ache. Bark crumbled from the branch.

And Adella began to scream.

"The ears are weak, all flesh and no bone, so it's the best place to test if someone can use magic," Dimas said, hands stained red and black. "If the ink remains and their ears are whole, they can't use magic. If the ink eats the flesh like an infection, they can. It means there is power in their bodies they can still harness."

Adella howled, back arching, and Dimas unhooked her chains from the trunk. She writhed on the ground, legs tangling in her binds and hands clawing at her neck, as close as they could get to her ear. The dark ink vanished. The guard hauled her to her feet.

Lantern light streamed through the new holes in her ear.

"Good," Riparian said, voice barely carrying over my frantic breathing. "She'll do perfectly."

No part of me moved.

A trick of the light. Lady, let it be a trick of the light.

An alchemical agent. An acid, a poison, anything but magic.

The runes he'd drawn had burned away, leaving the scent of singed hair drifting on the breeze. I gagged and covered my nose. Riparian left, unaffected.

Maud vomited in a bush.

And the runes, Lady, the runes, writhed in Dimas's hand, dark specks tearing in and out of his uninjured hand, blood dripping down his fingers and the wounds burning shut before they could bleed too much. He helped Adella back onto the trunk and pulled the bandages from where Maud had dropped them. Adella flinched away from him.

Maud raced over, grabbed the strips of cloth, and began doing up Adella's ear. Dimas fell back.

I stayed in the tree all night, awake and watching, spinning the ring along my finger until my nail chipped and the ring was much too warm, because if magic was real again and Erlend was using it, had been using it, the shadows were within their grasp.

In the morning, Riparian's group moved out and sunlight scoured all the shadows from the woods. I watched Maud pass under me, in the wagon with the trunks, and picked a scab from my arm till it bled.

"Don't let Riparian find her out," I whispered. "Don't let Dimas give her up. Don't let Adella and the others get sent to wherever they're sending them. Don't let me be too late for Cam."

I dropped from the tree and followed after them, steps sure and quick. Their path was perfectly clear.

"And don't let anyone kill Riparian before I get to her."

Runes or not, shadows or not, war or not, she was mine and mine alone, and I'd make her pay.

I never strayed far from camp. The dark that crept around it lingered at my back, keeping my heart pounding in my chest every moment of every day. The whisper of shadows was never far—wind rustling the leaves of the forest floor, the stench of mold and rot beneath a fallen tree. It was like I was running again.

Like they were grasping at my back again.

So I watched Maud and Dimas. They'd reversed roles. Maud, chin held high and wearing the sneer she'd stolen from Riparian, dismissed him at every turn and followed at Riparian's heels. On the third night of being ignored, Dimas turned his attention to Adella and whispered through the air holes of her trunk. She didn't fight when he opened the top, but she was ready to run, from the press of her bound hands on the trunk edge to her sideways glances. Dimas only unwound and redid the bandages covering her ear. There was no blood.

There was no flesh at all where the runes had eaten away her skin.

Not runes. A single Nacean word. A command.

*Eat.*

I didn't know how runes were supposed to work, but watching Dimas was as enlightening as it was sickening.

Riparian had called Adella "useful medium." He'd agreed. I'd gagged.

"Why bother making her feel better?" Maud's voice carried in the quiet dark, and the guards might've mistaken the disdain as directed at Adella.

Dimas didn't and flinched. "It's not a pleasant feeling."

"Like fire ants," Adella muttered. She kept speaking, but I couldn't hear.

I crept closer. The guards were at my back, but it was Dimas who worried me. Maud bent over the trunk, using the still-open lid for cover, and slipped a little bundle of food into Adella's hands. Dimas pulled back. I settled beneath a tangle of overgrown bushes and shook my head.

Maud was trusting Dimas to not turn her in.

"Why are you here?" he asked softly. "You're too kind for Lady de Arian."

Maud rounded on him, braid slapping her back as she spun, and raised her chin. "Speak to me again and learn how kind I can be."

Lady help me. She was going to get herself killed.

"If you keep saying things like that, she'll know and she'll kill you." He scratched at the ink staining his skin. "This is dangerous, Maud, and I know—"

"You don't know anything about me." She stepped toward him, away from Adella's trunk.

He stepped back. "I know everything about you."

I rose from the underbrush behind Dimas. Maud raised her hand.

There was no part of this world hurting Maud so long as I still breathed. Not when she stared into the dark and knew she was staring at me.

She trusted me to be here, and I always would be for her.

"You know all the silly things about me. You know where I was born, how old I am, how long I lived in that orphanage, how much I hated it. All the worries and facts and fears I shared with you while you were lying don't mean you know me."

"We were both alone." He stumbled back, freezing only a whisper from me. "If Erlend had your siblings, if Erlend would kill them if you didn't help, what would you do? You would do what I'm doing, but this"—he gestured at the clearing around them—"is not you."

"No," she said. "This is me. This has always been me because no matter who you serve now, if Erlend gets what they want, we'll all be dead soon enough."

Dimas's mouth opened in a little gasp. She'd given herself away.

"But Lady de Arian likes me." Maud lifted her face to him, teeth clenched, hands fists. Proper, thumb-out fists. "My siblings are safe. I am safe. You're the only one with blood on your hands."

Dimas fell against the tree at his back and buried his face in his hands. "It's either my family's blood or theirs."

"As I said." Maud rolled her shoulders back and sniffed. "We don't know each other. I hope your mother and sister are alive, and I hope you know what you're doing, but don't speak to me again unless Lady de Arian requires it."

Dimas didn't. We traveled two more days, and I stayed as close to Maud as I could, sleeping a handful of hours in the highest branches of thick evergreens to hide me. There was only one way into Lynd proper, and I'd need my strength to do it.

Needle-thin paths twisted up the hills and mountains of northern Erlend and merged into one great road leading to the main gate of North Star's capital, Lynd. It was his last great land, the bastion of all of Erlend's old ideas, and it had enough farms and workers to outlast any number of sieges. Riparian—Lady de Arian—was in charge of keeping the records straight and the city stocked, counting down everything to the last single grain. Guard towers lined the hilltops, and mountain posts could probably see folks as far as a half day off. I stayed in the trees.

North Star's lands were the farthest north, stopping at the peaks of the mountains looming over Lynd, and they were impassable. The only way into Lynd was the front gate.

No wonder Our Queen had wanted a thief as her Opal.

Course, I'd no papers and an Alonian accent, so my stealing myself inside was the only way in, and given how handsy the guards were being with everything, it'd be tricky.

Riparian's carriage lined up with all the other folks traveling and she sent Maud out to talk to some guard. Maud looked around, nose crinkled, and I knew she was looking for me because I had caused that same tired look on her face plenty of times before.

Erlend wasn't even good enough to steal that from me.

Maud and Dimas ended up in the cart carrying the trunks. Riparian's carriage was directed around to the front of the line, ahead of the travelers and farmers and traders vying for time inside the city. The cart of trunks filled with kids and one bandaged cheater had to wait in line with only three guards, Dimas, and Maud to watch over it. The guards at the gate checked each part of each wagon, opened every bag and trunk, and flipped through the citizenry papers of each person. Maud had been gifted a set by Riparian. She'd cried.

I'd not liked watching it, but Riparian had seemed convinced Maud was who she said she was: a servant loyal to her.

But I'd no papers and no friends capable of helping me pass through. If I'd been with Rath—my chest ached at the thought, a tight memory of his arms around my shoulders, his cheek against mine, his salted eyes glittering so brightly in the evening light it brought tears to my eyes—he'd have caused a distraction while I snuck in, but Rath would never grace this earth again. He was gone, and I was alone. Only I could get to Cam.

Grief was a fickle thing. It twisted in my stomach and rose in my throat, a burning pain so sharp, blinking didn't stop the tears, and I pressed my palms into my eyes to keep from sobbing. It was quick and hot. An uncomfortable prickling like roaches scurrying across your skin. There and gone.

No time to think, only enough time to react.

I hated it.

"Cam." I swallowed the snot gathering in the back of my throat and rubbed my nose. "He'd want to save Cam." Rath would want to save everybody. "So I'm saving Cam."

I crept as close as I dared to the road. Maud was scanning for my face among the small crowd and frowning each time she looked up without seeing me. A woman leading a herd of goats and children was resting by the side of the road, papers in hand, and I dropped a twig on the nearest goat. It bleated and kicked, leaping over its leash mate. Maud whipped her head round at the sound. She'd know.

Maud trusted me. She'd trust me to be here, and goats bleating was close as I could get to talking to her. She'd snuck out of an orphanage in a laundry cart, and there weren't any of them here, but there were plenty of carts and the road was well laid with stones. I could take a wagon in, reverse the order. Just had to find one tall enough.

I moved up and down the queue, staying out of sight, and looking beneath the wagons and carriages. Maud's wagon and one filled with straw were perfect. I climbed up an oak to study the guards at the gate. None looked under the wagons.

Good. Just needed a distraction.

I had no idea how to say that to Maud in goat.

No Rath to do it for me either. I squeezed the ring on my finger. It didn't spin so much anymore as squeal against my knuckle, but it helped. Was something to do.

Least he'd think my way in hilariously rash. But the guards checked everywhere except beneath the wagons. No one was rash enough to hide under there.

This would be fun.

Protective plants lined the wall, green veins breaking through the thorny underbrush and winding up the wall until they thinned into curling points that fell away from the wood. Wagon wheels and horse hooves clattered over the stone road, grinding fallen leaves into a foggy dust that swirled around the waiting people's feet. I slipped down my tree and shimmied into a bush near a slight bend in the path near where Riparian's wagon would pass. Thistles scraped through my shirt.

Fun.

When the wagon stopped, I rolled beneath it and hooked my arms and knees over the axles. They were fixed to the wagon, the wheels turning round them, and the rolled-up canvas strapped to each side—stored there until they needed it on a rainy day—hid me from view. So long as I shifted with each lurch and didn't slump, I'd be hidden. I collected splinters with each stutter-roll forward though.

But the gate came and went, the guards never looking beneath, and I was in Lynd.

I owed this world a debt of blood, and I'd pay it in any way it saw fit.

The stomach-clenched pain of balancing now would be nothing compared to killing North Star.

Once we were on a well-worn street with more holes and bumps, I rapped on the bottom of the wagon in the same little tune Maud and I had used during auditions. She tapped back with her foot.

"What are you doing?" Dimas asked, voice softer than I'd ever heard it.

Maud huffed and probably gave him that annoyed sneer I knew so well. "Keeping myself occupied?"

"Just be careful," he muttered. He shifted, the boards creaking above me. "We're going to the labs. You shouldn't come with us."

"I take orders from Lady de Arian, not you." Maud's voice rose to a sharp, bitter pitch. "But please continue to offer an opinion I didn't ask for."

I tucked my face into my shoulder and laughed.

"I don't know what that woman has offered you, but if it's not your family, then there is nothing worth what you are doing." Dimas sighed loudly. Sadly. "You could leave. At the very least, there will be blood."

Maud was squeamish but determined, and she knew her limits. If I knew her well as I thought I did, she'd not leave something half done.

"Or I could stay in this wagon until we pass through the royal gate and arrive at the place Lady de Arian specifically told me to go to," Maud said loudly, and I withheld my shout of thanks. "Deal with your own mistakes, Dimas, and leave me to deal with mine. If I ever make any."

All thorns today, then.

We rounded a bend and the wagon rocked as if someone had thrown their body against the side.

"His estate's carved out of the mountain?" Maud's shock escaped as a whistle. "How?"

A pair of soldier's boots stomped along the side of the carriage and a voice roughened by talking all day said, "Lot of hard work and hope, mostly."

"Does it go back?" Maud asked, and I knew she asked for me. "Into the mountain? That's so clever."

People were always more likely to talk when you complimented them.

"No army's getting through these gates and tearing down those walls unless they're capable of leveling mountains." The guard grunted. "I heard the south's all wood."

Maud stood, the cart creaking beneath her. Must've been

handing over her papers. "It depends where you are, I suppose. I've seen hills, never mountains."

"Greenhouses?" Paper crinkled. The guard muttered something low and rapped on the side of the cart. "Why do you need so many trunks for the greenhouses?"

Lynd didn't know about the magic? Did Elise?

Would she care?

"You have mountains," Maud said. "We have plants."

We started rolling again. Armored, knee-high boots paced up and down the paths around us. I couldn't see North Star's estate or the mountains. Sweat pooled along the dips of my chest and gathered in the trembling crooks of my arms. I closed my eyes and breathed.

Lynd—and the rest of Erlend probably—didn't know about the magic or the test Riparian was running on kids. Why?

Having magic would be a boon to the war and would bring hope. Erlend depended on the shadows last time; it was their whole army. Our Queen wouldn't stand a chance.

Damn.

Even if Erlend wasn't all the way there yet, they were trying. Igna needed to prepare. Our Queen needed to know.

But they'd have to realize it soon. Dimas's escape only made sense when you added magic to it.

If I killed North Star and Riparian first, found Cam, freed Adella, and put a stop to whatever monstrosities Erlend was committing, it wouldn't matter. There'd be no shadows.

The wagon jerked to a stop. Dimas leapt down first, unsteady feet tapping the wagon bottom, and Maud's feet appeared slowly. He must've helped her down.

"Where are we going?" she asked.

"There." Dimas's shadow shifted, raising its hand to gesture, and the bare skin at the back of my neck prickled. "You don't have to come."

"Thank you for reminding me that I asked for your opinion," Maud said sharply. "How forgetful of me."

I peeked out from under the wagon. We were at the back of a dozen or so ramshackle buildings for servants and soldiers, and the horses were being led away by the only person in sight. I rolled out from under the wagon and set off in the direction of Maud and Dimas. North Star's estate loomed.

White stone walls grayed by weather and age were carved straight out of the mountain side. They must've added to it, but the seams were worn away and fog wreathed the highest reaches of the pale towers, blending them into the storm-cloud sky. Dusk spilled over the eastern mountains like wine, a deep-purple stain seeping into the orange sun still sitting low over the western watchtower. Dishwater-gray snowcaps glittered days and days of walking above us. The castle was more ghost than building. A pompous show rising high above the plain soldier and servant buildings around me now.

Maud and Dimas had entered a place so squat and plain it looked more bump in the dirt than building. Even the plants growing out of the cracks in the ground bent away from it and avoided twining up its bricks. I raced to it, pausing in its shadow to check if anyone had seen me.

No one, and Maud had left the door ajar.

She was better than any thief or Left Hand member. She'd single-handedly infiltrated Erlend without so much as a plan.

I pushed open the door and found myself staring down a dark set of stairs spiraling deep into the earth. No rooms, no halls. Only the stairs leading Lady knew where.

CHAPTER
# THIRTY-ONE

Narrow stone stairs curving deep into the ground yawned
before me. Torches, dim and dying, lit the walls every
ten steps, but they did nothing for the flickering dark. Shadows
oozed out of the gaps in the stones. It was a hungry dark.

The sort that suffocated when the last light went out.

I spiraled down and down and down until the walls grew wet
and cold and my teeth rattled with each breath. There were no
servants here. No guards. There was only me.

And runes. Everywhere I looked, there were runes.

Odd runes, sharper than the ones Our Queen and Nicolas
wore on their arms. Darker than the moon-white turtles of
Isidora's wrists. There were even bloodred runes carved and
painted onto old, yellow bones.

The greater the tie to earth, the greater the control.

I shuddered and gasped. The cold gave my fear a foggy, wispy
shape. A ghost in the dark.

The floor evened out and suddenly the walls were lined with

doors. Thick slabs of stone cut with lines and shapes and patterns I couldn't see shook beneath my fingers. Not from me.

I wasn't strong enough to move them. No one person would be.

But they thrummed, like a heartbeat or a headache, the steady feel of sound shivering just out of sight. A low, deep call of the earth before it quaked.

Was this magic or fear? It was back—a phrase that set my teeth on edge and made my skin itch—but was this what it felt like? And why Dimas? Adella? Cam? I'd have said it was all about Naceans, but Adella and Cam were the odd ones out.

A shriek echoed down the hallway. I darted after it. Dimas's shaky voice bounced off the walls, and I pressed myself against the door he'd gone through, cracking it open so I could watch. Their voices carried into the hall.

"Tie her down," he said. "She'll thrash and might hit you. And don't undo her cuffs till she's tied."

How many times had he done this? To Igna? To us?

Maud's soft breaths quickened. "How do you know she'll thrash?"

"Just help me." He grabbed a rope, the strands of it rubbing across his hand and bandages, and looped it through metal hooks that clanged, metal against metal. "You're the one who opted to come with me, and if we do not have her prepared for tomorrow night's viewing, Lady de Arian will be upset. I do not care what she offered you, but it is dependent upon staying in her good graces."

If that was true, did he really think she'd let him walk away with his mother and sister?

"You keep saying things like that, Dimas." Maud sniffed. "Is it really that easy to believe I would stoop so low as to do all of this for money? You would really think that poorly of me instead of thinking I'm working for Igna still?"

"What? No. You can't say that aloud." He had his back to the door when I finally reached it, and his hands were above his head, working some rune on the doorjamb. "Lords, Maud, I would be glad for it, but if anyone heard that, you would be dead by midnight."

"You shouldn't worry about me." Maud smiled at me and stared up at Dimas. She pulled the rope in her hands taut. "Worry about Our Queen's Honorable Opal."

I pressed my knife to the small of his back.

"Hello, Dimas Gaila. No runes today. I'm not in the mood and neither's your spine."

He froze.

Maud peeked around him and grinned, her fingers curled into horns at her forehead like the goats I'd used as a distraction.

"Knew you'd notice that," I told her. I pushed Dimas into the room and shut the door behind me. "Now, about you."

I'd not worn my mask into Lynd, didn't look like Opal, but Dimas shrieked all the same.

Dimas looked up, unable to move from where I'd pushed him into the wall, and shuddered. "How?"

"Maud knew I could swim." I put my knife away—he was shaking too much to be a threat or draw a rune—and stood between him and Maud. "She's also not a terrible person. It was a good combination."

"Thank you," she said flatly. "Mostly."

"You know what I mean."

Dimas fell back against the wall, trembling. "You can't be here. Please. I have to do this by tomorrow night, or she'll kill them."

His sister and mother. Two more Naceans alive somewhere. Hopefully.

Lady, let it be true.

"I know, and I'm sorry." I punched him in the jaw only hard enough to unsettle him, and he stumbled to his knees. "But this is ending."

I yanked him up, fastened his hands to the table meant for Adella, and had Maud hold his flattened hands down so he couldn't rune his way out of this. He only sobbed.

Maud closed her eyes.

Would I have done this if it meant seeing my family again? Even just one of them?

Maybe.

Probably.

I'd killed so many to avenge them. What would I have done to save them?

Dwelling on it like this would get me nothing but grief and I'd enough of being sad already. I broke open the lock on Adella's trunk and threw open the lid, sure Adella would be out for blood.

Nothing.

I peeked over it. A blur of limbs flew out of the trunk and caught me around the middle. Maud shrieked. I grabbed Adella's bound hands and twisted her off me.

"Hello to you too," I said and sat up. "You all right?"

Blinking rapidly and staring round, Adella held out her hands to me. "How would you be?"

"Fair enough." I stood and helped her up, avoiding the sight of her bandaged ear. The edges were frayed as if something had been gnawing at it. "How's your ear?"

She groaned. "I was going to ask you. Lady de Arian kept going on about how she hadn't realized the cheaters were options too."

"She had me look at her books." Maud sniffed and looked up, hands continuing to keep Dimas still and runeless. "Some of the supplies were, well, like she'd been sending people up here for a while."

"She has been." Dimas laid his forehead against the table, and it was the first chance I'd had to look at him up close without wanting to punch him. His hair, so carefully brushed and shining when I'd been at auditions, was tangled up in a hasty bun. His skin was ashy, streaked the pale of cold winter months and relentless scratching. A stutter clung to his every word. "And I've been helping her for three months to find the kids. It's something to do with us—with our lack of magic—and Weylin wanted us all. My sister can't use runes, so she wasn't of any use. But I am."

I licked my lips. Hope was crushing. Deadly. "How do you know your mother and sister are alive?"

"Lady de Arian handed me an ear." Dimas shuddered. "That's the test. Magic changed something in people's blood and bones, something deep and constant, and a lot of children can use it still because their parents did. But my sister can't. They didn't need her, so cutting her wasn't a problem for them."

"You inherited it?" I asked. "Magic?"

Was it in me? Was the same slithering force that had flowed through shadows' veins as they tore apart my family living in me?

"No, I inherited nothing," he said. "Nothing at all—no runes, no magic—and that's why they needed me. They knew my parents, so they knew there was a half chance I could still use magic, and that's why they came after me. Weylin had them cut off my sister's ear, the one that had revealed her inability to do what I could, and Lady de Arian placed it in my hand, scars and blood and all. They'd iced it to keep it fresh. So I would know my sister was alive when they cut it off."

That meant magic hadn't been banished. Magic wasn't gone. Marianna da Ignasi, Our Queen of the Eastern Spires and Lady of Lightning, hadn't gotten rid of magic ten years ago.

She'd only banished mages' ability to use it.

People who had used magic or had runes used on them ten years ago couldn't use magic now. But people who'd never used magic, whose parents had never used magic, and who had never been touched by runes, could still use magic today.

People like Naceans.

"How do you know this?" I swallowed, skin aching. My parents hadn't used magic.

"She told me." He squeezed his eyes shut. "My sister was sick as a child, and a physician placed a rune in her heart. There's magic in her flesh, and she can't use it now. Lady de Arian told me that if I didn't help them find children who could be mages, my sister would meet an end worse than death."

The clawing itch within me stuck me to my spot. If I moved, I would split. Scratch. Tear.

"Shadows," I whispered.

"Children who have too much magic in their veins to be mages now make the best shadows," he whispered back, voice dragging itself from his throat. "The ones who can't be mages, the ones whose parents used magic and inherited its stain, are the most successful. It doesn't always work, you know. Sometimes they just die, body, soul, and all, and there are too few children untouched by magic left in Erlend."

The Carnival of Cheats, its real cheaters, didn't use magic to perform, but they got injured and have used runes to fix that. The perfect shadows. Nacea didn't deal in magic, didn't steal from the Lady and force her into runes. The perfect mages.

What had Erlend made us now?

"You've been finding Nacean kids?" I wiped my face, eyes burning. The Nacean in my mouth felt wrong. Hollow. Words that should never have been said. "We're all that's left and you're help- ing them find us? Use us? And you asked me about forgiveness?"

"Some will be mages, some will be shadows." The unfinished thought hung in the silence, raising the hair at the back of my neck, and he curled his fingers against the table. "But my family will be alive."

So many dead to save two.

Where was the line?

"There are more of us," I said in Nacean, "and you're killing them."

"Sal? What did you say?" Adella coughed and started to unwind the bandage.

Maud glanced between Dimas and me. "Are you speaking Nacean?"

"Yes." I touched Maud's arm and nudged her back. "We were."

"I could still feel magic when we moved here. I touched a physician's runes, and they lived." Dimas touched his bare wrist.

"My mother paid someone to take me away, to take me south and away from Weylin's lands. She said no matter how nice he was, how kind to let Nacean refugees resettle on his lands, he'd want the power he'd lost. He would want magic back one day, and that meant he'd want me. And I never saw her again."

"What did you do to Adella?" I asked in Alonian.

He raised his head, red eyes swollen shut. "All of us without magic in our veins can be separated, trisected—the body and mind peeled away from our souls. We're the only ones it works on."

I froze. The familiar cold fury of disbelief rippled over me. I turned to Adella and touched her chin. She flinched back.

"What?" she asked. "Is it bad?"

My fingers gripped her jaw, and I turned her head to the side so I could see her ear. She was warm. Dry. Not the clammy cold of death. I could feel her life, and I could feel the gnawing pinch of magic in her skin. The hole in her ear was like lacework, the runed part so delicately removed it might have always been nothing if not for the soft blur when she breathed. A trick of the light.

A shadow too slow to keep up with her. Separate—but not entirely—from her body.

"Will it spread?" I asked.

Dimas said, "I don't know. It's never worked for me, but I haven't tried very hard."

And a clearheaded, empty knowing came over me.

"Why bring her here?"

Adella and Maud backed away from him. Maud gripped Adella's arm, keeping her steady while she groped at the holes in her ear.

"Shadows can't pass through the doors."

I grabbed the back of my neck, the breath of air—not real, not real, not real—warming my shoulders.

The room was small. The low ceiling hung above us, more mold than stone, and the door leading out was ringed in runes so old the carvings were soft and pale like paint. Another door, as tall as the ceiling and as thin as Dimas, was an overgrown mess of moss and weeds opposite the entrance. I stepped toward it, the moss muffling my footsteps. Rune-scrawled iron dripping rust and dying ferns shuddered when I laid my hand against it. My dark handprint revealed the scratched-out edges of the door.

Nails clawing for a way out.

A sound so deep my teeth ached shuddered through the door. This was it. The birthplace of my nightmares. The home of my death.

Where Sallot Leon of Nacea had become damned.

"This was where they made the first shadows." I traced the flowery runes twining around the lock. The first shadows came from Erlend, but when Erlend was ready to put their work to the test, they used Naceans. Fitting. "And you were going to leave Adella here till she rotted away and nothing but a frantic soul remained."

Dimas didn't answer. He didn't have to.

I shoved open the door, sweat beading across my skin with effort, the chill in the air raising gooseflesh on my arms. The door opened slowly, a great yawn of a rusted-shut creak, and the dead air inside flooded the room. I stared into the empty dark.

Had the shadow that killed my family waited here? Trapped? Hurt? Tearing itself to shreds and forgetting who it was till it was nothing at all?

I held my hand out to Dimas. "Come here."

He didn't move. I pulled out my knife.

"I'll save your mother and sister, but you're not leaving this room. Not now."

Not for a long, dark while. Till he'd lived with what he'd done.

"I'm going to find every Nacean you sent up here," I said, "and all the ones Erlend kept trapped, and then I'm going to kill Gaspar del Weylin, Nevierno del Farone, and Lena de Arian. No more shadows. Not now. Not ever again."

I couldn't avenge Nacea.

I could protect the Nacea that still lived—stuck in Erlend, scattered through Igna—and the dying flicker of home that still lived in us.

"You won't let her hurt them?" Dimas asked, soft voice choked.

"If they're alive right now, I'll do everything I can to keep them that way."

Dimas, eyes open and hands still, stepped into the dark without a fight. I shut the door behind him.

And it sounded like a sigh.

Y ou're going to leave him in there?" Maud moved behind
me, hands fluttering but never quite touching.

I turned around. "For a while. We need to get to work without him interfering."

Adella was in the corner, her hand over her runed ear. Her
hair was flattened on one side, where she'd been shoved into the
trunk, but the springy curls on the other side trembled. A whole-
body shudder overtook her.

For someone always in control of her body, it was betraying
her now.

"Who are you?" I asked.

"Adella?" She tilted her head down, cracked lips quirking up.
"You knew me as Two?"

"Shadows don't know who they are. Were." I shrugged and
slumped. Could you stop making one? "So you're not one."

Right now.

"There's a second laboratory." Maud let her hand linger just above my arm, and in the warm, thick air of the room, I could feel it shaking there. "It was listed as 'fallow' in Lady de Arian's books, but it was still being sent supplies."

Fallow.

The Naceans still alive would be there. They had to be.

"I'll see if anyone's there and figure out what to do about it." I pulled the winter hat from the thin pack strapped to my back and tossed it to Adella. "Cover your ear." I turned back to Maud. "Get Adella out of here if you can and go about your day like normal. Just make sure that if you need me, you can send me a sign."

"I can lay low." Adella pulled on the hat, face twisted in pain. "Show me the way out, and I can hang around outside."

"You can stay hidden?" I asked.

"Obviously." She rolled her eyes. "Or did I imagine sneaking up on you multiple times during auditions and after?"

"Fair point." I took Maud's hands in mine. "You stay alive. I'll deal with Dimas."

"I'll find you a way in."

"Maud, you don't have to do that."

She squeezed my hands, face harder than I'd ever seen it. "I know why you're here. This is war. There are no rules. Weylin's out for blood, and you're out for him. Let's get him first."

"Deal." She was real. She was alive. She'd not betrayed me, and I'd see her again. One friend in this mess of a world.

And Adella was all right.

Alone in the room, my skin crawled with magic and shadows and fear. If magic was real, so were they. I spun the ring Isidora had gifted me and thought of high places.

And ignored the bit of me that thought of Elise in the moments before our fight. Lena de Arian—Riparian, one of the nobles responsible for Nacea—was her hero as Our Queen Marianna da Ignasi had been mine.

But Elise, no matter what else, would never have condoned this laboratory or Riparian's tests.

Maybe we weren't well suited, but Lady, it hurt. Thinking of Elise and what we'd said to each other hurt so much I didn't want to consider her at all, but not thinking of her hurt just as much.

I rapped on the door before trying to open it. No answer. Leveling my shoulder against it, I pushed, feet scraping through the moss and hands smearing the rust. It didn't budge.

I pushed harder, wanting to see Dimas, to talk to him, to know which parts of us were so similar and so different.

We'd both crossed lines.

The door creaked open, coughing rotten air into my face, and I fell back. A panicked prickling raced down my arms. Gooseflesh pimpled across my skin. I pushed the door open and let the light stream in. Dimas sat huddled in the corner.

His hands clutched his face. A constant shudder wracked him, and his muttering dulled the rumble of the room. Like whispering.

"Dimas?" I stepped into the small cell, skin crawling. I touched the wall and came away wet, and the urge to trace the lines along my arm nearly took over my hand. I froze. "Dimas, what did you do?"

He didn't answer.

A breath warmed the back of my neck.

And I was six again, legs wrapped around a tree branch while

I dangled upside down and begged my sister to stand. I was six and the summer was thick with heat and death, and I could taste the whispers of the shadows in the back of my throat. I was six and running for my fifth day straight, and I could still feel them at my back.

This wasn't real. I wasn't six.

I walked to Dimas. The scurrying of my feet across the stones sounded like whispered words. He wasn't bloody. He had skin and flesh and hair left on his bones, and the only thing wrong with him was what he'd done. My feet hit his.

"Dimas." I kicked his leg. "We're leaving."

He didn't move. "I can hear them. In my head."

I leaned over and touched his arm. Live, warm skin against my own and not the brush of leftover pieces dried by the sun. The sour stench of death—it was only stagnant air and my mind playing tricks—spilled over me.

"We're leaving." I grabbed his upper arm and hauled him up. "It's only guilt, and I'm glad we've that in common."

"It sounds like my mother," he whispered. "Why does it sound like my mother?"

I shivered, knees locking, teeth clamping together. All the words I had meant to say piled up in my throat. I grabbed him with my other hand too and yanked him to his feet, pulling him close to me and dragging him backward out the door. The uneasy itch to run grew stronger.

"I know who I am," he whispered. "I know who I am."

I slammed the door shut, falling on my ass and staring up at the top of the door. A nameplate, name long gone, hung half-broken from the jamb. Dimas raked his hands over his face.

"I made—" He tried to spit it out and gagged.

I finished for him. "A mistake?"

He sunk to the floor, sobbing, and buried his face in his hands. I stumbled away, but the sound followed me.

A whisper in the dark.

I raced out of the building to the older laboratory building Maud had told me about. It was a greenhouse, no tomatoes or garlic growing within. Great orange flowers drooping on their vines and purple-spotted petals crowned in thorns filled the glass walls. Poisonous plants.

Alchemical plants.

I'd left Dimas locked in that other room. He could get out, I knew, with magic, but the way he looked at his inky hands was so watery and sad, I didn't think he'd be using runes anytime soon.

A cat, the only living thing daring to touch the greenhouse, scratched at one of the windows of the attached wooden shed and batted a field mouse back and forth along the sill. I glanced round.

There were no other buildings nearby, and that struck me as odd. It would've made sense to build more here, would've saved space. There should've been something.

I circled the outside a few steps behind the patrolling

guards—nothing inside so far as I could see except two guards and a door to nowhere. I unlocked the shutters and windows farthest from them. Support beams crisscrossed the ceiling, all function and no show. The cat would be a good distraction.

I crawled into the rafters. It wasn't a big place, but they'd not look up with a yowling monster nipping at their heels. The cat, still scratching, meowed up at me through the wooden slats and glass. I reached down from the rafters and slammed the shutters, cracking the glass and letting the cat inside. The guards came running, and I crawled across the beams to their door. A terrible yowl split the air.

"Triad take me." One of the guards let out a loud, rumbling groan and clucked his tongue. "Come here, cat. I didn't mean that."

It must've gotten underfoot.

Least he apologized.

I picked the lock on the door—easy even with only a knife and a broken hat pin—and darted inside.

More stairs. More runes. More doors drenched in runes worn down by age.

"What're you hiding?" I whispered.

Let it not be Cam. Let him be far away from here.

I laid one hand flat against a door. The cold slithered up me, picked at me. Droplets of water pooled on my sleeve. Rose up.

Names lined the doors. Namrata, Mara, Thea, Cari, Prava, and more and more who had vanished under the wear of time. I tried to open the first one. Namrata was close to Namrantha, and Emerald had said the First Star of Nacea—there had been three, one for each of the Lady's main stars, one to protect each of Nacea's three regions, their families chosen by her centuries ago to be the leaders of Nacea forevermore—had possessed that name. It sounded like an Erlend or Igna thing to do.

Change the name a bit to make it more palatable. Even if it belonged to one of our queens, our protectors. Even if it was the only holy name we had left.

I shoved it open. The door rasped as it slid against the ground.

The racking, shivering fear that gripped me tightened, and I wrapped my arms around myself.

Cam could be in one of these rooms. The names were old, worn down, the nameplates used over and over and over. How many had died in this dark? I couldn't let Cam die in one of these rooms.

Rath had died to save him, and I wasn't letting Rath down.

Not again.

I pushed open the door, fully, totally, something I couldn't name pulling me toward the yawning black, and I heard it dripping across the dark. Skin scraped along stone, nails dragging, cracking in the dips.

*Drip.*

A breath soft as a breeze in summer rain coated my face in rotten, stagnant damp. "Hello."

*Drip.*

I took a breath, tongue heavy with sour rot, and muttered into the dark, "I'm looking for Cam."

"Who's Cam?" The sounds dragged across the still air, long and full of soft, slithering sounds. "Who's Cam?"

I shuddered. Fear, bitter and burning, filled my throat. A thousand images—Hia and Shea, faceless, red as dawn, as flames, as death, twitching in the grass—hit me hard, like my body hitting the surface of the Caracol. Splintered. Breathless.

Breathe. I had to breathe. This wasn't weakness.

This was a rational reaction to a stimulus, but I had reason to panic.

*Drip.*

Blood seeping into dirt.

This was real.

*Drip.*

"Cam?" Its words rattled in the air between us. A whisper. "Hello."

The shadow, more magic than flesh in the dim light, bandaged and bleeding, trailing moss and mold and the bitter taste of rot as it—she, Namrata—paced back and forth, stopped before me. There were gaps, great holes in her body where nothing oozed from the runed bandages holding her together. The last pieces of her green-marbled corpse vanished beneath a damp cloak.

"You're here for Cam," the shadow said, the name a death rattle in her missing throat. "The new child?"

A sickly, flighty feeling settled in my stomach. I wanted to run. Be sick. Sob. Give up and die because nothing could stand against the abyss that was this half-solid shadow hemmed in dust and dirty bandages. It slipped through the air before me like sound and touched my arm.

And it was real.

I threw my left hand up, the knife singing out of my sheath and tearing through the air where the shadow had been. It flinched back, like waves going out with the tide, and I darted out the door. It slammed shut behind me, my back against the stone, but I'd no memory of turning. I blinked, and I was running down the hall. Up the stairs.

LINSEY MILLER

And a hand grasped the back of my collar, nails scraping down my neck.

I screamed. It yanked me back, and I went tumbling down and down, back into the dark and nothing. I hit the hall floor ass first and crawled to my feet. Footsteps backed away.

Shadows didn't have footsteps.

"Who are you and what are you doing here?"

A girl, rune-drenched and wounded, black hair slick against her bruised neck, dark skin pricked with scratches and scabs, stood in a pitch-black doorway at the end of the hall. Blood and ink dripped down her fingers, pooling around her bare feet. The torch beside her flared.

And the runes—Lady, the runes—writhed within her skin.

The shadow maker.

Her gaze lowered to the knife in my hands, and she raised her hand to the wall, a line of runes so thin they might've been a torn strand of hair burrowed from her skin and into the stones. A prickling, scuttling pain held my empty hand to the wall. Blood welled up in the crack between flesh and stone. Red seeped into the carvings.

Runes.

Namrata's door opened, tendrils of shadow unfurling from the gap, and I jammed my knife into the mortar near my fingers. It crumbled. The blade bit into my skin. The magic's hold weakened.

A strip of nothing so dark that staring at it hurt slipped between my hand and the wall. I stabbed it.

"Stop!" The girl slammed her hand into the wall as the shadow reared back, my knife doing nothing.

Blood splattered down the hall, dripping between us. The

hairs on my arms rose, prickling and cold, like all the warmth was seeping out of me breath by breath. An ache rolled over me, oil on wet skin, and I stumbled to my knees. My ears rang. The shadow backed up.

A whisper.

A sigh.

The drip of blood and ink.

The girl crouched near me. "You were looking for Cam?"

"I—" The words wouldn't come. My hands shook, the knife clattering against the stones.

Shadows were real.

Real. Real. Real.

"They wanted Cam." The shadow Namrata flitted behind the girl, leaning over her and whispering in her ear. "Cam Nissa, son of Nissa Rin."

Namrata paused, though she didn't stop moving. The nothing of her body continued to twist and peel away from the wall before settling into a smoky blur before me. Her half-bandaged limbs, cloth stained green and yellow, mottled like a pear. She raised one hand to what might've been her mouth.

"You're scared of me," she—it, the shadow, Namrata?—said.

What had Erlend done?

Was this a soul and a mind bound to the earth without a body? Did that hurt? Was she always here? In this room, alone in the dark with no one for company but an eternity of pain?

Was this a person?

The girl glanced up at the shadow. She nodded.

Namrata vanished back into her room. The girl held her hand out to me.

"How about we go see Cam?" she said. "And we can take a break from panicking?"

She led me to a door at the end of the hall, and a cold, crushing fear of pushing open the door and seeing a shadow with salted eyes and the height of a child froze me. She tugged me harder.

"Just look. He's fine." The girl pushed open the door and a squeaky shriek came from beyond it. Light footfalls pattered away. "It's me, Cam. And a friend, I think."

I blinked, bracing for shadow, but there was only a boy. Tall for his age and missing a front tooth, he peeked out from behind a short cot. He stood, upsetting the layer of dead moss dust coating his dark-brown skin. Black runes flickered along his eyelid.

"I don't know you," he said, shaking his head.

"Rath sent me." I tried to smile. "He wanted me to make sure you were all right and take you back to Igna."

"Rath!" Cam grinned and tackled me in a hug, squeezing the air from between my ribs, and the touch made me shudder. "I knew he'd find me."

I patted his shoulder. "It's a long story, but he did. Traveled half the country doing it too."

"You're Sal, aren't you?" Cam sucked a poppy seed from his teeth and let me go. "You look like Sal. He talked about you a lot."

Course he did.

"Was it all bad?"

Cam shrugged. "Ninety to ten."

Course it was. I laughed and rubbed the tears from my eyes. The girl cleared her throat.

"Rath was your minder, yes?" she asked Cam, but she didn't wait for him to respond. "You know this person?"

He opened his mouth and shrugged again. "If they're Sal."

"I'm Sal." I swallowed and touched Cam's shoulder.

He was alive. He was real.

"Good." The girl touched my elbow, a barely there brush, and nodded to the hallway. "He's fine. He's alive. We need to talk."

I nodded.

She led me into the hall. It was like being a child again, afraid of the dark and getting led back to bed, but this time to the dark was alive and hungry, an abyss waiting to snatch my face.

Except Namrata had spoken. Had acted mostly human.

Was she just a soul?

I shivered. Nearly vomited.

The girl shut Cam's door behind us and turned to me.

"I am Moira Namrata, the Last Living Star of Nacea, and you are trespassing in my domain regardless of good intentions." The runes on her arms poked through her skin, sharp and bloody, and twisted toward me. Snake-line. Deadly. "I will ask you only once more—are you really named Sal and why are you here? Do not say for Cam. I know you were in the other labs."

The last sliver of Sallot Leon within me, the one of farmland winds and my father's voice, forced me to my knees. I bowed, face pressed to the floor. I knew that title better than I knew my name.

The three stars of Nacea had been our leaders, three royal families who could trace their way back to when the Lady still walked the earth and humans were only just beginning. The Stars of Nacea had been blessed by the Lady herself. Three stars to rule three regions of Nacea.

But this was the Last Living Star of Nacea. She was Lady chosen and alive.

And I was *dying*.

# CHAPTER
# THIRTY-FOUR

N acea lived.

# CHAPTER
# THIRTY-FIVE

I collapsed. The air within me tightened, chilled. Nacea lived and I was dead, drowned in the sudden crushing possibilities of it.

The girl—this couldn't be real and she couldn't be Moira Namrata—walked to me, bare feet dragging along the floor. I opened my mouth to talk, to beg, and swallowed a mouthful of air too sharp to just be air. The cuts across my skin burned.

"You're Nacean," she said softly, crouching before me. "How did you get down here?" She folded her hands behind herself, and the aching bite to the air went with them. "Why are you down here?"

"Broke in. I was looking for missing kids, other Naceans that Erlend's been stealing, and I found—" I spun my ring. Trees. Towers. Rafters. Roofs. They never looked up. "How are you here? How are you alive?"

She held out one hand to me. The runes on her arms, more scar than ink, sunk back beneath her skin and settled flat.

"They're runes," I muttered. "How've you got proper runes? We don't get runes."

Except we did. Dimas did. He said others did, the ones untouched by magic.

"We'll do this." She pulled back her hand, fingers curling. "We'll trade. My name is Moira. What is yours?"

She created shadows. She called Namrata mother.

Moira Namrata.

Naceans always took their mother's name.

Had she stripped her mother, the last Star of Nacea, bare? Had she bound her soul to this hungry earth, always searching for what she was?

But she wasn't searching. She wasn't hunting. She wasn't unsure of who she was.

Namrata knew herself. Knew Moira. Knew Cam.

Was she even a shadow?

Moira wasn't Dimas, wasn't going past the bounds of humanity because I knew shadows better than I knew myself. Namrata was not a shadow.

"Your name," Moira said. "What is it?"

Her voice was soft, her Nacean smooth, and the sound of it all made my tongue stick to the roof of my mouth. The Nacean I'd longed to speak for years clung to my teeth and refused to break free. A stone of words and fear.

What if I said it wrong? To a Star?

"Sal." I licked my lips—would they taste different? Nacean words from Nacean mouths—and stared up at her. "Sallot Leon."

She smiled. "Sallot. Good. I was here to visit my mother. You said you were here looking for the missing children? Most of them are well. We're not fond of the fact they're bringing us children, though we have found many lost Naceans that way."

"I'm Opal," I said quickly. "Our Queen's, the queen of Igna's, Opal, and I've been hunting the Erlends that ran the shadows through Nacea, and North Star—Weylin—is one of them, and you're dead. You're all dead."

"Oh, no." Her jaw tensed. "We were too useful to be dead."

My stomach rolled. Worth.

"You came from Alona? Through Nacea?" Moira brushed back her hair, strands as dark as the ink curled around the holes in her ears. Her fingers shook. "What do you mean 'we're all dead'?"

"Nacea," I whispered. "The shadows."

She fell back against the wall, eyes closed, hands up in prayer. "There are ten thousand of us in Erlend. I thought more would have—we sent people south."

Ten thousand? Ten thousand! That was an eternity of people, of faces, of souls, I didn't know and desperately wanted to.

"They're here?" The words stuck in my throat. "There are other Naceans here?"

"No." Moira slumped. "Weylin had different towns and cities quarter us when we first got here, and when he realized we could use magic several years ago, he separated us ever more. Until then, it had been normal. We were just Naceans in Erlend, waiting for his forces to clear Alonian soldiers out of Nacea— we thought the war was still going on, you see—and all of his updates about Alona sounded normal. But it was all lies. There are only a few of us here, and we don't know the locations of any of the towns housing Nacean families. It's been made very clear that if any of us step out of line, he'll kill an entire settlement."

I buried my face in my hands.

He couldn't.

He would. He would do it easily, but I wasn't losing Nacea after finding it. I wasn't letting Weylin destroy Nacea for a second time.

"Don't panic. He's been forcing us to work for him under threat of death, but his time has run out." Moira gently touched my arm, eyes wide and glazed with tears, and smiled. "Did you really meet no other Naceans?"

"I met another, Dimas. They told him his mother and sister were here, and that they'd kill them if he didn't help test kids for magic." I touched the shell of my ear. "He's got holes, and he said his mother snuck him out. Dimas Gaila. He's in the other laboratory. Or he was. Erlend said they'd kill family still here if he didn't help them make shadows."

"Gaila?" She tilted her head back. "There's a young woman whose mother was Gaila, but there are no others. And he is still in that lab."

I froze. "How do you know he's still there?"

"Because the shadow in that room is bound to me, and it says he is still there."

Shadow.

It had been real. It had been right there. Next to me. Behind me.

I was sick for real, and Moira pulled back my hair.

"You're scared of my mother, Namrata," she whispered. "Why?"

My last memory of hearing her name bubbled up in me and I cleared my throat. "Last I talked to anyone, they said the First Star was named Namrantha."

She laughed. "That's the Erlenian version of my mother's name. Namrata is a family name, one of my grandmothers decades ago came from the lands Eredan conquered far to the east and over the sea. It's one of our ways to remember that, and I will make them say it right."

"Oh."

"Come." She moved her arm within my grasp and didn't question my barely there touch or shuddering hand. "My lab. It's safer, and I have things." She glanced at me. "From home, from Nacea. We can talk there. I'd like to know more about Dimas and Igna, and I imagine you would like to know more about Nacea."

CHAPTER
# THIRTY-SIX

Clothes stitched into tapestries covered the gray stone walls. Deep, dark greens and blues, ribbons running through cotton like kelp through water, tightened the space, but I felt free, like floating in open sea. Like drowning.

There were books and cuffs and a pair of yellow socks peeking out from papers and scratchily inked diagrams on the table that took up half the room. There were no shelves, no chairs.

Moira sat on the clean edge of the table and cleared a spot for me. "Here."

"Thank you." Was I supposed to bow to the stars? Use titles? Look at them?

"I'm going to tell you everything I know," she said, "and then I need to know what's happened with the rest of the world."

I set my hand on the table. The diagram beneath it was of a human skeleton, skin peeled back and muscles bare, small runes burned into the underside of the skin.

Magic.

She was still a Nacean Star, but she was using magic. Drawing blood. Losing bits of herself and the Lady with every drop.

Was I still Nacean, then?

"You know magic?" I shook my head and pushed the diagram away. "I knew it was real, but how is it real? How can you use it? I don't know a lot, but I know we never used magic."

Moira folded her hands in her lap. "It has become a necessity. The alternatives were far more dangerous."

"How?" I asked. "Our Queen Marianna da Ignasi banished it."

But she hadn't. Everything leading up to this was proof of that. None of it explained living runes in Nacean skin.

"No, she didn't." Moira held out her hand, palm down, and traced the faded lines of an old, white rune. "I'm certain she did something akin to banishment, but to reject it completely would change the fabric of our world. She changed us, not it." Moira laughed and waved to the ceiling. "Well, she changed *them*, not us. She changed the mind, body, and soul of everyone who had ever used magic or been runed, and they passed on that change to their children. It will fade in time, most likely, but for now, there are a very few people capable of using magic and having it used against them, and a large amount of that few are Nacean."

My skin itched, the restless urge to scratch and claw until there was nothing left. I spun my ring. The soft hissing sound of metal on metal joined the thrumming in my ears.

"No one's got magic down south." My voice echoed and rattled. "I never felt it. I never used it. I've never had it, and my parents never used runes."

But that wasn't true. Dimas had said the same thing.

Magic wasn't gone. Shadows weren't gone. Nacea wasn't gone.

"It's not a thing you have," Moira said. "It's a part of the world, like air or gravity, and you can utilize it. Marianna some-how cut off the ability of people who'd used magic to sense it, manipulate it, whatever it is you want to call it. It's still there, it can still affect them, but I can only assume she took away their ability to sense it. It's why, once Gaspar del Weylin found out some of the people he had considered little more than refu-gees taking up his land and paying taxes could still use magic, he found the ones of us who could."

I laced my fingers together.

Us.

"The shadows came from the south, from Alona, or at least that is what the Erlend soldiers said. It's what we saw. It seemed reasonable. A simple lie." She wiggled her fingers, like running a coin across her knuckles but nothing was there. "Weylin started off slow, taking only one or two children away from their homes to Lynd under the guise of schooling and jobs. Helping us find new, better lives after Alona's shadows destroyed our old ones. That's what he told me when he brought me here five years ago."

How perfect that Erlend's monstrosities had driven Nacea here and Weylin had finally done the honorable thing and granted the survivors land, homes, lives. The lives he'd taken from them. Of course he'd lied. Of course he'd laid the blame at Alona's feet. Of course he'd made himself the hero.

She glanced at me from the corner of her eyes. "My mother didn't believe him when he said I was too busy to write so often. She visited. She found me, so he couldn't let her leave. We're not all in the same place, you see, so it's easy to make sure we don't know what's happening, but now I have you to add on to the news the others he sent north have shared. It's not like he let us settle in Erlend ten years ago with this in mind—he just let us settle. We built homes wherever we could and wanted, and we started paying taxes, paying tribute. We were just living. Like normal. We'd no reason to leave, no reason to not believe him. I didn't, at least, until he brought me here." She sighed. Slumped. "What's happening outside of Erlend?"

"What do you know?" I asked.

I should've brought Elise's notes.

I winced. Elise.

"Never mind." I shook my head. It didn't matter. "What don't you know? I'll fill in the gaps."

Moira knew of Igna but not greatly. It was, for all that mattered up here, still Alona. They'd known that half the Erlend nobles weren't truly loyal to Igna. There were just a few extras that Nicolas and Our Queen hadn't foreseen, and North Star had been plotting his little incursion for years. Winter and Five had moved too quickly and ruined North Star's plans. She'd hummed at the rumors of Our Queen making shadows.

And I'd nearly screamed.

Nacea had lived, still lived, and he's squirreled them away to use as scapegoats on some future day. Anyone farther south than Highwater, he'd told everyone in northern Erlend, was destroyed, the lands infected by whatever monstrous magic Our Queen had worked to destroy the shadows. He called them dead lands. Fallow.

Gaspar del Weylin—North Star through and through—had told his small Erlend holdout territory that after the war, the land was rotten. Igna was not a real nation but a collection of groups stubbornly holding out and refusing Erlend's aid.

And once North Star's Erlend and the old Erlend lands that had been integrated from Igna were united again, who'd care about the lie so long as they caught what they wanted?

"We had to defend ourselves." Moira scratched a shape onto the table and rubbed it away. "That was what he said. The old nation of Alona had risen from the ashes of the war and was trying to steal our land again. In the beginning, until five years ago, we'd no reason to leave. We were at war, and Erlend was fulfilling its contract of quartering us."

She talked of soldiers missing body parts—arms, legs, ears, noses, tongues. Shadow wounds. Runes carved into revealed bone but no magic buzzing in them.

"We didn't realize what he was doing at first," she said. "He'd been trying to bring magic back for years, reawaken his connection to it, but it didn't work. They just died. And then he noticed that our physicians were still using magic. We never considered it as such—scouring rot from wounds and ensuring those in need of lifelong interventions received it. He noticed. He offered my mother, a physician, many things if she would help him bring back magic or re-create shadows, but she refused. All of our physicians refused. Why would we torture a person so that the very core of their being broke? After that, he split us up. Divided us. There have been no more than twenty of us living in any given place since. We're not allowed to talk or teach anyone how to use magic. Not all Naceans can, but he is cautious. He stopped us from communicating so that we could not escape or, even if we did, find the other Naceans scattered about Erlend."

"He has hurt so many people." She dragged her nails down her arm, bouncing over the inky scabs. Her face might've been round once, but it was all softness turned sharp, hollowed cheeks and sunken eyes rimmed in red staring through me, never at me. "He has, by the sound of it, used Dimas Gaila to test children for magic, forcing him to rune their ears. He sends me children with bloodied, eaten ears and takes offense when I heal them. The other Nacean mages and I have done so much to avoid using the children he sends us. I have taught them to be mages at his behest and used my own blood as ink to make sure they spill none of their own. I have stripped my mother's soul even barer so that it may pass as someone else's shadow so that we need not make new ones. Every time he has threatened us with death, to kill or be killed, we have found a way around it, but now he wants a shadow army. He measures worth by blood, but how can he know till he's spilled it all at Our Lady's feet?"

Moira turned back to me, black eyes bright, and held out her hand again. The runes were still. The ink was dull.

"Gaspar del Weylin's death belongs to me," she said, "to Nacea as a whole. He forced his violence upon us, and I will make it his downfall."

I stilled, and a gentle, aching hum so deep I couldn't hear it, only feel it, rattled across my skin. In my bones.

"What have you got planned?"

"Survival, to which he is a detriment." She laughed, hollow and high, and offered her hand to me again. "A wounded limb steeped in infection will kill if not cut off, and I refuse to let our people be the rot-choked corpses Gaspar del Weylin wants us to be. We are going to free ourselves of the epidemic that is Erlend egocentrism." She offered me her hand. "What do you do when your flesh is rotten, when the skin is so dead even your blood turns against you?"

I took her hand. "Cut it out."

"Exactly," she said. "And if you would have me as your surgeon, I would have you as my knife."

# CHAPTER
# THIRTY-SEVEN

oira called killing Gaspar del Weylin self-defense.
I liked that.

Vengeance made righteous. He'd been terrible and he'd never stop, and now he'd get what he was owed.

"We don't know where we all are." She helped me from the table, the good bit of height she had on me making it easier, and unpinned a sprawling map from beneath the table. "And those of us he kept here he's got under guard. There's only about a dozen of us allowed in Lynd, and I know he keeps our numbers small in other settlements to prevent communication. The moment we try to step out of line, his guards will take us out, and he'll send messages to the others. We can only kill him if we can overpower his guards and messengers." She leaned in close to me. "I know how to do it, but I cannot do it."

She led me out the lab and down the hall. Watching her, the careful glide of her bare feet over the stones, the gold and silver necklace falling out of her shirt, the spill of loose hair down her

back, the unanswered question I so often muttered to the Lady—
Our Lady—welled up in me.

"Moira," I said softly. "How understanding is the Lady? About
blood and killing?"

She looked back at me. "Why?"

"I'm Opal." I'd no mask and few weapons, but surely a
Nacean Star would *know*, could look at me and see how out of
step with Nacea I was. "I've killed a lot of people."

She stopped. "Do you feel guilty?"

"Sometimes." I swallowed and tensed. "But mostly," I said,
stuttering, "they deserved it."

"Why?" She took a step to me. Calm. Careful. But the glint
in her eyes and tightness of her shoulders gave her away.

I stepped back. "They led the shadows through Nacea. Or
they were rangers. Or they killed someone else."

"If the child of someone you killed took revenge on you,
would you damn the child?"

I shook my head. "Probably not."

"Weylin and his rangers think they're better than us due to
their Erlenian heritage, and they have never had to face the consequences of their actions. They've been reprimanded but never
punished," she said. "You have become the consequences of their
actions. We will show them how wrong they are."

I blinked at her.

She smiled. "I've had plenty of time to consider morality
while watching my mother wither away slice by slice. You are,
like me, as Erlend forced you to be. They'd no right to leave us
like this, but they did. And so we can set it right."

I nodded. "Good."

"Now," she whispered, coming close. "What did you really want to ask of me?"

"Am I Nacean?"

I was. I was to me, and that's what mattered.

But I wanted her to say it in Nacean, to look at me, knowing all the things I'd done, and say it. I'd been acting for Nacea, but suddenly here it was, Last Living Star and all, and what if she hated that?

"You're Nacean." She let a breath out through her nose, a half laugh. "If you want to be, you are. There's not a test you have to pass."

I swallowed. "I remember some things. I remember the rules about magic and blood and prayers."

"Our Lady is understanding." Moira held out her arms, runes gathered in the crooks of her elbows like frightened creatures. "And more importantly, you are as you are. A debt of blood must be repaid in flesh—in service, in thought. It doesn't have to be literal. Do you think you're a bad person?"

I shrugged.

"Bad is relative." She took my hand. "Do you want to help me make the world a safer place for the people Erlend would murder and use and break?"

I nodded.

"Do you want the people who have killed for their own gain and comfort held accountable?"

Again, I nodded.

"And even though you feel in the right, do you feel guilty? Do you feel the need for redemption?"

"I do feel guilty." But did I crave redemption? Did I deserve it?

"I'll help you get it if you want." Moira let go of me. "But I don't think you need redemption. The world that made us does."

Let them try me after. Let a court of people just as hurt as I had been look at my soul and crimes and judge me as I was. Let the better world I wanted to make decide if I deserved to live in it.

At least, no matter what, the world would be better.

At least, of the two of us, it would be redeemed.

And I would have my revenge.

"You've only met one other Nacean since its destruction?" She waited till I nodded and stepped forward, pressing her forehead to mine. "Who you are is up to you, but for as long as I am Nacea's Last Star, you are as Nacean as me. Understand?"

I nodded.

"It's not a fact of closeness or place. It's a being, and I will never deny you that. No one can but you." She touched my arm. "I'm going to show you how we're going to get rid of Gaspar del Weylin. I think you will be the key to ending his reign."

We stopped before a door, footsteps muffled by the thick mat of moss creeping out from under it. The door was rune-scrawled iron and dripping, trails of rusty water catching in the carvings. Ferns curled out from under the door like fingers, twists of green against the dark, stained metal, and a wilting, white flower grew from the lock. A sound so deep my teeth ached shuddered through the door. I shivered.

Moira brushed brown leaves from the handle. "We found the idea of using flesh distasteful and gardening is quite calming."

She carved a rune and rapped twice. It echoed, long and loud. Longer than it should've.

"Please understand that while we had options, they were not good. There was no good path for us to take. If we did not do as Gaspar del Weylin asked with mercy, he would have done it with cruelty. He brought us people, and we let them decide. Many we smuggled out. It is easy to fake a corpse once you know death so well. At least, if we agreed to his terms, we could make sure as many lived as possible, us included. If we agreed to his terms, we could make sure to undermine him at every turn." Moira pushed the door open a crack. "We could destroy him. The expendable peoples he used to further his empire could break it down from the inside. So we waited."

The door creaked as Moira shoved it open and waved me in. "We are done waiting."

S he pulled out a diagram of the human body. I couldn't look at it.

"I know they're different and all, but I was in Nacea when the first shadows tore through." I covered up the stripped face on the diagram. "My mind doesn't always recognize that difference, especially if they get close or something, so if your plan involves shadows, I can't be a part of it."

"They're not really shadows though." She covered the diagram and frowned. "Weylin asked us for shadows, but we didn't know how to do that, and most importantly, we didn't want to. Making them was a process of trial and error. My mother volunteered to be the first so no one else would suffer the pain, and I did not torture her until she died and her body could no longer contain a soul. A shadow of violence is not the same as one of kindness. I broke her down, but it was not what Weylin would have done. These are not the shadows you feared."

But they were shadows still.

"How many are there?"

How many dead still walked this earth, killed with kindness and kept here by magic? It was unbelievable.

"Nine. A good, lucky number," Moira said. "And enough to protect the other towns where Weylin has hidden the rest of the surviving Naceans, I think. They'll be able to enter the towns and kill the guards and messengers before anyone gets the signal to kill Naceans."

I'd no idea what numbers were lucky or not in Nacea. I'd so little knowledge.

I ran a shaking hand across my face. "She's a shadow."

"She was my mother first." Moira's eyes narrowed. She spoke through gritted teeth. "All those shadows, they were souls, real people. Erlend made them as it made you."

I'd speared men and slit their throats, even made a few suffer, but I'd never stripped the face from a toddler's corpse and stitched it to their father's.

"You ever see them?" I asked. "What they did to Nacea?"

She slowly shook her head, and for a moment, the runes around her arms sharpened and cleared, jagged, black lines curled around her arms like thorns. "I don't remember."

No wonder she wasn't scared.

I laughed. Empty. Gasping. "When you strip us away, how much of the self remains? A soul? A mind full of a life that had come to pass? A soul without a person to fill it up is just a shadow. Like a body without a mind? I heard those stories growing up—tales of the War of Twelve Gods has got nothing on the shadows. And you're just unleashing them on the world!"

"I am in complete control of her. I hold dominion over her

soul." Moira led me down an empty hallway, all doors and no people. "Could you know everything about someone you love? Could you control them? Could you have pulled their memories from their head and carved magic so deep into their body it burned them from the inside out till they were nothing but a soul?"

As if that mattered. My last two encounters with shadows—or whatever they were—had left me so shaky I didn't think I'd ever be able to shake again.

Instead of answering, I asked, "Could you break a man's neck to get what you wanted?" I shuddered—Roland, if I'd been faster, could've been dead. "Even if he didn't deserve it?"

She didn't move, didn't speak.

I rubbed the back of my neck. Eyes. I could feel eyes on me. An itching, creeping prickle of eyes or hands or spider webs.

We were as we were.

And our bloodied, runed souls were going to destroy Erlend.

"I will do whatever you need me to, but I will not work with the shadows." I asked, "How do I help you kill North Star?"

I'd told her about their names, but she still scowled.

"Weylin is putting on a show tomorrow night for his officers and noble guests." She traced a rune on the table but placed no power in it. "I have been planning on taking over that show and demonstrating to Erlend what Weylin has truly done, but before I can do, I need the locations of the Nacean settlements. He separated us out. If we move against him, he kills a settlement, and we can't stop it because we don't know where the others are. They could be anywhere in Erlend, and they have no idea what's going on. No one outside of us has idea any of this is happening."

"I know how to find out." A vicious joy spread through me.

Maud had said Riparian was in charge of accounts, and she was meticulous enough to list those settlements. They'd have some sort of location marker on them. "Can you keep Dimas here? Tell him to pretend his job went smoothly if anyone comes for him? I only need into North Star's estate, and I can get the locations."

Riparian's bookkeeping records.

"Lena de Arian does all of Weylin's bookkeeping," I explained. "She has to have records of the settlements, Naceans, and mages in order to make sure Erlend can keep track of where you are. It's all about worth with her, how much it costs to do all this versus the payout. She has to calculate it some way."

Moira's jaw tensed, mouth stretching wide.

I shrugged. "Money's probably the only truth she and Weylin have."

"I will keep an eye on Dimas. The guards who check our progress can't tell the shadows apart. It will be easy to say he succeeded." She took me to a door cut directly into the dry dirt wall of a tunnel. We saw no other people, only footprints in the dust, and she laid a hand on my arm once we reached it. "We use this door to get around, but it is very hard to hide something in plain sight with magic. Don't let them see you leave or enter."

I paused. "Why not escape with magic? Why make shadows at all?"

"The runes." She held out her arm to me, palm up, and let the runes beneath her skin settle into place. "Do you know why we call them living runes?"

"No."

"Because they're exactly that. Alive," she said. "Bargaining with them, performing magic, takes sacrifice. If I lose control or attempt magic beyond my abilities, I will be devoured. And what's the point of me even trying to escape if in all likelihood I will end up dead and Weylin will kill the village I grew up in for my transgression? If I don't do what Weylin asks, he kills people. If I do what he asks, I kill people. He has forced me to walk a line, and I will walk it so that no one else has to make these decisions."

"How do you live like this?" I had asked Amethyst and Emerald the same question as Ruby's pyre burned. And I knew the words Moira would say before she spoke.

"Because I must," she said. "Because if it were not me, it would be some other child, some other Nacean I was supposed to protect, learning magic and making shadows and choosing who would die, and I would make no one else suffer this weight."

"I'll be your blade." I grasped her hand, the clammy touch of her skin so like mine. "I'll help you bear that weight."

"And I'll help you bear yours." She grasped my wrist and pulled me close. Her lips brushed my crown. The copper bite of ink and blood burned in my nose. "But Weylin is mine. We must show the world what he has done so that it is never done again."

"How do I find you after?" I asked.

She drew a rune on my arm. No power, but it still made me itch. "Draw that on the other side of this wall. It'll let you in. We're kept under guard, but they can't sense magic like we can."

I stared at the rune, stomach rolling, and thought of nothing but Namrata's hands, the ink holding the nothing gaps between her flesh together.

Moira sighed. "Never mind. I'll let you in after dawn. This street will be dark still."

"I'll see you then."

She touched me once before I left, her rough hands sliding down my arm and catching on my sleeve. "You have questions, but after this, I will answer all of them. And introduce you to the others here. There aren't many of us, mostly children, but they'll be as excited to meet you as you'll be to meet them."

I stared at her hand on my arm, the way her fingers curled across the wrinkled cloth, the neatly clipped ends of her nails darkened by grit and blood, how her spiked ring picked at the wool. It felt warm and real, real as my own skin. The runes curling round her knuckles were sharp. Arching.

"I'll make a list," I said. "I got lots."

She laughed as I left, the door cutting off the sound with a prickling snap.

*Magic.*

It was still night. It felt like it had been longer, a full day in the shuddering presence of Namrata. A biting chill had crept in, snow drifting down from the mountains, and I glanced around the empty dark. I was outside of the central grounds and the door was gone. The little alley opened onto one of the main streets of the eastern district.

I needed Maud and Adella. My hands were shaking and my skin itching, the little hairs on my arms standing straight up still. Like before a lightning storm.

CHAPTER

# THIRTY-NINE

Ice crusted every tree and rock on the mountain pass. Rivers of thigh-deep snow carved out by the wind soaked through our clothes and boots till I couldn't feel my toes. Flakes weighing nothing continued to fall—each soft, white insult easy to ignore, but with all of them pressing down on me. It was like drowning.

And there was no escaping it.

I should've worn the uniform Maud suggested. She was always right.

"No one comes up here." Adella, face turned into the wind, pointed toward one of the four towers looming over North Star's home.

"How do you know all this?" I asked through clenched teeth.

I was not made for the cold.

She shrugged. "Asked around, but not the folks Weylin likes, you know, the street performers and the like."

I held up my full arms. "What am I doing?"

"You're sliding down the embankment." Adella took an ax

and mimed slamming the point into the icy sheet beneath our feet. "There's a ledge a little ways down, and from there you can jump from the mountain to the tower. You're good enough at climbing." She grinned. "It'll be fun. You can't climb up. You'd never make it over the lip in the wall at the third floor, and the guards do circle the path at the bottom. They just don't look up here often. Too cold."

"Sounds like I'm going die in an avalanche." I wrapped my scarf round my face. My mask was hidden, hooked over the back of my belt. "Or fall to my death."

It was too cold for the clothes I wanted, and I'd so many sleeves it was a miracle I could feel my arms.

"Both better deaths than what Erlend has planned for us all," she said. "The windows have got bars. It'll be easy."

Lady save me.

Sliding was slow going. The cliffside wasn't straight and for all the blinding white around us, there wasn't enough snow to bury the handholds and bumps of the rock wall. And a good ways down, there was a little ledge jutting out toward the tower wall. Adella shouted something down. The wind ate it.

I could never tell Maud about this.

An ankle-spraining fall beneath me, a little balcony beneath a well-shuttered window gathered show and pine needles, and I leapt onto it. My feet slipped on ice, sending me to my ass. I groaned.

Only three stories to go till the next one.

I tossed up the weighted end of the rope. Took me three tries to loop it around the window bars above me, and I used it to climb up. Then the next window and the next until my arms were burning and my lungs too hot to be right. I just had to get to the next balcony.

I crawled onto it and laid down in the snow, arms buried, chest tight. The cold seeped in again.

"Up." I pushed myself up. I didn't want to be anyone else but me, but being Amethyst would've done me a lot of good right now. "No staring at the ground."

I left the rope and ax on the balcony and slipped a thin piece of wire into the crack between the doors. The hook popped up. I was in.

It was a furnished bedroom. The mattress was bare and the desk empty. There were another two rooms attached, an entryway and a bathing room. A set of two glass doors separated these quarters from another room, and I tried the handle, smiling as it gave way. The door in the other room opened. I dove under a couch.

Two people entered: a servant, pale-brown uniform dull next to the brilliant-green clothes of their companion, who wore a fancy mix of cloth and jewelry. The servant bowed, and a silver cuff at his ear, hiding a series of half-healed scars, glittered. Another Nacean.

"There's a room connected to it," the servant said. "Once your father arrives for tomorrow's demonstration, we can make sure he's comfortable there. A guard will escort you both to dinner and the city square."

The door to the room opened again. The fancy one jumped to attention and dropped into a bow, feet apart and back straight. The perfect height to acknowledge someone of higher rank than you. The servant dropped to his knees and pressed his forehead to the ground.

"Is it to your liking?" The new man was older, voice the rumbling gravel of decades of talking.

*North Star.*

The servant remained on his knees while the other man straightened and nodded. "Yes, sir. Thank you for your concern. I'm happy to be close by so that I can be part of this."

I braced myself, digging into the rug until my nails cracked inside my gloves, and closed my eyes. So close.

So close to the man who'd ruined thousands of lives to feed his hungry greed.

And I couldn't kill him. Not yet.

"Of course." North Star inclined his head and looked around, gaze glancing over the glass doors. "I am pleased you're taking an interest in your family's responsibilities at so young an age."

From my place in the dark, separated from North Star by practically nothing, he couldn't see me. Not through darkened glass and the seat of a couch. Not if his life depended on it.

Those in the light couldn't see out into the night. Elise would've called it a metaphor.

It wasn't. If it were, Weylin and I would've been facing off in the pitch black of the void, no moon or stars to guide our bloody battle. There was no light to guide our deadly ways.

"When is Roger arriving?" North Star asked. A sliver of a mouth set above a strong, clean chin wrinkled downward in a bored frown, and the thinness of his nose made the broken crook all the more crooked. He didn't so much as look at the servant still prostrate at his feet—even Our Queen acknowledged servants. There was no unnecessary gilt draped over him though. The dark green of his uniform and golden collar and cuffs brightened what little gold was left in his white hair. Round, brown eyes gazed from corner to corner of the room.

A crag of straight-cut mountain stone crowned in ice.

"Three days." The young lord smiled. "He wanted to see the borders personally."

North Star didn't answer, only nodded.

Everything about him itched at me: the sharp, exaggerated angle of his coat's shoulders, made to make him look wider and stronger than he was; the straight line of his spine as he stood unmoving while his people talked to him; the dismissive disinterest in the way he never quite angled his body to the lord speaking. North Star forced him to adjust to his stance.

Erlend men, back in the day, had prided themselves on how immovable they were, how stoic, how like the mountains they lived among, so Elise's history said. She'd a whole chapter on it. Erlend's culture had invaded Alona's like a weed and changed everything—food, language, gender. And I could see it in him.

North Star might as well have carved himself from marble, made himself into the ideal Erlend of old.

Eredan, wasn't it? The people who'd so ruined their own nation that all the folks they'd conquered and forced to be Eredan had fled? The people who'd traveled west across the sea from Eredan to Berengard and been denied as refugees for their hand in the ruin? The people who'd been welcomed in Aren out of mercy and wormed their way into the heart of it until they overthrew Aren and revived Eredan as Erlend?

Conquering. Ruining. Invading new lands to repeat the process until they'd an empire as vast as the one they'd made unlivable. A manifestation of the destiny.

Erlend was just a new name for it—Eredan greed at the expense of others, a driving force to see the world kneeling at their feet and declaring them the best. The greatest this world had to offer.

Weylin was selfish wants given mortal form.

And he made sure that all his men aspired to be him.

He made everyone and everything shift to accommodate him, made sure that everyone unlike him—male and noble blooded, pale beauty and able bodied—knew they could only pray to be like him. He was the ideal by virtue of his birth. A false upholding of blood as something that could be pure.

But no one was ideal. My heroes were as mortal as him, and marble could crack.

I would shatter him.

# CHAPTER
# FORTY

I waited for them to leave before sliding out from under the couch and into the visiting lord's room. There wasn't much in there to help, and I peeked into the little room off to the side for his servant. A stack of neatly folded uniforms that might be useful sat on a table.

I cracked open the door to the hallway. There was nowhere to hide out there, no rafters or furniture, and the only freedom was a window facing inward to what must've been a courtyard. The servant who'd been on his knees before North Star was the only one left in the hallway, and he stared at me, eyes wide.

I touched the shell of my ear where his cuff was, held out three fingers to his lips, and raised them to the sky, to the Lady's stars.

*Your lips to the Lady's ears.*

He grinned and did the same, turning his back to me and carrying on down the hall as if I weren't there. I slipped through a window facing the opposite direction as quiet as I could.

It was a garden closed for winter, the more delicate plants covered in cloths and the balconies stripped of their furniture and planters. I jumped to a little balcony beneath me and used the weighted rope to reach a large one backlit by a glowing window. Silhouettes drifted in and out of the light.

I crouched in the dark against the wall. If they didn't look hard and if I stayed far enough back, they'd not see me through the glass. The guards down below wouldn't either, and I could stand the cold for a little while. The sweat I'd worked up climbing had cooled as I waited for North Star to leave.

And Riparian was here.

Her dress was pale, a burnished gold decorated with reddish-orange sun rays, and the jewelry dangling from her ears and glittering at her neck was all for show. Dark green ribbons trimmed in gold—Erlend colors—were woven through the braids bundled against the back of her neck in a neatly tied bun, and she laughed along with the young lord seated next to her. Her smile was too wide, but he tilted his head back, neck bared, and chuckled. She glanced at North Star, lined eyes dark.

He arched one brow, just barely, and she laid a hand on the arm of the young woman next to her.

Maud.

She was dressed in a dark-brown dress the same color as pine bark, and a notebook lay open before her. No food or drink was set for her. She was only there to take notes. To serve.

The dinner paused. A door opened, and a servant announced something I couldn't make out. All the diners rose to their feet. I leaned left so I could see as far right as possible.

Elise glided into the room, chin up and shoulders back, and

stared straight at North Star till she reached his chair and bowed. He bowed back. Barely.

I looked away, chest tight, and squeezed my eyes shut. She'd be all right. She wasn't joining up with them.

Or she was. Just like Our Queen had let the fall of Nacea go unpunished to save the new nation of Igna, Elise could've been saving Hinter. She liked Riparian enough for it.

Would she do that?

I nudged open the balcony doors a hairbreadth.

"—glory in the name of Erlend." North Star raised his glass to the dozen or so nobles seated at the table. "Let us commit to making our country great once again, to make sure we are never robbed of our place in the world, to ensure our destiny for generations to come. Let's us not allow a queen of no significant blood deny us of our birthrights."

Elise and the rest raised their glasses, mouths moving in agreement.

I sat in the shadows and watched, too twitchy to listen to more.

If Erlend had ever been great, North Star and his nobles had ruined it.

The dinner lasted awhile, long past the time it should've, and the same young lord North Star had spoken to earlier turned his attention—with the urging of Riparian—to Elise.

She was dressed nice but nothing like how she used to look. It was all boring elegance and standard clothes, no cosmetics lining her eyes like sea waves or gold fishnets in her hair. A pale-green veil hid her braids, and she'd no jewelry at all.

Not even the locket with her mother's portrait.

She looked like only a part of herself, and she kept twisting her hands in her lap.

They all rose after dinner, mixing and talking over bite-size fruit tarts and pale wine, and Riparian and Elise spoke in whispered, grin-filled conversations anytime Elise freed herself of the young lord's attentions. Riparian stroked Elise's arm, a proud parent or particularly affectionate kennel mistress.

But when Elise turned her back on Riparian and no one could see her face, her smile dropped. Twisted.

Elise sneered.

And I *lived*.

So this was hope. She finally broke away from Riparian with a brief hug and walked as fast as she could to the balcony doors. I dove into the dark corner just to the side of them, and she pushed open the door, dress fluttering in the wind. A shuddering gasp filled the outside silence. I sunk down into the dark.

I missed her. I was furious.

She'd some bad ideas that needed fixing, starting with Lena, but that seemed underway. She'd come outside for a breather and was about to get an earful.

I took a deep breath, hands shaking, and whispered, "Elise."

She froze. Staring straight ahead into the dark, cold night, she whispered back, "How?"

"You know, spying, doing my job." I shifted a bit, gave her a chance to know where I was, and cleared my throat. "You and Riparian looked cozy."

She opened her mouth, hand fisted at her side, and a voice cut her off.

"Elise, darling, it's much colder here than Hinter."

Riparian—of course—slipped onto the balcony behind Elise and draped a heavy cloak around her shoulders. She straightened out Elise's ruffled veil with hands gentler than I wanted to admit. "You'll catch your death out here."

Elise shivered but smiled. "Thank you. I only want to take it in. This feels like Erlend in a way Hinter never did. I want to feel it. I'll come back in once I get too cold."

"Come in a bit before that," Riparian sad softly. She brushed a piece of fallen snow from Elise's cheek. "We need to talk about how to convince Gaspar you're as loyal as your father."

I stiffened. Elise sighed.

"Of course." She glanced up at the fog-white clouds seeping over the mountains and down to us. "I'm sorry I'm making this difficult. I really did think Erlend was over except for Weylin's lands."

"You were surviving." Riparian grinned, all teeth. "I won't let him hold that against you, and now you know all the little things about Igna I and your father don't because of your place on their court. That will help." She patted Elise's arm. "Come back inside when you're ready."

Elise nodded. "I will. Thank you."

The moment the door shut, Elise whispered, "You were right."

"I know." I tugged the hem of the cloak until she turned to me, hidden in the shadows, and wiped away the tears running down her cheeks. "Lena de Arian is Riparian, and a decade ago, she helped destroy Nacea. A few days ago, she murdered the only person living I could call family, and now, she's doing it all again—all those missing children, all those ears, all those flayed corpses on the border. She had a hand in all of that. She'll kill anyone to keep her power, to keep Erlend in power."

I couldn't ask the question I desperately needed an answer to, but Elise answered it for me.

"I don't know how to stop her." Elise sniffed and ducked. "She showed me her ledgers, her bookkeeping records, and it was the first time I'd seen them. She wants me to be her successor. But those numbers, they can't be right, or if they are, Sal, Triad save us if they're right, because it means she's been responsible for more deaths than you think."

More than a nation?

"Everything was so unsteady as a child, but she was always my constant." Elise took my hand in hers, fingers so tight it hurt. "I'm sorry. I'm so sorry I didn't believe you. She did so many good things, but at such steep prices. She funded my public school in Hinter." Elise shuddered. "She pulled the money from an Alonian-based business. We always had to stick together, Erlend women, but this—"

I pried her fingers from around my hand.

She laughed softly, sadly. "I feel like my entire life is a lie, and, any moment, the ground will fall away."

I wanted her to the know the truth, to be as good as I'd thought she was, but I didn't want anyone else to know this world-shattering pain. It was like having to remake yourself, finding out the one person you trusted was a lie. It was like dying.

"What're you doing here?" I asked. "With her, then?"

"She can't stay in power. Gaspar del Weylin cannot stay in power. My father cannot stay in power." She licked her chapped lips and shook her head. "I don't know what I'm doing, but I am not doing it or anything for Erlend."

I nodded.

"The missing Hinter children her guards took. They're here. I know they're here, and I need to see her ledgers again to find them." Elise tapped her temple. "I have lists of names, and I'm going to find them and save them from Lena. All the times I supported her—when she supported me—I have to make up for."

I nodded again, the cold, sharp pain that had lodged in my ribs after our last meeting melting away. "I know where some of them probably are, and they're mostly fine."

She stared, eyes glazed, and shook her head. "You're sure?"

"Yes."

"Sal," Elise said, voice dropping. "Lena de Arian is a monster."

"I know."

She sniffed. "How'd I not see it? I've known her since I was a child, and tomorrow she's set up a demonstration of how to make shadows."

"I know that too," I said.

"I trusted her." She leaned into the breeze and took a deep breath, flecks of snow catching on her veil like white blossoms on rolling, green hills. The wind stole her tears. "I trusted her more than I trusted my father, more than anyone else in this world, and she has—"

I laid my hand across hers, our gloves keeping us apart. "I know what she's done and what she's doing. You don't have to say it."

It hurt to speak the truth into the world when it was the last thing you wanted to be real.

"I know we have a lot to talk about that can't be said here, but we have to stop this." She turned her whole face to me, and the shadows brought out the bags beneath her eyes and red tinge to the whites of them. Her fingers laced through mine again. "I'll stop this if it's the last thing I do."

I smoothed down the wrinkles of her thin gloves and pressed my thumb into the underside of her wrists, where my ink once stained. "That's why I like you. I'm stealing Riparian's ledgers tonight. You want to help?"

The silence between us stretched—awkward, tense, an unwanted gap—until two voices from the room drifted onto the balcony.

"She's odd," one said.

"Her mother was Alonian."

That whole line of thought was why we were in this mess.

"Can you punch them as well?" Her huff escaped as a puff of white fog. "While you're stealing the ledgers?"

I nodded. "How many times?"

"I'll let you know how many times they utter more Erlend-bloodline nonsense and we'll start from there," she said dryly, scowling. She smoothed down the feathery, little hairs along her hairline and straightened her veil. "Lena's quarters are two stories up with a window facing east. She wakes at dawn every day. No exceptions."

And she was gone, the warm fit of her hand over mine fading. The door didn't shut all the way behind her.

I watched for a while, listened at the crack and turned our conversations over and over in my head. Two young lords watched her too. She called them over once and asked for their help translating the old Erlenian on a tapestry. I grinned.

"That can't be right," she said softly, glancing at them with wide eyes and a pout. Elise was many things, but she was not naive. "The old Erlenian conjugations aren't the same as modern ones."

He blushed. "Right, of course, sorry."

"You make it hard to think," his friend said. "Of course it's not that simple."

"Of course." Elise smiled. No teeth. No tenderness. "My mistake."

I nearly fell off the balcony from rolling my eyes. How'd they turn them not knowing Old Erlenian into her fault?

*Erlends.*

She was running circles round them with barely a dozen words and a glance, and I'd been shocked she lied to me. It wasn't even much of a lie.

It was just too much.

I was still attracted to her—not just her face and the way she moved her hands or how the scar on her lip stretched when she smiled. She knew me, all the good and bad, and being able to see that took knowing in a way others couldn't. We knew loss. We knew sacrifice.

She was still nice. It wasn't bad to think the best of people, to want people to be as good as you thought them. I'd done that with Our Queen and her Left Hand.

I'd been loving a simplification of her, the version of Elise de Farone my mind wanted her to be, not who she was.

That wasn't fair to her. I had to learn to love her fully, wholly, all the parts of her, good and bad and in between, because I definitely wasn't all good. Probably not even half good.

About as bad as these Erlend lords.

But only about.

Riparian's room was all function—a large desk full of locked drawers and covered in a writing pad, two chairs with just enough cushion to be bearable and straight enough to put anyone sitting in them for too long on edge, and a wall of carefully hung maps crisscrossed by green and blue threads. A series of brown threads, supply lines, hugged the river ways. No ledgers or papers in sight.

Most folks kept important things in safes or secret drawers, and Riparian was most people. The locks were good quality though, and she'd a flint-steel strike ready to light the whole blasted thing on fire if I hit the wrong lock pin. Nine pins, a keyhole too thin and long for most picks, and a soft ring of gold around the lock face. This was a dal Russo, handmade by the most popular locksmith in Igna. Figured.

I'd not pick this without help, but she had to keep the key on her. Wasn't like they blended in with normal keys. I placed everything back as it had been and peeked into the room connected to this one, which contained a large bed and a wardrobe blocked by a locked traveling chest. She must keep the key on her.

I clucked my tongue against my teeth—she did keep it on her and I'd thought it pretty, not purposeful.

The study door clicked, unlocking. I darted forward, left the bedroom door open just enough for me to see, and crept under the large wardrobe. Dust puffed up around me. I held my breath.

Don't let her walk in here. She was too clever to not notice the cloud.

"I need Hinter's updated numbers," Riparian said, voice the rough, low tone of travelers.

Trailed by Maud carrying a tray of two teacups and one slice of a large cream tart, Riparian led a nervous-faced Elise into her study, and North Star followed a little ways behind them, speaking softly with the guard at his side. Elise and Riparian waited for him to quiet and nod before sitting down. The guard ran off.

"I've memorized them." Elise sat in one of the chairs before Riparian's desk, well outside of my sliver of view, and Riparian sat at her desk. "How would you like them?"

"Relay them when I ask. Just like old times," Riparian said, smiling. "Gaspar, do you want to stay for them, or will my morning report suffice?"

"My curiosity can wait." His feet stopped near Elise's chair, the door blocking both their bodies. "I wanted to make sure our dear Elise was aware of her new responsibilities?"

"I believe so." Elise shifted, the familiar sound of her breath cut off by the movement.

Riparian leaned back in her chair, tea cup covering her

mouth. "It's only that with you living with them for so long, we didn't expect your loyalties to change so swiftly."

"They didn't." Elise's voice went up. She must've tilted her head to the side. Played naive. "You told my father to fit in, so we fit in."

"You were unaware of that plan," Riparian said quickly. "Though we don't fault you for your work in Igna, but we will need everything you know tomorrow morning."

Elise grinned, the soft, little look she used when playing at gentle charm. "Of course. Do you want me to write it down beforehand or only specific parts? Some of what I know is quite number and map heavy."

North Star patted the back of her chair. "You are in excellent hands."

I held back a groan at Riparian's slim smile. Excellent hands to strangle Elise. She might've been a good liar—and she might've been good at lying by omission—but Riparian wouldn't believe the Triad was being truthful if they spoke to her. She assumed the world lied as much as her.

"A rare specimen of her sex, possessing both logic and steadfastness," North Star said. "She is an excellent mentor, and I look forward to our upcoming conversations."

I winced. Elise recrossed her feet.

Riparian's only tell was the tightening of her jaw. "You're too kind, Gaspar."

Her tone didn't even change. How long had she been responding to backhanded compliments?

Elise's face never changed. "I look forward to what she can teach me."

Riparian watched him leave, her face dropping soon as the door shut. "I know you, Elise, and something is wrong. What is it?"

I edged forward to see better.

Elise leaned forward in her chair, calm and steady under Riparian's gaze. "The rangers took three Hinter children north. I just want to know what happened to them? I had been teaching two of them mathematics."

"Children?" Riparian pulled back. "Three children? That's all?"

"Yes." Elise stiffened. "They're from Hinter. I'm responsible for their well-being."

Her voice hitched.

"Lady de Farone." Maud bowed near Elise's shoulder and offered her a fresh slice of lemon for her inky hands.

Elise accepted it. "Thank you."

And in the moment when Maud paused to stand and blocked Elise from Riparian's sight, Elise let her expression fall into a weary-lined, watery-eyed scowl. She inhaled and shook the look from her face before Maud moved. Maud must've seen but she didn't so much as blink.

Lady bless her, but she was playing a dangerous game. Elise still had important things to do. People to save. Books to write. Thieves to stare down. She couldn't die putting herself in danger like this.

Elise balled a hand in her skirt. "Does he always talk to you like that?"

I was a fool for thinking her deathly honest—this was better. She knew how to play the game. She'd tear herself down to save her own, and I should've respected that.

LINSEY MILLER

Still, while some of what she said was rude, I was a killer.

I guess neither of us was perfect.

"A small price to pay, but if any of them ever approach you, come to me." She leaned across her desk and took Elise's hand. "It's a small price to pay, their disregard, for what our positions allow us to do for our people."

"All of our people?" Elise asked softly.

Riparian's lips pursed. "It would be best if you left your 'honorable' notions about gender in Igna. Marianna da Ignasi is failing for a reason, and her inability to keep order is part of that."

Least Moira was still going to let me kill Riparian. Course, Elise might get their first. She'd hooked her feet around the chair legs and nearly ripped a hole in her dress from grasping it so tight.

After that, Elise didn't speak except to relay a handful of numbers, settling for tightly wound silence that snapped every time Riparian so much as wrote a new number in her ledger.

And before Elise left for the night, after Riparian had tucked her ledger and key away, Riparian said, "I know it is hard stomach loss and young love, but your Honorable Opal is dead, and you cannot cling to him here."

"Don't worry." Elise turned and smiled. "They wouldn't want me to anyway."

I buried my face in my hands. Riparian let out a breathy sound somewhere between laugh and sob, and she shook her head.

"There's a guard outside. She'll escort you to your quarters next door and will protect you all night. If I were you," Riparian said, "I would use tonight to think about your place here, darling, and what losing it means."

300

CHAPTER
# FORTY-TWO

R iparian didn't take long to get in bed. She left two candles
burning, one on each side of the study, and bathed alone,
no maid to help her. She checked beneath the bed and locked
her bedroom door before crawling beneath her quilts and pulling
a book from beneath her pillows. I let her read and watched till
she fell asleep. She cried too, but I looked away for that.

The necklace with the dal Russo key never left her body.

I crept out from under the wardrobe. Riparian's steady
breathing didn't change, scattering her hair across her face with
each exhale. She slept on her side, and with her back to me, I
used a thin wire from my pack to snake the necklace out of her
nightgown and unhook the clasp. It took ages to tease the key
from the chain without waking her. My legs ached from crouching so long.

But it worked.

Key in hand, I returned to her study. Three shadows flickered at my feet and the knowledge they were real again, in the

depths of the earth beneath my feet, shuddered up my arms until I had to take a moment to breathe before unlocking the drawer. No fire flared when I finally got it open.

Three ledgers full of information sat atop a lockbox of old jewelry, and in the very back sat a bundle of old letters, each addressed to Lena from Elise. The first one was eight years old, in a child's shaky script. I tucked the bundle back into the drawer.

I'd not be able to take the ledgers to Moira and return them before Riparian woke up to miss them, but I couldn't copy the ledgers—even if I followed her numbers perfectly, it'd take ages and she'd notice the missing paper.

Elise.

I tucked the ledgers under my jacket and put everything else back in place. The door to the hallway rattled, and I froze. The handle turned, and I dashed for it, the handle slipping through my fingers.

The door opened. One of the guards, a young man with straggly, brown hair and the itchings of a first-time beard along his jaw, stuck his head through the crack. I froze.

"I'm sorry," Maud's voice echoed down the hallway. "Could you help me? I'm quite lost."

The guard pulled away without seeing me.

She kept him talking long enough for me to shut the door and work my way over to Elise's window on the outside of the tower. Adella's climbing knives kept me from falling from the tower wall, my fingers shaking too much to keep me steady. I leaned my forehead against Elise's window before knocking.

I wasn't looking forward to any conversations Elise and I would have, but I still wanted them.

RUIN OF STARS

The window creaked.

"Sal?" Elise's soft tone eased the itching at the back of my neck, racing up my arms and burrowing in my skin. A shadow in me. "Sal? What are you doing?"

"I need you." I lifted my head. "I need your help."

She opened the window and tugged me inside. "What's happened?"

She agreed to copy the ledgers before I'd finished asking, and I let her have them, choosing to collapse in the corner of her quarters instead. She'd been in bed but not asleep. Her braids were wrapped in a plain silk scarf, and a robe covered her night gown. She curled her bare toes up against the cold.

"I'm sorry I didn't believe you about Riparian," she said softly after a long silence had passed and my breathing was under control. "And that I never told you I'd been sent to be robbed and pick which thieves got posters."

"It's all right." I rummaged around her traveling trunk for a pair of socks and tossed them to her. "I mean, it's not, but so far as happenings go, I get it. I'm still bouncing back and forth on Our Queen."

Elise paused, one sock half-on, and then thought better of asking for an explanation. There was no innocence left in us and no innocent intentions left between us. How could I fault her for something as simple as lying?

What I'd learned since then made her lies understandable.

"Elise," I said softly. "Erlend didn't destroy Nacea. Not totally."

She turned her face to me. "What?"

"They're here. North Star's using them." I leaned in close to her, the weight of everything that had happened, hadn't happen,

would happen, closing in on me, and I closed my eyes. "We can use runes."

"Runes?" She tapped her pen against the ink pot, its bone handle clattering, and took a deep breath. "There are Naceans here, and they can use magic?" She pulled back, mouth open. "Is that where those children went? They were Nacean? They're using you to make shadows?"

So clever. So concerned.

"Magic wasn't banished." I nodded, swallowed, and opened my eyes. If I slept now, would the world still be here when I woke? "Folks who never used magic and whose parents never used magic can still use it, and Weylin's making them create new shadows."

She took off here spectacles and covered her eyes. "That's worse. That's so much worse than I imagined."

"The deal is if any of the Naceans in Lynd try to move against him, he's got the rest of Nacea settled across Erlend in dozens of different homesteads and towns, and he'll kill them all as punishment. I need to know where they are so we can send shadows, new ones, different from the ones we knew, to prevent rangers from killing the other Naceans," I said. "There's too much to explain now, but those kids you're missing are probably in the laboratories. Erlend only wants the ones who can do magic or be turned into shadows." I slid from the sill and crossed to her, leaning against her desk so we could stare across it at each other. "Gaspar del Weylin, Lena de Arian, and your father all knew this. They've been funneling kids up here to test for magic. Remember the ears? Magic isn't gone, folks and families who used it just can't anymore, but Nacean kids, kids who grew up away from it, unexposed to it, they can, and magic eats its medium. That's what happened to the children and their ears."

She brought the three fingers of the Triad to her lips and muttered a prayer, chest heaving. "I had wondered how they picked, why only a few were missing. How many are dead do you think?"

I took her free hand in mine and muttered, "Too many."

"It always is." She started copying the ledgers again, marking places she thought might be kids from Nacea or Hinter kids she knew. "A decade later, and we're still mired in memories of grief."

Mired.

Good word for it. I always thought I was free, and then it sucked me back down.

"Sometimes I dream of running—barefoot and gasping, skin full of thorns—and I wake up with burning legs like it was all real, like I never escaped the shadows and they're still there, just out of sight. Still chasing me. And sometimes I don't dream at all," I said. "Grief's like that. Sometimes I'm still running with its claws in my back and my future nothing but endless night. Other days, I forget I was ever running at all."

And these kids were going to be stuck in this mire too.

Elise kept writing, hand steady and words perfectly inked. "I wake up hiding, crouched inside wardrobes and closets and chests. Just like back then. I never remember those dreams. Perhaps it's best."

She pushed her glasses up and smeared ink along her nose, covering the dark freckles and trailing a few drops along her chin. I took her hands and wiped them clean with my sleeves, dragging the cloth along each finger until the wrinkles of her palms were clean. She shuddered.

"It was Lena who told me it was all right to love girls. I had to be told it was. In Erlend, I didn't grow up knowing that. I was young when I went to live in Willowknot, but I still remembered my father's words, all the things he ever said about men and women," Elise said softly.

It wasn't a slight from Elise. Winter would never have acknowledged the existence of people like me just like he would never acknowledge his own daughter properly.

"What happened?"

"She helped me tell my father I liked girls. She said it was natural, that Erlend girls bonded in a way boys and girls never could, that our relationships were forged in fire." Elise laughed, barely, tears dripping into the ink on her chin, but she never stopped writing. Her penmanship became a frantic scrawl. "I should've caught on then that she meant Erlend women were better than other women. That she held the same ideas as my father but twisted to serve her. She was friends with my mother. I just wanted some part of my family to not be terrible."

"Lady knows we've not got the words for it all solidified yet, but we need them. Erlend keeps shoving us into roles—always one or the other." I leaned against her desk, head in my hands. "Everyone always defines me. I want to own myself. I should own myself. What gives anyone the right to tell me how I feel or who I am? Why's it only infallible when it's me? Why does every priest and judge rule that violating a person's self is sacrosanct and monstrous when it's everyone but me? I know myself. I get to say who I am, and you get to say who you are.

That's the world we have to help make—one where everyone is safe."

I was Sal, fluid and sure, and that was my Lady-given right—to exist as myself. To let others exist as their selves.

"I'm sorry about how things went when we talked in Hinter. I should've stayed to talk with you, instead of leaving the way I did." I took her hand in mine and bowed, kissing her hand. Knuckles. Fingertips.

She hooked one finger beneath my chin and pulled me forward. "Take your filthy boots and coat off before you get in my clean bed."

I felt the blush in my cheeks and breathed before asking, "Can I stay in here with you?"

"What?" Elise blinked at me, mind taking a moment to catch up with her moving mouth. She scooted her chair to the left and gestured to her empty right. "Sure. Pull up a chair."

I grabbed one of the wooden chairs before her desk and set it beside her, stretching out my legs under her desk and leaning on my left arm. Elise crossed her legs, hooking her left foot under mine. I sighed, the rough wool of her sock against my calf scratchy and comforting. Her breathing settled, and I twisted my chair so I could drape my legs across her lap. Elise laid her left hand against my thigh.

"Go to sleep," she whispered, thumb moving in circles. "I'll wake you so you have plenty of time to escape."

I closed my eyes and leaned back.

I didn't dream of running.

# CHAPTER
## FORTY-THREE

E lise woke me up with a hand on my calf and the singsong
call of my name on her tired lips. I thanked her, too much
probably, but she'd dark circles beneath each eye and ink on her
nose again, and the ache beneath my skin to take her face in my
hands and let her rest safe with me was too great for anything
else. She blushed, cheeks ruddy beneath her freckles and ink. I
bowed over her hand.

"Thank you, my lady."

"You're welcome." She caught my hand. "Question—was
that your servant with Lena last night?"

I nodded. "Riparian—Lena—took a liking to her back in
Willowknot, and I've been getting information from her since."

"Will you thank her for me?" Elise smiled. "She had perfect
timing. I was about to break."

"I'll tell her. Or you can," I said. "She's nice. Like you."

Then I told Elise to be wary, and she laughed softly as I left.
The day moved on, the world with it.

I returned the ledgers and the key, and jumped at every shadow creeping across the walls in the pale morning light. Adella waited at the very bottom of the tower. She unknotted the rope when my cold hands failed.

"I've been pacing the guards every round, hoping you'd show up." She worked in silhouette, the white expanse of Lynd blinding in the sun only just peeking over the horizon. "Just wind it up and let's go."

She led me around the city, dropping all the suspicious bits and picking up a mostly fresh rabbit carcass from a hollow tree off the guards' path, and we reentered the city with my Opal masks still hidden against my back. The knives, at least, hunters carried. I made it back to the street for Moira just as dawn began.

Adella stayed with me, and the two of us spent most of the new light avoiding the extra guards patrolling the streets above Moira's laboratories. No wonder, even with magic and even if the threat of North Star killing a whole town of Naceans wasn't hanging over her head, Moira wouldn't escape.

"You brought a friend." Moira flinched under Adella's gaze even though she was doing her best not to stare at the living runes. "Why?"

"This is Adella." I handed Moira the bag with the copies of the ledgers in it. "We're going to need her."

Moira's nostril's flared and she narrowed her eyes at Adella's ear. "Fine. She stays in my room. I need to make sure her soul is still firmly rooted to her bones."

"So we're clear," Adella whispered to me as we walked, "I would not have come with you if I'd known this was part of the deal."

I opened my mouth to agree and shook my head. I would have come. I would have.

I'd killed so many people. What was the point if I let Erlend kill even more?

We shuffled back down the tunnel, stopping once as a single guard went past, and Moira let me collapse on the thin mat in the corner of her laboratory. The rustle of the pages lulled me to sleep, but Moira's high-pitched hums of interest snapped me back out of it. She sounded nothing like Elise.

"Only coordinates," she muttered, "but I don't need names. I can work with this."

Adella, perched on a stool and wide eyes following Moira's fingers as they moved down each page, leaned her elbows on the table and rested her chin on her knuckles. Her thumb skimmed her lips. "You're been here this whole time? Learning magic and double-crossing Weylin?"

I covered my face with an arm. Fair certain watching a Nacean Star getting flirted with was against the rules. Of something. Surely.

I peeked.

"In short, yes." Moira glanced up, eyebrows coming together in an uneven line. "Who are you again?"

"Adella, Carnival of Cheats acrobat and knife thrower." She stuck out her free hand. "If you can use magic, why'd he not have you all fight for him or try to take us out?"

"He tried that when I was a child. It backfired. Only thing left of the people he sent out was the burned-on rune they were working with. Magic is fickle. None of us had ever trained in it and the runes we use are Nacean. The Erlend rules don't apply."

Moira chuckled but took Adella's hand. "I've never met anyone from a carnival."

"I worked at the Carnival of Cheats. The carnival." Adella's eye twitched. "The best one."

Too snippy. I needed them getting along. "Bet Weylin's scared." I stretched, arms and legs too sore for such an early morning, and sniffed. "The more you learn from making shadows, the more power you have over him. The shadows he controlled he could outrun and blame on Our Queen. But now the only thing keeping him safe is your fear for the rest of Nacea."

Moira said. "He wants our shadows in the next five days, and I've no intention of handing them over."

My tired mind cleared. "Did you talk to Dimas?"

She waved toward a cot in the corner. "Yes, but when we were done, he opted for a tonic to help him sleep. I think it was for the best."

Probably was.

"His family—"

"His mother is one of my shadows." Moira paused, glancing up from the ledger. "What's the word in Alonian?"

Dimas's mother? I shuddered, the memory of Namrata cold in my chest. "What word you want?"

The words came out as a raspy whisper.

She turned to Adella. "Do you speak Nacean?"

"No," Adella said. "Why?"

"Wasn't sure." Moira went back to the ledger. "I didn't want to be rude and swap if you didn't." She made a note. "Volunteer. Gaila was the second to volunteer," she muttered in Nacean. "He won't wake for some time, but I can't imagine he'll be over the knowledge till he sees his sister."

"Dimas's mother volunteered to be a shadow," I said to Adella in Alonian. It was easier, and now that they'd gotten me thinking about words, a whole host of ones I normally knew in Erlenian were stuck in the back of my throat and out of reach. We were all too tired to be plotting like this.

I was nodding off a bit later when the door creaked open and Maud poked her head in. She sighed when she saw me.

"You weren't in the other building, and I'm supposed to be checking on Dimas." She looked around, wondering if I'd let him out, and froze when she saw Moira.

I leapt to my feet and stumbled. "Maud de Pavo, this is Moira Namrata, the Last Star of Nacea."

Her mouth opened, closed, and she settled on nodding. "Should I bow?"

"Yes," I said as Moira snorted and muttered, "No."

"You and Dimas both bowed to me." Moira shook her head and stared at me. "Why?"

"You're one of the Lady's stars. You're important." I didn't look at her. I couldn't. "It's what you do for important people."

She let out a deep breath through her nose. "You don't have to bow to me. Stars are meant to protect, to be a light of hope. You don't owe us anything." She laughed, shoulders slumping, and wiped her nose. "You certainly don't owe me anything."

Maud nodded to Moira. "It's a pleasure to meet you then."

"And you," Moira said. "Dimas mentioned you, and I assumed the mistake he kept talking about was Adella."

"I could do without that nickname." Adella scowled.

"How is he?" Maud sat at the table with us, gaze sweeping over the cot in the back, and Moira shook her head.

"He's too stressed, using too much magic without enough practice." Moira sighed. "I hate bearing bad news, but at least only half of it was bad."

"Will we need him tonight?" I asked.

North Star's show of power had to be his last night on this earth alive.

"I will. I can't hold all of the souls on this earth at once, and it will be a start to repaying his debt." Moira traced one of the nine leaves—each one for a different tree, each one veined with white—inked onto her wrist. "I can only hold five at once. He will have to bind the other four."

"You mean control them?" I shuddered. No part of me trusted that.

"No, I mean bind." She frowned. "They're not here all the time. Not like the shadows Erlend made. I call their souls back from death when I need to, and their souls resettle into what's left of their bodies. It's easier on them. Unlike the old ones, they aren't stuck between two worlds. They're only traveling." She closed the ledger and laced her fingers together. "What I really need is the estate guards out of the way. The ones not at the square."

"Poison them," I said. It was the easiest way to take out many at once. "Knock them out for the night or something. Most of them eat and drink the same things unless Erlend does it differently."

"You say it so simply." Moira blinked at me, owlish eyes bright in the dark. "As if I need only acquire the poison and a way to administer it, not also the will to do it."

"You live beneath a greenhouse and brought the shadows back to life." I jerked my head to Dimas. "He blew up a wall without so much as breathing."

Dimas, still sleeping, said nothing. Moira picked at her scabbed-over arms.

"I will not kill them simply for being on guard. People change. Monsters don't. They're people doing their best in the world they occupy. Gaspar del Weylin has made me do terrible things, but he will not force my hand on this." She fixed me with a stare so strong it rattled in my teeth like skimming a metal spoon. My bones shivered. "No one else dies if we can help it. Nacea will not free itself of Weylin's reign to only to reinstate its nationalistic violence."

"I didn't say kill them. I thought maybe you could magic them to sleep for the night."

She shook her head. "People respond differently to different kinds of magic. Even if I had that much control, I still wouldn't know how much to impart or to who regardless. I could kill all of them or one of them."

"Use tartar then." Rath and I had taken it a few times ourselves for a good distraction, and most folks were kindhearted enough to help us to a drink or light lunch after we vomited. "The one physicians use to make folks vomit. And lots of people get sick if they see someone else get sick, and if they've got more than a handful of guards losing supper, they'll be distracted."

"I could find out where they keep their canteens." Maud shrugged. "They all carry the same type, and I bet they fill them at the start of every shift. That's what ours did."

If only we'd thought of this days ago and had swapped all their canteens out for antimony cups.

"Servants will be distracted too," I said, "dealing with so much sick."

Maud nodded. "Disgusting but true."

"That's the other thing." Moira leaned toward me, gaze darting to Adella. "I don't want the servants or soldiers there—I don't know which ones can be trusted yet and don't want to fight them if they would turn over easily—but I want the people of Lynd there. A good number of them. I want to show them the monster who abused their trust. I want him to confess. I want them to support his execution."

Oh.

I liked that.

Let them see the truth of him.

Adella smiled a crooked little half smile more hunger than happiness. "Are you asking me to put on a show so that Erlend can watch their king die?"

"No?" Moira paused, face wrinkling as she tried to figure out what to say. She was only nineteen at most and already had a deep worry line between her black brows. "Could you?"

"Because if so I love it," Adella said quickly. "I would love to put on a show for you before we die painful, traitor execution deaths."

Maud glanced at me. I shook my head.

"Hold that thought until after we successfully murder the king, yes?" Moira nodded, the corners of her mouth barely tilting up. "Traditionally, citizens must be present for all shows of military advancement in order to make sure they know what their king is capable of, but Weylin has made sure to summon only a select, loyal few. We are inviting more. Back before we knew all the new rules to magic, Weylin did not bother to find Nacean children. He took Erlend citizens under the promise of physician treatment, and we're going to invite their families."

"Finally an Erlend tradition that isn't garbage," I muttered.

"The problems with Erlend aren't their traditions. Tradition is not counter to progress," Moira said. "Unfortunately, they have conflated their traditions with violence and erasure." She glared at me, shaking her head. "Weylin has put this show off until midnight, so he will sleep beforehand, as will most others. I need you to kidnap him while he sleeps. We will start the show once everyone is there and we have him."

"I'll get him." I pulled my pack into my lap and lifted my Opal mask to my face. "Which one do you think is scarier? This or the midnight one?"

"Your actual face," Maud said without so much as blinking. "I can handle the guards. We can do that earlier, so they have time to drink, and after that, I'll gather up servants to take care of it. They'll think it's a stomach sickness before anything else. You get Weylin while that's happening, before they have a chance to warn him."

Maud was turning into a strategist.

I loved it.

"Can you find Elise de Farone?" I pinched the ring on my finger to try and keep the blush at bay. "Maybe she can keep the nobles busy."

"Yes, I can find your lady." She smirked, nose crinkling. "What after all of that though?"

"Come to the square once you're done." Moira held up her hands. The runes slithered into place and settled. "I've been planning this for a very, very long time, and Gaspar del Weylin has been an excellent teacher on how to show off your power and how to make people believe you. Did you know Erlend thinks torture reveals only the truest of confessions?"

"So it's settled." I held out my hand to her. "Gaspar del Weylin—North Star and liar king of Erlend—dies tonight."

## CHAPTER
# FORTY-FOUR

I slept in Moira's laboratory until that evening. Maud was searching out Elise and the canteens, and I'd be no use until the cover of night. We couldn't plant the poison too early.

They had to be dealing with it during the show.

Maud returned a while after dusk with a servant's uniform in hand.

"It might not fit, but I wanted to have one just in case." She tossed it onto the table and pulled a silver canteen out of her pocket. "They all carry one to drink on shift, and they pick them up from the kitchens right before. It's crowded, but they leave them out to dry on a rack. I can just walk by and drop them in."

"Good. That'll make it easier on you." I pulled on my gloves—no use making myself sick—and checked myself over. Mask, knives at my belt and in the sheaths on my ankle, and a set of lock picks. I'd not need rope or anything else. "With any luck, they'll think it's the pump first and recall the guards.

That'll take a whole third of them out of commission without any murder."

Moira set a small packet of white balls before Maud. "One per person. Only one. And be careful—if you jostle them, they'll all go back to being one handful of powder instead of balls."

I pulled out one of the little balls. Soft. Easy to palm but easier to crush. "Maud, watch this."

I laid one in my palm and closed my fist over it, catching the ball with my first and second finger. I opened my palm. The ball, tucked gently in the little divot between the bases of my fingers, was out of sight. Maud nodded.

"Do it ten times." I handed the ball to her. She couldn't wear gloves indoors without looking suspicious.

She got it on her fifth try and kept getting it right after that.

"A shadow will trail you." Moira, nose deep in the copies of Riparian's ledger, didn't look up. I'd been sure she wasn't paying attention any more. "If anything happens, it will help. Don't be scared."

Maud smiled. Close-mouthed and tense. "Great."

I rounded on Moira soon as Maud left.

Moira waved me off. "There won't be one with you. Don't worry."

"Thank you." I nodded to her, resisting the urge to bow as Ruby would've made me, and pulled up my hood. "See you in the square."

I retraced my steps up to the mountain path, through the window of Elise's room, and into the garden courtyard where I'd spied on supper the night before. Elise was there with a whole herd of young Erlend nobles dressed to impress in muted, militaristic outfits of pine green and mountain-clay brown, and she had cornered a young Erlend lord against a wall while his friends all watched. Elise gestured wildly, upset. Or at least pretending to be upset. He cowered.

Good look for him.

I cracked open the window.

"—harmless comment."

"You don't get to decide that." Elise spun away from him and pinched her nose as though she were holding back tears. "So many of our subjects have Alonian heritage now. You are more than happy to accept the taxes of your Alonian-born citizens, but you're not happy to offer them the same protections? You cannot see the issue with that? How will you decide who is Erlend enough? How do you know who's Alonian?"

"Again." The young lord raised his hands in defeat, answering none of her questions. "It was only a comment. I meant nothing by it."

A few more nobles and a handful of servants slipped inside to watch.

I laughed.

"A pity, you said the other night, that I was half Alonian." She turned away from him, gaze falling on the windowpane, opened so I could hear, and smiled. "I want you to understand very clearly that I am not a balance of two opposing sides. I am a person forced to balance your expectations—how Erlend, how Alonian, how those expectations make me neither and both and completely separate all at once. I know who I am and it's not my fault if that threatens you. I am here to make Erlend a better place. All of Erlend. Even you."

And that wasn't even a lie.

My cue to leave. She was nodding me to go while they were distracted.

"Do you understand me?" she asked softly. "Or should I say it in Alonian since you think the language is better at sounding angry? I would say it in old Erlenian, but you wouldn't understand."

Righteous. Fury.

And some of the other nobles were nodding, not all of them and not a lot, but enough to keep Elise safe. There had to be others—like me, like Elise, like Nicolas and Emerald—who Erlend had hurt. They'd be the first ones to believe Riparian, Winter, and North Star were bad. They'd see the problems.

They'd believe Moira tonight.

They ushered her outside to the balcony I was on, and I darted behind the door. The door shut. Elise laughed.

"I think I'm distracting them fairly well." She looked down at me, smiling softly but cheeks still dimpling.

I glanced back into the room in time to catch one of the servants leaving in a rush. "You and Maud really don't need me, do you?"

"Well, no," she said, stepping into the shadow behind the door and taking my hand. "But I know that I want you."

"Do you?" I held back a shiver that settled low at the base of my spine. "I'm glad."

She squeezed my hand. "Don't die. Tonight or any night."

"I can't refuse an order from a lady of the court." I wrapped my arms around her shoulders and pressed my forehead to hers. "Don't you die either."

"Sal?" Her nose brushed mine. "May I kiss you?"

Life was too short. Love to brief. Fickle.

I nodded.

She pressed her lips to mine—hot, bitter like too-long-steeped tea, and cracked by the winter wind—and pulled away. I followed.

"I'll be fine. What trouble could I get into?" She hugged me tight and let me go, gesturing to the room behind her. Riparian, wearing the closest things to trousers I'd ever seen her in, had entered the room. "She wants to talk to me about navigating Weylin's court as a woman."

Her eyes rolled up and she sighed.

Such strict rules on how to appear feminine and masculine. How to be whoever you were.

I grinned. "I'll see you after."

"I know who's on your list, Sal," she said as she left. "I've made my peace with that, but remember—death isn't the end result of justice."

"People will know." I wasn't killing them to kill them. Not anymore. They'd debts to pay to Nacea and Igna, and I was collecting. "It's an execution waiting for them, not assassination."

"Still, be wary."

The door shut. The cold returned.

"No more," I whispered to the dark above Lynd. "No more kids growing up in Erlend and thinking they're wrong. No more Erlend ideas seeping down south and ruining that safe haven too."

Weylin had used ill and injured folks as readily as he'd used Naceans. Anyone outside of his narrow Erlend view wasn't worth anything to him, and he'd no right to weigh worths. Our lives weren't defined by how useful we were to him.

Elise looped her arm through Riparian's and left under the stares of every person in the room.

*North Star. Riparian. Winter.*

*Weylin. Arian. Farone.*

Soon, only two to go.

## CHAPTER
# FORTY-FIVE

T here were no servants in the halls and only two guards crossed my path. They patrolled the hall near North Star's room in rounds, and I timed my way around them. There was plenty of time for me to pick the three tumbler locks on his door, top to bottom. That was always the order, and tumbler locks required so little skill after a while. It was shocking how trusting people were of buildings to keep out danger.

An uneasy, trembling fear awoke within me the moment my foot crossed the threshold. I shoved it away, feet sliding over the stones, and the prickling in the back of my mind snapped. I glanced down.

A trio of runes burned with power beneath me.

*"It's about willpower," Moira had muttered to Adella and I during one of the only quiet moments in her lab. Adella had asked how magic worked. "It takes effort to walk, to not fall, to talk. You can feel it, can't you, moving over you like wind? It wants to move. It wants to be used. Like a river dammed must break free, magic stifled*

*seeks to be used. You'll feel it now I've introduced you. You have to know exactly what you want, or the runes will eat you alive. Your want has to be absolute."*

So this was magic.

"Lady take you," I whispered and stepped over it.

The runes dulled and died.

I didn't like it, not the shuddering tiredness it left in me or the way it urged me to want more, to do more. No wonder North Star loved it.

I could use magic, but I wouldn't. Not to fight him.

He would take no more of Nacea from me.

North Star's quarters weren't as lush as I'd expected. He'd plenty of fur rugs, the bear heads glaring at me in the dark. Old swords and spears and tapestries hung from the walls, and even the lantern holders hanging from the ceiling were gilded antlers and molded-together helmets from Alonian uniforms. I shuddered and pulled my lock picks free. The double doors to his bedroom had three tumblers too, each sporting a separate key by the looks of them. I knelt before the door.

Maybe, if North Star's ancestor had just accepted their loss of leadership ages ago, if North Star hadn't sunk his teeth in and let those old ideas fester, we'd have all been different. But he'd split me and all the other kids.

I was torn—part of me thinking of the life Sallot Leon might've lived had shadows never crossed the land. The Sal that grew up with parents and siblings, neighbors and Nacean culture so ingrained I knew I was Nacean no matter how far I wandered and didn't wake up asking who I was. The Sal who knew all the folks too dead to teach me things I could never learn now, my family's history, my mother's dreams, my father's favorite memories. I'd been robbed of so many things but none so cruel as the what-could-have-been part of me.

The part that didn't wake up screaming or scratch at raw skin just to know I felt something. The part of me that couldn't pick three locks in the time it took to a normal person to use the key.

The part of me that didn't know the aching *want* of North Star's thieving blood on my hands.

There wasn't anything wrong with it, one foot in two worlds, but I wanted both, and he'd no right to deny me myself.

"I am as I am," I whispered. "I know who I am."

And North Star would know me too.

I pushed open the doors and stepped inside.

Winter—Elise's father, Nevierno del Farone—sat in a chair across from the large desk. He was in his old uniform, a green-and-gold set fitted to look good, not move well, and his sword was at his side. North Star wasn't here.

He knew.

"Nice of you to show up here." I shut the doors behind me and locked them. "That window's a lot higher than the one you pushed me out of."

North Star knew we were coming for him tonight, and he'd left Winter in his place. Just like Nacea.

He was throwing Nevierno del Farone at me in hopes he could escape.

Had to do this fast.

The room was large. Lantern light flickered in every corner of the room, glinting off saw-toothed hilts and time-worn swords mounted to the walls. A set of three shields hung behind North

Star's desk, the sigils scratched away by the civil war, and Winter leapt to his feet. His boots creaked against the hard stone floors, and he unsheathed his short sword. I pulled out two knives.

"You're supposed to be dead." His lip pulled back in a sneer. He'd the same eyes as Elise. "Twice over according to Lena."

I pulled the opal mask from my belt and fastened it to my face. "Please, Winter, you killed me in Nacea ten years ago. I can't die by your hands ever again."

I couldn't bring Moira North Star, but I could give her the Erlend Winter. I could save this mess of a plan.

I lunged. Winter stepped back, sword slicing up. It ripped through the air at my left, tip nicking the lantern hanging above us, and the light bounced around the room. Shadows flickered across his face and light burned in my eyes. I blinked.

He flung a coat over my head. I stumbled back, caught in the cloth and cursing. A pair of arms grabbed my middle and rammed me into the wall. Metal hooks and wooden frames cracked beneath my back. A fist slammed into my stomach. I gagged.

"I would throw you out the window," he said, ripping the coat from me and pinning me to the wall with a forearm to the throat, "but I thinking I've earned watching the life leave your eyes, don't you?"

I tried to swallow, buy time for my aching head, and his muscles tensed. My throat closed.

He dropped me, hauled back, and punched me straight in the nose.

I came to a second later, facedown on the floor. Blood pooled in the back of my throat and dripped out my nose. I rose to my knees.

If Winter was here and North Star knew Nacea was coming for him, Riparian knew.

And Riparian had Elise. I had to end this fast.

"Kill me then." He'd stab me in the gut, surely. A slow death. A painful death, and I spread my arms wide to give him a clear shot. "See what Elise thinks of you then."

He jabbed his sword toward my stomach. I lurched right, catching it in my shirt, and the blade skimmed over the leather vest beneath. I twisted.

The flat side of his blade smacked into my ribs. The hilt flew out of his hands. He reached for another weapon.

I raised my leg and kicked him in the chest, heel connecting with the soft squish of flesh right beneath his ribs. He doubled over. I kicked him again, heel to temple.

Wasn't a safe hit, but I wasn't looking to live through tonight.

He fell to his knees. I sniffed and spat, all the blood he'd stolen from me splattered between us. I yanked an extra knife from the sheath in my boot and pressed the point into the thick muscle of his shoulder, right where his neck met his arm. He hissed, shuddered. I pushed harder.

"Move and I'll pull this out," I said. "You'll bleed to death before you get out that door."

"Mercy, please." He grasped at his impaled shoulder. "Please, Elise would—"

"She'd hate you dragging her name through the list of wrongs you've committed. She knows you're on my list, Winter. She knows all about you." I ripped the knife from his shoulder and waited for his screams to stop. "And don't you remember?"

He groaned.

"Mercy's dead," I whispered. "Thrown from a window into the Caracol. You killed mercy, but vengeance remains."

He'd stolen everything—my family, my language, my innocence.

And I couldn't kill him. Not yet.

"An Erlend winter is nothing. Beware me."

I let go of the knife and slammed my fist into his head hard enough to knock him out for a few breaths at least. I didn't have the strength to carry him, but with no one around, how would I get him out?

And how would I get to Elise?

I dropped him on the floor, grabbed my knives, ran to the door—ears ringing with the ache of his hits—and peeked outside. Maud stared back at me.

"You're much shorter than everyone here," she said, shoving a laundry cart through the door. "I figured you would need help."

"Yes, I do." I grasped her shoulders. Froze. "Have you seen Lady de Arian?"

Her eyebrows bunched together. She nodded. "In Lady de Farone's room. I brought them tea."

"Tie him up," I said, darting around Maud and down the hall. "We've been found out. She knows."

Riparian knew.

She and North Star had set Winter up to die, but Elise—was she worth more dead or alive to them?

# CHAPTER
# FORTY-SIX

The door to Elise's room was open. I flew through it, knives in hand. There was no one there, only empty seats and pinched-out candles, the woody scents of tea and smoke still in the air. I crept forward, quiet, shaking. Riparian, for all her faults, loved Elise. She would be fine. She would live.

I pushed open the door to Elise's sleeping quarters. Elise was laid out in bed.

Unmoving. Fully dressed. An empty set of cups and two damp bags of tea leaves sat on the table. My world narrowed to the stillness of her chest, the redness around her eyes, and I dropped my knives. Her chest didn't fall. I picked up the cup nearest her bed. Her chest didn't rise.

Mold and mice and must beneath the bitter scent of black tea.

Poison parsley.

I let the empty cup fall and dragged myself to the edge of Elise's bed. My shadow crossed her face, darkening the tired dips of her eyes beneath her spectacles. I couldn't shake the memories of her moving, writing, smearing ink across her cheek and down the underside of my arm. The image of her, bloody and brilliant, kicking me out of the carriage the night we first met. The ruddy flush of heat in her cheeks as she recited poetry I didn't know and danced in the circle of my arms, avoiding my clumsy feet.

*I am safe.*

I was broken.

And a great, yawning nothing opened up in me, the shadow of my soul ripping free from my bloody body and finding some new, safer home where no one died and death didn't linger. I was a child again, running through the mire of corpses and grief. I was alone again.

"Elise?" The rusty freckles dotting her nose were paler now. Tears stuck her lashes together. I laid my hand against her cheek.

"Sal?" She opened one eye.

My heart stopped. "What?"

"Sal." Elise—alive, moving, speaking, no poison-stillness in her skin—shot up from bed and threw her arms around my neck, breath warm against my neck, heart pounding against my shoulder. She gasped. Sniffed. "Is Lena gone?"

I nodded. Touched her arm.

"It was a trap." Elise let me go—moving, taking in breaths as though she'd been holding hers, gnawing at her cold-cracked lips and drawing blood. Only the living bled. "Lena knew you were alive. She knew you were plotting something tonight. They're running."

Let her run.

I touched Elise's lip.

"Sal?" She stopped, half out of the bed. Her shoulders slumped. "You thought I was dead?"

"There's poison parsley in your cup." I smeared her blood between my fingers. Hot. Red. "You weren't breathing."

She pulled my hand into hers and wiped the blood away with the edge of her skirt. "I didn't drink it." A watery, uneasy frown pulled at her face. "Lena tried to kill me."

I nodded.

"She prepared my tea," Elise said, voice low and flat. "Just like she did when I was a child and we had first arrived in Igna, but it wasn't right. She wasn't right."

I glanced back at the cup on the floor, Elise following my gaze, and she laughed. Barely. Painfully.

"I grew up with the Left Hand," she said. "I know how to make it look like I'm drinking something I'm not."

I laid my forehead against her shoulder. "I need a bit."

Wasn't time for this. Maud was on her way with Winter to Moira while Riparian and North Star got farther and farther away. To where? Were they abandoning Lynd? Erlend? For what?

What could anywhere else offer them?

"Lena said they were giving you my father." Elise's voice cracked. "Did you—?"

"No." I took a deep breath and pulled myself up. Together. "We were killing North Star tonight, publicly making him confess, but your father was there instead, so I sent him to Moira Namrata, the Last Living Star of Nacea. He was alive then."

Elise kissed her three fingers and pressed them to her heart, tears splashing against my hands. I brushed the tears away.

"A confession. A public execution." I let her go, the mess of our lives shaking in my hands. How could we live like this? After this? "I have to go after North Star and Riparian. They knew, they must've have known, and they left Winter in his place. They tried to kill you. They're tying up loose ends, but we got Winter. We got Lynd. Everyone will know what they did."

Elise nodded. She kissed my cheeks. "It's high time Weylin's reign ends."

## CHAPTER
# FORTY-SEVEN

I raced out of the building, mask on, knives in hand, and no one stopped me. The city streets were lit with lamps and flecked with people whispering back and forth, limping away from the gate separating North Star's estate from the city proper. A small crowd shouted at the poorly manned gate. I grabbed a man near the wall and yanked him down to face me. He yelped.

"Weylin just left," I said. "Which way and how long?"

"Straight out." He pulled away and crossed his arms before himself. His eyes couldn't settle on my face or my knives. My mask was a full moon in his dark eyes. "Ran through the amphitheater line."

The show. The execution.

Moira was having Adella collect people to watch, and North Star hadn't been able to escape without passing through them. But if he was up to angering Lynd, his home, his people, he wasn't coming back.

I ran faster.

The streets closer to the main gate in and out of Lynd were chaos. Soldiers and citizens crushed together in a many-armed battle that was getting nowhere, and in the distance, at the edge of the gate, one small carriage built for speed forced its way through the small crowd of people trying to get inside and home before the night was too dark to travel by. Rangers decked in scars and steel shoved the confused crowd out of the way. I darted into an alley.

The streets were too crowded. I was too angry. They didn't get to just leave. They didn't get to be free of this. I climbed onto the roof of a nearby building, stumbling across the clay tiles. Erlend didn't keep roof gardens or balconies. The buildings were sloping works of wood and thatch and tile. I sprinted across them toward the carriage.

People shrieked, horses neighed and reared, and the rangers cleared the way as I cleared the last roof. The carriage took off.

I slammed on top of it, knives digging into the roof. The driver spun round. We were racing down the road out of Lynd, rangers on each side, and an arrow ripped over my head. Too high.

Too much going on too close to North Star and Riparian.

I ripped out my knife and pushed myself up, stabbing down into the roof a good hand's width ahead of where I'd been. Shouts I couldn't make out echoed around me. A sword tore through the roof where I'd been laying.

Rath would've loved seeing this.

I dragged myself to the front of the carriage. The driver pulled a sword. I threw myself at him and caught him around the middle, knocking us both to the floor. The carriage jerked to the side. He stood over me, sword in hand. I kicked his knees out.

The driver crumpled, falling off the side with a thump and

rattling crack. I stayed crouched. The rangers riding on either side kept their arrows nocked.

I needed a shield.

"Horse!"

The carriage door burst open. A ranger edged their horse as close to the carriage as they dared. They went stumbling off, and North Star hauled himself into the saddle. Riparian's pale face appeared in the doorway.

North Star, Gaspar del Weylin, the man who'd plotted with Riparian to let the shadows destroy Nacea so Erlend's army could escape, wasn't going to risk his escape to save her.

I laughed and cut the carriage horses free of their bonds. North Star glanced back, gaze slipping from Riparian to me, and he turned away from her. The carriage toppled forward, tossing me to the ground. The carriage skidded passed me. The Lady's constellation flickered above me. Riparian shrieked.

Her lips to the Lady's ears.

I sat up and watched all but three rangers ride on.

"You and me, Riparian," I shouted, cackling through each word. "You, me, and the Lady judging makes three!"

I forced myself to my knees, my feet, and rolled out the soreness settling in my bones. The nearest ranger was the one who'd given up his horse for North Star. He pulled the pole weapon from his back—more Mizuho blade than spear. I glanced back.

No one from the city dared get close.

I flipped one of my knives down and balanced my stance. "Sorry," I said to the ranger, "but the dead don't count."

He lurched forward, feet slipping in the mud and blade going high. I dropped to my knees and kicked my right leg out. His ankle cracked, buckling his knees. I leapt onto him.

The blade clattered to the ground next to us. I slammed him into the dirt back first and slipped my knife into his throat. He was dead before he could blink. The other two rangers approached on horseback. One held a crossbow, the other a spear.

"I'm killing Lena de Arian tonight." I pushed my mask to the top of my head, wiped the blood from my face, and pulled the mask back on. "And I wasn't planning on killing all of you, but you're making a real compelling argument."

A crossbow bolt cracked against my mask. My ears rang. A heady, bright-eyed pain shot through the left side of my face and white flecked my vision. My head snapped back so fast my teeth clacked together. One chipped.

I picked up the dead ranger's blade and walked backward to the carriage. Riparian's uneven breaths and frantic nails-on-wood clawing rang in the small confines of the crash. I risked a look back. Riparian was pinned beneath the broken carriage floor.

My blade pricked her neck. "You two—drop your weapons and get off those horses."

They did. One ran. One stalked to me, shoulders back and gaze narrow. I drew the blade from Riparian's throat, blood welling across the wavering steel, and jammed it into the earth too far away for her to grab. The ranger drew a short sword from the sheath across the small of his back. I advanced and grabbed my knives. The ranger attacked.

I let him, only slipping aside enough to avoid the worst of the blow. The blade cut through my leather vest and nipped my side, and I grabbed the ranger's wrist, pulling him close and driving the sword farther through me. A flesh wound.

A debt repaid.

"Your lady already killed me once—drowned me." Rath's dead eyes open and staring. Hia and Shea rotting beneath the safety of my tree as shadows slipped their faces from their skulls. She'd left me to tread in a sea of grief. "What makes you think you can kill me now?"

The hilt of the sword hit my side. He swallowed.

I slipped a knife into the crack between his leather chest armor and belt. He gasped. A gurgling, lung-pricked breath bubbled in the back of his throat. I yanked my knife free and stepped away. He collapsed.

Riparian was still stuck in the carriage wreckage, shoving, scratching, screaming at the boards holding her to the ground. I knelt behind her.

"You want me to call your Erlend friends to help with this?" I asked. "Or think they're a bit sore after you running them down? Think they'll support you now?"

She threw a handful of dirt and splinters at me. I laughed.

"They'll get over it," Riparian said, words hissing through her teeth. "No Erlend will follow your shadow-making monster of a queen."

I twirled my knife in one hand and tipped back my mask with the other. "Not till they find out who Weylin made into shadows before you sent him Naceans, they won't."

She turned her head to the side, staring at me from the corner of a bloodshot eye. I grinned.

"I'm not killing you." I laid the point of my knife against the hollow of her throat. "Not yet. Not till all of Lynd knows all your little, bloody secrets."

Not till her soul was flayed and bare and every Erlend knew how much she thought they were worth compared to her. We didn't have North Star, but we'd two.

Winter.

Riparian.

And Erlend would know them as well as I did.

# CHAPTER
# FORTY-EIGHT

M aud and Moira met me at the gates of the city, Namrata hovering over their backs.

The people of Erlend hid in the dark corners of their shops and streets, and I didn't blame them one bit.

"Well." Maud handed me a bandage. "That was the most foolish thing you've ever done."

"Don't joke. We both know it isn't." I yanked Riparian before me and pushed her to the ground at Moira's feet. "And I'll say this with words you understand." I knelt down till I was staring Riparian dead in the face, her eyes staring through the holes of my blank opal mask. Blood dripped from the crack between mask and skin. "Worth it."

"Worth." Namrata's rotten breath brushed my cheek. One long, crooked finger cut a line across Riparian's cheek.

Moira nodded. "You will confess before your citizens, Lena de Arian, and we will let them decide your worth. After all, you and Weylin taught them that confessions under torture are the most trustworthy confessions of all."

Namrata marched Riparian to the city square, where the other eight shadows stood watch over the gathered crowd. There were few guards and fewer nobles, but Elise and her gaggle were standing at the bottom of the amphitheater steps. Adella sat with a group of families nearby, pointing out Moira in the crowd. We descended the stairs slowly. I stopped at the edge of the stage.

"Come." Moira held out her hand. "You are Nacean, and you are my blade. You have a place here as much as me."

The other Naceans—I hadn't spoken to them, didn't know their names, and couldn't when my vengeance was so fresh and my clothes still bloodied—stood runed and still along the edges of the stage. One of them pulled shackles from their belt and closed them over Riparian's wrists. Winter was tied to a chair in the center of the stage. Moira met me before him.

"We needed North Star for this," she muttered, as though the rest of the crowd would've been able to hear.

I shrugged. "Your shadows might catch him. I can't."

"Take off your mask." She glanced at Winter and Riparian, black eyes glittering like a night full of stars. "I'll trade you. We will put them on trial, and you will kill North Star."

Fury rose in my veins. Winter was mine. He'd killed Ruby, nearly killed me, kidnapped Elise, and wreaked so much havoc I didn't know enough words to express my hate for him. He was mine.

He should have been mine.

"It will be better this way," Moira said quickly. "They'll have a trial. People will know."

She was right. If they went on trial, if Moira got them to confess in North Star's place, everything could change.

She touched my arm. "And North Star will be yours to kill."

I handed her my mask, the red-smeared names inside of it facing her, and she ran her thumb across their gouged names. She led me to the center of the stage, behind Riparian and Winter, and left me there. The Nacean nearest me, their tall frame more failed runes than flesh, smiled and mouthed, *Hal Avery*. They touched their chest.

I tried to smile but it only made me cry. Another Nacean whose name and face I knew. Another Nacean not dead.

"Lynd!" Moira sliced open her finger and drew a line of blood along her throat. "Tonight, Gaspar del Weylin was going to show off his newest weapons, his newest way to win the war against Alona, but instead of facing his creations, he ran. So I will show you what he made instead."

She said it without screaming, but the words stretched across the space, impossibly loud and everywhere at once.

The torches around the square sparked to life, magic prickling in the air, and I gasped. Nine shadows, dark and looming, encircled the theater. The crowd screamed. Adella grasped the hands of the Erlends around her. Elise's gaggle shifted.

"They won't hurt you unless you try to hurt us," Moira said. "They are the weapons your dear Lord del Weylin wanted to show off." She lifted her head, the bloody runes at her throat a bright, vivid red in the light. "Tonight, Lord Gaspar del Weylin was going to provide his noble court with a demonstration of his last decade's work, but I realized it would be more fitting if instead of showing off his work, we listed the names of every Erlend, Nacean, and Alonian citizen he killed to fuel his work."

A handful of people leapt to their feet and moved for the stage, but the Naceans around me raised their hands and runes, black as the void above us, and bound the people to their seats. The families near Adella whispered to their neighbors, to anyone they could reach.

"Weylin fled once he realized he had again created shadows out of his control." Moira ripped the gag from Winter's mouth.

He lurched and spat. "I'll kill you!"

"Unlikely." Moira backed away to the box sitting across from him. "Weylin wasn't capable enough to kill my mother, and you weren't even capable enough to realize he was setting you up tonight."

"You'll eat those words." He struggled with the ropes and shackles holding him to the chair.

Moira grinned, teeth bared. "Good. I'm ravenous, and you're not even the one I wanted. But tell them, Lord Nevierno del Farone, why you are here."

He stared at her. The crowd thrummed, an uneasy half silence of whispers and quick breaths at his name. My skin tingled with it.

"You always used torture and told your people it revealed the truth." Moira pulled out a long-bladed knife curved like the crescent moon. "So if torture reveals the truth like you always said, what's your truth? Or were you a liar?

"Do you know who I am?" she asked, leaning close to him.

His jaw tensed. Through clenched teeth he muttered, "Moira Namrata."

It reached the whole square despite his attempts to swallow the words, and Moira nodded.

"I am Moira Namrata, daughter of Namrata Vera, the First Star of Nacea and Protector of the Northern Reach, and now, I am the Last Living Star of Nacea." She raised her arms to the crowd, palms out and runes bared. "You know Naceans resettled in Erlend. Gaspar del Weylin told you it was from the kindness of his heart. He granted us land and saved us from the slaughter of our home country when Alonian shadows invaded us from the south. He told you half truths—they were not Alonian shadows. They were Erlend shadows made by Celso de Lex. I know this because Weylin taught me to make shadows with Celso's notes. I know too that Weylin ordered the release of those shadows in northern Alona to fight their army, but he didn't know they couldn't control them. So when they started heading north, they let them through Nacea instead."

She turned to him. Her arms fell. The knife slapped against her thigh.

"Weylin did not think of this on his own. Lena de Arian, Nevierno del Farone, Caden de Bain, Horatio del Seve, and Mattin del Aer decided that it would be better to let the shadows destroy Nacea, slowing them down and giving the Erlend army time to retreat." She turned to the crowd, silhouette a jagged blur of runes poking through her skin. "Do you deny that you had a hand in this?"

"They would have destroyed Erlend!" He jerked. The bonds held. "I will not apologize for saving the lives of the people I swore to protect when I took up my title."

"So you admit to damning Nacea to the shadows," Moira said, "but claim it was to save Erlends?"

"Of course."

Moira pulled the copies of Riparian's ledger from the box. "This is a list of all the people Weylin tested magic on when trying to bring it back and all the people who died when he forced us to make shadows."

She began to read a list of names. A dozen names and then a dozen more, and plenty of them were Erlend names. Erlend, Nacean, Alonian, and a few from Mizuho as though the terror hadn't spread far enough. I found Elise in the crowd, her spectacles two stars among the sea of unfamiliar faces, and stared at her. She shuddered at each name.

She wasn't the only one. A quarter of the crowd was screaming, sobbing, tearing down the steps to be closer to the stage and proof of their loved ones' fates.

One shadow, slight, lanky, barely a smear of dark before the torchlight, slipped through the crowd without so much as touching another person and stopped before a woman at the front. The shadow wore a ragged cloak that only just hid the remnants of their body—a bony leg, a flayed hand, and a blank, bleeding face. And the woman called the shadow "daughter." Embraced it. Her.

People.

So many people.

Moira spoke till her voice grew hoarse and tight, crackling with each detail and death—a flayed person and failed shadow strung up at the border, a group of rangers trained in flaying so that Our Queen could know Erlend's wrath, and a long, long list of the children Winter helped send from the south to Erlend for study. The last name a man's, convicted of desertion. His brothers denied it until Moira described his face and scars.

"Leon Margo and Perrin Cal." I choked on my parents' names. "Shea Leon and Hia Leon, my siblings. They weren't even five yet. I don't remember my sister's laugh, but I know the color of her skull at dawn. And you made more shadows? Killed more children? Started a new war? Because Our Queen of Igna—you can't even call her country by the right name—didn't start it. You did."

"We were killing a war criminal that your queen let live." Winter tried to look at me, but his ropes kept him still. "Rodolfo da Abreu murdered our mages after the treaty was made. He tortured them to death."

"He cut the runes from their skin so that no one would ever know how to make shadows again, but you couldn't let the world forget." I shrugged. "And you can't speak of war crimes. You nearly killed Royal Physician Isidora da Abreu. The only reason she's not dead is because I stopped you then. You threatened to kill the family of a servant if he didn't assassinate Our Queen."

It was easy to pick out the Erlends who'd seen the shadows. They were crying or shaking or staring in horror at the lithe-limbed shades above us.

"The Erlend nobles have made shadows twice now," I said. "The first time, you destroyed an entire nation. What if it hadn't worked? What if they'd escaped into Lynd?"

Moira laughed. "Weylin had a plan for that. It was only for him and his court—not the citizens, not the soldiers, not the servants. They were to be his new Nacea and slow the shadows down."

A rock flew from the crowd and slammed into the stage at Winter's feet.

"I had planned this to be Gaspar del Weylin's confession and execution, but Nevierno del Farone is just as guilty, just as monstrous." She reached out and pressed the point of her blade to his cheek. "Don't worry. I won't flay you like Weylin made me flay my mother. I am not the monster Erlend's nobles tried to make me. I will end your monstrous reign.

"This is what it's like when people really know you," Moira said to him. She raised her face to the crowd. "Is there anyone here who would speak in defense of Nevierno del Farone?"

Namrata, rotten limbs dragging across the ground, dripped blood down the steps as she walked down the center stair of the amphitheater and onto the stage. The crowd rippled as she passed, leaning away from her. The last human parts of her sloughed away.

"I would." Her voice shook. "But he would not speak for me, my daughter."

Moira nodded, hands shaking, and opened her mouth to speak, but Elise beat her to it.

"I, Elise de Farone, would." She stood, cheeks damp and spectacles pushed to her forehead to keep them clean of tears. "But I was there when he tried to kill Isidora dal Abreu and when he sent the children we were sworn to protect north to be used and hurt and killed, and I cannot speak for him anymore. He doesn't deserve it."

"I'll kill you!" He tried to launch himself from the chair and tumbled back, nearly falling over altogether. His teeth clacked together. "All those kids, all your Naceans, they'll be dead by dawn. Gaspar made sure of it."

"I hear your words," Moira said, "and I am not compelled toward mercy by them."

She stabbed the knife into the wooden stage at her feet. Winter collapsed back, shoulders slumping. His eyes rolled from side to side.

"You can't kill me. You're Nacean." His voice cracked. Blood dripped from the ropes at his wrists. "You can't spill blood. You can't. It's not allowed. She'll disown you."

"It's not?" She laughed, head thrown back, and cut his cheek. "Are you sure?"

He shuddered.

Moira let out a shuddering breath, mouth half-open, eyes wide, and lips pulled back in a taut sneer. "Do not tell me how to live my culture, a culture you have tried to destroy time and time again. You know nothing. You're so shortsighted. All these years with us, and you think it's about spilling blood? Death isn't an equivalent exchange. I can't simply erase the blood killing you will leave on my soul. But I can repent for it. I can bear my guilt." She reached into the box at her feet and pulled out a pitcher the size of her torso. "You don't even know what guilt is."

Moira closed her eyes, took a breath, tilted her head to night, and when she opened her eyes again, I could've sworn the Lady's stars shone in them.

"You and your confidants tried to kill us." The runes beneath her skin writhed and tore and ripped free from her, pooling at her feet till nothing but blood and bone and skin remained within her. "I wish I weren't like this, but this is our choice, and you will not take another one from us. Making us be like you, making us give up our traditions to take up yours. You tried to kill us twice."

The words rattled in my chest.

It *was* a different kind of killing.

Moira hugged the pitcher to her chest. "So every dawn of every day since you first had us carve souls from skin, I bled and cried. I regretted something that wasn't even my doing. No more. The pain you caused ends tonight."

Winter quivered.

"I offer my blood, blessed and saved, as payment for past, present, and future indiscretions against others." Moira tipped the pitcher and blood trickled down and down until the clot-speckled puddle of red at her feet encompassed us all standing on the stage. She pulled free the knife. "Do you have last words?"

He shook his head. "You can't."

She raised the knife to his throat, pressed the blade to his chin, and didn't draw a single drop of blood.

"I can't." Moira laughed, sobbed, and stepped across the river between her and Winter. "But your crimes are great and demand a fair trial. So, citizens of Erlend, what punishment fits Nevierno del Farone's crimes?"

Lady, she could have me till my veins ran dry and my bones were dust, till everything within me had rotted and returned and the only words that left my lips were the winds through my cracked teeth.

She was better than he could have ever been.

"Give him to us," the Erlend woman in front, arms still clasped around her daughter's shadow, said. "To his shadows."

The crowd surged, some stepping forward and some moving

back, and three of the nine shadows drifted to Moira. They whispered to her, dripping blood across the stage. A dozen people waited before it.

Winter had pushed me from a window. He had killed Ruby. He had been part of the plot that killed my family.

But Winter was not my kill.

He'd hurt so many more than me. His fate belonged to everyone and not just me. Moira was right.

Moira undid his shackles and ropes. Elise buried her face in her hands, and he started running, stumbling, away from the stage. The shadows flickered, thorns through flesh. A line of red welled across his neck. He fell.

I closed my eyes and turned away.

And the Erlend Winter died screaming.

CHAPTER
# FORTY-NINE

There was no body. There was no blood. There might have been no death at all if not for the weary-eyed stares of the grieving. The other Naceans dragged Riparian to the chair, and she, still quiet as she had been all night, only sneered. Elise did not look up.

"I read your ledgers, Lena de Arian." Moira pulled the knife from the wooden stage. "I know how much you think a Nacean life is worth. How much an Erlend life is worth. How much do you think you're worth?"

Riparian didn't answer.

"No answer?" Moira asked. "Did you never take stock of your life as you did ours?"

The thick, green leggings covering Riparian's legs were torn and filthy, splinters of her carriage caught in the creases, and a jagged wound cut across her left cheek. Fresh blood on new snow.

"I know who I am and what I've done, and I regret nothing. I know what the people of our future will think of me. The only reason Lynd still stands is because we directed the shadows through Nacea. If we hadn't, Erlend, the whole of it, would be dead. So no, no begging, no regrets." Riparian's gaze slid across the crowd. "And it brings me great comfort knowing that in two days' time, all the Nacean homesteads will be razed."

Moira, the runes along her throat crumbling and her voice fading, stilled before her. "What?"

"Gaspar sent the rangers to kill as many Naceans as they could two days ago. They'll reach the closest one in two days. You won't." Riparian laughed deep in the back of her throat, tears dripping down her chin. "We knew you'd pick tonight. The only things we didn't know were the details."

Moira stilled. A shuddering hum rose in me, shaking through my teeth, my ribs, and an unnatural quiet settled over the crowd till all I could hear was Moira's unsteady gasps. The nine leaves in her arms bubbled over with blood. She cupped her hands together.

"The closest homestead is four days away," Moira said. The blood pooling in her palms dripped through the cracks in her fingers and overflowed. It turned to ash before it even touched the ground. "My shadows against your rangers. Who do you think is faster?"

The pile of ash at Moira's feet scattered in the cold night air. Nine figures, bandaged and bloodied, rotting bodies held together by nothing but will and runes, stepped into the lights of the stage. Namrata, more shade than flesh, stepped between Moira and the crowd. I stared through the dark nothing where Namrata's lungs should have been and met the eyes of an Erlend girl, hollow-stare deadened even more as Winter's blood dripped down her shirt.

"Gaspar del Weylin commanded me to make shadows. If I didn't, he would kill me, my family, the town I grew up in, and anyone else he deemed fit to die." Moira's voice shook, and she held out her hands full of blood and ink and ash to Riparian. "He watched as I stripped my mother from flesh to muscle to bone to soul, and when I cried, he reminded me of how many would die if I stopped. And every success, every failure, you logged in your ledgers next to the monetary worth of the person used."

Namrata and the other shadows grew darker in the bright lights, their wispy silhouettes taking shape, and began to march from the amphitheater.

"And?" Riparian arched one perfect eyebrow. "The people of Erlend were always the most important part of my life. They were always the people I protected. All those people I saved, all those people I've spent my life caring for, will not let you walk away from killing me."

"All the good you did," Moira said, pulling out a copied page from the ledger, "but does it make up for the twenty Erlend children, the twenty Lynd citizens no older than fifteen and too ill to live without a physician's aid, you told Weylin to use when you couldn't send others to use instead?"

She huffed. Shook her head. "Of course. That's absurd. Just because you know their names and recite them near me doesn't mean I killed them."

Moira glanced at me. The shadows were gone, racing to catch the rangers before they reached the Naceans, and her skin was the ashy pale of blood lost too quickly.

"If Erlend does not want her death, Our Queen Marianna da Ignasi does." I tied my opal mask around my head and took the long-bladed knife from Moira. "Whatever good you did here, Lena de Arian, you are still responsible for the attempted assassination of Our Queen, kidnapping, and murder." I cut her free from the chair. "Weylin abandoned you, left you here with us to die so that he could escape, so where will you run?"

She stood and fell, stumbling off the stage. I followed.

"What do you know of the south?" I asked the people nearest me as I descended the stage. Riparian fled up the steps. "Of what Lena de Arian has been doing?"

"The southern holdings were political prisoners." The blood-splattered girl looked from Riparian to me. "They escaped. The queen retaliated. The war restarted."

"No," I said, "they were trusted allies, and they tried to assassinate multiple members of Our Queen's court before seceding from the nation and rejoining Weylin. They're traitors, and they started the war."

"It's true." Elise stood, eyes teary and hands shaking. "I wasn't a prisoner. My father wasn't a prisoner. Lena wasn't a prisoner. We were members of the noble court. We were normal people there. It was my father who took me prisoner when he brought me here. When he tried to kill the people I grew up with just so he could blame the start of the war on them."

Riparian spun, chest heaving. "Elise—"

"You tried to poison me tonight," Elise said. "I did not speak for my father, and I will not speak for you because I know how guilty both of you are and you do not deserve my mercy."

"I was saving you!" Riparian broke for the first time, a shaking through her. "Gaspar would've slit your throat. I was only going to put you to sleep."

Elise's mouth tensed. She sniffed. "I would rather have died like that than found out the people I loved had murdered so many and would have added me to their lists."

"Let's see how much you're worth then," Moira said, voice low and scratchy. "Run, Lena de Arian. Perhaps someone here thinks you're worth helping. They won't be harmed. No other innocents in Lynd will be harmed if I can help it."

Tomorrow, when the sun was high and the people with no missing loved ones awoke, the city would be harder to control. A few thousand people and only a hundred or so with reason to be here, with reason to cling to the promise of knowing what happened to their missing. Would the rest believe them? Would the people who'd no reason to doubt North Star, Winter, and Riparian their entire lives believe Erlend was capable of this?

But for now, with the victims of Riparian's life lining the streets, no one helped her. No one hid her. She'd worked her whole life to make Erlend a safe place for herself, and now all the Erlends she'd brushed aside wouldn't even look at her.

They only cleared a path for her and said a prayer.

Moira grabbed my arm. "Executioner, not assassin."

"Shadow," I said, shaking her off. "I will be her shadow."

They might all take offense tomorrow, but they'd learn that a handful of good deeds didn't outweigh a nation. I'd done bad things for good reasons, bad reasons too, and my hands were still red. Riparian didn't get to wash herself of this.

"We can make this fair." I tossed her one of my knives.

She snatched it.

"You killed a boy named Rath," I said as loud as I could. My voice cracked. "Rath went looking for you after you abducted one of the kids he looked after to be used as a mage or shadow, and when he found you, when he tried to save a child's life, you killed him."

She took off, and by the time I reached the top of the stairs, she was sprinting down an alley. Out of sight.

I took off running.

She didn't make it to the corner before I caught up to her, a small collection of the grieving at my back. She stopped in the middle of the empty street. Turned.

"Will you really pretend you're doing this out of devotion to your job?" She swallowed, tilting her chin up. Her fingers tightened around my knife. "They'll kill you."

"And?" I shrugged, circling right. "How much am I worth? I'm Nacean, but I bet there's much more about me that offends you. At what point does my life become worthy of caring about? You slaughtered a country and then kept on doing it once you found out a few of them lived. You threatened to start a war and get your people killed just to make sure you lived and Erlend stayed around. What're you worth?"

Riparian circled left, head slightly tilted and mouth barely open, like the words coming out of my mouth were a jumble of nonsense instead of Alonian.

"I saved fifty thousand people by suggesting we lure them through Nacea instead of east," she said slowly. Like explaining "sit" to a dog. "Nacea had only thirty-five thousand at the time of the last census, and ten thousand made it to Erlend. I will take twenty-five thousand deaths over fifty thousand every day until die."

How many Naceans would have been too many? How many Erlends too few? Where was the line?

"Tonight, then," I said in Nacean, "and then you'll never take anyone else's life at all."

I grasped my knife tighter and took off my mask.

"What are you worth?" I asked again, revealing the list of names on the inside of my mask. I carved a line through hers and laid it on the ground. "Bargain with me."

"What do you want?"

My family. Rath. Ruby.

To have more happy memories than I had ghosts.

I laughed. "I don't want anything. I want nothing. I want you to be nothing. I want your memory to be a blank spot on our history. I want your legacy to be an ink smear on a blank page. There is nothing I want from you."

She dove to run around me. I leapt, catching her around the waist. We tumbled to the stones, my knees against her chest, and she drove her little knife into my arm. I knocked her arm away. The knife shuddered in the wound.

I'd cut myself there once, to hide a ring and make deal—a little pain, a pretty payoff. But my arm didn't hurt now.

There was no pain in death, and there was only death in me.

*Lady, let my debts be paid. Let the world be better.*

No Rath to bandage my wounds now. Never again.

"I'm your shadow, Lena de Arian. You made me. You made this death." One hand holding the knife to her throat and one hand pulling her blade from my upper arm, I let the blood drip across her. Nacean blood on Erlend skin. "Our Queen sent me after you and didn't put a price on your head because this is the only legacy you will ever have. You're a tragedy. Nothing else."

A debt of blood repaid in flesh.

She took a breath. "I—"

And I slit her throat.

CHAPTER
# FIFTY

Elise pulled me from the alley. I picked up my knife, arm
aching. Her hands slid across my shoulders, my jaw, and
wiped the blood from my nose. I let her help me to my feet and
stumbled from the alley. Maud met us at the mouth of Riparian's
grave. She covered me in a clean cloak. Everything hurt.

Everything always hurt.

"One left," I whispered. "One left."

Two stars, two titles—one granted by the Lady as a symbol
of protection and one a secret name meant to hide a murderer.

*North Star.*

But I felt no better for these deaths.

Just tired.

They walked me back to the amphitheater. Moira, perched
on the edge of the stage and showing Riparian's ledgers to desperate onlookers, swayed with each word and breath, the quick
rise of her chest too fast to be safe. I sat next to her.

"They'll catch up to the rangers by dawn," Moira whispered

to me as the crowd around us thinned. "And he's still out there. Running."

Was this Nacea? Lost stars and tears and ashes?

Or was this Erlend?

Winter and Riparian were dead.

But North Star still lived free.

"What now?" I asked, but the rough drag of my voice was too soft to be truly mine. Had I always been this tired?

"Nacea." She coughed and wiped her face, wincing at her own voice. "We protect Nacea and Erlend. Lynd will rebel—the officers and low-born nobles won't like us turning them over to Igna—but we have to keep control. We have to end this. Those here tonight will be on our side. They all lost someone to Weylin's schemes."

Nacea.

There were others out there. Whole families and friends and towns still breathing and living. Together. Digging their toes into this same earth. Snoring beneath the stars I couldn't see. Unaware of the rangers racing toward them.

It wasn't Erlend that had ruined us. It was North Star, Deadfall, Riparian, Caldera, Winter, Coachwhip, and all the other folks who placed themselves higher than others. Who thought living equally meant taking a loss. Who viewed the world through a lens of Erlend worth and found us lacking. Who'd tried to reshape the world into their image so many times they'd nearly broken it.

Had broken it.

Had dragged dead souls back to life and left them confused and in pain to wander the land. Had let us die so they wouldn't be devoured for their own mistake.

No more.

"Moira." Her Nacean name stuck in my mouth, unfamiliar, awkward, and I knew that North Star was at fault for that too. But she wouldn't mind. She'd understand. "What do you need your knife to do?"

"I'm glad they're gone," she muttered. "I'm glad no Naceans will have to suffer in Weylin's labs again."

I looked around; the only ones left around us were Elise, Maud, Adella, and the other Naceans.

"They're hanging the bodies of Nevierno and Lena from the city gates like Weylin did to deserters during the war." Adella shuddered. "The whole city will know soon."

Moira wiped her face and looked around. The remaining people watched us, uneasy, and the few soldiers who'd come to see the commotion stayed on the outskirts. A few had been stripped of their weapons by furious Erlend onlookers shouting about betrayal. "I will take care of Lynd and Erlend if you will take care of Gaspar del Weylin."

"Gladly." My dead were a part of me—the seven from auditions and the countless others I'd added since—and I had to make their deaths worthy. I had to put an end to this. "We end this now. No more war. No more shadows. Peace begins with us."

Not an end but a beginning.

The tall Nacean who'd mouthed their name to me—Hal Avery—and nothing else, crouched next to us. "Moira, time to sleep."

"I know." She nodded and nearly collapsed. Her gaze found mine. "I didn't use Dimas, didn't trust him, but I can't do much else while bound to the shadows. This is Hal. Let them heal you."

"Nice to meet you, Sal." Hal grinned, strained, but held out their hands palm up before touching me.

I scowled, slumping against Elise behind me. "I don't like runes."

"You need help." Elise carded my matted hair. She sighed, breath warm at the back of my neck. "If I'd trusted you, this wouldn't have happened."

"You thought she was better than she was," I said. Just like I'd thought Our Queen was better than she was. "She gave you hope when you had none. I'm sorry I got up in arms about you trusting her."

"And I'm sorry I didn't trust you." Elise smiled, close lipped and tight. "I'm sorry no one—and none of us—are how we appear."

I grinned and nodded to Maud. "Maud's always how she appears."

Nose scrunched up as she sneered, Maud glared at me.

One bright spot among my bloody memories.

"See?" I waved to her. "She's always annoyed at me."

"You make it so easy," Maud said. She helped Hal and Elise haul me to my feet.

"One rune," said Hal, "and then you can go on your way. Only one."

I nodded. They drew a Nacean word I didn't know on the soft skin of the back of my hand, and their blood sunk into me with a shudder. The bruises of that hand began to darken and fade. Riparian's last wound stopped aching. I opened my mouth to thank them, but magic prickled in the back of my throat. I groaned.

"Thank you," Elise said for me.

Hal nodded and gathered Moira up in their arms.

"My quarters." Elise hooked her arm through mine. "It has locks and plenty of space."

I leaned against Elise. "So I get to sleep in your bed?"

The words barely made it past my lips.

"Of course," she said softly. "How else am I going to make sure you don't run off to do anything dangerous before resting?"

"Thank you." The rough rub of her tired voice in my ears set my teeth on edge, and I touched her shoulder to make sure she was still there. My feet kept moving but my eyes fluttered shut.

Elise led me into her bedroom and locked the door. I kicked off my boots and crashed on the bed. Elise laughed softly. Her fingers worked at my coat.

"Come on," she whispered. "No blood in the bed."

I shifted till she could pull my coat free, and there was a rustle as cloth hit the floor. Elise settled next to me.

My legs dangled over the edge, and for a brief, panicked moment, all I could think of was shadows crawling from the dark beneath. I pulled myself fully onto the bed and buried myself beneath the blankets. My heart calmed as soon as I covered my head.

The metallic, stinging scent of ink burned up my nose. I sighed. Safe.

*Leon. Perrin. Shea. Hia. Sal.*

*North Star. Deadfall. Riparian. Caldera. Winter.*

One more.

CHAPTER
# FIFTY-ONE

W e have a problem." Moira's voice snapped me out of
sleep. "You've had two days. We have work to do."

I jerked up, tangled in the blanket, and blinked till the world
righted. Two days and I still felt raw. I hadn't even wanted to
wait. "What's it?"

"Weylin." Elise sat next to me, hand taking mine. "He con-
tacted Our Queen."

"About what?" I rubbed my face and picked the gunk from
my eyes. "How he got his court killed and fled his city?"

"No, it was before you even got here. About how he's still got
control of the largest army on this continent and also has a bunch
of shadows working for him," Moira said. "About how, if she
doesn't sign over control of the northern lands of Erlend to him
officially and withdraw her troops from the seceded holdings,
he'll kill every Alonian and Nacean here."

Of course he did. "How do you know this?"

"A friend of yours was found freezing to death this morning."

Moira turned her head to the doorway. "He said he was hunting Dimas Gaila."

I peered around her.

"Nice to see you alive." It was Roland, road weary and nose nearly frostbitten but still breathing. He grinned at me.

"You too." I nodded to his plain clothes. "Scouting?"

"Got a note a little while ago instructing every scout to grab as many folks as they could and get out of Erlend." He shrugged, the bandage on his arm crinkling, and gestured to Elise. "Lady de Farone explained what happened."

I took the moment to glance around—Elise's quarters were mostly bare, save for my neatly folded and cleaned clothes in the corner. Elise, Moira, Adella, Roland, and I were the only people in here. Moira was sitting, knees shaking against each other. I sucked on my teeth.

"So," I said, "what's the downside here? Who cares if they make a deal?"

Elise squeezed my hand. "Because it's a wartime treaty."

"Because Weylin had Dimas draw up a treaty days ago—using runes." Moira flinched as she spoke. "It is magically binding, and once your queen signs it, she and Weylin will be bound to uphold it, politically and magically."

Elise collapsed next to me. "So we'll have peace, but he will still be the hero, alive and living out his days in tranquility."

Still a king. Still able to plot. Still able to write his own history.

"Is there a chance she won't sign it?" Moira took a deep breath. "It would shift the borders. She'd be trapping scouts and soldiers and you all and whoever else is here, in Erlend under Weylin's rule. He could try all of you as traitors."

"What's the alternative?" I threw off the blankets and stood, spine cracking and ash crumbling from my grimy skin. I wanted to run, hunt, have North Star bleeding beneath my blades. "Shadows and soldiers and a war she fears Igna couldn't win? If she thinks the shadows are on his side and more could die from the war than could die up here right now, she'll sign it. Wouldn't you?"

Moira nodded.

"She'll sign it." I buried my face in my hands. History was endless—less dead if she signed. She would kill us all to save Igna. Hundreds of thousands of people would live if she signed it and only a few hundred would die. She'd weigh those lives, not with worth like Riparian had when given the option of letting a few Erlends die to save all of Nacea, but she'd still weigh them. She'd justify them as a better exchange. "We can't get word to her, can we?"

The shadows were out saving the Nacean settlements. We had magic but barely any knowledge of how to use it outside of violence. We had only us.

"Not fast enough," Roland muttered. "Our line of communication is cut off at the border—we can get in quickly but out only slowly."

"The queen of Igna will sign it," Moira said slowly, stepping to me with each word. "You may be her Opal, but you are and always will be Sallot Leon, and Gaspar del Weylin must pay for his crimes against Nacea. Against us."

Elise's quick inhale broke me. "That's a war crime. Even if it's right, you'll be put on trial. She'll execute you to appease the other nobles and keep peace, to make sure they don't view it as Igna breaking the treaty and reason enough to attack."

Like Ruby.

Rodolfo da Abreu, the dead war criminal—dead and disgraced before he even turned twenty.

"I'll do it." I cracked my spine and yawned, stretching out the sore muscles of my arms. Hal's rune had healed the worst wound in my arm, but I still ached. "I'll kill him before he signs the treaty."

I would be her blade.

Elise opened her mouth. I shook my head.

"I became Opal to end Erlend, to avenge Nacea, but it's more than that. All this killing is just killing if I don't leave the world a better place. Weylin and his arrogance don't belong in this world anymore. People need to see the old world die. They need to see the consequences followed through."

Ruby would've understood. Emerald and Amethyst too. Somethings had to be done.

"There is a debt." Moira met my gaze, the red light of the evening sun spilling across her feet, the reds and golds of a new day swallowing the snow-crowned mountains out the window behind her.

I bowed my head. "And debts must be paid."

"Remember," Moira whispered, "you are Nacean, Sallot Leon, and Nacea made no deal."

# CHAPTER
# FIFTY-TWO

I wasn't just Nacean though. Sal, Twenty-Three, Opal—each part of me was of Igna. I couldn't give it up. Me being Nacean wouldn't stop folks from lashing out if Our Queen's Opal slaughtered anyone with whom she'd come to an agreement.

It would be a war crime.

Wasn't like the treaty was under false pretenses—not at the time he sent it, anyway. They thought Weylin could go to war if Igna refused and thousands would die for no reason.

I had to kill him before Our Queen was forced to accept the deal. After that, we'd have time to figure out what to do to keep the next ones in charge from pulling the same thing.

But if they got it signed, Opal would have to die. Because I would kill Weylin, war crime or not.

"The places they were holding Naceans, they're safe?" I asked while Moira checked my wounds and prepared me for traveling through snow. My mind was spread too thin, too many new people and places and words I couldn't keep up with. My skin burned with it. Even clothes were unbearable. The dim lights too bright. The dinner conversation deafening.

It was all too much. I needed to go.

I needed North Star.

"I know a bit about what is happening through the shadows we sent. They are for now, but they're weaker this far from me. They're not like the original shadows, and the soldiers will realize that soon enough. It's here that's an issue. The nobles are trying to step up and fill the spaces and take over what North Star was doing. I can only scare them into submission with magic so many times before they realize I'm not as skilled as the feared mages they remember. We need Erlend to surrender fully."

No matter what end it came to.

If folks learned that attempting to slaughter entire populations different from them was bad for all of us, they'd stop, but they'd not learn if nothing happened to Riparian and Winter. And if it was after a deal, they'd call for blood but my point would stand.

North Star didn't get to strong-arm his way into peace after leading a life of violence.

His idea of peace was still violence—erasure of their crimes.

I would not let him go unpunished.

"It's finally stopped snowing." Elise touched my arm, fingers gripping the sleeve. It had started snowing after Winter and Riparian's deaths, and it hadn't stopped since. Even if I'd known how to ski, it would've been near impossible for me to survive traveling. I'd had to wait. "The passes won't be cleared out until dawn. You still have some waiting to do."

I glanced at her, the hitch in her words clear.

*We have time to talk.*

It began with silence. Moira left, Hal came and went with a nod to me, and Maud had brought the food, smiled when I asked where it came from, then left the milk rolls when she took the plates. I tore one apart while Elise took a seat on the edge of the bed. She sighed.

"I might've overreacted." I offered her one of the rolls and paced a bit, getting used to walking again, working the uncomfortable sore of sleeping too long from my limbs. "Back in Hinter."

She waved away the roll. "I should've told you, but it never really came up. I didn't think it was important."

We'd both played each other.

"I should've told you when you said you were lying to me." Elise glanced over, staring through cracked spectacles. "That would've been best."

"It would've." I shrugged and sat next to her. "Course, I was lying to you forever."

"That really didn't bother you, did it? The lying?" she asked. Her left side pressed against my right. Not a lot. Not side to side. Just enough that the warmth of her thigh seeped into mine through her dress. "It was Lena."

"She was a monster," I whispered. "And you were defending her."

Elise nodded. "Lena didn't raise me, but she was part of my life for a very long time. Like my father. I trusted them both, and in just one year, all that trust has been broken."

"Elise." I held out my hand, palm up, not wanting to grab her with the words I was about to stay stuck in my mouth. "I know they're dead and that's a lot to think about, but—"

"I'll mourn after I've cleaned up the mess they made." Elise, eyes glazed with tears, turned to me and laced our fingers together. "I spent all day with Moira. I met Namrata. Gaspar del Weylin is a man made monstrous by his arrogance, Lena de Arian was a woman made monstrous by her cunning—there is shrewdness and then there is the careful execution of people by devaluing them to numbers—and my father was a man made monstrous by greed. We could have lived happily. We could have lived as we had been, but he wanted more. They would kill thousands and start a war just to reclaim power they don't deserve. We cannot have peace because they continually destroy it. Igna was doing well, and they had to do this? There's no excuse for it. Others might not see it that way, but I remember Hinter. There is no amount of power or wealth or personal gain that can justify returning to that."

She laid her cheek against my shoulder. Her nose brushed my ear, breath shivering along the shell, and I wrapped my other arm around her waist.

"Will you stay with me till I leave?"

Then, at least, the unease of waiting within me would be stifled. She hummed into my neck.

"I'm probably going to die," I said softly. "I liked knowing you though. That was good. There were a lot of good parts, but I'm glad at least a part of the world's in your hands."

Rath.

Maud. Who'd be pissed enough to bring me back to life only to yell at me for not saying goodbye.

Emerald and Amethyst. I'd never figured out how to shoot properly. One of ten arrows? Sure. Anything more than three was a crapshoot.

Moira and Nacea. Hal and the others I didn't know. All the little things I'd not asked yet, the little details I didn't know. But Moira would do right by me.

By Nacea.

Elise whispered, "We could still make good memories."

*Oh.*

"Do you want to?" I said quickly. My breaths came faster, nothing to do with the warmth of her hand or gust of her laughter against my neck. "You're so many things I wish I were, not now, not after all I've done, but when I was a kid. You're clever and nice, and you care. You care about so many people you've never even met. You're a good person. You'll be a good leader. And I know it's selfish of me, but I want to show you how much just knowing someone like you meant to me. You deserve good things, better things than all this."

Elise lifted her head. "Are you asking my permission to kiss me?"

"I'm asking your permission to do a bit more than kiss you." I turned so I could look at her, meet her eyes, and she shifted against my side. Her right leg crossed over my lap. "I mean, we could just kiss. That'd be fine too. You're just...good."

She laughed, neck arching. "Sallot, if you want to kiss me, kiss me, but please stop second-guessing."

"You're real bossy." I touched her chin, tracing a line up the rounded corners of her jaw, and pushed her braids behind her shoulders.

She pressed her lips to mine. Warmth and safety and affection I wasn't sure I fully deserved crept over my skin, the point between her thigh and mine, my hand and her neck, and sunk into my bones. Peace. Nothing. Everything. So she'd surprised me once. She still felt safe.

"Is that a complaint?" she muttered against my mouth, tongue flicking against mine, hands dragging up to my face and down, down, to the very bottom edges of my hips. Her hands found the skin beneath my dress.

I pushed her back till she sunk into the bed and tugged me down with her. I kissed the hollow of her throat, pressed my ear against her chest and listened to her heart through the thick layers of her dress, lowered myself to the round hill of her stomach and kissed the spot above her navel, and settled against the softness of one thigh. My fingers skimmed her sides, and she laughed. My head bounced against her leg.

"You're ticklish." I crawled up and laid my cheek against her stomach.

She grabbed the hair at the nape of my neck. "Don't you dare tickle me."

"I think I might love you." I pulled her up a bit and pried apart the knots at the back of her dress. "Or could have. Or might. You're clever and kind, and sometimes when you're thinking, you rub your nose and get all inky or do the glasses glare, and your eyebrow hooks up just right, and you look like you can't believe you're stuck there and I love all of it. I want to love you. I want to know you. All the little parts I don't know yet."

That I might never know.

She yanked, and her dress went flying over her head in a wave of wool and cotton. Her underdress bunched under my hands, pulling tight across the curves of her stomach and breasts.

She pulled my hands free of the fabric at her sides and placed them low on her hips. My breath caught in my throat.

"I would like for you to know me." She unbuttoned the top part of my shirt and shoved it back, baring my shoulders and half of my chest. "Really know me."

I shuddered. "Yes?"

"Oh, yes."

I ducked to taste the skin at her throat, ribs, hips, her breath escaping in a little gasp, her hands grasping at my hair. I kissed the soft skin of her inner thigh.

And I broke as she broke, my name shivering from her lips.

"Sal," Elise whispered in the dark of the night when we were half-asleep in the warmth between our tangled bodies. "I think I might have loved you too."

The words followed me into sleep, filling my dreams with soft skin laid over frozen grass and the gentle taste of honeyed tea on worried lips. Elise's arms kept finding me in the night, curling around my shoulders, my hips, my stomach until I woke up with her nose buried in my armpit and the whole of the bedding bundled up at my feet. She snored softly, and each point of warmth between us ached in my chest. She could have loved me.

If I stayed.

If I lived.

If the world were unjust enough to let killers walk free.

I slipped from bed and draped the quilts over Elise, goose-flesh rising up her legs. Her toes peeked out of the edge.

"It's sideways." Elise tugged the quilt edge, curling up her legs until they were safe beneath it. She blinked at me. "Sal?"

"Yes?" I straightened out the quilt, tucked it under her feet, and braced myself against the edge of the bed. I was sneaking out without so much as saying goodbye. I was a coward, leaving while it was still dark and she still slept.

I was sure of what I needed to do, but the sacrifice that came with it hurt.

Feeling her shift and sigh in bed next to me had sang in my bones. The brush of her hip against my thigh, my arm against her breast in the soft movement of the afterglow still prickled over my skin, but the knowledge of what was to come muted the memories. I dredged up the feeling of her fingers tracing "Opal" along my arm. The press of her lips against my palm.

A hand cupped my chin. "You were going to leave without saying goodbye."

"Sorry." I crawled back into bed and sat tailor-style before her. Tense. Waiting. "I've been told I don't handle emotions well."

"Whoever told you that is brilliant." Elise, bundled in the quilt like a hooded cape, leaned forward till her nose pressed against mine. "You overthink things."

Maud was brilliant.

I wished I'd said goodbye properly.

"I know what you have done and what you are going to do," Elise said, voice unwavering despite the bright sheen of sleep still over her eyes.

I touched the little bruise at the curve of her throat. "If you tell me to stay, I might not be able to leave."

"You can and you will, and I'm not holding that against you. You should've woken me up though." She leaned into my touch. "Live through it. If they've already signed the treaty and made the deal, just come back. If Opal kills them, you'll be committing war crimes. You've got so much left to do."

"All right." I kissed her—old tea, me, sweat, morning breath— and savored every breath I lost between her lips.

She shivered, fingers skimming my ribs. "All right?"

"All right," I said and kissed her once more. "I'll see you after. If they've signed it, I'll leave."

Elise did know me, understand me better than most.

"Yes." She wiped the tears from her cheeks and pulled away. "After."

And Elise knew I was and would always be a liar.

# CHAPTER
# FIFTY-THREE

Maybe I wasn't in the right. Maybe nothing was worth it. Maybe the treaty was justice and the people they'd lied to would break out of the lies just fine without seeing them punished.

Maybe I didn't care.

I wore my opal mask out of the city. It was cold, the stinging sort that burned until you sweated it out and then chilled you all over again. They'd offered me a horse, but I'd no clue how to ride, and stomping through the snow was faster than a cart. I'd not stop till I had to.

I'd not stop till I reached Weylin's safe house in Hinter.

Ice cracked behind me. Someone shrieked.

I spun, knife out, and the blob struggling on a sheet of ice so thick the earth might've died and turned white glanced up at me.

"I've been following you—loudly—since you left." Adella grinned, smile just peeking through the tightly cinched hood over her face. "You need company?"

"You need a hand up?" I waited for her to nod and slid back to her. "So."

We walked for a bit, neither of us mentioning what we were doing, and she nudged me.

"So," she drew out. "You want to hear about how Four got bit on the nose by a grass snake?"

"Please."

We talked about a lot of things—Four and Two and Adella's slow breaking after their deaths, her mother's reaction to her joining the carnival, her apprentice's crush on the carnival physician. We'd days and days of nothing to do but talk.

I didn't remember much of it.

Adella understood.

"I don't like silence," she said our fourth night, the lights of Hinter too far to see but the closeness of it looming. "I don't think you do either. It lets you dwell."

"Look, we're all good at something, and I've got dwelling." I downed my last canteen of cold soup—no fires, no warm food, no dry cloaks—and fell back against my tree.

Adella threw a snowball at me. Missed. "Don't sleep there. Snow'll fall and you'll die."

"Maybe that's how I'll kill Weylin."

"We could write a ballad about it." Adella swallowed, head falling back against her bag. "How are you going to kill him?"

Good question.

I only knew where they were because of Weylin's slighted heir, the lord who'd been told to flirt with Elise the other night at dinner. Weylin hadn't taken the lord with him, picking instead his oldest, most trusted advisors. Weylin had left him to die by our hands.

Erlends didn't handle losing power well, and the lord had told us of Weylin's hideout as soon as we promised him his life and home.

Roland had confirmed the story—five nobles and a handful of rangers heading where the lord said. He hadn't seen that it was Weylin.

I would kill five people to stop them from killing five thousand. I was fighting fire with fire, but forest fires were necessary things, clearing the underbrush from the land when the time was right and regrowth was necessary. The nobles of Erlend had been left to rot for far too long.

I could rationalize any way I liked, but they were still dead and I still a killer. There was no coming back from this. For any of us except those who would come after.

And I'd made my peace with the dark parts of my soul. I'd made my peace with being dark so the rest of the world wouldn't have to be.

"Tomorrow's my nineteenth birthday," Adella said softly. "Myra and I shared one. It gets better."

The empty drop of grief opened up in my chest.

"No, it just gets different, sometimes easier, sometimes worse. Grief's a mixed bag of different kinds of shit." I tossed a handful of snow at her. "I thought you were older."

"And I thought you were better looking when you wore a mask, but we all make mistakes." She was quiet for a while after that, and then, when the clouds overtook the moon and I could barely see the glint of her earring it was so dark, she muttered, "I finished my list."

"What list?" I asked.

She'd not wanted to kill anyone. Had she already?

"We made a list. The three of us each picked things we wanted to do no matter what—things we couldn't live without, and our plan was to do them all. I did. What do I do now?"

I wasn't sure what to say to it. I wasn't one of those people who'd make her feel at home.

"Well, we got five folks, a whole bunch of guards, and one house to destroy. Think you can figure out something you want to do with them?"

"Burn it." She cackled, mouth open beneath the sky like she was trying to swallow it up, taste the stars and laugh them up. "Weylin deserves to die, so let's give him a kingly funeral pyre."

He would die. Course, I wanted him to know why I was killing him. Fire was too quiet, too passive.

"We can't both be the reckless one," I said. I played with the edges of my Opal mask, the proper one, the blank one, the one so white it was as suffocating as the endless drifts of Erlend snow. Maybe he'd think he was looking in a mirror.

Adella shrugged. "Ma always said I'd more scars than sense."

It would make sure the rangers didn't come running in. I touched the names on the inside of my mask, the warmth of Ruby's funeral pyre a distant memory even though it hadn't even been a year. I wasn't scared of fire—I'd been to too many funerals—and it would be fitting. A pyre fit for a king. Nothing left of us but ghost.

And he'd die afraid.

"It's not bad though, but how we going to get in?"

"How'd you normally rob a place?"

"I'll need a distraction—a good one." I sat up, leaned my

elbows on my knees, and waited for her to look at me. "I'll need to steal the key to the door. My bet is it'll be on whoever's in charge outside just in case something happens, and lifting stuff from soldiers is only a good idea when they're new or distracted."

Adella pulled my bag to her with a foot hooked through the strap and dug through it. "You got another mask?"

"Very bottom."

She yanked free my second Opal mask and held it up. "What're they going to do to two of you?"

CHAPTER
# FIFTY-FOUR

T he guards never looked up. Adella crawled from giant pine
to pine to pine, stringing a series of wires far above their
heads while I found the leader. She'd put on a show, half-threats
and half-carnival, falling from wire to wire in the dark like a
shadow, too fast to be human. I circled the building—a squat
wooden house built to blend in to the woods with no windows
and a wooden lock on the wooden door, each piece painted to
match the trees crowding it. Fifteen guards, two of them in fan-
cier coats. One never went far from the door.

I settled against the trunk of a fir near him, hidden in the
thick branches. A thin chain ran from his belt to a pocket low
on his pants leg. I covered my mouth to keep from laughing,
branches shaking around me. Not even a secret one. Just stuffed
into the pocket above his belt and attached to a chain hooked
to his buckle.

I had wire clippers for just this reason. Rath had always
laughed at me for carrying them.

"Who's laughing now?" I whispered.

Him, probably. He was always laughing.

A torch flared high within the trees. No, not a torch—Adella. She'd soaked a sword blade in oil and set it aflame. The guards at the door looked up.

The white mask covering her face flickered like the moon waning and waxing in quick succession. She raised her arms and shouted, "Who here hides the damned?"

The soldiers drew crossbows and longbows and spears, each staring straight at her.

"Our Lady demands retribution." She turned and walked along the wire, a midair stroll on nothing for all it looked, and one of the men beneath her gasped. "Erlend made more shadows of the surviving Naceans, and for this indiscretion, Erlend owes Our Lady a debt of blood. Who will pay this debt?"

She ran her other hand along the blade, extinguishing the light, and around me, the dozen guards lit their torches. They held them as high as they could to her old spot.

Nothing there.

I crept forward till I was in arm's reach of the guard, and he started loading his crossbow, shuffling all about. Another light appeared above us. He spun round.

"No one?" Adella pitched her voice low, dragging out each word and making her words carry farther than I thought possible. She stood atop a fir on the other side of the house. The light cupped in her hands didn't smoke, didn't burn her skin. "Shall I call the shadows you made of my family and friends?"

The guard took aim. I clipped the chain dangling from his leg, fingers steady. His bolt flew, the snap of his crossbow loud between the low rumbles of the other guards and Adella's drawn out cries, and I pulled the key from his pocket. He whistled.

And a dozen more arrows flew. Adella fell, too fast to see. I couldn't tell if any hit her, but I couldn't stay.

I darted forward, key in hand, and unlocked the door.

"Lady, let her live." I shoved open the door. "If only one of us leaves here alive tonight, let it be her."

The door locked behind me.

Good. The guards couldn't get in.

Let North Star understand true loneliness for the first time.

There was no one in the entrance way. A hallway with four side doors and a set of double doors at the end flickered with low light and rumbled with hushed conversations from the room at the end of the hall. Only one side door was open.

Empty.

A thick letter laid on the desk. Our Queen's blue seal was broken and crumbling, and North Star's signature shone in the flickering candle light. Wet, red ink boxed in by two bloody thumbprints. I picked it up.

"A pyre fit for a king." I held the signed treaty over a candle and set fire to every paper and cloth in sight.

The room burned slowly, and I left my bag in the hallway. I locked the doors to each room in turn. No windows. They'd killed themselves.

"The last star of Erlend!" I undid the chain on the double doors at the end of the hall, and threw them open. "About to burn out."

The room stilled. North Star, the exact same as when I'd last seen him, sat at the head of a large table, and the others flanked him. They glanced from him to me. North Star only sighed.

"We made a—"

"I don't care." I paced the length of the room, dragging my knife across the wall, shredding tapestries and maps. A saw-toothed hilt was mounted to the wall and I ripped it off. "You're all going to die tonight. The only question is what we do until then."

The door to the office I'd set on fire collapsed. The other nobles panicked, pushing each other out of the way to escape. North Star pulled a sword from his belt, the thin-bladed standard of Erlend. I laughed, the sound echoing in my mask, and switched my knife to my left hand. The saw-toothed hilt bit into my right palm.

Smoke poured in through the open double doors. Screams, choked and dying, roared over the sound of flames. Footsteps pounded down the hall. Fists hammered against the door leading out.

"My guards outside will break through the door before the fire spreads." North Star rose to first position, his shoulders relaxed, his hands steady. Only his jaw tensed. "You've failed to kill me. Again."

"I'll kill you before that happens." I glanced back once to make sure the front door wasn't open and guards weren't coming. "You're not leaving this room."

He lunged. A shudder rolled down my arm, raising gooseflesh across my skin, prickling against the back of my throat like smoke, until it settled in my ears. It sang. Like the wind. Like my mother had. I clenched the hilt, splitting my palm open.

"*Let the blade run red if you want me to kill him,*" I prayed in my head. "*My soul to the Lady's open arms.*"

My blood sunk into the runes of the sawtooth hilt, red to black to boiling, and burned away to ash. The pain peaked and sharpened to a single point of contact in the center of my palm, and I raised my hand.

A sword of blood and ash, mottled red dripping into solid, serrated edges, lengthened.

North Star would rule no one else. He would hurt no one else.

For all that we had done, neither of us deserved to live.

I swung. My blade ripped through his, sending steel clattering to the floor. North Star stared at my sword, eyes wide and hands trembling for the first time. He dropped his ruined sword to the ground.

"Does it infuriate you?" I slashed my runed sword across his chest. Blood dripped across the table and shivered, reaching for the sword. His blood seeped into mine. His debt became my blade. "You killed us only to find out you needed us—the people you didn't even think twice about killing."

He stumbled back. I let the mage's sword fall and raised the knife in my other hand. I didn't need magic to kill him. I drove the knife into the flesh beneath his right shoulder, through and through and through till he was on his back against the floor and I was kneeling on his chest. He coughed, blood on his teeth.

"Nacea's dead whether you kill me or not," he said in Nacean.

He tried to punch me, and I ripped the knife from his shoulder. He shuddered and screamed. I pinned his other arm to the floor, knife through his hand.

"Don't you remember?" I whispered. "You made Nacea learn magic. You made Nacea make shadows. You gave Nacea the means to beat you. No one's dead or dying but you."

He'd stolen everything—my language, my family, my innocence.

I pried the hilt out from the skin of my hand. The blade attached to it shuddered and froze, red turning black. It drifted away piece by piece like ash, leaving only the hilt behind.

"My name is Sallot Leon."

I shoved the hilt of the sword between his teeth, working them open, till the pommel dug into his soft flesh at the roof of his mouth and he groaned. His lips split.

"My family—Leon, Perrin, Shea, Hia—were good people. You killed them." I pressed down harder. "And I've been told good people find it within themselves to forgive. If my family was good, am I? I showed mercy once. I was going to let Winter live. He threw me out a window and started a war. But you'd just do it again, wouldn't you? To some other land and some other kid? That's what you do—flee when you lose and declare yourself king of wherever you run out of breath? For all the years I looked up at night, to the stars I should've known names for, to the Lady I should've known how to pray to, to the world I should've felt a part of, you should have to feel that loss, that lack, of knowing so much that the sky might swallow you up and the world won't even notice. You made me feel singular and small, a speck of leftovers clinging on long after I should've been gone. And I couldn't even properly explain the pain, the loneliness, the wait, because you took those words too."

His teeth cracked. Scattered.

He howled, blood splattered from his flailing tongue, breaths bubbling in the back of his throat. I let him escape. Let him crawl away from me.

"I can explain it now." I followed him, the sawtooth hilt falling from my hand. "But I don't think you'd understand, North Star, because you've always had a name and language and family to return to in your mind. You had safety. You've never *wanted* like I have."

The yellow-gray flecks of broken teeth crunched beneath my boots, and North Star, bloody hands clutching bloody mouth, dragged himself toward the door. I stumbled after him, head hazy from smoke. I pulled off my mask.

"You'll die!" He laughed, blood splattering against his paling face. The words were garbled, but I knew them. I knew that laugh. "You'll die."

Like it was the funniest thing in the whole damned world.

Like I cared about Opal dying.

"I know." I coughed, more ash in my mouth than words. "We'll die."

The screaming behind us softened into coughs and gags. Wooden beams crashed to the ground. Guards shouted through the burning cracks in the building.

I could not ask for forgiveness—there was none to give for all that I had done—and I could not carry on as though my soul weren't a deep, red river overflowing with a dozen names. My life wasn't worth all the lives I'd save tonight. Igna needed me dead to keep the truth-deprived Erlends at bay until the long, hard work of undoing North Star's lies was done. They'd never trust Our Queen if she let Gaspar del Weylin's killer and Lena de Arian's executioner walk free. This was the only way no one would turn out like me again.

I had not become Opal because I was Nacean, because I was displaced, because I was Sal.

This was my choice, and North Star would take no more choices from me. From anyone.

But for every reassurance, every sorrow, I'd still killed more people than I'd ever loved.

And death was final; my hand in it was a mess of blurred, uneven moral lines and questions no one could straighten out.

Complexity.

I was infinite and understandable, a dozen inaccuracies and uneven edges held together by gentle memories—my mother cutting my hair and letting me wear her earrings on my birthday; stealing a tray of smoked venison with Rath and having to toss it to the dogs giving chase till we were left with nothing but sweaty clothes and laughter; the swish of wool over wool beneath the hum of words as Maud, knowing I hated the quiet but never wanting to presume, moved her chores into my quarters and read Elise's history books aloud to me; Elise, a smear of charcoal along her jaw and a twister-tight curl bouncing with each breath, staring at me from across the pages of a book and translating lines of poetry faster than I could think while teaching me Erlenian; the soft sounds of Nacean in my ears as Moira read off the names of all the living from my country just to prove it survived and calm the fear inside of me.

Beneath all the grit and love and blood, I was and always would be Sallot Leon.

And Sallot Leon I would always be whether the rest of the world liked it or not.

Opal would die as Opal had been.

Brilliant and bloody and short-lived.

North Star laughed through all of it, choking on his blood and spit. "You'll die!"

As if that were the worst fate that could befall someone.

"I'll die." I kneeled next to him, dipping my mask into the pool of blood at my feet, and I let the ash in the air catch hold of it. Speckle it. Bury it. "You'll die."

An uncomfortable, seeping pain crawled up my throat and tightened around each word. Beams cracked. He tried to speak again and gagged. I tossed my mask into the flames.

"Maybe of smoke. Maybe of fire. Maybe the roof will collapse and crush us side by side, but no matter what, we're dying tonight, North Star. We've debts to pay."

# EPILOGUE

W here are the bodies?" Emerald asked.

She still wore mourning gray, wools dark as storm clouds and light as frost clinging to grass blades. The Left Hand weren't assassins any longer—publicly at least—but they still wore masks. A "scare tactic," Our Queen had called it.

Igna was trying to be more truthful.

Which meant no more assassins employed by the court. The Left had transitioned to elite guards, protectors of those still in danger—Our Queen, Moira Namrata, and the other leaders all scrambling to figure out what to do with Gaspar del Weylin's old holdings up north. Wasn't a hard transition.

Emerald and Amethyst were the only Left Hand members alive, and the audition for the new Ruby had been sparse.

"Wherever they walked off to, I'd imagine." I wasn't used to wearing the thick, black mask they'd given me at the gate. It itched. The stitches holding the red ribbon of 4 to the front unraveled against my mouth. "Probably eating breakfast."

Amethyst cleared the table in one smooth jump. She reached for my hood.

I flinched.

She froze with her fingers against my cheek, breath catching. I knew that sound, I knew that masked look. I'd known her for only the better part of a year, but the familiarity of her knocked the air from me too.

"Hello," I said. "Again."

"For Triad's sake," Emerald muttered. She ripped my mask off. "Sal?"

"Nice to see you too." I smiled. I'd more scars since the fire but looked the same. Adella and I had spent months building up the strength to travel back north and join Moira. Maud and Elise had left by then, returned to Willowknot for peace talks and truth telling. "Sallot Leon and Opal are dead. I thought this'd be fitting."

My mask slipped from her hands. She didn't move.

I swallowed. They could arrest me.

The assassination of Gaspar del Weylin—North Star—and the others at the house in Hinter had been a high crime since they'd been due for court. The old Opal had died with them, treasonous and disgraced.

Opal was dead. Forever.

At least until they'd time to hold auditions for Opal.

"Or, since I'm Ruby, I should be saying this is poetic."

Emerald crushed me into a hug. The edge of her mask nipped my shoulder till she ripped the metal off and tucked her cheek against my crown. A puddle of tears pooled between us.

I patted her back. "I thought I'd be the crying one, not you."

"I could make you cry," Emerald said, voice hushed and

heavy. "I should. You were dead. You were very dead and very out of line."

She pulled back, letting her hands linger on my shoulders. The brass nails cut into my skin.

"How have you so spectacularly mastered infuriating me?" She touched my cheek. "And now you think you can be Ruby? After your dismal performance as Opal?"

Dismal?

"Wasn't a dismal thing about it. You're the ones who—"

"You did nothing right. Ever. At all." Emerald smacked my arm—not hard but not gentle either—with each word. "Whoever Four was, whoever Ruby is, cannot be tied to Opal."

I swallowed. "Opal is dead. How could anything be tied to them?"

"Good." She grinned and wiped the tears from her neck. "Right answer, Honorable Ruby."

I could not be Sal again. Not in public.

But when Elise had returned to Lynd to take her place as the heir of Hinter and help rebuild Erlend and Nacea, I'd been Sal with her in private.

And in the crowds of Naceans traveling south to search for long-lost family and friends, no one spoke of Sallot Leon. They knew not to, and Moira helped all those looking find me. My father's northern family had been more than happy to keep my secret. I wasn't so scattered anymore. So lost.

It was nice knowing the deal though. The Left Hand made me wait. Amethyst and Emerald didn't press for all the details while we talked all day, but they waited all evening to announce their selection. It had only been one night.

Not even that if I was being arrogant.

I'd been welcomed into Willowknot by Roland—he'd lived, thank the Lady—and his new scars, and he'd paused before letting me in, gaze lingering on my knives. I'd told him I'd forgotten the hand.

He'd have found out who was I was sooner or later.

There'd only been four of us auditioning. The Left Hand wasn't what it used to be. We were to be protectors and aides. If Our Queen needed protection, we were her shield. If Erlend's soldier holdouts, few and far between, rebelled, we arrested them. If Nacea needed help with the harvest, we picked up a sickle and figured it out. We existed to keep the peace and Our Queen safe.

Course, Marianna da Ignasi wasn't my queen anymore.

I followed a new star.

Marianna da Ignasi wouldn't be queen for long either. Her search for an heir was underway, and the new Left Hand would be the heir's personal guards. I'd chased the other three auditioners for Ruby off, but Amethyst sent a messenger to give them invitations for Opal's mask. There'd be a party that night, and the memory of my last one shuddered through me. I had nothing now, no vengeance and names, and Ruby was all I was. A new name. A new job. A new chance to start cleaning the blood from my soul. Moira, at least, would understand. Growing up in Igna, doing what I'd done, not all the Naceans I talked to got it. Moira did.

Her letters had been nice.

After enough hugging for years, Amethyst and Emerald let me retreat to my old quarters. They'd been cleared out, my things moved to storage or garbage somewhere, and Maud's careful touch was gone.

I traced the smooth angles of my coat, nails catching over each stitch. Ruby's old mask felt odd and uneven against my face—too cold, too sharp, too confining.

"You asked for me, Honorable Ruby?" Maud, the same, the exact same, bowed in the doorway, and I braced myself against a chair to keep from tackling her. The voice she used for folks she didn't want to talk to but had to because they were ordering her around sang in my ears.

Dimas and Maud had been the only familiar faces absent from auditions. Dimas was in prison, punishment for his treason and attempted assassination. When Our Queen or Moira had need of him, he was escorted out to act as a mage or healer or whatever people needed, but otherwise, his future for now was a cell overlooking nothing, near nothing and no one. His sister, Moira said, had visited once. He'd turned her away. The only runes he used now were for healing.

I could've been a mage, but the sight of runes still made me shudder.

Cam was having fun with it though. He and the other kids taken north were inseparable now. They'd made a new family, tight-knit and loving. New beginnings.

"Your honor?" Maud frowned. She'd held a funeral for me, and it had nearly killed me all over again, but it and her reaction to my death had been the final pieces of evidence to make the world think Opal was dead. "You called for me?"

Nicolas had offered her a job working with him, but she'd not taken it. Too dangerous. Too much time away from her siblings.

"Yes," I said, "I had a question for you."

"Of course." She nodded her head, but her eyes flicked up to get a look at me. "What was it you wanted to ask?"

I pulled Ruby's mask from my face. "Do you think I look good in red?"

She froze. A tense shudder rolled her shoulders and upset her neat bow. Her fingers grasped at nothing, opening and closing at her side, and an odd, unwelcome panic settled over my skin like cold sweat. I'd let Maud think I was dead, and she'd mourned me. She stepped forward. She didn't cry.

Thank the Lady.

If Maud cried, I'd break.

"Sal?"

I nodded.

Maud yanked her arm back and punched me in the face.

I shrieked and stumbled. She let me fall, flinging her hand around.

"Triad, that hurt." She clutched her hand to her chest. "You utter ass."

I moved my nose around to make sure it was still in one piece. "That was good. How's your thumb?"

"Fine!" She hit me again, not hard, and collapsed on her knees next to me.

I wrapped my arms around her shoulders. "I'm so sorry."

"You were dead." She sniffed, sobbing, and buried her face in my shoulder. "You were dead. You were dead and a criminal and you didn't even say goodbye to me."

"I know. I'm sorry. I am. Really, Maud, you're the only person in this world I'm sorry about leaving out of that." I rubbed my eyes. "I was always a criminal though."

"I'm going to punch you again," she said slowly, "if you keep talking."

I tightened my grip on her shoulders and shook my head.

And we stayed like that for a long while, till she laughed and hit me again without any malice and I got up to wash my face. She asked me what had happened. I told her everything.

"You're a better friend than I deserve."

"I know." Maud grinned, nose crinkling, as she left to find me clothes for tonight. "But the pay's good and someone has to save you from jumping out of windows."

I laughed and fell back into bed.

At least someone had mourned Sal.

Moira had held meetings for days about how to remember Nacea. No one wanted a giant statue or a building full of names. We wanted the unsettling punch of grief that hit when you least expected it, when you heard your sister's favorite tune or tasted your father's favorite meal. The sort of grief that snuck up on folks even on the brightest days and reduced them to an uncertain, aching mess of memories.

My mother's favorite sound was late-autumn rain on damp earth and the distant crack of thunder.

My brother's laugh sounded like a wayward lamb calling for its family.

And so they—we, I had to say we, had to get used to belonging, Moira said, because I did even if I didn't feel like it—scattered grief throughout Nacea. Polished, mirror-bright silhouettes haunted the land.

Shea's glittering form, delicate and playful, tiny hands grasping at just-out-of-reach wildflowers, glowed red in the rising sun every morning and was near invisible when I'd seen it for the first time at noon.

She wasn't there, but she had been. I'd draped a crown of daisies, poppies, and clover around her mirror throat. She was so small—in life, in death, in memory—and kissed the flickering surface of her cheek.

Grief was fickle and ever changing, bright and dark and endless as the space within her polished form. And sometimes, when the light was right, it was me.

The elected Erlend ministers in charge of shifting Erlend to Igna had called it creepy. Most of the Igna ministers had agreed. Moira had laughed and approved the project on the spot.

"Good," she'd said in court. "Your memories of Nacea should make you uncomfortable after what you did."

Elise had written out the entire exchange—still preserving everything for the future, to make sure folks never went back on their words—and sent me one of her many safeguarded copies along with a needle and thread for the flower crown. I was terrible at knotting the stems together.

She'd picked purple, the same color as the wildflowers that grew around Shea.

I'd spent the day sobbing.

Into a handful of flowers.

It was ridiculous, but that night, when my throat was raw and my eyes swollen, I'd felt better. Someday someone else would crest the hill where my home had stood and stand in shock at the sight of Shea. The uncertain grip of grief would steal their breath. They'd maybe stop. Maybe pick a few blooms and place them at her feet.

I'd not be alone. Never again.

And one day far, far in the future, when grief didn't lurk in me like a long-forgotten pox waiting to burst forth, her silhouette would crack and crumble. The world would move on but the remnants of her would remain.

I was all right with that.

I was all right.

I was.

Fine, I was getting there. Mostly.

So when Maud helped me get dressed in a dark-gold dress stitched with yellow and red poppies around the hem, when Emerald and Amethyst came to retrieve me and brought all of Nicolas's Nacean books he'd not had a chance to send Moira yet, when I tied Ruby's mask around my head and looked in the mirror, I didn't cry.

I'd done enough of that while Maud was gone.

I raised my head to Our Queen. She shifted, sea-green dress folding across her lap like foam at low tide. She wore no crown, and the corset lined with whalebone to keep her back from aching was woven with blue-stained steel and fish scales. She held out her left hand to me. I kneeled.

"My new Ruby." She let me kiss her ring and take her hand, pulling me as close to her as propriety allowed.

"Make me Moira Namrata's guard," I said. "I'll never leave her side, and no harm will come to the Last Living Star of Nacea or Nacea. Ever. Even if you try to let it die again. I will not be yours, I will not serve you out of love, but I will make sure people who will make the world a better place survive."

She frowned and covered her shock with a gauntleted hand. "Yes."

"Good," I whispered.

She cupped my cheek, fingers warm despite the mask between us. "I won't let Nacea down again. You could've stayed there."

I pulled away from her. I was not hers. She was not my queen, infallible and perfect, Lady-sent to save us all from the shadows. She was a person who'd tried her best, but that was no longer enough for me. I would protect what she couldn't. What she hadn't.

We were the same. She'd understand.

"No, I couldn't have." I needed to repent, to make up for the death I'd wrought, and this was a start. "I made them pay, and now I've a debt."

She took my hand and pulled me into the center of the room with her, the court silent around us.

"My friends." Our Queen raised her arms wide, still holding on to my hand. "My new Honorable Ruby is with us. Be kind."

And with that, I was Ruby.

Returned.

But she pulled me back, fingers tangled in mine, and whispered, "Dancing first. I believe you have some explaining to do."

"Thank you." I bowed. Low and proper.

Nine out of ten.

"Your Honor?"

I turned.

Elise, dressed in the same starry, silver dress she'd worn last time, bowed to me. I grinned.

"My Lady de Farone." Ruby's mask let me see every bit of

her face, from the ruddy blush in her cheeks, to the way she arched her back as the music pitched. "You look lovely."

"You used that line last time." She hooked our arms together and pulled me to the center of the dance floor. Her hand settled on my waist. "Come up with something better."

"I could rob you." I laughed and spun her round. "Steal a kiss."

Isidora stared from the edge of the room, and Emerald leaned down to whisper in her ear. Her gray eyes went wide, the dark circles hanging beneath hollowing when she turned—a testament to how well infant Rodolfo da Abreu was living up to their noisy, needy namesake. Nicolas had them too, and she grabbed his arm. He nodded.

"Later." Elise smiled. "I keep all of my expensive jewelry in my bedroom."

We turned, Elise leading, and my hand crept up her back to play with the beads at the ends of her braids.

"This is nice," I said.

No assassins. No threat of death hanging over folks who were trying to be better. No empty space in the land and my soul where Nacea used to reign.

Elise murmured her agreement and pulled me closer, pressing a kiss to the thin skin near my ear.

The song swelled. Amethyst danced with Lark next to us. Isidora watched me from the corner, whispering to Nicolas the whole time, and Our Queen danced with Emerald in a playful, twirling step. Moira wouldn't be back for days, and I'd life as Ruby to get used to. A new mask.

A bare mask with no names and no memories.

My shadows were dead. Peace spread under the careful watch of so many too intimate with war to care for it again. Nacea, busy and thriving in the lands that sprang back to life soon as Moira's feet touched the ground, lived.

And so did I.

# ACKNOWLEDGMENTS

To my father—thank you for showing me how to love science fiction and all the different possibilities within it.

To my mother—thank you for letting me steal your mystery novels even when I read them twice and left you to deal with the overdue fines.

To my grandmother—thank you for teaching me to know when to follow the recipe and when to break the rules before I was even tall enough to reach the counter.

Thank you, thank you, thank you, everyone who read, reviewed, and supported Sal through their harrowing journey. I can't put into words how thankful I am to everyone who read *Mask of Shadows* and *Ruin of Stars*, and the last two years have been an amazing time thanks to all of you.

My husband, Brent, was a constant supporter and sounding board for world building woes and fantasy idioms, and I couldn't have done any of this without him. He believed in my work even when I didn't. Rachel Brooks is one of the best agents an author could meet, and none of this would've been possible without her. She didn't just believe in the silly color-coded assassin novel I wrote, but believed it could be better. When Annie Berger took a chance on Sal and me, it changed my life for the better, and I feel so lucky I got to write a second book, finish Sal's story, and do it all with such a wonderful editor. The team behind the duology was fantastic in every way.

Then there were my writing mentors and partners for whom no gift would ever be great enough. I still remember Jessie Devine's advice and keep the edit letter hanging over my desk; Kerbie Addis is still one of the best writers and editors I know for dark fantasy, and I can't believe we met by chance because, without her, my writing wouldn't be what it is today; Kara Wolf was one of the first people to read both *Mask of Shadows* and *Ruin of Stars* and was amazing both times; Rosiee Thor and Maria Mora—the best Pitch Wars mentees ever—helped me edit and stay calm even in the most panicked of times; and Carrie DiRisio continues to be one of the most thoughtful writing partners I've ever had.

I can't even begin to explain how lucky I feel to have found a home with Sal at Sourcebooks. Thank you Alex Yeadon, Kathryn Lynch, Stefani Sloma, Cassie Gutman, the designers and artists who brought these books to life, and everyone at Sourcebooks for being a part of this journey.

And to all of the early readers who are clever and patient and deserve the world, I can't say it enough.

Thank you, thank you, thank you.

So this is the end of Sal's story—from Sallot Leon to Twenty-Three to Opal to Ruby—and it wasn't always happy, but it was

Sal's. They've a whole new set of adventures to live now, and so do you.

Live.

# ABOUT THE AUTHOR

Linsey Miller is a wayward biologist from Arkansas who previously worked as a crime lab intern, neuroscience lab assistant, and pharmacy technician. She can be found writing about science and magic anywhere there's coffee. Visit her online at linseymiller.com.

# FIREreads

## — ❂ #getbooklit —

## Your hub for the hottest young adult books!

Visit us online and sign up for our
newsletter at FIREreads.com

 @sourcebooksfire

 sourcebooksfire

 firereads.tumblr.com